LOVE WAS THEIR DESTINY...

The King gazed at Bronwyn in the firelight, his blue eyes filled with longing. "I'm glad we are back on speaking terms once more, my songbird." He leaned over, laid a hand against her cheek and whispered in her ear, "So you love me again, eh?"

Bronwyn bridled. "You, sir, are a fickle knave, talking of love when you don't even know me!" Pretending indignation, she gently pushed him away, though she didn't really want to. When he was near, she seemed to forget everything . . .

"Ah, but there you are wrong. I do know you. We met in a dream one night."

The simple words couldn't have shaken her more. Just pretty words spoken in jest—or were they? Bronwyn couldn't be sure.

The whole day Edward had cherished the vision of her gentle smile and emerald eyes like a talisman in his heart. He couldn't put her out of his mind. He had never felt this way about a woman before. Hearing her voice and seeing her smile filled him with peace. She healed his weary soul.

Bronwyn realized she wasn't afraid of him any longer. "Well?" she raised her eyebrows slightly. "What was I in this dream of yours, good sir?"

"My own true love, the one I have been seeking so long. I thought I would never find you, and now here you are," he replied, unsmiling, in a husky whisper that no one else could hear.

Bronwyn lowered her eyes. No, he wasn't a stranger to her, either. "It is true—we have met in a dream," she breathed.

Bending over her, he kissed her swiftly and gently on the lips. When he drew away and smiled into her stunned eyes, the warmth of his nearness put her in a kind of trance . . .

THE HEART OF THE ROSE

Kathryn Meyer Griffith

LEISURE BOOKS ☙ NEW YORK CITY

For our beloved Christopher, who was taken from us far too soon, and who is still missed by his older sister and the rest of the family.

A LEISURE BOOK

Published by

Dorchester Publishing Co., Inc.
6 East 39th Street
New York, NY 10016

Printed in the United States of America

PROLOGUE

England—1461

THE NIGHT was cold and black. The only light was reflected from the snow that had been falling steadily the whole day and now lay in high, powdery drifts against the inn and the outbuilding clustered around it. The wind was cruel and stung Bronwyn's thin red cheeks as she worked beside her tired father. The snow clung to her rag-wrapped feet as she cleared the horse droppings from in front of the inn and dumped them on the growing dung heap.

"The horses are fed and watered, but they seem restless tonight for some reason," he said to her, walking back from checking them again. It was their job for tonight. They'd stood in front of the Red Boar and collected the patrons' horses as they arrived, took them out back to the stables and fed and groomed them for a small fee. But it would buy food for the next day and it was the only work her father could do now. Tomorrow they would seek employment elsewhere.

"We're almost done." Bronwyn grinned up at her father. All she wanted, she thought tiredly, was to warm her frozen bones before a good warm fire and to eat something. It had been such a long day!

"Aye, little one, nearly done," her father replied. He was a thin man with long hair the same shade of grey as his melancholy eyes. He stretched and straightened up with a groan. "And I'm glad of it. I'm not as young as I used to be and my leg is giving me a fit tonight. Damn leg!" He muttered in disgust, slapping at it as if that would do any good. Bronwyn had noticed that most of the night he had barely been able to hobble around. He had been wounded many years ago when he had fought for the old King in France, and it was both the old wound and the memories that plagued him forever after. He had been a good soldier once and now, crippled, he'd been tossed aside like an old useless nag, reduced to doing odd jobs for a living. But, Bronwyn knew, it was his pride that hurt him more than the wound.

He put his hand on her thin shoulder to help support himself. She searched his pained face in the faint light and smiled wistfully at him. "Let's collect our pay, Father, and go home," she offered.

He nodded. "Aye, I'm for that. A warm bowl of stew and your mother's smile will put things right again. I'll see to our pay." He gave her a swift kiss on the top of her head as she stood there shivering and went off through the deep snow to the inn's back door since servants were not allowed in the front entrance. "Be right back, my poppet." He waved at her and then disappeared into the bright, noisy inn.

Bronwyn stood out in the shadows, waiting, his usual words teasing at her memory: "*The Red Boar is no place for a beautiful woman like you. It is filled with wicked women and lustful men . . . a soldier would lay eyes on such an angel as you, child, and surely do you harm.*"

At the thought, Bronwyn would always laugh and say, "Who would want such a skinny girl with big feet and no chest?" She was only thirteen and she knew she was no

6

beauty. She was too tall already and too thin. She thought she was ugly, but her father saw her differently.

"You will fill out someday, and you will be *beautiful* . . . like your mother. I promise." It was as if he could already see the woman inside the girl. Her father—how she adored him! Her mother and her two younger sisters, Samantha and tiny Mary, she cared for deeply, but she loved her father above all others. He made her feel like a queen, though she was only a poor man's daughter.

She tried to pull her ragged cloak tighter about her thin frame, but it evaded her efforts to capture it and continued to flap wildly in the wind. She raised her face to the dark sky and began to hum an old tune her mother had taught her when she was a child. She had a hauntingly husky voice for such a small body, but she didn't know that any more than she knew that she was indeed beautiful. Her long, silken blond hair that usually fell to her waist was bound in a tight braid that hung down the center of her back and moved softly when she walked. Her skin was white and smooth and her intelligent eyes were an emerald green. Bronwyn had a way of looking at a person as if she knew a secret they did not know and it amused her. She was unselfish and kind to everyone. It wasn't so much that her individual features were lovely, rather that when she smiled and tilted her proud head in the way she usually did, people knew that in her touch there would be tenderness.

"Hurry, Father, hurry," she sighed into the night air, shivering. It had been the coldest winter she could ever remember. There had been so much snow . . . and so much sickness. She frowned slightly. Bronwyn wasn't like everyone else and over the last few years she had learned to accept this. She had the gift of healing in her hands and the knowledge—from where she did not know, though she preferred to believe her gifts were from God—*to make sick people well*. But she couldn't heal everyone, nor could she heal all ailments. It was curious, this gift of hers, and it frightened her witless at times. She was a *healer*, yet she and her family had to conceal her gift from those around them who feared her powers and might do her harm. Some people, those who had seen the softness and love in her eyes as she had tended to the sick, called her a saint. Others called her a witch and her talent, not a gift from God, but a favor she had received from the devil for the sale of her immortal soul. *Witch!* Just the word was enough to strike terror in anyone's heart these black days. *They burned witches at the stake . . . tortured them and threw them into pits in the belly of the earth and let them rot. They burned them . . .*

Bronwyn knew that. The Lollards were being tried and burned at the stake in droves these days. Anyone who thought differently than Mother Church was said to be in league with the devil and therefore destined for the rack or the stake. It was like a plague. The stench of charred flesh was thick in the air. Between the burning of heretics and King Edward's men hungry for the blood of their enemies, the Lancasters, there was little peace in England. But it had been thus since before she was born, her father had often told her. The Yorks against the Lancasters, the white rose against red as they fought for the glittering crown of England. The country had been at civil war so long that no one could remember what peace was like. But it was the poor people who suffered most, like her poor crippled father, they paid for the wars and gave their lives in the battles the noblemen waged. It would have been far better, she had often heard him say deep in the night in a whisper to her mother, had he died on the battlefield than to live as he was forced to now, better that he had died a soldier than live a cripple.

She stamped the snow from her feet again and slapped

her arms against her body, trying to keep warm. Where was her father? It was very late and her mother would be worried. She had been sick lately with a high fever and it worried Bronwyn that all her special herbs and care had been of no avail. There were terrible times like these when Bronwyn's skills could not cure. The patient had to want to get better and she feared that her mother had lost the desire to live. It was as if the harsh winter and the bitter poverty of their lives had drained the sap of her very soul until her mother was just a shell. Bronwyn didn't know what else to do. The fever refused to break, and the cough became steadily worse.

Bronwyn had a heavy burden of worry upon her thin shoulders.

She grew weary of waiting out in the shadows and was just about to go look for her father inside when she saw the doors swing open wildly and a group of men come stumbling out into the snowy night. They were drunk. She heard their slurred words on the night air. They were richly clad and she could see the sparkle of jewels as they moved out into the dark courtyard.

"Our horses! You there! Get us our horses!" one hiccoughed to her father, who had come running out behind them. "Can't leave without our horses . . ." the same voice mumbled. She saw the man fall over, and her father stopped and helped him to his feet before he ran off toward the stables.

Bronwyn frowned. Would they never get to go home? Rich men! How she hated their spoiled, greedy ways. All they cared about was themselves. They looked down on poor men like her father and treated them like their own personal slaves. She ached to see her father dance to their tune.

She could see him coming back now, leading their horses. The animals' breath was smoky white in the air and the heat from their large bodies clouded the cold air around them as their monstrous hooves stamped on the snow.

Bronwyn heard the galloping horsemen coming from somewhere in the woods behind her long before she saw their cloaked figures bearing down upon the drunken men and her father. Startled, she spun around. They rode so close to her that she could have reached out and touched them if she had wanted to. They hadn't seen her. Suddenly she knew what they wanted and her scream was lost in the night amidst the death cries of the drunken men outside the inn's doors as she caught up her long skirts and ran toward her father. Later, she didn't remember what she screamed as she ran, stumbling through the clinging snow. It didn't save his life. She only remembered the terrifying glint of raised swords, the rearing horses, the screams of pain and death. She saw her father fall under the flashing hooves of a huge black horse and, as if frozen for all eternity in her horror-filled eyes, the profile of the man astride that horse as he spun the beast around and brought his sword heavily down upon one of the other men on the ground.

"*Father!*" Bronwyn screamed, throwing herself to the ground to protect him as he lay bleeding. She cradled his head in her lap and looked up, for just a second, into the eyes of the man upon the horse towering above them. "*Murderer!*" she cried, rocking her father's broken body in her arms. The other men lay still or moaning in the bloodstained snow. "*Murderer!*" She saw the white rose insignia against the dark man's chest, as he glanced down at her. She heard his voice as he wheeled his mount away from her and the bleeding bodies in the snow. Then she looked down into her father's still face as the other riders spurred their horses through the bloodstained snow into the night.

It was as if something had snapped inside her. Bronwyn jumped to her feet and ran after the dark man who had

10

killed her father. She threw herself at his leg, clawing at him like a crazed, wild animal. Through the darkness, he stared down into a child's tear-streaked face and laughed at her fury.

Without a word, he tossed her frail little body aside as if she were a bothersome fly. *"You killed my father! You—killed my father. . ."* She crumpled to the ground in a heap, weeping in the snow at the edge of the woods and watched through her tears as the men galloped away until their forms were specks against the night sky and their presence only a dreadful memory. Sobbing, she pulled herself to her feet and numbly walked back to where her father's body lay. Bronwyn knelt down beside her father after she had checked the other men, all dead. They had done their job well. Not one had been left alive, not even an innocent bystander like her poor father. What had he ever done to deserve this?

As people poured out of the inn to see what had happened, her thoughts were on the stranger who had done this. Who was he? She knew nothing, had no answers. But she swore that whoever he was, she would hate him until the day she died. Deep inside as she stared across the snow in the direction he had disappeared, she vowed that one day she would meet him again and avenge her father's murder. *One day* . . .

She was a child, but her anger was not a child's. As she sat there in the snow, cradling her dead father's head in her lap and listening to a hungry wolf howling mournfully miles away in the woods, she also knew there was nothing she could do now to wreak her revenge. The knowledge made her grief even harder to bear.

What could she do against the King's men, soldiers, armed, and skilled in the art of killing? It was insanity to let herself dwell on such thoughts, and Bronwyn was no fool.

She swore silently under her breath. *"Tis lucky for them*

that I am not truly a witch, or I would place such a terrible curse on those bloody butchers that they would wish they were dead instead of my good father! At that moment, Bronwyn would almost have sold her soul to have that power.

CHAPTER I

London—1463

THE INN called the Red Boar had a reputation all over London as being the secret meeting place of certain noblemen who desired to remain anonymous as they took their pleasure or furthered their plans for political intrigue. But Bronwyn didn't believe a word of it, or she wouldn't have been huddled by the inn's closed doors that night as she was so many nights, mesmerized by the laughter and singing inside. She couldn't tear herself away from the merriment she could only listen to and dream about, but dared not partake of. The Red Boar was no place for a young woman and she knew it. Yet the delicious aromas that drifted past her nose made her eyes water and her empty stomach growl. She hadn't eaten all day and even if she had any money, which she didn't, she'd never spend it behind those doors, not while her sisters, all alone now since their mother's death last winter, were waiting at home with empty bellies, too. She had found no work today and therefore she had nothing to take home to them. Bronwyn worried about this, but she was too weary to care much at the moment. So she leaned against the wooden doors of the inn and pretended she was a rich lady with servants to wait on her as she took supper inside. Pretending couldn't hurt, she reasoned. She hummed the songs the revelers were singing and tapped her small feet to the music within. But whenever someone came in or out the door, she'd turn and flee like a scared little mouse. She was so tired of tears, so tired of worrying about things she couldn't change. Her mother had died of fever only a few months after her father had been killed and for the last two terrible years Bronwyn had begged for work or food in any place that would have her, anything to put food in their stomachs and to stay alive. Her life had been so full of tears and now, standing before the inn's door, secretly wishing she were one of the fortunate laughing and eating inside, she was sick of it all. Something had to be done, she knew; something had to change. She was tired of being frightened of everything and everyone. Wasn't she almost sixteen? Wasn't she almost a woman?

Bronwyn had changed a great deal from the gawky child she had been when her father had died. She was tall, with a graceful figure and large, beautiful green eyes that could smile as if they could see deep into your soul, haunting eyes that according to those who came to her for healing held secrets. Word of her gift had spread in the last two years and she and her two sisters were usually left alone. Some feared her special powers and some respected them. All kept their distance unless they needed her services.

Bronwyn tossed her head and her long golden hair fell in a shimmering cloud about her shoulders down to her narrow waist. Suddenly apprehensive, she glanced around her into the shadows and then nervously retucked her hair back under the hood of her ragged cloak. She was far from home tonight and if she wasn't careful, someone might see or hear her, someone she didn't know. A lusty soldier or an arrogant dandy could make trouble. Here, she knew she wasn't safe.

"Careful, wee mouse . . ." she said to herself, "or you

will find yourself in some clumsy soldier's grasp, and never be heard of again!'' But she wasn't really afraid. The protective cloak of her reputation as a healer had lulled her sense of danger over the years. She noticed how men looked at her at times and she knew she was not a child any longer. Her breasts were high and full and strained provocatively at the coarse brown wool of her gown. Yet the men who knew her left her alone. *She could stop bleeding from an open wound just by the laying on of her small hands* . . .

The payment for her healing services kept them all alive, for the poor paid in food. But even that had been scarce this winter and as Bronwyn stood listening to the music from inside the inn, she knew that she must somehow find work. Her sisters' welfare meant more to her than anything else in the world. Nothing must hurt them. They would not know hunger if she could help it.

A second longer, she promised herself. How she loved music! She loved to sing. It eased her fears, her hunger and her sadness. And it cost nothing. *I wish I were a gypsy!* she thought. *I could sing and dance for my supper. I'd never worry about tomorrow and I'd be happy.* She sometimes felt in her heart that she must have been born a gypsy and someone had stolen her away to live this drab, unhappy life. She could almost see herself whirling in the campfires in bright skirts, laughing at her gypsy lovers in the firelight, her hair flowing in the wind as she danced. All she knew was responsibility and worry. She was only fifteen . . .

Would any man ever love her? she wondered. Who would want a waif, an orphan . . . a *witch*? Yes, that is what they sometimes called her! She knew, too, that soon she and her sisters would have to leave the place where they had always lived. It was getting far too dangerous to stay there. *They burned witches!*

She stretched slowly. It was freezing out in the winter

night and the cold had seeped into her bones. It was totally dark now and she knew she had stayed out too long. Her sisters must think some terrible mishap had befallen her. She had been cruel to stay away so long. How she loathed winter and the ugly memories it always brought back to her! Her father dying, her mother . . .

She was so deep in remembering the past at that moment that she didn't become aware of the men approaching her until it was too late to run and hide as she usually did. Too late, she heard the unmistakable crunch of boots on the icy ground and twirled around just as two strong arms grabbed her firmly about the waist. How long had they been watching her?

"*Let me go!*" she cried, as she was lifted from the ground. She kicked at the tall stranger, but her feet hit only air. "Let me go!""

He laughed down at her then. "Nay, sweet maid—stay awhile! I must see what it is I have caught." His voice was deep and his strength seemed to mock her struggles. His grip was secure and tight when he grabbed the arm that lashed out at him and he pulled her up close to his large body. She was trapped! Her mind reeled at the horror of what could happen to her as she glared up into a pair of cunning dark eyes in the lean, dark face so far above her. She had been so foolish to linger here in the dark . . .

"You've caught nothing, sir," she boldly spat back at him, still fighting to free herself from his iron grasp. "Nothing that is yours. So please, put me down! I'm no wild animal. I'm just a girl!" She was angry, using anger to hide her fright. She was determined not to let him see how afraid she really was. *Nothing will happen*, she kept telling herself to soothe her growing fears. Nothing. It was silly to believe that this man would want to do her harm.

"*Only* a girl?" He laughed wickedly as his eyes raked across the length of her face and twisting body as she tried to fight him off. "You are no girl, my sweet, but a woman

16

to my mind,'' he told her in a husky whisper, and laughed knowingly at the two men who had suddenly appeared, as if out of nowhere, behind him. His hands were roaming unbidden about her waist and then cupped her breasts possissively as his lips found hers and kissed her greedily.

Ashamed and terrified at her helplessness, Bronwyn wrenched one of her hands free and with a cry of utter desperation, reached up and scratched his leering face from eyebrow to chin so deeply that she could feel blood seeping from under her fingernails when she snatched her hand away.

Yelping like a kicked dog, he threw her violently to the ground, and one of his gloved hands flew up to explore the wound unbelievingly. ''Why, you little vixen!'' His voice roared down at her as she cowered in the drifting snow at his feet.

Horrified at what she had done and knowing there would be a terrible penalty to pay, she scrambled to her feet and tried to run, but a strong hand yanked her back into his arms. ''Hold still, you little wildcat, or I will snap that slender neck of yours!'' he growled into her ear, as he bent her body back painfully to stare into her frightened face. His grip had tightened mercilessly as he continued to glare down at her in the dark. But still she didn't cry out or even whimper, glaring back into his eyes balefully.

Finally, to her amazement he burst out laughing. ''Wild cat, that's truly what you are. Why, you even fight like one with those sharp claws of yours! Nay, you aren't a girl or a woman, but a wild animal. I think I will teach you some manners. You have spirit. I like that in my wenches,'' he told her. ''But now,'' he commanded, ''hold still or I will break your neck, pretty as it may be. I will have no animal disobeying me.'' She could tell he was used to being obeyed and, beaten at the moment by his greater strength, she went limp in his arms. There would be another chance to escape, she told herself, but she could never escape if she were dead and, right now, there was murder in the man's cold eyes. Her heart was thumping so furiously in her breast that she could hardly hear his next words.

"Yes, you have spirit. I hate wenches who whimper and beg as if they hadn't a brain in their heads. I detest weeping women." He wiped the blood from his face with the back of his hand and grinned down at her, the hunter observing his freshly caught prey. He shot a glance back at his friends who had watched the whole episode and were now laughing as they nudged each other knowingly.

They usually shared the wenches. But this one was different. They could tell by the way their friend was glaring at them. *Hands off*, his expression said plainly enough.

"Cousin, she is all yours," one of the men said. "I am in no mood to fight a wild cat's claws and teeth this night! No, no—all I crave is a mug of hot buttered rum and a *willing* wench. This one is all yours." The other shadowy figure beside him laughed in agreement and both of them disappeared into the warm, brightly lit inn; letting the light from inside shine out into the dark night and showing the tall stranger a brief glimpse of Bronwyn's face before the door closed all the way—and showing her his face, a dark brooding face with high cheekbones framed by long dark hair that almost touched his broad shoulders. He was a very tall man, but it was his eyes that captured her gaze and made her gasp. Dark, piercing eyes that seemed to burn right through her, as if he could see what she was thinking, predict her next move. Eyes that hid many secrets. Those eyes, she realized, held her prisoner more than his iron grip, for there was power in them. He was quite a handsome man, she thought then with surprise, in a wickedly dark way, handsome like a hawk or perhaps a wolf.

He loomed over her like a figure in a nightmare and seized her face between his strong fingers, pulling her close to him. He studied her with a strange glitter in his angry eyes and with one swift movement, he reached out and freed her long hair from her hood so that it cascaded down about her face and shoulders. Silently, she met his stare, her chin held high.

How she hated such arrogant men! She was trembling inside. Something vague and nameless was nagging at the edge of her memory as she stared at him. He seemed, somehow, familiar. It bothered her. Some inner sense told her that this was no ordinary man and to show him any weakness would be fatal.

"Well, sir, you've had your fun. You've shamed me enough and you've earned the scratch I've given you. We're even. A kiss for a scratch. And you have ogled me long enough. *Now*—let me go!" She was shocked when he not only refused to answer her, but simply lowered his lips until they brushed her cheek softly. She shivered at his touch even though his lips were hot on her cold skin, and tried to pull away.

"Will you apologize for scratching me? Beg me to forgive you?" he said in a maddeningly calm voice. Its sinister tone made her blood race. He wasn't going to let her go!

"Will *you*, then, apologize for grabbing *me* and stealing a kiss in such an intimate manner? A kiss you had no right to take?" she threw back at him, knowing she shouldn't have said such a thing the moment the words slipped from her mouth. This man was dangerous. She shouldn't be toying with such a man. She didn't know enough of the ways of men to do so.

"Apologize for taking what I want?" He smiled. "Never! You are far too pretty not to kiss. You were made for kissing. All women are." And as if to prove it to her, he yanked her away from the doorway of the Red Boar and dragged her out into the yard behind him, as she frantically kicked and squirmed to escape. He pushed her roughly up against the hard wall of a building in the shadows and pressed his lips cruelly upon hers again. Forcing her mouth open, he thrust his tongue inside, probing. His large, powerful body thrust up against her, pinning her against the wall so tightly she couldn't move.

"So anxious to get away from me, little wench?" His breath was hot on her face. "Well, you shall pay dearly for that as well as for my wounds. I shall take you here and now, for no one defies me and gets away with it. You will learn to enjoy it once we start. So, my little wildcat, put away those claws and make it easy on yourself. I always get what I want. And I will have you." He chuckled, kissing her again.

Panicking, she kicked at him wildly and they tumbled to the ground, entwined. She couldn't believe what was happening. Wouldn't anyone come to her aid? No, she realized with terror. No one would interfere. He was a soldier and she was a peasant.

"Stop fighting me, wench!" He slapped her. She didn't cry out, stunned at the unexpected violence.

"*You have no right to do this!*" she murmured, her voice low and husky. "Have you no honor? *You cannot* . . ." But he stopped her words by kissing her again, his hands grabbing her shoulders and twisting her slender body to mold it to his as they struggled in the snow, rolling over the hard ground. He was far too strong for her and she felt his hands tearing at her bodice, ripping the cloth away from her young breasts; his warm mouth and teeth found them. Bronwyn screamed, but he immediately brought his lips back down on hers as his hands stripped her bare to the waist. The cold air stung her naked skin but everywhere his hands touched her burned like fire.

He was amazed at how lovely she was. He knew as she fought him that she was no street whore that he could treat this way—and yet the very way she defied him, the pride that flashed in her brilliant green eyes as she had scratched him enflamed his lust. He could have had any woman he desired. He rarely had to force them, for they always came willingly to his bed. Why, he wondered, was he in such a fever to possess this worthless wench? How could he bend her to his will?

Money! That was it. He could offer her gold. Didn't every woman have her price? Yet, staring into her wild eyes and feeling her warm body struggle under his, he knew that this was one woman who might not be bought. He had heard that there were such women, but he had never met one. And he had to have this wench! Her resistance only made him desire her the more. His lust made him cruel and he slapped her again. One lone tear slid down her pretty face and fell across his hand. Suddenly the brutality of his actions pulled him up short. "Give in and enjoy it, little one. I will not hurt you any more," he said, almost gently. "Give in and I will reward you afterwards. A good meal . . . gold," he promised.

The look she gave him then could have killed. "Never!" she cried. "Never! Let me go!" Her eyes were so full of hate that the fire in him was rekindled.

She could smell the heat of his lust and she could feel his heart beating strongly in his chest so close to her. When he refused to let her go, she bit his lip until she tasted blood and he retaliated by biting at her exposed breast. She didn't cry out. Instead, she stopped fighting completely and he thought he saw defeat in her eyes as she watched him.

Bronwyn knew he would rape her right there on the frozen ground under the innocent moon if she didn't use her wits. She must be cleverer than he.

"That's it, wench, be easy. Just hold still," he growled as he tried to position himself and dispense with some of his clothes. He unstrapped his sword and tossed it next to them.

It was at that moment that Bronwyn realized how she could escape.

"Wait!" she gasped, smiling up at him as beguilingly as she could manage under the circumstances. " 'Tis true! You are right—if this is to happen, I might as well benefit from it. Perhaps, I will give in. I will take that generous reward that you have offered me." She hesitated. "I am very hungry and I do have small mouths to feed back home . . ." Her heart skipped a beat as he peered down cynically at her, trying to read her true meaning.

"So. You, too, have your price." She was sure she heard contempt in his voice. He was wondering if he could trust her. Then he seemed to make a decision. "Aye, it would be easier for both of us," he finally said.

"I am not a complete fool, my Lord." The words were spoken softly; she had stopped struggling completely.

"No, of that I have no doubt." He studied her a moment or two longer and then abruptly laughed out loud. "Here," he exclaimed, and rummaging around beneath his cloak for a second, he placed something hard and cold in her left hand. She heard a clink. Coins!

She was relieved. He had *believed* her!

Now he was in a good mood. "But," he teased her, kissing her again, "the coins aren't only for your favors, as much as payment for that sweet voice of yours I heard before. You are not only lovely, but you sing like an angel." He laughed, his hands roaming freely now over her body. How she hated him for touching her so!

She had been so stupid! He had heard her singing before in front of the inn's doors. She cursed her foolishness and vowed that if she survived this encounter, she'd never do such a stupid thing again.

"You may even sing for me . . . later." He chuckled, releasing his tight hold on her.

"Perhaps," she replied, her mind lighting on another idea. "Isn't there someplace we could go, someplace warmer and dryer—more private?" she asked. "The inn yard is no fit place for this."

He nodded and pulled her to her feet in one swift movement. "You are right. I do have a place I can take you. It is near here. Ha! I can even buy a nice warm fire and a good meal; a nice soft bed, too." He chuckled. "Come, I'll take you there." He grabbed his cloak and his discarded sword. Why not have the wench in more comfortable surroundings? Besides, he wanted a better look at what he was buying. The soft bed and warm fire sounded better and better to him. He wouldn't have to worry, either, about anyone coming along and spoiling his fun. Some place more private . . . He grabbed her arm and strode off down the street, dragging her behind him. In desperation, Bronwyn tried to cover her nakedness with her torn gown as they made their way down the dark streets. Her mind was whirling over how to use this to her advantage.

He was smug now. "You didn't need to put on such a good act, my saucy wench," he said. "You didn't need to scratch quite so hard." He lightly traced the uneven slash along his face in the dark. "If you wanted money, all you had to do was ask. I am a rich man." He looked down at her with an amused grin on his shadowed face. They passed by doors and then turned a corner. "We're almost there," he said.

"But you *hurt* me." And her voice reflected the pretty pout she had set on her face. They stopped before a large building that was alight with bright torches burning in sconces. She knew that if she was going to escape, it had to be now.

"You like to play games, then?" He had placed her in the torches' glow to look at her as they stood before the door. She was so beautiful that he couldn't help admiring her. The most beautiful thing about her was that she herself didn't know how lovely he was. There was some-

23

thing in her eyes, something that mesmerized him. He wanted her more than any other woman he had met in a long, long time. When she smiled at him coquettishly, mischief danced in her face.

Out of the corner of her watchful eyes, Bronwyn had spied the progress of a group of merrymakers coming their way and she could hear a carriage coming. Now was her chance!

Suddenly, the group of laughing men and women were upon them and the tall rogue who still firmly held her by the arm let his eyes drift their way for a fraction of a second, just enough time for her to place a swift, well-aimed kick to his groin. When he howled and doubled over in astonishment from the pain, she pushed him over into the snow at her feet and darted through the crowd and then around the carriage that was rapidly approaching. The wheels narrowly missed her as they rumbled past and she ran on down the street as fast as her legs would carry her.

Bronwyn didn't slow down until she was sure she had left him far behind her. Then she flattened herself up against a wall in a deserted alleyway and doubled over in relieved laughter. How funny he had looked after she had kicked him! And how richly he had deserved it! She clutched her sides as she laughed, congratulating herself on her narrow escape. Now, that hadn't been so hard, had it? she asked herself. And hadn't she taught that lecher a thing or two! She looked around her and knew exactly where she was. When she had stopped laughing and trembling and had rearranged her torn clothing as best she could, she climbed the broken fence at the end of the alley and started for home, careful not to let anyone see her. She put her hand up once to keep her torn gown from falling and was genuinely surprised to find the coins the man had given her still clutched in her cold hand. For a second she thought of flinging them aside, but thought better of it and thanked God for them instead. They would buy food and warm clothes for herself and her sisters. Bronwyn told herself it wasn't as if she had stolen them. Hadn't he given them to her, not only for her favors, as he had said, but for her sweet voice? So in keeping them she wasn't doing wrong. In fact—she frowned down at the glittering coins in her thin hand—didn't it in part repay her for the brutal way he had treated her? She touched her face where he had so recently slapped it. Her body ached where he had roughly handled her. No, the money was hers and she would put it to good use. He had told her he was a rich man, so he wouldn't miss these few coins.

She continued home, her mind made up, following the familiar peals of the Gabriel Bells that reminded all good Christians to bow their heads and recite their Ave Marias. Her fears of what had almost happened to her that night subsided and her steps grew lighter as she neared her home. Wouldn't Samantha and little Mary be surprised to see what she had brought them!

Bronwyn called out to her sisters to keep them from being afraid as she came upon their small dwelling. It wasn't much of a shelter, she thought, as she pushed aside the heavy old wolfskin that served as a door—a trophy from one of her father's long ago hunts. How she longed to come through this doorway and find him waiting for her as in the old days! How happy the coins would have made him! How she missed him and her mother.

"Mary . . . Samantha!" She greeted them both with a kiss and a wide smile. "Look what I have found!" She held out her open hands so they could see the coins glitter in the weak firelight.

"Where did you find them?" Samantha squealed as Bronwyn laughingly dropped her treasures into her sister's anxious hands. Even poor little Mary seemed to brighten at the sight of so much gold. Her deep brown eyes flew open wide in disbelief and she actually smiled for the first time in days from her pallet by the fire. Bronwyn bent over and touched her hot forehead gently; then, frowning, turned to build up the fire. It was so cold and damp in their tiny home.

Samantha, still clutching the coins, threw her thin arms about her older sister. "Where did you get them?" she persisted, her eyes sparkling.

"A rich man must have dropped them in the street when he left the inn drunk, my poppet," Bronwyn lied, "and I found them." She shrugged. "I would have been a fool not to have picked them up. Someone else would have found them for sure."

"Aye." But Samantha's sharp eyes didn't miss the guilt that flickered briefly across her older sister's tired face. She said nothing, however. Then she sighed. "Now, at least, we will have food!" She grinned, brushing her long blond hair from her face. "Can we go and get something to eat right now? I am so hungry!" Her teeth flashed white and even in her round face. "Please!" Aye, she would be a charmer some day, Bronwyn thought.

Mary, always the serious one, said, "You had been gone so long, we were sure something terrible had happened to you." Her weak little voice trembled as Bronwyn knelt down beside her, smiling softly.

"No, nothing terrible happened to me, my tiny sweet poppet. How can anything happen to me when God is watching over me?" She smoothed her sister's damp dark hair back from her feverish brow. The child's face was so thin . . . "How do you feel?" she asked, concerned.

"Her fever has gotten worse, as her cough has since the sun went down. It is so cold in here, sister." Samantha supplied, hovering behind Bronwyn and looking down over her shoulder at her little sister. "I have given her all that hot broth that you brewed earlier," she said. "It helped a little, I think. She did sleep a long time."

"Good." Bronwyn sighed, standing up. The broth was

a special one made from the strongest herbs she could find in this weather. It brought on sleep so the patient could rest and help the body heal itself, and she'd made it even stronger than usual.

"I was almost ready to come looking for you." Samantha's eyes couldn't hide the worry she felt.

Bronwyn blushed, remembering her torn gown, and she pulled her cloak more tightly around her so Samantha wouldn't see the condition it was in.

Bronwyn remembered the man who had almost abducted her and started at what her sister had just said. "*No!* You must *never* go out into the streets alone at night, Samantha. *Never* come looking for me, do you hear? Promise?" She held her sister's surprised gaze and waited until she nodded obediently.

Bronwyn sighed and dropped a kiss on Samantha's blond head. "You're both hungry, I know, and so am I. Stay here," she directed the words to Samantha, "and I'll fetch us some cheese and bread and some tea. Would you like that?" It felt so good to be able to give them something to smile about. Such thin, sad-eyed little waifs! There was always hunger in their childish faces and she felt the familiar twinge of guilt as she heard them both say, "Yes, yes! That would be grand!" They asked so little of her, but their care demanded so much—maybe too much—from her, little more than a child herself. There were many times she felt as if her burdens were too much to bear. She could barely take care of herself, let alone her two helpless sisters. Hungry, loving eyes followed her every move and she shivered. How she wished she could turn to someone else for help! Bronwyn shook her head again. She didn't want to dwell on it any further—she couldn't solve that problem tonight.

So she went back out into the freezing night and searched until she found a light in a neighbor's cottage. One of the coins immediately persuaded the neighbor to part with some bread and cheese. The stooped, crooked-toothed cottager eyed her suspiciously when she handed over the shining coins, but he didn't ask her where she had gotten them. Gold was far too seldom seen to question its source.

As she made her way home again, bone-weary and aching with cold, her thoughts were troubled. What would she do if she happened to run into that black-eyed stranger again? And why had he seemed so familiar to her? It bothered her, but she couldn't remember. Surely she had met him somewhere before, but where and when?

But later, her sisters' joy over the food wiped all those troublesome thoughts swiftly away. "Tomorrow," she said brightly. "We'll go to the market. It's time we had some cloth for new warm gowns." She was content to see their smiles as they gulped down the food and sipped their hot tea.

"Mary, I'm going to make you the prettiest red woolen gown you've ever seen!" They all laughed.

That night, for the first time in months, the three girls went to sleep with full bellies, huddled together under the thin blankets.

In the dim, eerie light that pervades the earth right before dawn, Bronwyn awoke, clutching her throat. She had been dreaming. She shook her head, trying to scatter the disturbing remnants of the uninvited dream, but it still clung to her like a heavy mist on a chilly morning.

She had had this particular dream many times before and it still terrified her as it had the first time. She tried telling herself that, after all, it was just a dream, but to no avail. She stared unseeing into the fire's dying embers with glassy eyes, and her fear was so real she couldn't escape it.

Some called her a witch, and thus the dream was shattering for she feared being accused of that crime, and of being burned at the stake. She lowered her heavy head onto her knees and trembled. She feared the prison of her dreams, with its thick, windowless grey stone walls. Water dripped down over the cold stones; there were no sounds but the pitiful moans of other wetched creatures locked away in pain and agony. A stench of blood and death was everywhere. In her dream, she cried for mercy over and over, but no one could hear but the other prisoners. She had the feeling she had lingered there for years.

But the last few times she'd had the dream, she saw a fair-haired man whose eyes were gentle and full of compassion, and on whose brow rested a glittering crown. He would come to her and stoop to speak to her and calm her terror, but then he would fade away into the grey mists surrounding the walls from whence he had come. What did it all mean? She wondered if she would ever know.

Bronwyn's eyes grew heavy again as she listened to the heartless wind whispering about in the frost-encrusted trees outside. Was there a message in the wind? What was it trying to tell her?

Looking down at her sleeping sisters, Bronwyn brooded. She was almost sixteen. It was time she faced the great world out there, frightened of it though she was. For her sisters' sake, if not for her own. Mary needed a safe, warm place to live. She was so frail and Bronwyn worried so about her. They could not stay here much longer. It was time to move on.

Bronwyn yawned sleepily, and soon she drifted back off to sleep. This time she didn't dream.

It snowed heavily throughout the long night and Bronwyn awoke the next morning to a grey and white world, shrouded in mist.

Samantha was sitting next to her and Bronwyn ran her fingers through her sister's long, tangled hair. "Bring me the comb," she yawned, still half-asleep. Samantha smiled and went to fetch the comb that had belonged to their mother.

"Bronwyn?" Samantha pouted. "You promised we'd go to the market today, remember? Are we still going?" Her voice was petulant, coaxing.

"When I've built the fire up again, we'll talk about it," Bronwyn said. Then seeing the disappointment flash across Samantha's face, she added, "Your sister won't be able to go, but we'll figure something out, I promise." Then, shivering in the icy morning air as she stepped out into the snow, she ran toward the woods, careful not to wander too deeply into them for fear of the wolves.

Later, after she had rebuilt the fire and tended to Mary's needs, Bronwyn melted a bowl of snow and washed herself and her sisters as best she could. It was too cold to do anything but dab at their hands and faces. She found herself shivering. It had never seemed so cold. She touched Mary's feverish face and her heart was heavy.

Mary would never get well here in the cold and damp. The place was full of drafts, no matter how hard she tried to fill the cracks with new mud and straw. They must leave this place . . .

But frightening images kept swirling around in her mind—that man's angry, lustful face . . . the empty, hungry faces of those she met on the streets every day . . . her father's murder . . . Bronwyn shivered not only from the cold.

"Sister," Samantha tugged at her sleeve and sat up, playing with her hair lazily. "Are you going to stay in here all day? You promised we'd go to the market!"

"Go ahead." Mary's weak little voice chirped behind them. "I'll be fine here by myself for a little while. No one will bother me. No one ever bothers us, Sister." She was looking pointedly up at Bronwyn as she spoke. "*You* know why. And I want that new red gown you said you'd make for me. I am so cold, Bronwyn.'' Her eyes were bright, too bright.

Bronwyn was thinking about Mary's words. Everyone was afraid of her. They kept their distance unless they needed her . . .

"Bronwyn!" Mary was still talking to her. Silly sister, her tone seemed to say, always somewhere in dreamland. "Did you hear me? I'll help you make the gowns. I know you aren't handy with a needle." Both younger sisters giggled. It was true—Bronwyn's hands held a special kind of magic for the sick, but none for working with cloth. The gowns she'd made for them last year looked like sacks. Mary, only seven years old, was already the best seamstress in the house. Her stitches were much neater and stronger than her older sisters'.

"Are you implying that I can't sew?" Bronwyn feigned anger.

"But 'tis true, sister, you can't." Mary said smugly. She and Samantha giggled until tears were running down their cheeks.

"All right, you've convinced me. But are you sure you'll be all right alone until we return?" Bronwyn asked as she and Samantha prepared to leave. The fire was crackling and Mary was warm and well fed under her blankets.

"Yes!" she sighed, waving her tiny hand at them. "I'm a big girl, aren't I? I can take care of myself!"

Bronwyn couldn't help but smile. The child had far more courage than she herself did at times. She could always depend on Mary. Samantha was the one who needed watching. She was more headstrong and sometimes rebellious.

Bronwyn and Samantha, bundled up for warmth, headed out into London's teeming streets. "We must fetch what we need and hurry back as fast as we can to Mary. I hate leaving her alone," Bronwyn said as she held Samantha's hand tightly and maneuvered through the bustling crowds that thronged the noisy marketplace. They needed some warmer coverings for their feet, too, she mused as they hurried along. They stopped at the cobbler's first and Bronwyn ordered three pairs of sturdy boots.

"They might not be the prettiest things you ever set your eyes on," she told Samantha, clutching her sister's hand and touching the little pouch full of coins that she had hidden within her bodice so no clever thief could snatch them away, "but they'll keep our feet warm and dry."

"Sister, couldn't we have some fashionable, pretty shoes for once?" her younger sister begged.

Bronwyn laughed and shook her head. "I'm sorry, Samantha, but sensible boots will keep our feet from getting frost-bite, not fashionable, pretty shoes. Time enough for that when warm weather arrives." They continued on their way, purchasing yards of thick woolen material that they would sew into warm gowns, under-clothing and cloaks. No one questioned where she had gotten the coins she spent. The town was so full of people that no one wondered how two young girls, shabbily dressed, happened to have a surprising amount of gold. But Bronwyn knew she couldn't trust anyone and no one would trust her. On the London streets, life was cheap. Cutpurses and murderers abounded, ready to prey on the innocent or unwary. Under her belt, tucked away safely between the folds of her old gray gown, she had strapped a tiny dagger that had once been her father's. She had no doubt that if she needed to, she'd use it to protect herself and those she loved. What had happened the night before would never happen again. She knew the streets of London were dangerous, except for the mighty and the rich who made their own rules. One learned to be cautious in order to survive.

They stopped later to buy hot oatcakes soaked in honey when they got hungry; Bronwyn carefully wrapped in cloth a portion to take home to Mary. The coins had been a Godsend, she thought, as she and Samantha crouched in a doorway and gobbled the cakes hungrily. She'd never had so much money in her life and she was determined to make it last as long as she could. Bronwyn wondered what it would be like to be truly rich, to have anything one wanted. Just thinking about it made her giddy and light-headed. The coins in her little pouch made her forget her usual worries in the excitement of the moment and she and Samantha giggled over their newly bought treasures as they skipped down the streets, bundles held close against them under their cloaks and on their lips, melodies their mother had taught them as babes.

A short, fat, smiling fellow in a green woolen tunic with a capuchon dangling down his back winked at Bronwyn. In a moment, he was lost again in the milling crowd around the open stalls.

The girls made their way up Bowyer Row and past the precincts of St. Paul's where tradesmen who were caught cheating their customers as well as other sinners did public penance.

"Get out of the way, Samantha!" Bronwyn cried suddenly, yanking her younger sister, just in time, out of the path of a band of galloping horsemen who wore the badges and the colors of the King. King's men! They rode through the city as if they owned it, she thought angrily, watching as the last rider dug his rowels deep into his stallion's sweating side, urging it to more speed. Sometimes they trampled an unobservant wretch under their flying hooves. It was though the common people didn't exist.

A moment later, however, Bronwyn's attention was distracted by the exciting scene around her. Samantha paused to speak to a wool merchant they both knew and patted the donkeys that he had led to market, all of them laden with large panniers of raw wool on each side of their lean flanks.

Then they moved on, swept along by the crowd—fletchers with their bows slung across their shoulders and warmly dressed in homespun jersey wool, scurrying scribes, their writing implements dangling on a chain about their skinny necks and tightly rolled parchments clutched in their hands, farmers who smelled of manure and sheepmen smelling of their sheep. Stewards and pages bustled about the heavily laden produce stalls searching out bargains for their masters' dinner tables. Smiling people hurried past them and frowning, complaining housewives shoved them aside in their haste to purchase the best piece of meat or the fattest chicken. London! Sometimes Bronwyn hated the city and sometimes, like today because she had money in her pocket, she loved it.

"Isn't it wonderful?" Samantha seemed to read her thoughts. "Not to be hungry, and to have money? And to know that soon we'll all have new gowns. Which cloth will you have?" she asked her smiling sister as they finally headed home.

"The green, I think. It matches my eyes." Bronwyn was laughing as they turned down a side street—and were engulfed in the midst of a shouting mob.

With a cry of terror that could not be heard over the loud voices of the people milling around them, Bronwyn looked up at the scaffold towering above the jeering, ugly crowd.

They were torturing someone up there . . . she could hear his screams . . .

"*Oh, my God, no!*" Bronwyn wailed in outrage and pity, grabbing Samantha's cold hand and yanking her as best she could back through the crowd of bloodthirsty gawkers. "*We must get away from here!*" she sobbed, the terrible image still vivid in her spinning mind.

A poor pitiful excuse for what was left of a human being pleaded and screamed on the bloody scaffold behind them. He screamed in agony and horror because he had no hands.

Bronwyn finally tore herself and her frightened little sister away from the abominable scene and the horrible sounds. As soon as they were far enough away in a deserted alleyway. Bronwyn collapsed and emptied her stomach there and then of every bit of food she had eaten. Poor Samantha was unable to do a thing but stand behind her, holding her waist to keep her from tumbling to the ground, until she was through.

It was only then that Bronwyn noticed that they had been followed.

"Samantha," she whispered to her sister. "Don't look back and don't say anything, but when I say the word, *run for it*. Do you understand?" Bronwyn's voice quivered and her grasp on Samantha's hand tightened. She kept her eyes ahead of her, wary of looking backwards, afraid their pursuers would realize that she was aware of their stealing up so silently behind them. It must be the gold they were after! No doubt someone had watched as Bronwyn had removed the precious pouch time and time again to pay for her purchases. What a fool she'd been to think it had gone unnoticed!

"Run!" Bronwyn cried and they pushed through the thinning crowd, pushing people roughly out of their way as they ran.

"Bronwyn . . . slow down . . . I can't keep up with you!" Samantha panted in fear behind her, sobbing.

"No! You must run faster! Look, they're right behind us!" Bronwyn pulled her along mercilessly, nearly dragging her through the streets.

In one swift backward glance, Bronwyn saw that their pursuers were gaining on them.

"Maybe they only want our packages," Samantha offered breathlessly.

"Then drop them!" Bronwyin commanded. "Maybe that would satisfy them."

The precious bundles tumbled into the filthy snow and Bronwyn and Samantha turned abruptly down into a long, narrow dim alley.

"Oh, no!" Samantha wailed. "They took the packages, Sister, but they're still coming! What do they want of us?"

Bronwyn stole a look back and saw it was true. They were so close she could see the leering grin on the leader's face.

"I'll scream, Bronwyn! Someone will hear me and come to help!" Ah, the innocence of a child, Bronwyn thought.

"No. No one will hear and no one will come to help us. We must take care of ourselves, little sister."

Suddenly Samantha stumbled and fell sobbing to her knees in the snow clinging hysterically to her sister's gown, refusing to go on.

"Samantha! You can't give up now. Get up!" Bronwyn snapped angrily.

"I *can't*! Can't go on . . ." she wept.

"You must! Get up! *Now*!" Bronwyn ordered.

". . . *Can't*." Samantha huddled at Bronwyn's feet in the filthy, cobblestoned street. Bronwyn felt a twinge of disgust but Samantha was her responsibility, and she must protect her.

With a last final desperate tug, Bronwyn brought her hysterical sister to her feet and shoved her around the next corner, only to cry out in alarm when she saw it was a cul de sac. "No place else to run . . ." She uttered the words in a long moan. Then, squaring her thin shoulders, she turned to face their pursuers with a determined expression in her face. *I have no choice but to stand and fight them*, she realized.

"What is it you want of us?" She stood straight and her voice was a low growl in her throat as they surrounded her and her sobbing sister. "You already have everything of value we own . . . there is nothing else. Why don't you leave us be?" Her angry eyes searched the flushed, grinning faces of their tormentors. Some were barely more than boys, gaunt of face from the long, hard winter and clad in dirty rags. Their guilty, nervous eyes kept shifting from their cornered prey to the boy she assumed was their leader. He was a pathetic scarecrow of a man-boy with deep pockmarks pitting his ugly face and evil, squinty eyes that openly appraised his prize catch. He stared at her and laughed, breathing hard, eyes glittering.

"Let us pass!" she demanded, yet he only stared at her as if she were an animal caught in a trap and he a voracious wolf.

A feeling of rage began to blossom deep inside her very being and grew like a raging fire. Her eyes flashed. She had been hounded and abused, had almost starved these last few years since her father's death. Something was happening to her now. There was this great anger inside her.

Suddenly, she was no longer afraid. She shoved Samantha behind her skirts and leveled burning eyes at their leader, her mouth a grim line. She slipped her hand under her cloak and pulled her dagger from its leather sheath. Its blade glinted in the sun. The snickers suddenly stopped and the looks on the boys' dirty faces turned to surprise and dismay.

Her voice rang out like steel on the frosty air. "I promise you, if you touch one hair of my sister's head, your blood will be shed, red and thick, I warn you!" Her tone was as deadly as the blade in her steady hand.

"Ah, we've caught us a live 'un, we have!" The leader

grinned nervously back at his unsure comrades. They'd already backed up a few steps, out of range of the sharp blade in her small hands. He was studying her with his heavy-lidded eyes and wiping his drooling lips on a tattered shirt sleeve.

Bronwyn glared at them silently, waiting for them to make the next move. Cowards, she thought, disgusted. They were all filthy cowards!

One of the ruffians far enough away from her knife to feel relatively safe jeered, "Dearie, do you really think you can fend us all off at once?" He laughed a little weakly. "Mayhap it's your sweet kisses we're really after. Give us a kiss or two and off we'll be, as pretty as you please." He grinned at her and a few of the others laughed, but the laughter faded away as she stepped towards them.

"Try it, then." Bronwyn said coldly, her anger making her brave.

The seconds ticked away, but no one made a move towards her. They seemed afraid of her—if only a little.

The jackal who was their leader told her, "We outnumber you, my pretty. Perhaps we'll just take what we want."

"*Try.*" Her voice was just a harsh whisper. The knife flashed out in front of her. Samantha was speechless with fear—Bronwyn could hear her uneven, wild breathing.

Bronwyn felt her growing fury push her over the edge; without warning, she lunged at the lout closest to her and sunk her dagger into the palm of his outstretched hand. He stood there, a shocked and stupid look on his ugly face, then dropped to the ground screaming in agony, clutching his wounded hand. Blood gushed through his fingers as he tried to stop the bleeding with his other hand.

Bronwyn knew that her only advantages were surprise and courage and she spun around and thrust her bloody dagger deeply into the leader's arm this time, just above the elbow, twisted it, and smiled fiercely as he yelped in pain and grabbed at her. She dodged him easily and he fell onto the cobbles, then struggled to his feet and, cursing loudly, ran off, followed by his henchmen.

As suddenly as it had begun, it was all over. She heard one of them shout. *"We're not finished with you yet, witch! You'll regret this. You'll pay for this, witch!"*

Bronwyn slumped down beside a trembling Samantha and took the child into her arms to comfort her. She had thrown the dagger to the ground, overwhelmed by what she had done. She was a healer, and today she had wounded someone! She was no better than they, no better than the murderers who had ridden down her innocent father or the executioners who mounted those bloody platforms behind their pitiful prisoners. She wiped the tears from her hot face, and wearily helped Samantha to her unsteady feet.

"Let's go home," she said without feeling, gathering the bundles that their would-be attackers had left behind in their hasty retreat. Some good had come of her standing her ground, after all.

But as they cautiously trudged back through the busy streets toward home, Bronwyn could feel only despair. They had called her witch. Oh, it was a common enough epithet when you were angry at someone. To accuse someone of being a witch was an easy way to get rid of someone you hated. Yet it haunted her. It was dangerous to bandy that word around. Why had they called her that when she was only defending her sister and herself? They were total strangers.

Perhaps their assailants would make good their threat. They had to pack up their belongings and go away—far away—and soon. It filled Bronwyn with dread to imagine what might happen to her and her helpless sisters if they were found and cornered one dark night.

They must leave. With no strong protector, they were at the mercy of brutes and thieves such as those who had just attacked them. Bronwyn must find a better, safer life somewhere, a sanctuary, someplace warm and safe. She must conceal her healing gifts and she must find work in the city somewhere. She wasn't a witch, but anyone who bore her the smallest grudge could simply point a finger at her, and soldiers would come and drag her off.

CHAPTER II

London—1463

IT WAS musty and smoky inside the Red Boar and cool, even though a great fire blazed on the hearth and the walls were lined with huge torches. Bronwyn had hoped that the inn would be empty. The place reminded her of a large cave. The stink of ale and whiskey hung everywhere, mingled with the odor of sweaty leather, and the mildew and dirt embedded in the stale rushes spread over the wooden floors.

The sound of a lute beckoned her from one of the shadowed corners, soft and haunting, its audience almost concealed by the shadows around a trestle table as they quietly talked and ate their midday meal.

No one noticed her entrance, or so she thought.

She walked slowly over to another long wooden table near the fireplace and found herself suddenly peering into two suspicious beady eyes that made her think immediately of a ferret she had once captured in one of her traps.

Behind the man, roasting mutton sizzled on a spit over an open fire and Bronwyn could smell the tantalizing sharpness of bacon in the air, too. It made her stomach growl. The coins had long ago been spent. Another sound reached her ears—the distinctive scrape of metal on metal. Only the wealthy ate from plates with metal utensils; the poor ate their meat on thick slices of bread or used their fingers, as God had intended.

She faced the innkeeper, for so she assumed him to be, and drew her hood back, revealing her perfect features. With Mary's help, she had made the green gown she had promised herself. It bared her white throat, and the fire's warmth caressed her cold skin. It felt heavenly after the bitter cold outside. The gown was simple, accenting her slim figure and womanly breasts. The skirt brushed against the rushes as she moved and the long sleeves fell open to reveal undersleeves of cream-colored wool. Bronwyn didn't comprehend how beautiful she looked. The color matched her brilliant eyes perfectly and contrasted strikingly with her white skin and pale golden hair that she had plaited into two thick braids that hung on either side of her slender neck. She didn't know that from the moment she had entered the inn, two warm blue eyes had intensely followed her every move.

"Sir, are you the innkeeper?" Her voice came out in a tiny squeak and she found herself repeating the question so he could hear her.

"Aye, that I am," the man with the fat, greasy face and bald head replied curtly, looking her over with a sharp, experienced eye from head to toe. His red tunic was covered with a dirty, wine stained apron that must have been white at one time and beneath his apron, his bulk was huge. She backed up a bit because his breath reeked of whiskey and his fat body stank of sweat. He grinned then, displaying broken yellow teeth as if he were proud of them and emphasizing the wicked scar that ran the length of his left cheek. The scar disappeared under the neck of his gown; she wondered if it was a souvenir from some long forgotten war.

"What do you want with me, lass?" His tone had

already dismissed her and his hands had already gone back to filling the tankards in front of him on the tray with frothy ale. "Looking for work, I bet, like everyone else . . . you're not a whore, are you?" Sudden interest caused his eyes to flicker momentarily over her body.

"No!" she retorted, a little too loudly. She felt a flush creeping up into her face. Her hands were shaking no matter how hard she willed them to stop.

"Now that's a pity. There's always a demand for 'em, young and pretty like yourself. Pity." He shrugged and looked at her fully as if for the first time. "Then, pray tell," his scarred face broke into a grudging grin, "what can you do?" He had taken note of her soft white skin and the full curves under her simple gown, the pretty face and the wide green eyes. There were always uses for someone as pretty and fresh as she. An innocent smile beamed at him shyly and he decided regretfully that she probably wasn't that kind of woman after all. What a shame.

"I . . ." She bit her lip anxiously, unsure of what use she could be in such a place as this. But she had to try. "Perhaps . . . I can be a serving maid, clean the rooms, cook . . ." She gulped at the amused look he gave her, hesitated, then blurted out the rest of her prepared speech. "And . . . and . . . I can . . . sing a little." Her voice had faded to an embarrassed whisper. She felt his beady eyes laughing at her. Who was she to claim to be a singer? Her audacity made her feel faint.

"Oh, that's all?" He shrugged again and gestured vaguely to one of the serving wenches to come and take the tray of tankards he had just finished filling. He seemed disinterested and began wiping the table in front of him off with a dirty rag.

"Yes . . . but I could *learn* how to do anything. I need a job badly," Bronwyn pleaded. In another second, she swore to herself, she'd take to her heels. What was she thinking of, begging for work in a place like this?

Sensing this, and thinking that her fresh young beauty might appeal to the patrons of his inn, the man looked back up at her and smiled. "Have you ever done this sort of work before, lass?"

She could have lied, but what was the purpose in that? Sooner or later she'd be found out. "No," she breathed, expecting him to tell her to leave. Then she added again, "But I *can* learn! Just give me a chance and I can learn to do anything, I know it!"

He sighed heavily. Her eagerness touched even his hard heart, but it was her beauty that finally convinced him. "We serve a lusty clientele 'ere. I'll warn you first. The soldiers are a rough, unruly lot, and the rich are used to getting what they want. Do you think you can handle them?"

Bronwyn was speechless with amazement—he was actually considering her for a job! She didn't know whether to laugh or cry.

"I know I can!" She thought of all the problems she'd dealt with over the past few months using her wits and courage alone, and she believed that she could.

He scrutinized her a moment longer and then laid one huge hand intimately over her small cold ones that gripped the edge of the table. "I believe you mean it, girl. You're a determined one, you are. And you say you can sing, too?"

She was repulsed by his touch and wanted to make it clear that she was nothing other than what she said she was, yet fearing to make him angry because she needed the job, she gently but firmly pulled her hands away from under his. "A little. But I've been told many times that I have a pleasing voice."

" 'Ave you, now? Well, we shall see." He nodded and, wiping his dirty hands on his apron, winked at her. "All right, lass, I'll give you a try. But if you don't work out, out you go!" He cocked his thumb towards the door.

Her mouth fell open. "Really?" was all she could utter. She couldn't believe what he had just said.

He grunted. "I just happen to need another serving wench. Business has been good lately and one of my girls walked out this morning. You're lucky. Aye, and you'll do well enough . . . How old be you?" He didn't really care how old she was; she looked a woman grown and that was all that counted.

"Sixteen," she fibbed. Not quite, not yet; but what did a few months matter? Sixteen sounded so much more grown up than fifteen. She wasn't sure he really believed her but he didn't say anything further and she left it at that.

"When do I start?" she asked politely, and was taken back when he said, "Now. Good time as any to break you in. Not too many customers, and by tonight it'll be so busy you won't know which way to turn. Best to start now when it's quieter."

Her heart sank, but she only nodded.

"You can begin by helping in the kitchen and doing anything the other serving wenches need done—or whatever Martha, my wife, thinks needs to be done. She's been pestering me for months now to get her more help. Been doing so well she can hardly keep up. She'll show you what to do. And about your singing," he said with a touch of humor in his voice that she didn't miss, "you can try it out on my customers tonight and we'll let *them* decide if you have a voice or not." He chuckled, finding it somehow amusing. Apparently, he didn't believe she could sing at all.

She felt a twinge of nerves. Had they ever hanged anyone whose voice was truly bad? She devoutly hoped not.

"Well, what's keeping you?" he barked.

She was suddenly frightened. Could she really do this? Mingle with rowdy, drunken soldiers and make a spectacle of herself before all those strange men? Bronwyn pulled herself together with great effort. She wasn't a child anymore. She kept seeing Samantha's terrified face on the day the thieves had chased them and she knew she had to try.

The innkeeper was talking to her again and she concentrated on the matter at hand.

"Molly's taking care of that table back there," he pointed towards the rear of the room. "But my other customers need some attention too, so here—take them some more wine." He put out some mugs and expertly filled them with a pungent-smelling red liquid, then pushed the tray into her hands.

Bronwyn took a deep breath and picked up the heavy tray. She glanced apprehensively towards the table full of hungry, thirsty men and swallowed nervously. Her throat was suddenly dry. *Don't give yourself time to think about it, girl—just do it!* she told herself.

"You can hang your cloak over there by the door." The innkeeper nodded toward the pegs that were holding other cloaks along the back wall. With her courage fading faster every second, she self-consciously walked over and hung up her cloak.

The man who had been watching her from across the room was completely intrigued by then. He had been watching her with more than usual interest, positive that he had never seen her here before. He gathered that the girl worked here or was just starting. In the firelight, when she stretched her slender body up on her toes to hang up her cloak, he was aware of the grace and beauty of her every movement. But she looked so very young—she couldn't be much older than seventeen or so, he'd guess. Something about the way she smiled, the easy way she moved, reminded him of a cat and intrigued him the more as he studied her from a distance. His companions had already noticed his interest in the girl and were gleefully nudging each other and making lewd remarks.

But he was a shrewd judge of women and this girl had him completely baffled. He wasn't sure in which category to place her. He couldn't believe she was a common whore—too much innocence in that sweet face, he decided quickly as he propped his handsome head on his hands. She was easily one of the most alluring women he had ever encountered. There was something vulnerable and child-like about her. But of course, he pondered with a small flicker of a smile, his friends would say he always saw the best in women at the beginning. But no, he knew this one was somehow different. There was something special about her but he couldn't put his finger on it and it bothered him. What? He knew there wasn't a lady at his court despite their silks and furs, jewels and painted faces, who could outshine the simple maid he saw now before him. So, he mused, even peasants could produce beautiful women. It was something he had never considered before. He should mingle more with his subjects if many of their women folk were like this one. But then, he thought, it was time he got to know his people better—more than time.

His men were staring at him, but he merely smiled and ignored them—until one of them spoke up, making a derogatory remark about the girl's probable lack of virtue. "Don't you think she is exceptionally fair . . . for one of her kind?" He turned his cool eyes on his comrade as he spoke.

"Yes, Sire, she is a very pretty little thing," his friend finally acknowledged, then added, "but her beauty is simple and I know how you detest those ridiculous court fashions and the way the ladies paint their faces so garishly."

His Lord silently nodded in agreement. They were

spoiled, pampered, silly women who carried little in their pretty heads and even less behind their scheming, sly smiles. His gaze returned to the girl. She was so breathtakingly beautiful, her face unpainted and her shining braids hanging over her shoulders, wearing a simple gown with no gaudy jewels to detract from her natural beauty. Those huge, innocent eyes of hers seemed to pull at him in the strangest way . . .

It was absolutely crazy to let a peasant girl affect him this way. She was nothing but a penniless wench that he could have just by snapping his fingers. Yet he sat there staring at her like some lovesick lad who didn't know his left foot from his right. Why did this particular waif attract him so?

Her voice might be soft and husky, he daydreamed, her laugh sweet and innocent. She turned and he found himself staring directly into her frightened doe-eyes. A shock traveled like wildfire deliciously throughout his whole body, startling him. It was as if he had met her long, long ago, perhaps, in another life, if one believed in such things. He had the strongest desire to jump up and wrap her safely in his arms and press soft kisses upon her full lips.

She must have sensed that someone was staring at her. Her eyes suddenly flashed and her face went cold as stone. Did she really see him staring at her, or was she deep in her own thoughts? He couldn't be sure, but he did know that he wanted to see her up close and find out if she was as beautiful as she appeared to be from here—to see what color her eyes were. Her hair gleamed like silver in the firelight; would it feel like silk if he were to run his fingers softly through it? Would she be soft and warm nestled like a tiny baby kitten in his arms? And would her kiss . . . He sighed aloud, and his Captain seated next to him looked up in amused surprise from the middle of his meal, his fork halfway to his open mouth. *The King lovesick for a peasant maid*? Strange, he mulled, and so unlike Edward.

"Sire?" The Captain caught his master's attention with a concerned whisper. "If you want her, tell me, and I'll have her brought to you." It was as simple as that. Edward IV, King of England, could have anything or anyone he wanted. No one refused a King. The Captain spread his gnarled hands and raised his eyebrows. People disappeared every day in the streets, pretty women especially; some went to private masters and many more to the whorehouses along the docks of Kent or Essex.

The other man meditated a second and then replied gently, "No, good friend, I don't think she is that kind of maid. Don't ask me how I know it, I just feel it here." And he lightly tapped his chest above his heart. "I feel as if I knew her well." He sighed again, wishing in a way that she was just another doxy so he could use her and have done with it. Yet in another way he was glad that perhaps she was different. He was tired of grasping strumpets who only bedded him because he was powerful and rich. No one had ever loved him for himself. He sensed that this girl might be different, not like Jane Shore, that treacherous whore who passed herself off as an actress these days and who had dangled him on a cruel, greedy tether these last few years only to milk him of more money and jewels. Because he was King, they all thought he was rich. He wanted to laugh. If only they knew how empty his state coffers and his pockets were these days! Yes, he was thoroughly sick of these conniving, greedy women! He was twenty now and had never really loved a woman the way a man was supposed to love, nor had one ever loved him in return. His glittering crown had always blinded them to the real man underneath.

"Ah . . . she is lovely, though." Edward muttered, still staring.

"I've seen fairer." His friend Captain John Hawkins laughed now. The King frowned at him good-naturedly but his eyes were still on the wench. Captain Hawkins inspected her himself a little more closely, trying to see what his Liege had discerned. There was indeed something . . . *unusual* about the girl. He had watched as she demurely pulled her hand away from the innkeeper's intimate grasp and had seen the King stiffen until the man had let go of her.

"As little as I know him, I have no liking for that rascal . . ." Edward confided to his friend under his breath. "I know his kind well enough. He'd probably sell his own mother if the price was right. He's the kind that thinks all women are just for one purpose . . . ah, see how she fends him off, though!" Edward smiled then and slapped his well-muscled thigh.

The Captain laughed. "Aye, and if I were a woman, so would I! He's a filthy creature, with those pig-eyes and that fat stomach. But, Sire, I think it is all an act on her part. I'd wager that she's just another street whore, perhaps a little younger and cleverer than most. Clever the girl who knows all men want most what they cannot have easily," he said cynically, amused that he was arousing the King's ire over such a little thing as a peasant girl. He saw the King's eyes flash and he knew he should stop now while he was ahead in the game. "Besides, if she's innocent, if she stays in this rat's den very long she won't be." Captain Hawkins had little use for most women. Women and power never mixed well. Look at that hellion Queen Margaret and that last little piece of baggage the King had just got free of, Jane Shore. He cared about and worried over his soft-hearted young Liege. A pretty face could turn his head so easily. It was his tender age, Hawkins supposed. Edward had enough problems resting on his young shoulders—the weight of a kingdom and a war brewing in Scotland. What he didn't need now was another piece of worthless female baggage weighing him down—the crown was heavy enough.

"Why, John! how calculating you have become. Remember, not all women are to be had for the asking and I feel that this one is the exception to the rule, my friend. You just don't know any other kind of women." Edward smiled fondly at his Captain, laying a hand on his shoulder in a gesture of comradship. "You've spent too many years fighting my father's, and now my, battles. You know only the camp trollops, admit it! I'll make you a wager that she isn't that kind of woman at all! Are you game?"

"Done. A bag of gold, then?" the Captain chuckled, raising a bushy eyebrow over a twinking grey eye. All in fun, though, because he, better than anyone, knew how poor the new King really was; it was a standing joke between the two that they would bet unbelievable sums over the most ridiculous things and neither would ever be able to collect. Only the infamous Earl of Warwick was still rich these days. And Hawkins loved to tease the King—had since he was a small pimply-faced lad—because Edward had no sense of humor in most things and he was so naive when it came to games.

"Why not make it two?" Edward surprised him and bandied back.

"Ah, my Lord, you still believe in the basic goodness in everyone . . .in true love and loyalty, as well?" Hawkins laughed aloud, stroking his dark, grey-streaked beard and slamming his tankard down a few times loudly on the table, a well-understood signal to the innkeeper that he needed more wine. "This will get their attention . . . and then I'll see about buying her for you for the night, at least if she isn't *too* expensive."

"If you can, my good man," Edward retorted, his warm blue eyes dancing.

Their four companions at the table were listening to their conversation with interest, now that a wager was on. Three were of lower rank, a corporal and two men-at-arms, to protect their foolhardy young King as he played at being a commoner, a ploy they couldn't understand, for they were of the common people themselves. Why would a King want to hobnob with the poor? It was said that he wanted to get to know his subjects in order to understand them better. But they all knew it could be extremely dangerous for King Edward to mingle with the rabble in such a lowly tavern with so little protection; they were as nervous and cautious as cats, eyeing everything and everyone with mistrust.

The fourth man was a short, stocky man with a bright red beard, red hair, and the strength of a bull with a temper to match. He would gladly lay down his life for the young King and consider himself lucky to do so. He was a loyal King's man, but he didn't approve of what his Liege was doing. It wasn't right. Hertford grunted, turning his eyes towards that crazy Hawkins. What were those two up to now?

Hertford had also been with the King since he was a lad. Edward was a lion already on the battlefield and a shrewd diplomat, and he was swiftly growing into the strong and able leader the strife-ridden country badly needed. But Hertford, too, was aware that Edward had a few weaknesses—women and good food and wine—and he had to be gently led away from them or it would cause him trouble in the end. He was a strange man, Edward; he could be as cold as ice when dealing with his enemies, but a mere puppy when it came to women. He'd overheard the last part of the conversation and wondered what the King would do if the woman accepted Hawkins' offer.

Hertford rolled his eyes when Hawkins slammed his empty mug down on the table. What the hell did the King want with a common whore? They were often riddled with disease. He looked at the maid and studied her. She was pretty enough; the word "unspoiled" came to him as he looked at her and shook his shaggy head. She looked so very . . . *young*.

To the surprise of all, it wasn't Hawkins who made the first move but Edward. Suddenly, as if mesmerized, he rose and walked toward the girl like a silent, stalking lion until he was directly behind her as she stood listening to the innkeeper. She didn't know he was there. He gestured silently to the innkeeper until the stupid man suddenly comprehended what it was he wanted him to do. *Ah!* the beady eyes glinted with understanding. *Yes—I'll send the wench in your direction! Yes, I see what you want.* Inside, the innkeeper smiled greedily, thinking that it would surely mean something special for him later if he sent the girl to that wealthy gentleman. He'd been a procurer far too long not to understand.

Satisfied, Edward went back to his table, aware that the innkeeper had understood his silent message completely.

The tray was heavy in Bronwyn's arms "Over there, go ahead; don't pussyfoot around, wench—they're thirsty and don't keep 'em waiting." Jack, the innkeeper, impatiently waved her away. "And you can sing them a song or two as well if they wish it! We'll see how good a voice you have, then."

She made her way cautiously to the table with the heavy tray balanced in her hands. She cringed at his casual disclosure. Now there was no turning back, and now she'd have to do that, too, if they wanted her to.

As she set the tray down before the men at the table, she tried not to look at them nor to call attention to herself.

"You're new, eh?" one of them asked her. "I've never seen you here before."

"Aye, I'm new." Bronwyn looked up nervously. The lute's music had stopped suddenly.

"You are very pretty," the man said, startling her. He had deep blue eyes that sparkled at her, and thick blond hair. Suddenly he reached up and softly brushed a stray wisp of her hair away from her flushed face; in the same movement he lightly traced his fingers gently down across

53

her cheek in a caress. Her eyes turned towards him as if she were seeing him for the first time, and she took a step backward.

"No! Don't run away," he pleaded. "I'm sorry. I didn't mean to frighten you." When he smiled up into her eyes, it was as if everything froze for her . . .

He had long blond hair . . . eyes the color of sky . . . a smile that reached down deep inside of her and touched her very soul . . . and Bronwyn shivered. She stared at him and her confusion was mirrored in her eyes. *He was the man—the same man—of her dreams!*

He slowly leaned back in his chair, frowning. "You know me, then?" he whispered.

She shook her head slowly. *"No, no . . ."* But she couldn't pull her eyes away from his face. He was a stranger and yet, he could never be a stranger.

He sighed and closed his eyes a second, deep in thought, the tankard still in his hand, then looked back up at her with that same puzzlingly familiar smile she had never seen before but knew so well. He put the tankard down. "Did I hear right? That besides being the loveliest serving wench I've ever encountered, you can sing, too?"

The sincerity of his smile finally made her smile weakly in return. His eyes captured hers and again she felt as though she were falling into the world of her dreams, losing touch with reality. He seemed to have such a hold on her that she knew she should run—flee—now. But he was so *beautiful*! She'd never seen anyone as beautiful as he. He was dressed in a wine-colored tunic edged with white fur and covered with a burgundy leather vest laced across the front. His hair was wheat colored and his eyes reminded her of cornflowers in the sun. His head was bare but a velvet cap lay on the table next to his sword, and his cloak also trimmed in white fur was carelessly slung over the bench. She knew that when he stood up, he would be tall; his legs, clad in dark hose, were well-muscled and his high leather boots shone in the firelight.

So beautiful that he would steal any woman's heart away . . .

And he knew it. Here was a man used to getting what he wanted; she could see it all in his eyes.

Her heart was thumping wildly in her breast as she replied, "I sing. A little. But I'm really just a beginner, I'm afraid, Sir." She lowered her eyes shyly. "You are probably used to much finer music." Why were they all staring at her? Had she said something wrong?

"You look like an angel, so I've no doubt you must sing like one as well. My friends and I are not hard to please, you'll see." The man of her dreams touched her hand lightly with his as if to give her courage.

"I . . . used to sing for my father at night before the hearth. The songs are the ones my mother taught me when I was a child and my father always told me I have a fine voice, but then, he was my father." She shrugged lightly and turned to take the tray back. But before she could walk away, the blond man reached out and took her hand, holding her back.

"Where are you from?" he asked, and she was relieved that he hadn't asked her to sing just yet.

"I live on the edge of the city, Sir," she replied, surprised at such a question. His hand surrounding hers was warm and firm; his hold gentle enough, though, that she wasn't really afraid. He wouldn't hold her if she were to pull away.

"Do your parents approve of your working here, little one?" Why was he asking all these questions? she wondered. "It can be a rough place."

"They're both gone now," she said sadly. "My father died two winters ago and my mother last year." Her eyes grew cold and distant for a second. "I have small mouths to feed, so I must work."

The King hid his surprise. She looked far too young to have children already—yet he had heard that the peasants married very young. Was it possible that she had children at her tender age and a husband as well? Hertford threw him a warning look.

"How old are you?" Edward exclaimed. Why, she was just a child herself, surely! Hawkins was chuckling behind him. But, Edward fumed, no one had won the bet yet. The joke was on them. She was neither a whore nor an innocent if she was a married woman with babes of her own. Married! That could cause problems. The more he saw of her, the more he desired her. But he wasn't one to come between a man and his wife. He let her go, but he still had an almost overpowering urge to touch her, hold her, husband or no!

Bronwyn looked back at Jack. "Almost sixteen," she whispered, blushing." But don't tell *him*, he thinks I'm sixteen already." She stole another glance at Jack who seemed very interested in everything she was doing. "I have to get back to work . . . is there anything else I can get you, Sirs?" She was eager to get away, petrified that they would ask her to sing. They were looking at her so strangely, especially the one with the blond hair. What did they really want of her? What did it matter who she was or where she was from? It wasn't any of their business.

"What . . . no song?" He shook his tawny head at her. "You must sing at least one little song."

Looking down at their expectant faces, Bronwyn's heart sank and her legs grew unsteady. What would happen if her voice wasn't as sweet as her father had always told her it was? What would they do to her? On the other hand, what did she have to lose? If she was bad, they'd never ask her to sing again, and if they liked her voice it would mean extra money.

Still she tried to get out of it. "Perhaps later . . ."

"Oh, no, *now,* of course!" the blond man teased, his eyes telling her that he knew what she was up to. "You shan't put us off so easily. We want to hear how pretty a voice you have." He waved a slender hand toward the boy with the lute who stepped from the shadows behind him. He remarked casually, "Leon has only been with me a short time. He was my father's page since he was a little lad, but my father made the mistake of sending him to one of my cousins a few years back. They not only failed to appreciate his musical talents, but mistreated him as well—until I stepped in and bought him back. The boy's lute is sheer magic, though his voice is a little thin for my taste. But I have no doubt that some day he will sing as sweetly as he plays." So he was a patron of the arts? It made Bronwyn even more apprehensive about her debut.

Yet when the boy stepped to his master's side, the smile they exchanged was warm as the boy touched his slender fingers to his beribboned lute and expertly played a few simple melodies.

The gypsy boy had a thin, dark face and the biggest, softest brown eyes she had ever seen. He wore a blue tunic belted around his waist and his face revealed past sadness and hunger, of the kind she had known herself. Bronwyn was amazed at how young the boy was for one so talented, and how deep the pain that shone in his eyes when he looked up and smiled at her, nodding.

"Hello, mistress," he said in a soft voice as he bowed to her. She estimated that he couldn't be much older than she. When he led her gently back to his stool by lightly taking her hand, she couldn't help but smile back at him, some of her earlier nervousness dissolving as they discussed the songs they loved to sing the best. The others, too, were encouraging her and laughing. Perhaps, she thought as she hummed a well-known tune to the boy, it wouldn't be so bad, after all. Leon had a sweet voice and he seemed to know instinctively how to blend it with hers in harmony. As they quietly went over the song they had finally chosen for the last time, she found herself thinking about the cruel man who had mistreated Leon before his present master had rescued him. It didn't seem fair, yet it was the way of the rich to brutalize the poor and it was something she knew would never change. At least, when she looked at Leon's smiling face, she knew that he was happy now, and when she looked up later at the blond gentleman, she saw him in a different light.

Edward, too, was thinking about Leon's previous master as he sat there and listened to the two young people test their voices. His great, cruel cousin Warwick, *Warwick the Kingmaker* . . . Warwick with his power and his immense wealth . . . his dark charisma and his blatant cruelty toward those he couldn't use and didn't need . . . Warwick, his most staunch supporter and the man who almost singlehandedly two years ago, along with the mighty Neville family, had placed Edward firmly on the English throne after his father, the late great Duke of York, was murdered. Warwick, his great friend and protector, who had proved his loyalty by fighting many a bloody battle and literally handing a young, bewildered Edward the crown on a silver platter, blood-splattered though it was. He had won the crown the same way for Edward's father before him.

Edward, as he sat listening in this noisy inn so far removed from his usual world of pomp and glitter to a peasant girl hesitantly testing her voice, was actually years and miles away. *If it had not been for the great Warwick, he would not be King today. He owed the man his very life.* But he was beginning to doubt if he could trust the man any longer; he'd become so ambitious lately. *Too ambitious.* As Edward sat there brooding, his heart was heavy. *Why?* Ever since his triumphant coronation on Palm Sunday two years ago, he was aware of a change in

Warwick's attitude. This man who had always obeyed and followed him with more loyalty than any man on earth, who had loved him like a true son since he was a babe, perhaps could not be trusted. And that made Edward sad. And Warwick, he'd be the first to admit, would be much too powerful an enemy! It was an endless dilemma, especially now, when Queen Margaret was still prodding her dethroned, idiot husband Henry to rouse and gather yet again those forces in Scotland still sympathetic to their cause, hopeless as it was—to regain the English throne that had been wrested from them two years before. Edward knew that if they succeeded in gaining the support of the rebellious Scots, they would descend upon England like a plague of locusts. *Christ!* Edward thought darkly, rubbing his fingers across his tired brow. Henry had always been unstable as a monarch, but now, if Edward's spies were correct in their information, he was half-insane and was rumored to be led around like a docile dog by his greedy, scheming, ambitious wife. She hungered for the crown again for that idiot husband of hers, or as some were saying, for her young son, Edward. *Strange, another Edward* . . . It didn't matter which one they put on the throne, idiot or boy; heaven help poor England if they succeeded. Neither would stand a chance against England's formidable enemies such as the wily Louis of France. Henry must never sit upon the throne. It could be the end of England. Edward needed Warwick's loyalty more than ever. As it stood now he was sure that his cousin was still on his side—but for how long? He must be clever and court Warwick's favor. He'd invite him here later tonight for supper and show him his new discovery; it would be just like old times. Warwick had a great deal of vanity and was easy to flatter. He'd reestablish their bond by sending Warwick on a special mission, one he found distasteful but that was always necessary—the killing of a traitor. Warwick loved nothing better than to root out treachery to his country, Edward and the white rose! It was a brilliant idea, Edward mused, that would kill two birds with one stone.

He must never lose Warwick's support, never.

Bronwyn was laughing softly with the gypsy boy, and their voices brought Edward back to the present. He watched the two as they talked, one with hair so fair and the other with darker hair bent over the lute as she taught him one of the songs she knew best. Edward was suddenly struck with the premonition that this girl would mean something to him; that she was destined to play a major part in his life. It was as if he had known her before somewhere, somehow.

Leon soon caught on and was playing the song her way. She seemed pleased. She began to sing in a rich, true voice, as if they had no audience at all. Edward was surprised at the change in her. She was like a wild flower blooming before him. She and the boy seemed to be cut from the same cloth, both dreamers yearning to be free. Innocent children, they could have been brother and sister. Edward was reminded how young they really were. He sighed, wondering what her world was like. He couldn't believe she was already a mother . . . Perhaps he should call off the wager and leave her alone. Then she looked up for a second and caught his eye. She smiled at him before she went on. *No! Damn it!* he fumed. He couldn't let her go now. There was something about her that he needed. Craved. It was as if there had always been something missing from his life and when he looked into her eyes, he found it *there*.

He watched as she leaned over to whisper something into the boy's ear. They made such a pretty picture, he reflected soberly. He felt a twinge of jealousy and it astonished him. She was nothing to him, nothing and yet . . .

"Well, we're waiting," he said, drawing their attention

immediately as he drummed his fingers upon the table. He was no longer smiling.

Bronwyn turned to Leon and asked him to start again. "A little slower, this time."

"Is it to be a love song, then?" the blond one demanded to know, a touch of ice in his voice that Bronwyn didn't miss and was puzzled about. Had she done something to offend him?

She stared into his blue eyes and saw anger as well as naked passion at war there. What did he want from her?

"There are many kinds of love, sir," she replied softly. "Love is what you feel for a father, a mother or your home—your country. Sometimes that is the best kind of love. This is a song my mother taught me when I was a small child and it brings back many good memories. Therefore, yes, it is about love."

Everyone became quiet and, crossing her nervous fingers behind her back, Bronwyn began her song softly just as her mother had once sung it to her and her sisters many long years ago. At first, scared and unsure of herself, her voice would crack or falter on a high note, but as she went on the approving and encouraging smiles on the faces of her rapt audience gave her confidence. Her voice grew stronger in harmony with Leon's, and in the refrain he played his lute so sweetly that it brought tears to her eyes.

When she finished the song and then sang them another, she was delighted and amazed when they stood and clapped, begging for more. Even the haughty gentleman with the blond hair seemed surprised. *They had liked her*! Suddenly her knees stopped trembling and for the first time in her young life she felt proud and special. It was like a lovely, impossible dream. She couldn't get enough of their applause and admiration; it lit a fire in her heart that had never been there before. They begged her to sing again and then again until she was almost exhausted. When she finally put her hands up and begged to be allowed to stop, they laughed and threw coins which she and Leon happily scooped up from the floor and tucked away, smiling and flushed with triumph. Even the innkeeper was beaming at her.

Edward was completely entranced. He stole a glance at his Captain, who simply threw his hands up in surrender. "I told you she was not a whore, Hawkins." Edward told him simply.

"She sings like a little nightingale!" Even Hertford was praising her.

"Ma petite belle chanteuse!" Edward whispered to her above the clapping, his eyes blazing. "You are a prize, my little nightingale," he told her, smiling. He watched her so intensely that Bronwyn was completely flustered and felt faint.

Her happy face suddenly clouded as she remembered everything . . . her problems, her sisters.

"Where did that beautiful smile go?" the man with the blue eyes asked. "You were splendid. You must sing for me again. Did you hear that, Innkeeper? You have quite a prize here. She has a beautiful voice!" And all the time he was watching her, wondering how he could pluck this lovely rose for himself. Or should he leave her to her husband and family? She wasn't one of the common rabble, even he could see that. But then, what did he really know of his subjects? Perhaps she could teach him about her world, help him be the just and good King he so wanted to be.

"Maid, what did your father do for a living, may I ask?" he said.

The mention of her father cast a shadow immediately over the joy of the moment and it served to bring Bronwyn back to reality·like a splash of icy water. *She had been entertaining the same sort of men who had caused her father's death*! She was betraying every promise she had ever made to herself. Her eyes grew distant as she recalled the night her father had died. "He was a soldier. A good, loyal King's man." She turned cool eyes on the rich gentleman. "He was wounded in France and never served again. It broke his heart to be so forgotten."

"I'm sorry," Edward, taken aback, said sincerely. So she was a soldier's daughter. Curious. "England owes such brave men a great debt."

A debt that it seldom repays, she thought scornfully, thinking of how unhappy her father had been in his later years, useless and poverty-stricken.

"He enjoyed serving his King; they were the best days of his life, he always told me," she said sadly. There was nothing else to say. She didn't need to tell this rich stranger anything about her father's brutal murder. He wouldn't understand and he wouldn't care. His kind never did. He was one of the spoiled rich and not part of her world at all. She found herself glaring at the gentlemen in their fancy clothes and glittering jewels, and the others in their hated uniforms. She was reminded of who she was and who they were. *Her enemies.*

It was only then that she noticed that they all wore the King's colors and the soldiers sported the badge of the white rose. Her face paled. *She was that helpless, grieving child again out in the falling snow, fighting heartless soldiers on that wintery night so long ago; she was that child crying over her poor father's grave in the woods.* She let out a faint cry.

Maybe, she thought, *they might be the very devils who had killed him!*

Edward saw the abrupt change sweep over the girl's features as she stared at the insignia his Captain wore; that they all wore proudly on their caps and engraved on the hilts of their swords. He was at a loss to explain her strange reaction, and the way she seemed to turn to stone right before their eyes. The hatred was so palpable one could almost see it emanating from her flashing eyes.

63

"What is it?" He touched her hand, trying to help, seeing the pain in her eyes. But when she looked at him, he saw such hatred that stunned him like a blow. What had he done? Had he offended her in some way?

"Nothing, Sir." But she tore her hand from his as if his flesh burned her. "I have work to do now . . . I have dallied long enough. I must make my living by the sweat of my brow. I have no more time to laugh and sing songs." And her sullen, cold eyes seemed to say: I am not rich and privileged. I am not one of you.

"Then go!" Edward felt a wave of conflicting emotions. Anger. Pride. He was a King; no one treated him like that! He waved her away and turned his back on her, dismissing her like the lowly peasant she was.

After all, she was only a bar wench and not worth a second thought, and he was a King, not some mewling milksop.

The way he so casually dismissed her, galled her and she spun around, skirts in hand, and fled the room like a rabbit from the hunter, not knowing or caring where she was going as long as she could get far away from all those beastly arrogant men.

She ran through the first door she came to and leaned against the wall, cringing as all those terrible memories she had resurrected assailed her. She stood there as if frozen, staring into space with tears streaming down her face. It was strange, she hadn't cried like this in a long time.

Edward had silently watched her disappear and then turned back to his men, a tight frown on his handsome face, his eyes angry. Hawkins knew the King well and at that moment, he felt truly sorry for the man. Edward always wanted his own way; he was used to getting it. Opposition, of any kind, couldn't be tolerated. The King, he sighed to himself as he quickly lifted his cup to his lips, was like any other nobleman, spoiled and pampered, and sometimes his power went to his head. Edward would never know the simple pleasures no matter how often he mingled with his people, nor be sure he was being loved for himself alone. It was a harsh truth that Edward belonged to the country and not to himself. His pride and his duties encompassed him too closely.

Hertford, a little wiser perhaps in the ways of love, muttered to himself that nothing good would come of all this. Edward was obviously infatuated with that wench. He'd seen that look before in the King's eyes.

Hertford knew as sure as he was sitting there drinking wine, that they hadn't seen the last of that proud songbird. Edward would not be able to forget her. Then heaven knows what would happen, he fretted.

"Come!" Edward stood up and slung his cloak over his shoulders. His blue eyes were ice chips still. "We're going!" He turned on his heel and was out the door in a second.

"*I knew it!*" Hertford mumbled, as the rest of them found themselves scrambling to pick up their gear and follow him into the streets. But Hertford, unlike the others knew that they'd be back before the night was over.

CHAPTER III

London—1463

"HA! I'LL LAY you odds that it's a man who brought tears to those pretty eyes of yours. It's always a man, eh my girl?" A woman's understanding voice boomed out at her as Bronwyn pushed herself away from the wall, self-consciously wiping her wet face with the back of her hand. Bronwyn looked at the plump matron who had asked the question as she continued to stir something in a great black kettle that hung over a roaring fire. The woman's face was red and sweaty from the heat and her wild red curls about her plump tired face looked as frazzled as she did. She took the corner of her white apron that was tied around an ample middle and wiped at her hot face. Her shoulders were rounded and stooped from the work as if she had been at it for a long time.

"A man! Am I not right? Martha's always right." The woman looked at Bronwyn sympathetically, shaking her head.

Bronwyn nodded mutely in reply. Then she sighed and said, "I really don't understand why I'm crying. He means nothing to me. I don't even know who he is. It was just that he made me remember something I would rather have forgotten."

The other woman sent her a curious glance and then smiled as she bent back over the steaming kettle and ran a hand through her curly hair. "Aye, it's always a man at your age, deary, believe me. They steal your heart and break it, then run off to war leaving you to put all the pieces back together. Ay, love is strange, that it is." She chuckled then." I wouldn't be your age again for all the gold in the world." She ladled a few spoonfuls of whatever she was cooking into a large wooden bowl and held it out to Bronwyn.

"How about *half* the gold in the world?" Bronwyn smiled back, taking the offered bowl, her tears all but forgotten. She had hardly known the knave, after all.

The other woman laughed, wiping her hands on her apron. "Well, eat every drop of it. You looked starved to me. You need more meat on your bones. That's how men like their women, not skinny as a blade. Go ahead and eat it over at that table. Bread and butter's there, too. Eat as much as you like."

"Men!" Bronwyn sighed as she sat down at the table, tore off a hunk of fresh bread and hurriedly buttered it. She *was* starving and the bread was delicious and so was the stew. "The one out there that upset me so—it was just the way he treated me . . ." Bronwyn shook her head and stuffed another hunk of bread into her mouth. A flash of guilt hit her as she remembered her two hungry sisters at home. Maybe, she thought as she ate, she could bring a little home to them.

The woman was chuckling again as she watched Bronwyn wolf down the food as if she hadn't eaten in days. Her voice was calm and motherly as she said thoughtfully, "Oh, I've seen it all, lass, and believe me few things can make a grown woman cry for no reason—and a man is one of them! They can be so cruel—or so stupid—without even knowing it."

When Bronwyn didn't answer, she went on. "I heard

68

you singing out there, child. You have a lovely voice. 'Tis a true gift from God, that talent of yours. Me, I cannot carry a tune in a bucket but I envy anyone who can.'' She was studying Bronwyn. "And you're pretty as well. You'll have all the men mooning over you and pestering you if you stay here. Just don't let them bother you; you're pretty enough to get what you want, hold out for it and don't ever settle for anything less, you hear?'' She was waving the spoon at Bronwyn. "Remember, you're only young and beautiful once and beauty quickly fades. So get what you want out of life *now*, before you get fat and wrinkled like old Martha here.'' She cocked her round pleasant face towards Bronwyn and shrugged. "Besides being a singer, knowing stingy Jack, I assume you're also the new kitchen help he's promised me?''

"Aye, that I am.'' Bronwyn had emptied her bowl and without asking, Martha filled it again. She knew a starving girl when she saw one, thin and pale-cheeked. "I'm Bronwyn, and you are Jack's wife?'' Bronwyn ventured.

"Ha! Jack's *slave*, would be more like it!'' Martha laughed a full hearty laugh. She was a short, stout woman somewhere in her forties, Bronwyn guessed. She wore a tattered gray gown and her eyes were the same shade of gray. "I have bread in the oven,'' she said and smiled as she went to pull the steaming loaves out skillfully from the large ovens and placed them out on the table to cool. "Lord!'' She wiped her sweaty face. "There's always far too much work for one woman to do here these days. Business is good.'' She heaved a big sigh. "So I'm glad you're here to help. Any experience? Do you cook as well as you sing?''

"No, I'm afraid not. I haven't had much experience, really, in either. But as I told your husband, I can learn and I'm a hard worker,'' Bronwyn replied eagerly as she swallowed the rest of her stew and picked up the crumbs of crusty bread left on the table. "It's the men out there that

I'm not sure I can handle," she said. "I haven't had much experience with them, either." She shrugged and smiled ruefully. "I've always been afraid of men." She turned her eyes away. Why was she telling this woman everything? It was because she was so easy to talk to, so friendly. You didn't meet very many like her. It had been a long time since she'd had a real friend.

"Child, child, don't fret your pretty head over it. I'm probably three times as old as you and I still don't know how those blowhards think!" She threw up her hands. "Who does understand men? But out there, you'll develop a thick skin soon enough. When the soldiers are in their cups they're a little hard to handle at times, but I'm sure you'll learn how to fend them off. And the rich ones . . . well, they're not for us. Not of our world, so to speak. In time, you'll learn to handle them, too. *Men!* They'll pinch your bottom or steal kisses—or more—if you let them. But *only* if you let them. Some of the girls do, you know, for money. It's common enough. If you know what I mean." She eyed Bronwyn meaningfully. "It's up to you, lass. I never make judgments about our girls. A body has to live, you know. It's up to you."

Bronwyn understood, and was grateful to this woman who talked to her as if she were her mother.

"So you think that I'll be able to do the job?" Bronwyn asked.

"Of course I do! You're far prettier than any of the other girls. Even Molly." She stopped then and winked at her. "Now, you could have a bit of a problem with that one. Molly's a harpy. Can't stand for men to notice any other woman when she's around. Ha, ha! wait till she gets a look at you! Ooh, she'll die of jealousy, the saucy bitch!" Martha snickered as if at some private joke.

"Tell me more about this Molly." Bronwyn came up behind Martha as she returned to stirring the pot. Martha handed Bronwyn the spoon and Bronwyn continued stirring while Martha checked something else in the oven. She then went to the table and began to cut fresh vegetables she had just laid out.

"Molly is one of the girls here. She lords it over all the others. She says jump and they jump. She's gonna *love* you, child." Martha chuckled. "You're too young and too pretty; not to mention that lovely voice of yours. Wait until the customers get a good look at that innocent face of yours, and hear that lovely sweet voice! Molly'll want to scratch your eyes out before the night's over. Mark my words, Molly would rather slit another woman's pretty throat than give up any of her power over the men. She paints her face like a common whore—on a real hot day, I bet, that face'll melt, she slaps it on so thick!" Martha was beaming at her as if she found this all very funny, but Bronwyn was beginning to feel very apprehensive.

"She sounds like someone I wouldn't want to have angry at me," Bronwyn said haltingly, stirring the pot, her eyes downcast.

Martha glanced at her. "Just *being* here will do that. So just a small word of warning—stay out of her way. She's mean. She's trash, that one!"

"Thank you for the warning," Bronwyn faltered.

"Unless . . . you're not a whore, are ya?" Martha suddenly asked.

"*No!*" Bronwyn protested. Why did everyone ask her that? Did she look like one?

Martha laughed loudly. "No, I didn't think so. Just asking. So, since you're probably pure as the snow, you had best know the rules before you start. Mind you, as I said before, I don't exactly approve of what some of the girls do for a coin, but I don't condemn them unless they take advantage of the customers—making the men so drunk that they don't know what they paid for come morning. Some of our girls have families to support and they'll do it here or out in the streets; but, my Jack now,

71

he's a greedy one and he allows too much to go on in those rooms upstairs because he gets a cut. Aye, he even encourages them. So watch your step, stay away from those upstairs rooms and you'll be fine." She saw the look of revulsion in the girl's eyes. "No. Don't fault the girls for wanting better'n they have. I've seen all kinds and I don't blame them. The streets are hard. You know what it's like to be poor, fighting to make ends meet. We all do the best we can, even if sometimes the best ain't good enough. You got to survive. I'm just glad that you're not like the rest of the girls, from what I can see; maybe we can be friends. I'm in sore need of friends these days," Martha whispered tiredly. Looking at her, Bronwyn could see that the poor woman carried a heavy burden on her shoulders and she hoped that when she knew Martha a bit better, she might be able to ease it.

"I just hope you can stomach the place; that you stay." Martha glared about the kitchen as if it were her prison and shook her head, a hopeless expression on her plump face.

"Why wouldn't I stay? Haven't I got a friend already?" Bronwyn teased. *Why not?* Here there was food and warmth and a job . . . a whole new way of life. It had to be better than what they'd gone through the last two long years. Old Molly and busy bedrooms weren't going to change her mind. She'd seen all that and more out on the streets. Martha could never understand how badly she needed this job. "It can't be all that bad here," Bronwyn offered.

"Ha!" Martha huffed, but Bronwyn noticed she was smiling. "For one thing, there's too damn much work. Jack can work ya right into a grave, if you let him. He's been trying to do it to me for years." She laughed. 'Make 'im happy, too, I bet. Well, at least now I'll have some help. No one wants to work in this hot kitchen. No one wants to help old Martha. They'd rather be out there flirting and playing up to the customers. Ah, I don't blame 'em.''

The woman was lonely and Bronwyn could understand that. She felt sorry for her and at the same time found herself admiring her. Martha seemed to be everywhere at once and doing everything.

"Well, ma'am, I'll do my best to help you." Bronwyn said earnestly.

Martha turned thoughtful eyes on the slender girl standing over the bubbling pot. "Bless you for that, child. I do believe that I can count on you." She wiped her red hands dry on her apron and putting down the ladle she was stirring with, she sauntered over to face Bronwyn. "What this place needs is another two or three like you." She laid a hand briefly on Bronwyn's thin shoulders and then went back to her baking. She was making meat pies and summoned Bronwyn over to watch. "The stew's done. You can take it off the fire, if you can lift the pot," she said. Bronwyn lifted the heavy pot from the hook and set it away from the fire, then went to help Martha shape the little pockets of dough. Bronwyn learned quickly how to roll the dough and fill it with the fresh vegetables and meat. "Perfect!" Martha finally proclaimed as Bronwyn pushed the finished ones aside and smiled up at her. "You've got good hands for the dough. A soft touch. You'll make a good cook after I get through with you. There! Already you have more going for you than all the other girls here have . . . and you have a kind heart to boot. You're lucky."

"I'll learn anything you wish to teach me," Bronwyn said firmly. "I'll help you in any way I can."

"Well, well," was all the older woman said. They found themselves talking of other things as they worked and the time passed rapidly. Something about Martha reminded Bronwyn of her own mother, something about her voice or the way her eyes smiled without the mouth actually doing so; something about the caring way the older woman treated her, as if they were good friends.

Bronwyn's thoughts as they talked were far away. She was remembering something Martha had said before. *"What this place needs is another two or three like you."* Bronwyn wondered if maybe there might be a place here for her small sisters. Martha had said there were lots of rooms. Bronwyn knew that they couldn't work as hard as she could—they were only children, after all. But she'd work twice as hard and for less pay if they came in the bargain . . . if there was a tiny closet somewhere in the vast inn where they could sleep. She frowned. Mary wouldn't last the winter, she was afraid, unless she could be someplace warm and safe. They were such small girls. They didn't eat much, really. Samantha was old enough to help in the kitchen or clean out the rooms upstairs, and Mary was good with a needle, little as she was. And . . . and . . . Bronwyn began to hope just a little. Martha seemed so kind. If she'd talk to her about it . . .

Bronwyn tried not to think about what the rooms upstairs were used for. No matter what went on, it could be no worse than living in the hovel at the edge of the woods, unprotected and starving. Bronwyn was confident that she could handle the soldiers and the rich men, Molly and the whole crew if only she had her tiny poppets here under the same roof. To keep them safe, she would do anything.

As the hours went by helping Martha in the kitchen and talking about her new job and the Inn, Bronwyn began to worry about the girls. They were probably hungry and worried about her long absence. She'd been gone much longer than she had anticipated. She'd never expected to find a job and a friend all in one afternoon.

"Jack'll have a fight on his hands if he takes you away from me, child! You're a Godsend. You're quick as a fox.

A hard worker, too." Martha's gray eyes sparkled for the first time since Bronwyn had met her.

"I'm the one who should be grateful to both you and Jack. I needed a job more than you know." Bronwyn thought, *I have nothing to lose and maybe something to gain*, so she plunged ahead. "It's been so hard for my two little sisters since our mother and father died . . ." Bronwyn saw instant pity and interest in Martha's look.

"You have two small sisters and no mother or father? Who takes care of the three of you; where do you live?" Martha seemed incredulous as she stared at Bronwyn, her mouth open. "Orphans!" she exclaimed. "How long?"

"Two years since my father died. A year since our mother . . . and I've taken care of us since. Mother was sick a long time." Bronwyn sighed as she shoved the finished meat pies into the oven and wiped the flour from her hands on a towel Martha supplied her with. When she looked up at Martha there were tears welling in her green eyes. "It is hard to talk of either of them. I loved them and now, I miss them so." She had planned to ask Martha about bringing her sisters to the inn, but now it seemed like too much to ask of anyone. They were *her* sisters and her problem. No one else would care what happened to any of them. No one else ever cared about anyone but themselves in this world, she reflected bitterly, remembering past experiences.

"*Two years*? Two years you have taken care of your sisters?" Martha stared at the frail girl standing before her. She couldn't believe she could take care of herself, much less two young children. "It must have been hard. These last two winters have been so cold." Martha had seen children living in the streets, shivering in their rags; she'd seen them huddling in a doorway to stay out of the rain and snow, frightened and starved. Her heart went out to this brave little thing before her and she turned the girl's face toward her and looked into her eyes.

"It hasn't been that hard . . . I . . ." Then, quite unexpectedly, Bronwyn's tears escaped and poured down her cheeks. Without a word Martha folded her into her plump arms and cradled her head as she cried, her frail body trembling in her arms as she sobbed. Twice in one day, Bronwyn had weakened and cried. *Twice!* What was wrong with her? Bronwyn thought, fighting desperately to stop the flood of tears.

"There, there, now, child. Not bad, eh? No, go on and cry. It's time you let it all out. You have had a hard time of it, haven't you? And you can't fool old Martha, so don't try. I was an orphan out in the streets before Jack found me all those years ago and brought me here." Martha patted her gently on the back. "I know what it's like out there . . . The streets are no place for a pretty maid like you and no one to take care of you and the two little ones." Martha pushed her away and leveled a steady gaze at her. "All three of you must come here. *Tonight!* I'll have no back talk, either." She shook her head meaningfully. "There's plenty of room here. There's a tiny loft up on the third floor that's only been used for storage for years now. It used to be my Johnnie's . . ." She stopped, her face so full of melancholy and remembered sadness that Bronwyn was speechless. Martha went on. "But he's been gone a long time now and the loft's empty. No use to anyone. Well, now it can be used again. You'll go fetch those two wee ones right away and all three of you will live here at the inn!" Her voice was resolute. She wanted this girl and her two small sisters. It was the only thing she had really wanted in years, since Johnnie's death.

"But what will your husband say?" Bronwyn was dumbfounded by the yearned-for offer. It would solve all her problems! Could it be true? A new job, a new life . . . a new home, all in one day!

Martha rolled her eyes. "Bah! That old slave driver I'm

76

married to? If your sisters are anything like you, I'm sure they'll be more help than trouble. Jack'll just see two more pairs of working hands and he'll not say a thing against it, you'll see. These days, too, he does well to stay out of my way, if he knows what's good for him. He'll do as I ask; I ask little enough from him as it is." Martha's voice had grown cold and bitter but when she looked back at Bronwyn, she was smiling again. "We'll work it out, child. Don't fret over it. Just answer me: will you bring your two sisters here to stay as well as yourself?"

Bronwyn didn't have to think twice. She nodded her head silently, her eyes still shining with tears, but this time happy tears. *Who was Johnnie?* she wondered. *And what had happened to him?*

"I've been alone too long." Martha said. She looked around at the kitchen as if she hated both it and the inn. "If I can help you and your sisters just a little, it would give me great pleasure. As for Jack, he doesn't give a fig for me! I have no one that cares about me, nor do I care about anyone here. Once," she lowered her voice and looked so sad it wrenched Bronwyn's heart, "I had someone I loved very deeply. My son, Johnnie . . . but he's dead now. Dead a long time. He was a sickly little fellow and not . . . Jack's." Her eyes misted over and she turned back to her kettles. "It was a long time ago and it's all over now. He's gone." Her shoulders seemed to droop a little farther and she wiped her eyes, sniffling as Bronwyn followed her.

"I'm sorry," was all Bronwyn could say. She laid a small hand on Martha's plump shoulder. "So sorry," she whispered.

" 'Tis better so. Jack hated the boy almost as much as I loved him. He was a good boy, though, truly he was. A bit of a dreamer, and sickly; but he had a good heart and a warm smile. You . . . remind me of him in some ways." She looked over her shoulder at Bronwyn. "He didn't have much of a voice, that boy, but how he loved to sing!'' She laughed sadly. "Why, he'd scamper all about the place, hiding in the loft or any dark corner he could find and sing his little heart out, he would—silly little tunes. My Johnnie. . .'' What she didn't say was that he'd hide from Jack, who detested the boy and used every excuse he could find to hurt him, to punish him for nothing at all, except that he existed. Except that she loved him so. Since the boy had died she had never been able to forgive Jack. Her eyes wandered around her, full of sadness for what was gone, never to return. *"Aye,* sometimes, I swear I still hear his pitiful little voice going from room to room, seeking me still. Lonely always, like me. My poor little Johnnie.''

"I'm sorry.'' Bronwyn said again. The woman's grief hung about them like a pall.

"Don't be sorry. It was a long time ago . . . and now, why, God's seen fit to give me something to smile over again! You and your sisters. It will be good to have children around the place again. I've missed children's laughter.'' Then she said something that surprised Bronwyn. "And Jack won't care. He has Molly and as long as I keep my mouth shut, we get along. And I *have* kept my mouth and eyes shut now for a long time. He owes me this.'' Her tone was menacing. *"He owes it to me.''*

Molly! Now Bronwyn understood why Martha had talked of the woman with such open hostility. Molly was Jack's mistress. It was sad, but life was like that at times. It was the way of men to have many women, while a woman could only have one man, no matter how badly he treated her. She found herself almost hating this woman she had never met.

But Martha wasn't the kind of woman to brood over things she couldn't change. "Well! Enough of wallowing in pity over myself and my life. What is done is done; what is past, past. Life goes on.'' She smiled bravely. "And Jack'll have my hide if I burn this supper!'' She laughed, herself once more. "I want him in a good mood tonight when I spring our little surprise on him."

"Will Jack be angry at me for not going back out there after what happened?" Bronwyn asked, worried. "I just ran out and never told him why or where I was going." She'd acted like a child, and she couldn't afford to act like a child anymore. She looked at Martha and ruminated on all the advice the woman had given her. She was right. You had only a short time to make your place in this world before you got too old and tired. Look at Martha . . .

"Lord, no. Don't underestimate Jack just because of what I've said. He's clever enough to have figured out that you've been in here helping me all this time. He'll not be angry at you." The words were uttered almost fondly and Bronwyn was confirmed in her earlier suspicion that Martha still loved the man, regardless of what he had done to her. She'd heard people say that love was strange. All Bronwyn knew was that if she had a husband who took a mistress, she would never be able to forgive him. "Oh, Jack knows you're in here helping me, I'll wager. *Someone's* told him." The emphasis left no doubt in Bronwyn's mind to whom Martha was referring to—Molly.

"In a bit, I'll break the news to him about you and your two sisters staying up in the loft. I'll send old Harry, our stableman, with you on some horses to fetch your sisters and whatever possessions you'll want to bring. Lord, I hope you don't have any furniture! There's little enough room up there in that tiny loft for the three of you and your beds, much less having to squeeze in a cartload of furniture."

Bronwyn shook her head. "No furniture. We had to burn almost everything this winter, when I couldn't get out to find fire wood." Her eyes closed a brief second as she remembered that terrible time when it was so cold and Mary so sick that they'd had to burn the last of the lovely furniture her father had so painstakingly crafted years before. He'd told her once when she was just a tiny child watching him sand a tabletop so carefully, that when he had been a lad he'd always wanted to be a carpenter; but his father hadn't the money to have him apprenticed to a master craftsman to learn the trade, and so her father had become a soldier and fought in foreign lands.

"There's not much but a few clothes and special things that belonged to our mother. We could easily wrap all we have in a few large bundles. It'll be no problem at all." It was better that way; she didn't really want any of the old life to clutter the new. Her father had always promised them that they'd live in a grand house someday . . . Her poor father. What a dreamer he had been! He'd never given up hope that the King would someday recall him for some useful service in his twilight years. Just fantasies, that was all they amounted to in the end. Old soldiers were put out to pasture and forgotten; not all his prayers and plans (he'd even had their mother teach both Samantha and Bronwyn to read and write in preparation for the glorious days ahead. What a folly that had been! Who needed to read or write in the gutters?) had ever changed their meager life after he had come back wounded from France. Now she, Samantha and Mary were left to face the real world.

"Good," Martha replied, taking her apron off and smoothing back her damp hair. "Now first, let's go up and see exactly what condition that old loft room is in. Then you go and get those sisters of yours and I'll talk to Jack. While you're gone, I'll tidy up the loft a little bit and get it ready for you."

Hesitantly, Bronwyn tagged along behind as Martha made her way through the main dining area again. She looked around to see if the blond man and his friends were still there, but they were long gone. The place was almost completely empty and Jack was nowhere in sight. Martha's shoulders stiffened but she didn't utter a word. Bronwyn noted that the serving wench who had been there earlier was no longer in evidence, either.

"I'll just have to talk to Jack a little later," Martha said as she led Bronwyn up a narrow staircase that coiled up through the inn's two other floors. They passed a tiny dark landing on their way up and Martha lit two candles that were waiting there for them on a shelf. "Watch your step, it's dark up here. Wouldn't be so bad if we were bats."

They came out onto the third floor; Martha puffing. "You'll have your work cut out for you tonight, child," Martha told her. "Maybe you can take a little rest before you begin, it'll be a long night." Martha didn't say it aloud, but she thought that the poor girl looked as tired and weak as a kitten who'd been out in the cold too long. "I'll ask Jack about it."

"Thank you, ma'am."

"Call me Martha. We're all the same here—no fine ladies and gentlemen. By the way," Martha continued when they finished climbing the last flight of decaying steps up to the loft room, "how old are your sisters? I never even thought to ask."

"Mary, the youngest is only seven and Samantha, the elder, is eleven."

"Just babes! You must have your hands full." She tossed a glance back down at Bronwyn as she pushed aside the spiderwebs and shuddered. It looked as though no one had been up here in ages, Bronwyn thought, a chill running through her. She carefully lifted her skirts up off the dusty floor and tried not to brush against the dingy walls. She could hardly breathe, there was so much dust in the air. Something seemed to stir behind them, whispering in the empty spaces. Bronwyn trembled; she could have sworn she heard someone laughing far away. It was the laughter of a child and her heart began to race. A child, here? No wonder Martha believed at times she could still hear her poor dead Johnnie wandering through these corridors at night as if he were seeking her. There was a forlorn air about this garrett that made Bronwyn's skin crawl. But she sealed her fears away, setting her lips in a tight line. Beggars couldn't be choosers and Bronwyn was just grateful that she and her sisters would have a room to stay in, haunted or not. As long as they were all together nothing else mattered, she told herself firmly.

"Here it is." Martha shoved against a small door at the very end of the hallway and it opened with a loud creaking and scraping. They had to stoop to get through it. "It isn't much, as I warned you, and it needs a good scrubbing, for sure." She grunted as she ran her plump fingers along the wall and frowned at the dark smudges on her hands in the candlelight. "Filthy!" She slapped her hands against her skirts.

The loft room was tiny, no larger than eight by nine feet, Bronwyn mentally calculated as she looked it over, holding her guttering candle high above her head. There were old dusty crates stacked to the ceiling in one corner and bits of old broken furniture strewn everywhere. As she walked across the room, the dust swirled around her skirts like a clinging mist. There was a solitary window at the far end and Bronwyn determinedly tugged and pushed at its rusted latches until the casement swung open and fresh, cold air poured in. It was late afternoon and as she looked out she was surprised to see how dark it was. She had to get her sisters soon; Mary was too delicate to be brought out into the sharp night air. She breathed deeply, trying to clear the dust from her throat, and coughed. "You're right, Martha, it does need a good cleaning!" Without another word, together they began to dust, dipping rags they found in a chest into the snow outside the tiny window.

After a little while, Martha threw up her arms in defeat and said, "Just leave it for now. While you're gone, I'll come up here with a mop and broom and give it all a quick going over. I'll have one of the girls bring up some clean bedding and make places for all three of you to sleep tonight. I'll do the best I can, but it's getting late and soon the inn will be packed and I'll be busy. But tomorrow, we'll give it a real good cleaning, I promise. It's been a long time since anyone slept up here." Bronwyn knew she was thinking of her dead son. It showed in her face. It was as if she was hearing something—or someone—that Bronwyn herself couldn't hear. Suddenly the hinges of the window groaned as if unseen hands had slapped it shut; Martha jumped. They just stared at each other, then finally began to laugh softly. "Well, enough of this dawdling. We can't dally up here any longer or Jack will have my head for neglecting my work." Martha picked her candle back up from the floor where she had set it and led the way back down the dark stairs into the bright kitchen full of the lovely smells of baking bread and bubbling stew. Bronwyn couldn't wait until the girls got here; wouldn't they be surprised! The food Martha had given her had been so delicious that she could almost see her sisters' happy smiles when they sat down to eat.

As if Martha had been reading her mind, she said, "I'm anxious to meet your sisters and to get you all safe and settled in. They must be worried over you by now; hungry, too, I imagine." Martha watched as Bronwyn went to get her cloak and slipped it on. "You'd best hurry, child. Soon it'll be dark and even on horseback with old Harry, the streets are dangerous. Harry is no longer a young man but he is a faithful servant and I trust him. But I won't rest easy until you three are all back here safe." Martha was already working again. There had been a huge roast in the oven the whole afternoon and now she was basting it. Bronwyn thought she had never smelled anything more delicious.

No one else was around and when she asked about it,

Martha shrugged and told her that sometimes the girls took short naps at this time of day, before the evening crowd filtered in. Only Martha was up slaving over her chores; it didn't seem fair to Bronwyn.

Bronwyn smiled at her, ready to go. "You're a lot like our mother," she remarked softly then added, "Are you *sure* you really want us all here?" She feared that Martha might still change her mind and snatch this wonderful new life away.

"Aye." Martha was touched by the girl's remark about her being like their mother. "And after tonight, when he sees the looks on the customers' faces as they listen to you sing, you will be Jack's prized possession, you'll see. He'll give you anything you desire. Jack knows when he's struck gold and you, my girl, are pure gold. Old Harry's out back, most likely, in the stable. Go tell him I want him to saddle the mares and take you to get your sisters. Be careful, and hurry back. Soon there will be a lot of work to do." Martha smiled and waved her off. Bronwyn slipped out the door and walked around to the stables. It was getting even colder and she pulled her cloak tightly around herself, shivering in the wind. The sun was going down and the wind was blowing in great gusts. She was so glad that they would all be here tonight, safe and warm.

Bronwyn found the stableman, Harry, and explained who she was and what Martha wanted him to do. She was amazed at how young "old Harry" really was. He was a quiet sturdy-looking man of middle height, with pale eyes of washed-out blue and white hair; he was not much taller than Bronwyn herself, though she was tall for a woman. The white hair made him look older than he actually was, she surmised, watching how gentle he was with the horses. He talked to them as if they were friends. There was a great peacefulness about Harry as he moved about the stable, saddling the two mares and asking Bronwyn about herself as he did. Bronwyn knew instinctively that with Harry she would be safe, just as Martha had said. "We only keep a few mounts here, missy," he told her in his gruff, thick voice, "just for our own needs. The rest of the stalls are for the customers' horses. This roan, he's my favorite. Big and strong, but gentle as a lamb." Harry stroked the tall horse lovingly as he brought the mares out into the stableyard.

He helped her up into the saddle. "You've never ridden before, then?" he asked, astonished. To him horses and riding were second nature. "Well, it isn't hard and Rabbit here," he gently slapped the bay mare on the neck and pulled her head around, "is the sweetest-natured girl we have; wouldn't hurt a fly . . . you and her will get along just fine. Don't pull too hard on the reins and she'll thank you for it."

He swung up into the other mare's saddle. He instructed Bronwyn on how to control her horse and soon she was riding along behind him, feeling fairly confident. "I've always loved horses," she told him. "All we had at home was old sway-backed Sassy. When I was tiny, my father used to put me on her back and lead her around. But she died before I was old enough to ride her by myself. We never did get another. I used to dream of having a beautiful mare like this one." She caressed the mare's silky neck fondly. "I wanted to gallop across the hills and fields; to run faster than the wind," she said dreamily, gazing at the back of Harry's white head as they trotted out into the street. "I love all animals."

"And they can sense that, missy." He looked back at her, noting how she was handling herself and her mount. She was doing well, but then Rabbit was the gentlest of horses. "If she didn't like you, well, you might not still be up on her back but in the snow."

Bronwyn laughed and leaned back in the saddle, straightening her gown and her cloak to cover her legs. "I guess I'm like my father. He was a soldier and he used to tell me of the warhorses on the campaigns. He used to take care of them. The stories he told me about them! Aye," she said wistfully as they rode through the narrow streets, "he was good with horses, he was. He taught me a lot about them." Bronwyn felt like a queen on Rabbit's sleek back. She was so happy that she began to sing softly to herself, smiling, as they trotted along. Harry glanced back at her and smiled too. He wasn't much of a talker, she thought, but she didn't mind that. He listened to her sweet voice and kept an eye out for trouble. Bronwyn had no idea how deeply he had fallen under her spell by the tme they had reached their destination, didn't notice the adoring way he looked at her. To Harry, she was a vision, with her kind smile and simple beauty. "You were born to ride, that I can see," he told her and Bronwyn glowed with pride.

"You've lived here since your parents died?" He looked about him, his eyes registering his curiosity and then astonishment at the poverty of their surroundings. A small blond child came running out to meet them and threw herself at Bronwyn even before she could slip from the saddle. "Bronwyn!" Samantha cried, talking a mile a minute as Harry got down from his mount. He couldn't understand how they had all managed to live here unharmed all these years. Three little lasses living by themselves? Unheard of! They had been very lucky. He knew what could befall children in this wicked city.

He thought about it as he helped them pack up their sparse belongings into large lop-sided bundles and load them up on the horses' backs, tying them securely. No, it wasn't luck that had protected them here all alone, he decided, but a miracle!

When they were ready and Bronwyn had turned her back on her old home, Harry helped her back up into the saddle and lifted up an excited, giggling Samantha behind her. Bronwyn had no feelings of regret as they moved away from the cottage. Only unhappiness had come to them there and she was glad they were leaving it forever. She never wanted to come back, never! Harry had put little Mary up in front of him, and now they headed back towards the inn. The sun was slipping down and as he looked down on the pale, thin face of the little girl that he held carefully in his arms, he worried that she was sicker than any of them knew. When she breathed, there was a rattle deep in her tiny chest. It was getting dark and very cold. He wrapped her tighter in his cloak and listened to Samantha and Bronwyn talking behind him in excited whispers. The sky was heavy with the promise of snow and Harry knew a storm was coming, a bad one. He also knew, halfway back to the inn, that the child he carried might not live through the night unless another miracle could happen. He'd seen that look before many times, during the last plague. None of them had lived through the week. He could feel the heat radiating from her frail body as she slept quietly and securely in his strong arms while they cantered through the twilight. His heart ached for her.

"Missy . . ." He leaned back to speak to Bronwyn, "we must hurry our mounts a bit more. A storm's coming this way." He didn't tell Bronwyn that the real reason they broke into a gallop was because her tiny sister had fallen into a sleep she might not wake from unless she received care and warmth.

As they galloped through the darkening streets over the cobblestones, Bronwyn was very worried about her youngest sister. She had been a healer too long not to have seen that same look in Mary's feverish eyes that Harry had seen before. Bronwyn knew well how sick Mary was. The look was so familiar—like that in their poor mother's eyes the night she died. Bronwyn held on to the reins and dug her heels into the warm heaving flanks of the mare, praying that Mary would recover this time as she had so many times before. Surely the promise of a better life would pull her from the brink of death!

At one point she looked up and met Harry's concerned eyes. He nodded and they rode a little faster as the sun disappeared entirely. Bronwyn shivered beneath her cloak in the chill of the winter night.

CHAPTER IV

London—1463

BY THE TIME they reached the Red Boar, Mary's body was burning with fever.

Harry scooped her up tenderly and carried her into the warm kitchen. Martha was waiting for them and she snatched the sick child from his arms. "My goodness, this wee one is sick!" she exclaimed, laying a hand across Mary's hot brow. She looked up at Bronwyn. "Why, she's burning up! The poor little thing!"

"I'm Samantha," the older of the little girls said shyly as Bronwyn knelt down next to Martha who was cradling the sick child to her ample bosom, clucking over her like a mother hen. Bronwyn stood up. "I have a special broth I can make that will help her. If you don't mind, Martha, I'll prepare some now before I start working. Is that all right?" She would do it anyway, no matter what Martha said, but she was relieved when Martha simply nodded. "Anything to help the wee one. Go ahead, and if I can help you in any way don't hesitate to ask," Martha said sincerely, her gaze lingering on Mary's pale features. She was such a pretty little thing . . . "How do you make this special broth?" Martha asked, curious.

"It's an old recipe my mother used when we had the

fever. She taught me how to make it." A lie. But Bronwyn couldn't stand to see that look she knew so well in Martha's eyes. Not now. Not yet. Nothing must jeopardize their place here. How could she tell Martha that the uncanny knowledge she had of the medicinal herbs she carried with her always in a tiny pouch hung from her belt was something she had simply always *known*; that she could heal the sick at times with just a touch of her hand, and that she always knew what to do for a sick person even though she had never had any real training or help? The word *witch* roared in her ears as she met Martha's unreadable eyes.

"Use anything here you need, child. I'll have Harry take the little one up to bed and I'll see to it that she's warm and comfortable. While you were gone I cleaned the loft and prepared the beds with plenty of blankets. I'll heat some bricks in the fire to lay at her feet. This child needs attention immediately," Martha stated, standing up slowly with a still sleeping Mary snug in her arms. With a sharp look at Bronwyn as she began to gather the necessary ingredients for the broth, Martha disappeared up the stairs behind Harry, who was now carrying Mary. Bronwyn sat Samantha down with a large bowl of Martha's stew and slices of warm bread. That would keep her busy.

Swiftly, Bronwyn began to heat water in a small kettle over the fire. After first looking around to make sure no one saw her, she lifted her skirts, took the small pouch from her belt and selected the herbs she would need. Nightshade . . . just a pinch, would be enough to let Mary sleep for a long time and give her weak body the rest she needed so badly to fight off the fever—but a pinch too much of the dangerous substance and Mary would never wake again.

She dug deeper into the leather pouch and found the other herbs she would need and threw them all into the bubbling water, her heart thudding like a prisoner against her rib cage. The broth alone might not cure Mary, but Bronwyn's touch would help as well. Together, it must make Mary well again, Bronwyn prayed as she stirred the mixture. There were other things, too, she could do for Mary, things no one else must witness, if worse came to worst. Bronwyn's eyes were filled with worry. *Please, let no one see me!*

Martha reappeared so suddenly behind her that Bronwyn, startled, jumped when she spoke. "What have you put into your broth?" Martha asked.

Bronwyn tried to smile innocently. "There are all kinds of good things in it . . . do you mind—I took some of your boiled chicken off that plate and some of the vegetables for it."

"Lord, no, I don't mind, child," Martha responded, watching the mixture simmer in the kettle, a slight frown on her face. "I think part of that poor child's problem is that she's half starved and frozen from the cold."

Bronwyn merely nodded. Her mind was upstairs with her sick sister. "Here, it's not bad . . . would you like a taste?" She turned to Martha with a ladle full of the broth, seeing the curiosity bright in the older woman's eyes. "It's really good."

Martha shied away as if Bronwyn was going to burn her. "*No!*" She gulped. "No, thank you . . . I'll take your word for it." But it was too late. Bronwyn sighed wearily. Somehow Martha *knew*, or suspected what Bronwyn was . . . or what people thought she was. Her heart felt very heavy and there was a numbing ache deep inside her. Would her gift always alienate her from all others? Would she always be an outcast because she had a gift no one understood?

"Where did you learn . . . this *skill* of yours?" Martha finally asked softly, aware that Bronwyn had sensed her reservations.

Samantha was still busy gobbling down the stew and

was on her fourth piece of buttered bread. She looked up now and smiled across the room at her sister and Martha as Bronwyn told Martha how she had acquired her unique ability. She didn't lie to her. Martha was too good a person to be deceived. If they were to live here under this woman's roof, at least Bronwyn could be honest with her, about everything.

Martha stared at her for a long time after she had finished speaking.

" 'Tis not magic . . . I only use what people have known about for centuries." Bronwyn's eyes pleaded with the other woman. She felt the old fear rise up inside her at Martha's familiar guarded look. Then the older woman smiled and nodded, patting Bronwyn on the back and saying, "It's all right, child, I know it's not witchcraft." But she was staring at the pouch that Bronwyn still held clutched in her hands. Without a word, Bronwyn put it back away, out of sight. "I know you . . . you are good. And Martha always goes with what she feels in her heart. My heart tells me you are no witch." She whispered, "God gave you the gift for helping people and I see no devil's hand in that."

"Some say it *is* the devil's doing. But, Martha," Bronwyn lowered her voice, "I only use my talents to help people get well. *I have never hurt anyone, believe me!*" More than anything, she wanted Martha's friendship and trust. It was comforting to be able to talk about it freely.

"No," Martha said, smiling at her. "I'm not condemning you for I think it is a gift from God, but some would and my advice to you is to keep your skills and abilities to yourself, especially around here. If not for your own sake, then for your sisters' . . . there are ignorant clods who would use it against you out of jealousy, especially now. Since you sang this afternoon, the girls have been talking about nothing else but your voice and your youthful beauty; some, I hear tell, with malicious envy of your talents. You already have enemies—you don't need to give them anything else to gossip about.''

Relieved and grateful, Bronwyn squeezed Martha's hand. "Then we still can stay?''

"Aye." Martha sat down wearily at the long table. Bronwyn spooned some of her special brew into a cup and gave orders to Samantha to take it up to Mary. It was better if she called as little attention to what she was doing as possible. When the girl was gone, Bronwyn sat down next to Martha after she had hidden away the remainder of the broth.

"I knew a woman once . . ." Martha began in a somber voice barely above a whisper. "She could heal anyone of almost anything. She lived up in the Surrey Hills years ago." She faced Bronwyn. "Not much of a woman, mark you—tiny and withered up like a dry leaf in the winter. Ah, but she had a kind and generous heart. Cured my little brother, Jesse, once of a mysterious pain he had had for years in his legs. Some days, poor tyke, he could hardly walk, it was so bad. He'd cry out in the night with the pain sometimes. I, too, was just a child at the time and our family were as poor as churchmice. I never knew the old woman very well myself; I, like most of the other children, was fearful of her. Called her witch, we did." She said this with shame and regret. "We were cruel, foolish children. But we were no different than all the rest of those hypocrites who used her talents and then spoke spitefully behind her back. I imagine it was because they were really afraid of her powers underneath it all. People hate what they cannot understand . . . and they destroy it, if they can." Martha's face was clouded as she stared away into nothing. "You see?" She looked directly into Bronwyn's eyes and Bronwyn saw fear there.

"What happened to the old woman?" Bronwyn asked anxiously.

Martha took a deep breath and stood up slowly, looking down into Bronwyn's face. "What usually happens to witches?" She asked caustically. "One dark night when there was no moon to light their crime, they gathered together after drinking a little too much at the local tavern and dragged her screaming and kicking from her tiny home. They strapped her to a tree in the forest, with all her pitiful possessions thrown about her feet, and set fire to it all. *Righteous townspeople! Bah!*" Martha spat out the words bitterly. "They believed she had stolen a little girl from her bed in the dead of night to concoct one of her 'evil enchantments,' so they swore. The mother cried for vengeance when she found the child missing and rallied the townspeople to help her. They were stupid, cruel people who hated her just because she was different, that was all. So they burned her and she had done nothing but good all her life."

"Did they ever find the child?" Bronwyn's voice was trembling.

Martha laughed then. "Aye, the next morning they found the brat cowering under her own bed. Her mother had yelled at her the night before and the child hid, thinking that her mother would come back to punish her. She hid the whole night through. The old woman hadn't taken her at all."

"*Oh, my God*." Bronwyn moaned. "They burned an innocent woman for nothing!"

"Aye, and one that had at one time or another helped each and every one of them in some way . . . she had never harmed anyone. But worst of all, my dear, was that afterwards they acted as if nothing had happened and slunk away in their guilt to try and forget what they had done. Some bragged about what they had done and how the old woman had begged for mercy and screamed at the end . . ." Martha shook her head, unable to bear going on. "Mind, child, there are those in this world that care not how they harm another human being. So *be careful*."

Bronwyn had a sudden flash in her mind of the poor wretch weeping that day on the bloody scaffold in the center of town. Oh, how well she knew that!

With a sigh, Martha told her she had some details upstairs to attend to before the crowd descended on them; it was late and the inn was already filling up. Bronwyn could hear the noise growing outside the doors. Martha gave her a few instructions and left the kitchen. Bronwyn kept thinking about Martha's story as she went about her chores. Would she never be free; never feel safe? She worried, too, over sick little Mary and decided to slip upstairs for a few seconds and check on her.

She didn't hear someone softly close the kitchen doors after the person had listened and watched with great interest everything Bronwyn and Martha had been talking about and doing. Bronwyn never suspected that they had been spied upon.

Someone who loathed Bronwyn for no other reason than that she was the new, young, pretty thing with the dazzling voice who was already the talk of the whole inn. *Someone* who was seething with petty jealousy and vicious schemes to put the little bitch in her rightful place. *The pushy little twit*, she fumed as she quietly closed the door and then slunk away like a fox from the chicken coop. *Who does she think she is? Taking over the whole damn place and pushing Molly aside like she was a queen or something . . . dragging in those little rug-rats along with her . . . moving right in, she was, like she owned the whole damn place! Conniving witch, with all her fancy airs, fake innocence and pushy ways! Imagine her worming her way in here like that. Ugh! 'Twas all that idiot Jack had talked about the whole bleeding afternoon while he was in her bed . . . raved on and on, he had, about that bitch and her heavenly voice and how much money she would make for him; how she would delight his customers. On and on and on*! The woman's face was livid with jealousy.

I'll just have to show her who's boss here . . . teach her to step on Molly's toes, I will! The evil little bitch . . .

And the woman with the vindictive smile and gaudy clothes tip-toed away from the warm kitchen and back into the main hall, her painted face ugly with hatred. This was *her* place, *her* roost. No sniveling, prissy wench was going to oust her, not without a hell of a good fight. She snorted. She knew she should have gotten rid of that meddlesome old Martha years ago when Jack was still so crazy about her . . . now, with her looks fading, it was harder to make Jack do her bidding. He was getting hard to handle. *Aye, she should have made Jack throw that old hag out into the streets years ago.* She smiled slyly and her eyes narrowed in the dim light as she ran from table to table, lugging food and beer for the men she so readily flirted with and teased. She didn't want to think on it. Jack wasn't as sweet on her as he once had been. She was losing it, she brooded as she laughed with a tall bearded soldier, bending over just so, showing him a good view of all she had. *Losing it all.* Jack . . . and now, maybe even her position here. And just when she was so close to getting rid of that wife of his! Molly had Martha's husband already but she was greedy—she wanted all Martha had. She wouldn't settle for less. Jack had promised her soon. What was he waiting for? And now, all he could think or talk about was that new girl. That little *witch*!

She'd show her, she would!

It was sometime later that Bronwyn, after tending to Mary and cleaning up a little, ran into Molly outside the noisy dining room. Mary was finally sleeping peacefully and breathing much better. Bronwyn was smiling. The world was brightening up. The excitement of her new job and the happiness of having her two sisters here with her, as well as the friendliness of everyone she had met so far at the inn had added to her growing sense of contentment.

Samantha was with Martha now, helping to prepare the massive amounts of food the serving wenches needed for their hungry customers. The other servant girls, after a little teasing, seemed to accept her and some in the end had offered to show her the ropes. Bronwyn had friends here, especially kind-hearted Martha; and for the first time in years, she felt as if some of the burden of taking care of her two small sisters had lightened. Someone else cared about their welfare and Bronwyn was overjoyed to see them getting the attention and love they so badly needed. Already Martha was dreaming up a new wardrobe for the girls, declaring that what they were wearing was rags. She was right. Yes, this was home.

The woman came striding past her in the hallway between the kitchen and the dining room, with her arms full of food and drink. In the background Bronwyn could hear someone's shrill laughter. She simply turned and faced Bronwyn haughtily, eying her critically from head to toe. She tried so hard to look menacing and, instead, looked so silly, that Bronwyn had to force herself to keep a straight face. She didn't need a formal introduction to know that this must be the infamous Molly about whom Martha had warned her.

"So. You're the new girl?" Molly's laugh was coarse. "I'd say that old Jack is catching 'em a little green these days. But the men don't mind. They like anything with skirts on . . . and when they get drunk enough, why, they take a fancy to almost anything. In fact, they should like you just fine. Soldiers are always fond of little girls." Her eyes narrowed into slits as she continued to stare at Bronwyn.

Bronwyn, taken aback by the older woman's hostility, didn't know what to say back. She wasn't used to women like Molly, with her whining voice and rouged cheeks. Molly had declared herself Bronwyn's enemy and rival.

"You're Molly, then?" Bronwyn purred, determined

not to lower herself to the horrible woman's level. "I'm Bronwyn. And you're right, I've just started here. I've got a lot to learn, but I'm sure with everyone's help, I'll catch on well enough. They talk of you a lot around here, so I feel like I know you already." She smiled sweetly.

"I bet you do." Molly was glaring at her with hatred glittering in her hard eyes. "I've been here longer than any of the rest of the girls, you see. They kind of . . . answer to me, you might say."

"Oh, do they? But Martha is Jack's wife; I thought the girls answered to *her*. Don't they?"

So this was the infamous harpy Martha had spoken of. She certainly wasn't very pretty, Bronwyn decided. Really not at all, with that big nose and those brown eyes which were set much too close together. She was nothing but an old bar maid, so why was everyone so cautious of crossing her? Then Bronwyn had a sudden insight into Molly's character. She was just a tavern wench who had seen too many men's beds and heard too many broken promises and was now seeing her youth and chances slipping away like water through her grasping hands . . . *and she was frightened*! That was all. The heavy make-up and the low-cut gown, the dull hair dyed a raven-black all pointed to it. A woman her age shouldn't chase her youth so frantically. Bronwyn felt a stab of pity for the woman; but then, surprisingly enough, Molly offered her a piece of advice.

"Girl, take my word. Molly here knows how to handle those drooling beasts out there, all right." She jerked a thumb back towards the noisy dining hall she had just left. "I'll tell you how to treat 'em—just like the slavering dogs they are! Give 'em your backside, keep your pretty little mouth shut and don't get involved with any of 'em. They don't understand a lady like yourself, those dogs. Kick 'em and show 'em who's boss . . . it's the only treatment they understand. If you're too easy to get . . ." her eyes smiled knowingly and she grinned, showing a chipped front tooth between crimson lips, "they'll cast you aside when they're through with ya. Molly knows."

The woman had spirit, Bronwyn had to give her that. "Thank you for the advice, Molly. But so far all the men have treated me decently enough. In fact, everyone here has been very kind to me and my sisters. Are you really sure you know how to treat the customers? I've had no trouble with them at all," Bronwyn said.

"That's fine and good, me love. But that was today. Tonight, the inn is full of drunken sots and rutting soldiers and they'll try to lay their roaming hands on the little body you seem so proud of. You'll be singing another tune, I'll wager!" Molly snapped, her eyes flashing in her flushed face. *You little witch . . . I saw what you were doing in the kitchen before. I saw you brewing your devil's potion in that black kettle . . . I know what you are!* "But if you don't want to take old Molly's helpful advice, it's fine with me. Someday, dearie," she cackled like an old crone, then brushed Bronwyn aside roughly as she made her way past her, "you'll remember my words as you lie beaten and bruised in a gutter somewhere. *Then* you'll wish you'd taken Molly's advice, that you will!"

Bronwyn stared at her retreating back, frowning.

Almost at the dining room's door, Molly stopped and looked back at her new rival with a challenging gleam in her eye and hissed, "Don't tarry too long over that black kettle of yours, either, me love . . . people might get the wrong idea about what you are. And mind you," she said as a vicious parting shot, "I'll not be tripping over a clumsy new wench the whole night, so stay out there in the kitchen with your kettle and out of my way and we'll get along just fine. Jack don't abide laggards in his establishment." Then the door slammed shut and she was gone.

Bronwyn was fuming. What gall that woman had! *Don't tarry too long over that black kettle of yours . . . people might get the wrong idea*! A shiver of apprehension ran down her spine. Nothing less than her leaving would satisfy that harridan and *that* she wasn't going to do! No one was going to drive her away from this new life. No one!

But she was smart enough to know that she had better stay away from Molly. After what the woman had just said, she'd have to be very careful. Martha had been right again.

"Ah, I see that you've finally met our Molly." It was Martha, laughing behind her, her hands on her broad hips.

"*Met* her?" Bronwyn said. "She all but attacked me! I don't think she likes me very much." Then Bronwyn sighed. "In fact, I think she may *hate* me."

"Um-hum, I wouldn't doubt it. You're pretty and bright and I've seen how the men treat you . . . with real respect, like you were a lady. Molly'd hate you for that, if nothing else. The men treat her like the whore she really is. Only Jack doesn't seem to see it. That's another thing! Jack's been praising you and that sweet voice of yours to high heaven and running on about how the customers will love you tonight. Gets her goat, it does, 'tis all." Again Martha was struck by how lovely the young girl was. Those great cat's eyes and innocent face framed by that gleaming hair; the understanding intelligence in her eyes . . . "Just stay away from her, is all I can tell you to do," Martha said.

"I will." Bronwyn replied fervently.

"Have you had time to rest up a little?" Martha continued.

"Not yet," Bronwyn said with a rueful smile.

"Well, Jack's already asking when his songbird's going to sing. He's been telling all his customers that he has a surprise for them tonight. He wants to be sure that you come out there before it gets too late and they're all too drunk to appreciate you."

"He is, is he?" Bronwyn's eyes danced. "Then I guess I'll have to, sooner or later."

Martha wasn't fooled. The girl was nervous. Bronwyn's shyness touched her and she had to admit that she had grown very fond of the child and her two sisters. It was the first time in years that she felt needed and it felt good.

"Well, whenever you think you're up to it. But for now, you can give me that apron and I'll tend to the pots and the cooking . . . he wants you to go out and help wait on the customers now. We're so busy that the girls can't keep up."

Bronwyn nodded, her face suddenly frightened, and Martha slid her arm about the girl's slender waist and gave her an encouraging hug. "It will be fine, you'll see. You have a beautiful voice and the crowd will love you. I've tucked your two wee poppets in for the night. Mary's fever seems better and they're both sleeping warm and safe, their bellies full. I just checked them again, so don't you worry. Martha'll keep a close eye on them. It must have been hard on you three these last few months, with the weather so cold . . ." Martha trailed off, seeing the haunted look that crossed her young friend's face. "But now you'll all be safe. You'll see. Jack has already told me that you are welcome to stay as long as you want. For Jack, that's like giving you the keys to the kingdom!" Martha laughed, but inside she was a little concerned. Jack never did anything for nothing. What was he up to this time? she wondered. It bothered her but she was just so happy that they would be allowed to stay that she wasn't about to question it. You didn't look a gift horse in the mouth.

"Would you like it if I did your hair in a style I've seen the gentlewomen wear? It would look beautiful on you and I was always good at fixing hair. I used to love to fix my sisters' hair when I was a girl," Martha said excitedly. When Bronwyn nodded happily, Martha led her back to a corner of the kitchen where they could be alone.

She went to fetch her brushes and combs, hairpins and a few strings of cheap beads to loop between the coils of hair. She quickly undid Bronwyn's long shining tresses and brushed until it crackled and gleamed in the fire light, then adeptly braided it into an elaborate style, threading the strings of tiny beads in and out so that when Bronwyn moved her head, they sparkled. The hairstyle framed her face more effectively than the simple way she had worn it before. "It's lovely!" Martha exclaimed when she was done, clapping her hands like a young girl herself. "Wait!" she cried. "I've got something that you must wear . . . it would be perfect with that dress." She ran from the room and returned in a few minutes smiling, with something clenched tenderly between her fingers. "Here. I'm giving it to you as a present." She turned Bronwyn around on the chair and draped something about her slender neck, then backed up to have a look at her. How beautiful the girl was!

Touched, Bronwyn fingered the delicate necklace and felt as if she were going to cry. The woman was too kind. "Are you sure?" she asked softly.

"Of course. It fits you just perfect. My neck's gotten too fat to wear it anymore . . . even if I had a place to wear it to or someone to wear it for." Her eyes clouded briefly. "My time has gone, child, but yours is just beginning. You're young and pretty. Enjoy it!" She touched the necklace with love. "My Johnnie gave it to me for my birthday many years ago. I want you to have it; I'm sure he would approve." She added shyly, "Oh, it's only glass and brass and it's very tiny, but I always thought it was so pretty . . ."

"It is, Martha. Thank you," was all Bronwyn could think of to say. No one had ever given her such a gift before. She held the necklace away from her throat and gazed down at it. It was a simple chain, not very thick or very long, and on it hung a tiny glittering green stone that looked like an emerald in the firelight. Brass and glass, Martha had said. "It's beautiful," she murmured, swallowing the lump in her throat that always arose when someone did something kind for her, which wasn't often. "Thank you," she whispered again. It must mean a lot to Martha if her Johnnie had given it to her. Bronwyn decided that if she ever left, she would return it, if for no other reason than that. She couldn't keep Martha's beloved Johnnie's necklace.

"Now I'm afraid we've dawdled long enough. Soon Jack'll be bellowing like an angry bull if you don't get out there to work," Martha proclaimed, giving the girl a playful shove towards the door. "You can't hide the whole night in the kitchen. Time to face the crowd."

Two of the other serving girls were busy in the kitchen, filling trays with food for their customers. One of the girls smiled shyly at Bronwyn as she ran past. " 'Tis a hurly-burly out there tonight! I've never seen so many hungry people!" She was addressing Martha as she grabbed trenchers of steaming roast beef and loaves of crusty bread. She lifted the tray high above her head and headed for the door, taking a long, shuddering sigh. "Martha, I swear! If one more of those good-for-nothing soldiers in the back corner pinches me fanny just one more time I swear I'll smack 'im, the bloody sot!" The girl, a tiny sparrow of a thing named Abby, then giggled good-naturedly as she ran out. Bronwyn laughed along with Martha. She had met Abby earlier and she really liked the spunky little thing.

The other girl filling her tray was a big-boned peasant girl with wide hips and a full bosom, curly brown hair and pretty eyes. She was less vivacious than Abby, and Martha said she was a sly one, like Molly. Her name was Liza. Martha told Bronwyn not to be fooled by Liza's quiet manner. She had more men on the string and spent more time on her back in the upstairs bedrooms than all the other girls put together. But she wasn't really a bad sort and a hard worker, Martha had confided.

Now Liza turned to Bronwyn. "Jack told me to tell the new wench—that's you, isn't it—to get out there *now*." She cocked her curly head towards the dining room. "We've got more work than we can handle and Maggie—" She glanced upwards and started to say something, but caught the warning glance Martha was giving her over Bronwyn's head. ". . . is *busy* right now. We need some help. They're thirsty out there tonight!" She grinned, quickly smoothing her wild hair down with her free hand while the other balanced the tray. Then she was gone, too.

Alone again, Martha handed Bronwyn a clean apron from a peg on the wall. "Here. I wouldn't want you to soil your pretty dress. You can take the apron off when you sing."

Bronwyn smiled nervously, took a deep breath and went out to see what Jack wanted her to do.

After the girl had gone, Martha sat down at the table and rubbed her tired eyes. She was worried for Bronwyn. She was so fragile, so innocent. She worried that Bronwyn wouldn't be able to take care of herself if she really needed to. But then on the other hand she'd survived all this time on her own, as well as taking care of her two sisters, so perhaps she did know how to take care of herself . . .

Jack smiled a too-wide smile when Bronwyn had made her way through the boisterous crowd and stood before him. She was so nervous among all the people she thought she was surely going to fall over her own feet; or if she had to speak to someone, nothing would come out of her mouth. The words would have all been scared away!

"Well, about time the queen showed up. Humph!" He peered at her with those beady pig eyes and Bronwyn wondered what both Martha and Molly could see in the man. He was so clearly a brute. "Just wanted to tell you that your friends—those high-and-mighty gentlemen that enjoyed your company so much earlier today, remember?—are here again tonight and they've been asking for you," Jack said gruffly. He studied her closely. What was different about her? He had had to look twice to be sure it was the same lost little thing from that morning. Her hair was different, that was it. Much more elegant with those beads in it; made her appear older. He didn't miss the necklace about her white throat, either. He wondered if she didn't already have an admirer. He smiled greedily back at her. So she was a fast worker, was she? Ha, and here he'd thought she was so innocent! Perhaps it was that blond gentleman who had shown so much interest in her and asked a thousand questions. Jack was a smart businessman and he could see which way the wind was blowing; that gentleman would pay well for the wench and her favors. He chuckled to himself. The man was apparently very rich. He was sure the lass would be obliging. After all, women were made for only one thing, weren't they?

"What do they want?" Her knees began to tremble, just thinking of that arrogant man with the laughing blue eyes. She feared seeing him again, yet she craved it. What was the matter with her?

"Your friends are clamoring for you to sing again."

"They're *not* my friends, Sir." She pretended indifference, but her heart fluttered at the memory of those soft blue eyes, the hauntingly familiar smile and the strong handsome features. He was so beautiful! She had forgotten her earlier anger at him. She wanted to see him, and yet she didn't . . . she wanted to flee, and yet she wanted to be near him. Why did he upset her so, *confuse* her so? It wasn't his fault that he was rich, spoiled and pampered—or that he was the mysterious man who smiled at her in her dreams.

The innkeeper pushed some mugs at her, shaking his

head at her daydreaming. *Women*! "They've been waiting a long time—for you as well as their wine. Best not keep . them waiting any longer, *your majesty*." He smirked, pointing through the crowd. "And watch your step, lass, or the wolves will get ye!" He laughed at the frightened look that dawned on her face at his words. She turned and looked apprehensively where he was pointing.

But she couldn't fool old Jack any longer. She wasn't as innocent as she wanted people to believe, not if she'd lived alone like she said she had all these years. Pretty little act she had, though. Almost fooled him. The men liked it, though, he thought as he watched her make her way carefully through the rowdy crowd. He saw the way they looked at her and the way she smiled sweetly at them, like a child. He saw the way they treated her; the ripples of interest that went through the crowd as she passed. Just what the old place needed. Her tray tilted precariously as she tried to get past a couple of drunken farmers. "Don't spill the wine, wench! Or you'll pay for it!" he yelled at her and she turned to smile timorously at him over the crowd's heads. She looked scared to death. He shook his head and threw his hands up in exasperation. Maybe it wasn't an act, after all . . .

Bronwyn steadied herself and continued her way through the rambunctious sea of men and women eating, laughing and getting drunk. Did they have nothing better to do, then, but to carouse so?

Her confidence ebbed away like water into sand as she found herself facing a rowdy mob, a child not yet sixteen unused to this kind of life—just a child still, in so many ways. Looking at all the strange faces, eager smiles and hands grabbing at her as she walked by, she felt her skin crawl and all she wanted to do was run away and hide, have someone take care of her so she wouldn't have to face all this. What was she doing here with all these *wolves* (as

Jack had called them) looking at her as if she were to be their next meal?

Everyone was staring at her and she could barely hear herself think. It was so loud with all those lecherous, drunken men singing and laughing, devouring her with their bleary eyes. Did one ever get used to it? she wondered.

Then she firmly told herself for the tenth time, *Get used to it. Grow up! This is now your and your sisters' home.*

She threw up her chin and smiled at the soldiers. There seemed to be a lot of them tonight she thought. She tried very hard to laugh amiably when they grabbed at her, though she avoided their advances with quick steps. She stopped once to joke with someone and was pleased and surprised when she found herself actually enjoying their conversation. It was then she understood that none of them meant her any harm; they were just trying to be friendly. With just the right word or the right smile the men melted before her and she found it easy to handle them.

A group of soldiers, bowmen by their badges, were in the back singing an old war ditty she remembered well and when she came near them, they stopped her and soon she was singing along as she went on and after a while other patrons joined in. A battle was brewing with the Scots and rumors flew everywhere among the men. They might be at war in the next few weeks or months and might not live to see another year, so they were enjoying life to the fullest. She understood their fears and as she sang along with the crowd, she felt for the first time that she belonged somewhere. She could take care of herself.

Even seeing the blond gentleman again didn't dismay her in her present mood. He was throwing dice with his friends at the same table they had occupied that afternoon. They'd cleared a space in the middle and there were piles of coins before each of them. There was a much larger group with him tonight, but she saw only him when he looked up at her and smiled. His eyes were like blue gems. He was dressed all in black satin and leather and his blond hair shone like gold in the firelight; the shadows flickered about his lean, handsome face, making him appear older.

"Why, my little songbird, it's about time you graced us with your presence!" He stood up and gave her a mock bow in front of his interested companions, then smiled at her so winningly that she could no longer be angry with him. All the coolness of that afternoon was gone, on his part as well.

Bronwyn smiled warmly back at him and putting the drinks on the table, said, "I've been here all along, working out in the kitchen, cooking all that food you've been devouring."

"Aha! The lady can cook as well?" he teased her, sitting down. "Are you as good a cook as you are a singer?"

Bronwyn laughed lightly. "A beginner in both, Sir." She was fascinated by all the money glittering on the table.

"Ah, then you must be an excellent cook, too! What more could a man want in a woman? First she cooks him a meal that's fit for a king and then sings sweetly to put his heart and mind at peace," he exclaimed to his friends, "and she looks like an angel!" There was no sarcasm in his voice and when he gazed at her in the firelight, his blue eyes were full of longing. "I'm glad we are back on speaking terms again, my songbird." He leaned over, laid a hand against her cheek and whispered in her ear, "So you love me again, eh?"

Bronwyn bridled. "You, sir, are a fickle knave, talking of love when you don't even know me!" Pretending indignation, she gently pushed him away, even though she didn't really want to. When he was near, she seemed to forget everything . . .

"Ah, but there you are wrong. I do know you. We met in a dream one night."

The simple words, spoken with a soft knowing look in his warm eyes, couldn't have shaken her more. Just pretty words spoken in jest—or were they? Bronwyn couldn't be sure.

The King had fought with his pride and in the end he had lost. There was something about this particular maid that he could not forget. The whole day he had cherished the vision of her gentle smile and emerald eyes like a talisman in his heart; in his mind he had heard over and over again the magical lilting of her soft voice as she had sung. He could not put her out of his mind. He couldn't forget her . . . *and damned if he would, husband, babes, or not!* There must be a way to be with her, just to be near her. Edward had never felt this way about a woman before. Hearing her voice and seeing her smile filled him with peace. She healed his very soul.

Bronwyn was so close to him she could have reached out and touched him, and she realized she wasn't afraid of him any longer.

"Well?" She raised her eyebrows slightly. "What was I in this dream of yours, good sir?" she queried softly.

"My own true love, the one I have been seeking so long. I thought I would never find you, and now here you are," he replied, unsmiling, in a husky whisper that no one else could hear; his blue eyes were so penetrating that she felt herself blush. His companions had gone back to their game. It was as though they were alone in the world for an instant as he laid his hand gently over her trembling one and looked into her face. "Do you know how beautiful you are? How little else I have been able to think of since the moment I first laid eyes on that innocent face of yours? *Who are you?*" he murmured.

Bronwyn lowered her eyes, not knowing what to say,

No, he wasn't a stranger to her, either. "It is true—we have met in a dream," she breathed.

He hadn't moved or reacted in any way to what she had said. She thought he hadn't heard her and she looked up to find him staring at her in the strangest way. Then he squeezed her hand and, bending over her, kissed her swiftly and gently full on the lips. When he drew away and smiled into her stunned eyes, the warmth of his nearness put her in a kind of trance.

It was then she felt someone scrutinizing her. Like someone walking over her grave, the feeling was so strong that she shivered to her very soul. Then, her heart thumping wildly, something caught her eye; as if drawn by that powerful will, her eyes followed and she turned slowly to face the man who was standing like a stone statue at the other end of the long table, glaring at her. His face was as dark as storm clouds and his black eyes flashed savagely when they met hers. He nodded at her and then his thin lips formed into a wicked smile.

So you remember me, do you? Well, I remember you, too, it seemed to say. *I remember you well!*

Her heart was like a terrified caged bird fighting to get out at the sight of him. She was flooded with vivid memories. The hostility and open lust in his glance, the meaning behind it, held her mesmerized. *I've found you! I have you now and you won't get away this time!*

It was the same man she had outwitted the other night . . . the man she had ridiculed and left sprawling in the snow out in the street . . . the man from whom she had taken the gold coins!

Edward watched, perplexed, then worried, as the color drained from the maid's face and he followed her startled gaze. He turned slowly and was surprised to find himself looking into his cousin Warwick's furious eyes. But it was as if he were invisible; something about Warwick was clearly terrifying the girl. What was his cousin up to? Why was he staring at her that way?

But before Edward could demand an explanation, Warwick struck. Like the wolf he was so often compared to, he was at the maid's throat in the blink of an eye, his hand clamped like a band of steel around her slender throat.

"My Lord! Please, you're hurting me!" she gasped, struggling in vain against his greater strength as he brought her to her knees at his feet.

"I *knew* I would find you again, little whore! Only I had no idea it would be so easy or so soon. Such a clever little thief you were; but now, it doesn't seem so clever, does it?" he hissed malignantly in her ear as he pressed his fingers tighter until she was sure she was going to faint. He wanted her to cry out, to beg; but she only glared back up into his cruel eyes and refused to give him that pleasure.

"You . . . deserved . . . the treatment you received!" she cried breathlessly, her eyes defying him. "You deserved it and more!" Pulling away from his grasp, she spat into the face that hovered malignantly above hers.

"And you, little whore, deserve to be taught better manners, as I mentioned before! And I am just the one to teach you. *You will not get away this time*." His strong fingers siezed her again and she felt the world starting to spin away.

"*My Lord Warwick!*" Edward was suddenly on his feet, his voice like iron. "Let her go. *Now!*" Shock and outrage were chiseled into his handsome features. "What cause do you have to treat his maiden so? *Let her go,* I said!"

Royal command was implicit in his chilling voice and again Warwick was reminded who Edward really was. His King. The whole table was suddenly silent as a tomb. It was easy to see who was the master here and as Warwick's dark eyes traveled from one stony face to another, he knew he had lost—for now.

"Another time, little whore," he growled low in his throat, then pushed her into Edward's waiting arms as if she were a piece of discarded baggage he had no more use for. He turned languidly to face Edward, his lord and master, and bowed, eyes narrowed.

Ah, I see the way of it now, he thought, surveying the two; he understood that for the present he had lost his chance.

He glared at Bronwyn. Later. *Later!* his black eyes promised her and then, like the changing wind in a storm, his manner calmed and he smiled, shrugging his broad shoulders.

"As you wish, then, Edward, so shall it be. Forgive me!" He put up his hands and shook his massive head. "I mistook the maid for another. A simple case of mistaken identity, for this maid surely bears a striking resemblance to a notorious little pickpocket who palmed my purse in the streets the other night." Warwick continued smoothly, "Ah, but looking at her more closely, I see that it isn't the same wench." He turned to Bronwyn where she sat still stunned, her hand protectively about her throat, in the King's embrace, and his dark eyes glittered. "Will you forgive me, maid?" His voice was like silk, but he didn't fool her for a second and her reply was so faint that only Edward, cradling her in his arms, heard it. "Yes, yes."

Without another word or look at Bronwyn, he sat down at the end of the table as if nothing out of the ordinary had occurred. His eyes were hooded, concealing the hate and the envy of Edward's power and possessions that had grown like a cancer over the years.

Bronwyn looked at Edward's grim face, then scanned the silent faces of the men around them. Just a few words from this man and she was out of danger. Who was this man, then?

"Stop your gawking!" Her benefactor ordered his men curtly. "Go back to whatever you were doing or I'll have you all flogged!" It was spoken in good humor, though, and it seemed to break the uneasy spell that the whole table had been under. A smile played again on Edward's lips and he lightly kissed the bruises on Bronwyn's neck and held her close. He did not look at Warwick again, but asked her if she was all right, apologizing over and over for his brutish, stupid cousin's terrible manners.

"Little flower-face, I'm so sorry that had to happen," he whispered in her ear. She had just gotten over her fear of him and things had been going so well. Damn Warwick! "Excuse my cousin—he's not accustomed to the niceties of gentle behavior. He is used to his uncouth soldiers and the camp followers that traipse along behind them. But you must forgive him. He is a great warrior and he handles his men on the battlefield far better than he does his women." He chuckled, but secretly he was still furious with Warwick.

"I forgive him," she sighed, wanting to forget it all. But she didn't think *he* would forget.

"Well, so then shall I." Edward smiled tenderly at her. The noise of the crowd was suddenly so loud that she hardly heard him, so she simply nodded.

Bronwyn cautiously glanced over at her recent attacker. He was openly scrutinizing her still, anger flexing the taut skin over his square jaw, his arms folded tightly over his chest. He met her stare and his black eyes were as unfathomable as the depths of a grave. She had the same intuition as she had had the other night when she had been at his mercy—that here was that rare breed of cunningly strong man whom few would dare to cross. Now, she remembered—they called him . . . what was it? *Warwick*. Where had she heard that name before? Hard as she tried, she couldn't quite place it; yet it did sound familiar. She calculated that he was much older than his blond cousin. His face was rugged, lined and battlescarred. His eyes were dark and piercing, his hair thick and wavy, brushed back from his forehead. He was a giant of a man who emanated both strength and danger. He reminded her of a huge, vicious wolf.

Sitting there, the wolf was boiling inside over the humiliation he had just suffered in front of his men. He watched Bronwyn as she talked to the King. He was sure that she did not know Edward's true identity. After observing her for a while, he would have bet a gold piece on it. What would the little pickpocket say if she knew that the lap she so coyly lounged in was that of the King of England! It almost made him want to smile. He had to admit, all cleaned up as she was and in that pretty new gown with her hair fixed, she was very . . . bewitching. But it wasn't just her beauty that intrigued him, but the fire he'd seen in those green eyes and in her spirit, a magnificent spirit that he'd seen in few women, weak creatures that they usually were. He peered at Edward and wondered if he knew how rare this maid was? She was meant to be his, not Edward's. They were two of a kind, both fighters.

By God's blood, Edward would not have her! Warwick vowed as he watched the two smile at each other. He dug his fingers into his thighs until the pain brought him back to reality. Edward was protecting her. He smiled then to himself. He had already paid for this little hellion and though Edward had the title, the power and the glory of the glittering crown that rightfully, too, should have been Warwick's . . . *this one little wench he would not have*!

Edward was trying to hold Bronwyn in his arms, but she had other ideas. She felt conspicuous and it was making her very uncomfortable. This man, one minute so arrogant and condescending, was now so insistently charming that it unnerved her. She could see Molly off in a corner, glaring resentfully at her, and Bronwyn's heart sank. All in all, this day had taken its toll and all she wanted to do was to run upstairs with her sisters and collapse on her pallet, cover her head, and forget what had just happened. She was unsure of the intentions of this handsome man who held her, and terrified of the dark-eyed man across the table. She didn't feel safe with either of them. One wanted to kiss her, and the other wanted to strangle her!

She didn't belong here sitting on a rich stranger's lap. Her father had been right . . . an inn like the Red Boar was no place for a lady.

"What's that pretty little head of yours thinking now?" the blond man asked gently. "You are so quiet. You are all right, aren't you?" His blue eyes, troubled, searched the depths of hers.

"Yes. I'm fine," she answered, not sure what to say next. She noticed Warwick watching her and she cringed inside. "Sir, I have work to do. A job. Let me get up." She smiled at him appealingly and again tried to pull away from him. "It's my first day . . ." He laughed but finally released her from his lap.

"*Work*! Is that all you can think of, maid? You? Bah! You are much too pretty to worry over such mundane cares. You shouldn't be here, waiting on tables like a common serving wench. You're exquisite and you've a voice like an angel. You belong in a castle, wearing silks and jewels." He offered her a vision she couldn't begin to see. "You belong with me," he told her. "Can we not talk of this further?" he pleaded, his smile sure and strong. No woman had ever refused him. After all, even in disguise, he was King.

As she struggled to rise, he breathed in her ear, "Come with me and I'll give you anything you desire. You only have to ask. You do not belong here among this rabble. They don't appreciate true beauty and talent. They don't need you as I do." His lips brushed her hot cheek and his eyes were full of passion.

"Oh, but I cannot leave. I have responsibilities!" She pulled her hands from his with a sad smile. Yet she was flattered that he wanted her, when he could have had anyone. But, in the end, didn't he want what all men wanted? "I don't want jewels or silks," she exclaimed. "I'm happy the way I am. And I *do* belong here. These are my people. I know what you want of me and I will not sell myself. I can't! There are those who depend on me and I can't desert them." She was angry, but the pain in his face prevented her from lashing out at him further.

For a second, Edward felt angry as well. Then, looking at her sweet, innocent face and the truth mirrored in her eyes, he remembered. She was married . . . had children or something . . . *damn*! How had he gotten so carried away as to forget that? But she seemed so young. Looking at her unhappy eyes and her beautiful face in the firelight, he stared at her a moment longer, then slowly nodded. "I'm sorry." He turned his eyes away and let her go.

He wished that she wasn't such a virtuous woman. But then, that was part of what made her so special. She wasn't like the others he had known.

Seeing the sadness she had caused him, she offered, "Is there something else I could get for you or something I could do for you?"

Edward looked up at her and smiled faintly. "Aye, there is . . . sing for us, *ma belle chanteuse*," he said softly. "Sing us a song to make us forget . . ." At least she was still here. He could see and hear her. There was still hope. Something sparked in his eyes and his smile brightened. He would be patient and learn more about her. He'd ask the Innkeeper later about her husband and babies. Then he could decide what to do. He wanted her love, not her hatred. Perhaps she didn't love her husband. He wouldn't force her away from ones she loved, but perhaps he wouldn't have to. He had long ago forgotten the dice game and the rest of his men had continued playing without him.

Though with the "wolf" still snarling at her from across the table, Bronwyn would have preferred not to, she felt it was the least she could do in return for this man's kindness. She didn't ask him what he wanted her to sing, but walked over to where Leon had been sitting quietly all this time on his stool in the corner, his lute cradled in his lap. She moved as far away from Warwick as she could. Leon smiled at her. As long as the blond gentleman was here, Warwick couldn't touch her.

"Do you know this song, Leon?" she asked, laying a hand lightly on the boy's shoulder and began to hum an old peasant song that her mother used to sing in the fields. It was a message to all listening that she was a peasant born and bred and proud of it, not one to be bought with idle promises of wealth. She meant it especially for the man who watched her with longing in his blue eyes.

Coming up behind him, she sang the song softly as she remembered her mother singing it all those years ago as they gleaned the wheat after the harvest. In the heat, or the driving rain . . . she, a child herself, protecting the babies as they laughed and played, their chubby legs bare and dirt-covered as she chased them through the dust. Bronwyn had meant the song just for the few who sat around the table, but as she sang she was aware that gradually the crowd around them had quieted and many were listening. But by the time she had finished, she was no longer aware of the approving silence or the men, not even the dark-eyed rogue called Warwick. It was as if she had sung herself into a trance. When the crowd roared its approval, she blushed. Then she was asked to sing it again and as before the other customers joined in until the song echoed to the rafters. It was then she slipped back into the kitchen and back to work.

Jack beamed as he loaded her tray with wine and ale and sent her back out into the dining room. This time, everyone treated her with admiration and respect. No one grabbed at her or tried to detain her, unless it was to ask about or compliment her on her pretty voice. Even the roughest, most drunken of the lot treated her with awe. As she served the customers their food and drink the crowd launched into other familiar songs and they begged her to sing again.

Molly observed her from a dark corner of the room and her thoughts were spiteful. So . . . the little chit had already wormed her way into all the gentlemen's hearts, hey? She fumed as she fetched food and wine for men who could only whisper about how beautiful and talented the new girl was. Molly glowered at Bronwyn's back with envy and hatred. That settled it! The witch must go. Not one man had noticed Molly since that chit had entered the place! Somehow, she must be gotten rid of. Concerned with how to accomplish such a feat, Molly had been very interested in that little display earlier between the little witch and the tall dark soldier. She wasn't sure what exactly had happened, but she hadn't missed the look of mingled fury and desire in his face. It was something to check into. Perhaps, she rubbed her hands together with glee, it could all be turned somehow to her own advantage, perhaps even help to fatten that hidden purse she kept tucked under her mattress. Perhaps the girl was pure gold after all, she thought slyly, watching her smile at all the men. Bewitching them all, she was. Well, Molly would teach her to cast her stinking spells in her territory with her pretty little leather pouch of God-knew-what-all she carried under her skirts. She'd teach her to push Molly aside and make her look a fool. Burning was too good for the witch . . . And silently Molly's plan began to take shape as she followed Bronwyn through the crowd with her eyes. She spun around and pushed her way through the throng toward the man who had earlier had his fingers about the witch's throat.

Like Bronwyn, Molly had grown up fighting to survive except that she'd never had anyone to care about her or love her. Her mother had been a common whore who'd shoved her brats out into the street when they were barely old enough to walk—to steal and beg for her. Molly suspected who her father might have been, but she had never been sure. Right now the stupid old sot was rotting somewhere deep in debtor's prison and for all she cared, he could stay there! It wouldn't bother her one bit. She'd had four brothers and three good-for-nothing sisters; most were long gone, hanged for thieving or cutting people's throats—and good riddance, she thought. They had been stupid and slow-witted enough to be caught. But Molly was the clever one. Damned if she'd let herself end up out in the streets, an old hag selling herself for twopence or rotting in a damp cell somewhere because she was guilty of the foulest crime of all—being poor. Her eyes scanned the inn and its customers with smug possessiveness. Someday it would all be hers. There was no other reason for being that pig's mistress all these years. Ugh! He never washed and he snored. He took her like an animal. But if using her body thus could get her part-ownership someday in this place, it was worth it. Hadn't she always come out on top with her sharp wits? She didn't care about that old stupid fool, Martha; she didn't care who she hurt as long as it wasn't herself. She'd learned a valuable lesson years ago when she had run the streets as a decoy for her cutpurse brothers—she'd had many close calls—but in the end it had been *they* who had made the mistakes, been caught and finally swung from the end of a rope, not Molly. It was a lesson she had never forgotten. Jack, beast though he was, treated her well. Free room and bed (with him at times), yet she still took any man she fancied to the rooms upstairs when she felt like it. Jack knew better than to open his mouth, especially when he got a cut of it all—a tiny cut. Her sack of money was fat and still growing. Soon, she'd have enough to start her own little pub, if Jack didn't give her what she wanted. Tonight, maybe, she schemed with a gleam in her greedy eyes, she'd add some more gold to that sack.

Bronwyn didn't notice Molly's growing animosity; she was too busy the rest of the night to question the hurried conversation Molly had later that night with the man they called Warwick. She waited on the tables, dodging flying ale mugs as the night got wilder, until her feet and back ached. She sang a few more songs and avoided the table where the dark man still sat, watching her as a wolf must watch the cornered hare.

Finally, late into the night, the blond gentleman seized her wrist as she sped by. "Why have you avoided me the whole night, flower-face?" he asked. "Have I truly offended you so much?"

She smiled nervously down into his blue eyes, sensing Warwick's unblinking gaze. "No, Sir. I've just had work to do. I've been very busy . . ." But she was so strongly attracted to him, and she hesitated too long after her words. He took it for a weakening of her resolve and suddenly pulled her down into his lap and kissed her long and hard, his warm lips demanding and questioning, his arms about her like a vice.

Provoked, in a second of anger, she jumped up when he finally let her go and slapped him. "*How dare you!*" she said in a shocked gasp. She was exhausted and his breath smelled of wine. "Who do you think you are?" She glared at him.

The look in her eyes stunned him. He put his hand up to his cheek. "It was *only* a kiss!" He jumped to his feet, his eyes narrowed. "It is *you* who have overstepped." His anger was as swift and deadly as a thunderstorm. "*I could have you . . .*" He stuttered, unable to believe what she had just done, or even to finish his sentence. No woman had ever done that to him before!

"I don't care *who* you are . . . you had no right to take what I would not give freely!" Her voice rose.

"It makes so much difference to you?" he shouted, furious.

"Yes it does!"

"Good God!" he moaned under his breath." And it is my curse to *want* such a woman!" He threw up his hands, revealing how red his cheek still was.

"*No* . . ." she breathed. "It is your curse *not to have* such a woman; not if you treat all women as you have me!" One minute, she puzzled, he was so charming and the next he was an animal. Were all men like that?

The table was deathly quiet. Everyone was staring at her as if she had done something horrendous . . . as if this person ranting at her was someone special, someone of very high degree . . . as if . . .

Bronwyn cried out, putting her hands to her breasts and staring at the man before her. *The man in her dreams wore a golden crown on his fair head as if he were a King. The man he called cousin—Warwick. There was an Earl of Warwick*, she remembered. *Wasn't he the same man who had put the young King Edward on the throne a few years ago?* The whole land knew the legend of this man.

Bronwyn froze, her face going white. She stared at all the men around the table; the unsmiling way they now all studied her, their hands near their swords. The white rose of York was emblazoned boldly on their sword hilts; on their clothes . . . the white rose . . .

Oh, no! she cried inwardly as she saw the man before her as if for the first time. Could he possibly be Edward? *Edward the King*? Bronwyn stepped back as if his cheek had burned her hand. Here in this common Inn? *Impossible*!

As if he had read her mind, he sighed and nodded. No!

It couldn't be . . . had she truly *slapped the King*? God help her if it were true! She closed her eyes. She was going to faint, she knew it. *They cut off a person's hands for heinous crimes against a royal person. Cut off . . .*

Bronwyn tried to run, but he was too quick. He stepped in front of her, knocking over the table with all its contents. Her dress slipped through his hands and he cried out in astonishment and pain as he fell; she turned just in time to see him land at her feet amidst the food and shattered glass. And then she saw blood.

Appalled at what she had done, especially if he was who she feared he was, she instantly fell to her knees sobbing in the rubble and reached out to help him. Someone screamed, *"Sire! You're hurt!"*

But by then his bleeding hand was cradled in her trembling ones and she bent down and wiped the cut clean with the edge of her green gown. It was a wickedly deep slash across the top of his wrist and it was bleeding profusely. Without even realizing what she was doing, she laid her fingers on the bleeding cut and prayed. When she opened her eyes, he was staring at her in amazement; someone viciously grabbed her by the shoulder from behind and tossed her aside like a rag doll. Edward looked over to where she lay cringing. *"My God . . ."* he murmured. He stared down at the wounded hand she had just touched. "The cut is healed. It has stopped bleeding . . . You touched it, and it disappeared as if it had never happened!" His face was white with shock as three of his men bent down to pull him up. *"How did you do that?"*

"It was only a tiny cut . . ." she whispered. "Very . . . tiny."

If her heart had stopped at that very moment, she wouldn't have cared. She saw that *look* in his eyes, and the fear in some of his men's eyes who had been close enough to see what she had done. She slowly rose to her wobbling legs and began cautiously to back away from their accusing eyes.

This was the very thing she had feared all these years. This was the horror of her worst nightmares . . . to be discovered. *They burn witches.* The little voice laughed gleefully over and over in her spinning head until she could hardly stand it. And he was looking at her *that* way.

With a shriek like a wounded animal that knows it is cornered at last, she leaped up and ran from the noisy room, heading for the safety of her lair up in the loft. *I've done nothing wrong*, she kept telling herself like a prayer. She hadn't known who he was when she slapped him. She hadn't known!

As she ran, she bumped into Martha, and with tears in her eyes, she briefly told her what had occurred. "I'm so afraid! I did nothing wrong . . . what should I do?" She was shaking and Martha held her in her arms and calmed her. Bronwyn didn't dare tell Martha who the man she had slapped might be. It was too unbelievable. "What should I do?" she cried, looking around to see if anyone had followed her. But no, they were all too busy with the man she had hurt.

"Now, now, child." Martha soothed, "it will be all right. You go on upstairs and rest and I won't tell anybody where you've gone. I promise. I'll lie, tell them you ran away. Then later, we'll figure out what to do with you. Now, go!" she commanded and sent Bronwyn off with a firm push towards the stairs. "Don't worry, I'll see to it all." Bronwyn ran, not even bothering to light a candle. She stumbled through the dark halls, her hands sliding along the walls in the pitch black. Every shadow seemed to conceal a sinister pursuer and every dark corner warned her to run faster; run as far away as she could and hide.

"I know where she is right now," Molly divulged, her hands on her hips.

"Where?" Warwick's voice was curt. He disliked this greedy slut with the painted face and empty eyes, but if she served his purpose, what did it matter?

Molly's eyes glittered with malice and her smile was a slash in her pasty face. She held out her hand.

With a snort of scorn, he dropped a few coins in her open palm. She checked them and finally nodded as if they had passed her inspection. "Follow me," she said. "Though why such a handsome gentleman like yourself would desire such a high-and-mighty slut such as she be, I can't fathom," she continued. "She's too good for the rest of us, she is, with her prissy ways and her evil enchantments. She can't fool old Molly here. I know what she be! I tell you, she's a witch if ever I saw one! I saw her in the kitchen mumbling over her kettle, I did." Molly turned toward him half way up the dark, narrow stairs and the candlelight on her face flickered evilly, making her appear like a ghoul. "She's put a spell on everyone in this place, she has. That's why everyone is smiling and bowing to her. Take my word for it . . . she's the devil's own. And glad I'll be to see the last of her. Heaven knows what she'd be cooking up next," Molly spat as she continued up the stairs.

Warwick stalked silently along behind her swaying form and merely grunted. Superstitious bitch! he thought impatiently. Her spiteful prattle was grating on his raw nerves. He was taking quite a chance doing this, taking the wench right from under Edward's nose. He knew he didn't have much time, either. Edward, when the confusion cleared downstairs and he had time to think on it, would want the girl brought to him immediately, to ask her how she had healed his hand. Even Warwick, who had been close by, didn't understand what had happened. But what his mind couldn't comprehend, it brushed away.

Now, to get what he wanted, he must act swiftly. The innkeeper's wife had said that the girl had run away, but this wench claimed that was a lie and that she knew where the girl was hiding. Afterward, she would back the innkeeper's wife, saying the girl had packed all her belongings and had run away. Edward was naive enough to believe such a story. And what could he do about it? After all, Warwick grinned in the dark, she was just a peasant, one among many; no one would care if she disappeared and was never heard of again. As for her healing Edward's wound, well, that must have been some sort of trick. Even gullible Edward would see that after he sobered up a little. No one can heal just by touching. Edward had probably thought he had cut himself, but really hadn't. Warwick himself wasn't sure exactly what had happened.

"You *are* taking her away, aren't you?" Molly suddenly asked, holding her breath. It wouldn't work unless the wench was really out of the way for good. Molly hadn't asked what the fine gentleman wanted the wench for, and she didn't care as long as Bronwyn never came back to the inn. He could kill the girl or sell her for all she cared, as long as he took her far away.

"Yes. Very far away," he replied. He wasn't very talkative, Molly thought.

Puffing at the strain of the quick climb, she turned and handed the candle to him, but he waved it away.

"As you like," she replied huffily. It wasn't her concern if he fell down the stairs.

"I see very well in the dark, woman," he said. "Where is she?"

She pointed up the last few steps to the door. "There's a tiny loft room behind the door there. That's where she'll be. It shouldn't be hard to get in—the door is old and rotted, and the lock is rusty. Now I had better get back before someone misses me. I'll make sure no one disturbs you. You don't need me any more. I've done what you paid me for," she said and hurried back down the stairs.

Warwick smiled into a darkness that was as black as

death. Molly had told him that the girl was barely sixteen, and had two small sisters. He held his sword tightly against his side so it wouldn't scrape against the wall and announce his arrival. This had to be done with as little fuss as possible and he must leave no trace. He didn't want to alert the children if he could avoid it. He knew that if he was careful he could be long gone with the girl before anyone missed either of them, especially Edward. In a short time, the girl would be forgotten and Warwick would be back in Edward's good graces. In truth, Edward believed his cousin was now on his way to Croydon to accomplish the special mission he had given him.

Warwick was determined to have the wench, Edward be damned! And the Earl of Warwick always took what he wanted. This time she wouldn't escape him.

CHAPTER V

IN THE muffled silence of the dark loft Bronwyn threw herself fitfully down upon the straw pallet across the room from her sleeping sisters. Here she was safe. Someone as important as a King wouldn't follow her to such a place . . . if he even knew where she had gone.

She'd checked Mary before she had let herself lie down, relieved that the child's fever had abated. Then, her head spinning with the events of the day, she lay shivering in the dark, listening and praying that no one would come after her. An overwhelming wave of tiredness and hopelessness engulfed her and she wiped the tears from her eyes with trembling fingers. Why had everything gone wrong? She had met that lecher again, and slapped a King; wounded him and then shown the whole world her secret powers. And she had run away like a sniveling coward! She shuddered again in the dark. There was no other choice now but to give up her dream of a comfortable life at the inn; they couldn't stay. They'd have to pack their bags and move . . . *where*? Back to that miserable hovel or somewhere just as bad. She knew that dark-eyed brute would stop at nothing to have his revenge. She'd read it in his eyes as he had tried to strangle her.

Bronwyn feared he would not be put off so easily as the other one when Martha told her lie. He wasn't the kind of man to forgive a humiliation, and she was afraid he wasn't through with her yet. If she were smart, she'd pack tonight and escape with her sisters. *Now*. This minute. Something deep inside urged her to do just that. But then she let her eyes rest on the soft mounds that were her sleeping sisters and thought, *Mary is too sick to drag out again into the night air. I can't do that. Maybe later, but not tonight.*

Sad at heart and frightened, she sat in the dark and uncoiled her long hair that Martha had so happily fixed earlier. Had that really only been hours ago? When they left, oh, how she'd miss Martha with her good, understanding heart! All three of them would miss Martha. She stripped off her new gown with its bloodstained hem, taking off everything, including her pouch of herbs and her dagger, except her thin chemise and then huddled shivering beneath the blankets. Her mind kept telling her she was wasting precious time. *You should run, escape now!* She could look for work in another inn elsewhere in the city where she would be safe from all of them.

Tomorrow she would sneak them all out at dawn and not tell anyone, not even Martha. *A few more hours*, she pondered sleepily.

Outside, restlessly pawing and snorting horses waited below in the courtyard. The wind moaned and rattled the locked shutters above her as if in a frenzy. Doors opened and closed on the floor below and the muted sounds of the busy taproom could hardly be heard. She felt herself lulled by the unreality of what had happened down there tonight. She had sung, and the crowd had adored her; then she had slapped that man and the nightmare had begun. Perhaps, she stifled a yawn, it was all only a dream, all of it. And she would wake up tomorrow morning in their cottage as if nothing had happened at all. No inn, no Martha, no slap, no nightmare . . .

As exhausted as her body was, her fears wouldn't let her sleep. Images of what had happened kept running over and over in her mind until she finally crawled over to where their few belongings were still stacked in neat little piles. She hurriedly formed them into three bundles, tying them securely so they'd be ready for their departure at dawn. She had to do something. The walls were closing in on her like a prison, trapping her.

It couldn't have been but a second later that she froze. Were those footsteps she heard outside her door? Her heart pounded crazily with fear and she realized too late that her dagger was still in the pouch inside the gown she had just taken off, which was lying on the floor across the room.

The boards creaked and she heard someone grappling with the lock on the door. She grabbed a blanket, pulled it around her half-naked body and jumped to her feet. She searched frantically for the dagger, but couldn't find it among the folds of her gown. She stood paralyzed by terror as the door swung open and someone came in. In the dark, at first, he didn't see her standing there. Then abruptly he turned as if he sensed her presence.

Before she could move, she was brutally seized by steel-strong arms and spun viciously around, her arms yanked painfully behind her and lashed together with what seemed to be a piece of heavy cord. She would have screamed but for the lips that came bruisingly down on hers. The lips were instantly replaced with a large hand over her mouth as she was dragged fighting and kicking from the room and down the stairs through a sightless gloom. She fought like a wildcat but the intruder was bigger and stronger than she and it was all in vain.

He stopped on the first landing, and flattened her roughly up against the wall. As her heart almost stopped in shock, he held her firmly and kissed her again. His hands were exploring her everywhere. Then he put his hand back over her mouth and twisted her arms as he turned her to him, laughing deep in his throat.

She remembered well the brutal handling and the laugh. *Warwick!*

She held perfectly still, her mind whirling. How to get away?

"Ah, so you know who it is, ey, wench?" he snarled, his hot lips nipping at her ear. "We meet again. And this time, my clever little whore, not all your wiliness nor a powerful benefactor will save you. We'll just pick up where we left off the other night. No one will stop me this time. This time you won't escape. How would you like to go on a nice long journey—just we two?" He pulled her away from the wall and wrapped the blanket around her, stuffing the corner of it into her mouth so she couldn't make a sound. From somewhere, more rope appeared and he tied it swiftly about her and hefted her up upon his broad shoulders as though she were a sack of potatoes, then he fled down the rest of the stairs. After making sure there was no one about to see them, he slipped across the hall and out the door into the freezing night.

Trapped and terrified, Bronwyn continued to kick and squirm, though it did no good. Wrench and fight as she might, she couldn't tear herself free. How had she been so *stupid* as to let this happen! What was he going to do to her? Rape her . . . kill her? Perhaps he would rape her, then break her neck and leave her out in the woods for the wolves to feed upon. *Oh my God, no!* Hot tears flowed down her face. What would become of Mary and Samantha? Who would tell them that she had been abducted, that she hadn't abandoned them, nor forgotten them? *Who would take care of them now?*

If she only had her dagger! Her spirits sank further as her captor carried her across the courtyard, then stopped for a second, as if he were deciding which way to go.

She kicked as hard as she could and tried again to

scream. He slapped her so hard that the breath was knocked out of her.

He ran with long steps towards a horse that was tethered at the end of the courtyard. Since they were now far away from the inn, he dropped her to the ground and propped her up against the horse's warm heaving flank. When she tried to hobble away, he merely pulled her back and slapped her face until she tumbled, stunned, onto the snowy ground in a heap.

"Don't try that again!" he warned her as he jerked her back to her feet and shoved her against his mount again. She could feel the warmth of the stallion's body behind her. "I'll tell you this only once, my sweet," he hissed. "*You are my slave. My whore*—bought and paid for with gold coins . . . *do you remember now*? And you will do exactly what I tell you to do or you will get more of the same, do you understand?" He slapped her across the face when she refused to answer, then knocked her to the ground. She lay there, aching in every limb. His boot prodded her. "*Well?*"

She looked up in a daze, hardly able to see him in the darkness. He was a looming shadow against the black night. She finally nodded. Anything so he wouldn't kick her again! It felt as if her ribs were broken.

She winced when he dragged her to her numb feet again, then jumped effortlessly up into the saddle and just as effortlessly pulled her up and slammed her down in the saddle before him.

He laughed. "Oh, you'll learn to obey me soon enough, if you're as smart as I think you are." He rammed her cold, aching body up against his own and lashed her frozen hands to the pommel with the cord he'd taken from around her body, so tightly that it all but cut off her circulation. At that point, even the pain didn't bother her. She cared about nothing now. Her mind had fled into numbness and she heard his voice as if he were far away.

"*There*. That will keep you cozy. A good thing I thought to bring the blanket along, my little whore. It isn't proper riding attire, I'm afraid, but it is rather fetching on you. And so convenient for what I have in mind later."

She tried to scream but the gag muffled it and in any event they were far away from anyone who might hear. He only laughed at her efforts and prodded his stallion across the courtyard.

"You're mine now. You'll obey me or I'll thrash your backside; I, unlike my spineless cousin, am not a gentle lover when crossed. I don't coddle my women. You'll learn." He cupped her chin with his hand and tilted her face up so he could stare down possessively at her.

In the moonlight, she could barely discern the hated, rugged face, but she saw passion gleaming in his ferocious black eyes as his powerful hands caressed her small waist and full breasts under the blanket and she writhed in disgust at his touch. She managed to free one bare leg from the tangled blanket just enough to get in a kick at him in retaliation, not caring what he did to her. She could hardly think and she ached all over where he had already beaten her. He merely laughed and shoved her leg down with one hand.

Bronwyn wished she could die—anything would be preferable to what he planned for her. The only thing that kept her sane was that she still had some hopes of escaping somehow. At any time, her chance might come and she must be ready to take it. She would bide her time because she would need all her strength.

His hot breath warmed the nape of her bare neck as he buried his mouth in the loose, silken hair that cascaded down her back to her waist, and Bronwyn cringed. She hadn't felt such loathing for anyone since the night her father was murdered . . .

They rode through the gates and suddenly, out of

nowhere, a figure materialized directly in front of Warwick's horse. Startled, the spirited stallion reared as the man tried to grab hold of the reins.

"*Stop! Where are you going with that maid?*" the voice shouted.

With heart-stopping relief Bronwyn recognized Harry the stableman, blocking the stallion's path. Bronwyn tried to cry out, wrenching wildly at her bonds and kicking in frenzy. *Help me!* she begged silently.

"Why . . . that's the new girl you've got there! Why is she tied up? You knave—what are you doing with her?" Harry's anger exploded. He threw himself at Warwick, attempting to unseat him from his horse. "*Let her go!*" Harry yelled.

"*Get out of my way*, or I'll run you down! Let go of the reins!" Warwick barked as he fought around her writhing body, trying to break Harry's hold on his boot.

Warwick was a warrior trained to fight; poor Harry was no match for him. Bronwyn shut her eyes and prayed that Warwick wouldn't draw his sword. Sick with the fear that Harry might be hurt, she shoved her body up against Warwick's again and again as Harry tried to stop the horse. Cursing, Warwick kicked at Harry with his boot and spun the mighty warhorse around. The stallion reared, his flashing hooves coming down heavily as Warwick spurred his mount until she was sure its heaving flanks must be bloody.

Bronwyn watched in shock as Harry was trampled beneath the horse's frantic hooves.

They galloped through the gate and she closed her eyes in silent agony, unable to believe that the bloody heap of rags that lay unmoving in the snow behind them could possibly be alive. She prayed he wasn't dead because he had tried to save her.

It was all so much like the night her father had died that the horrible memories came flooding back. The wintry night, the snow, the smell of blood on the air . . . *No!*

Warwick sent the horse into a ground-eating canter. He wanted to get as far away as he could, as fast as possible.

Bronwyn, half conscious, kept seeing Harry falling under the sharp hooves, his blood spraying over the white snow. A tear slid down her cold face. Just like her father and those other unfortunates whose blood had stained the snow. *Her father* . . . She heard Warwick's laugh echo evilly on the still night air.

A skinny, ragged child helplessly pummeling away in vain at a laughing devil who rode away into the night on his black stallion, uncaring that he had just butchered five men. Laughing . . .

As Warwick was laughing now. Something foul and undefined began to swirl around inside her head, an insidious intuition that the man who had abducted her was that same man who had ridden away into the night all those years ago . . . *that this was the man who had murdered her father!* The dreadful realization sent her into a welcome blackness.

Warwick galloped through the frozen streets, aware that his captive had slumped forward lifelessly on his stallion's neck. Perhaps he had been too rough with her? He hadn't meant to beat her, but her defiance had aroused his rage. She would have to learn not to defy him. He pushed his horse to run faster. They had a long way to go before they met his companions and embarked on the mission with which Edward had entrusted him. Perhaps it had been unwise to have taken the girl now, but he had been unable to resist.

Poor Edward. He smiled into the biting wind, shifting the girl so she wouldn't fall from the saddle. To lose such a prize! For a brief second, he felt a flicker of pity for the wench, until he remembered what she had done to him at their first meeting. He knew that she was not a thief or a common street whore. He also suspected that she had kept those coins because of her extreme poverty; she must have been starving or perhaps she needed them to help feed her family. Whatever the reason, she had taken them and made a fool out of him in the bargain. Yet pity her or not, coins or not, the simple truth was that *he wanted her*. He wanted her for himself, for some reason he couldn't explain; he had to have her, and Edward be damned!

He looked down at her pale face and her hair blowing in wild silken strands mingled with the horse's dark flying mane and thought again how lovely she was. Young, vulnerable and somehow untouched by the world or men. She seemed strangely apart from the real world. There was a quality about her he couldn't put a finger on . . . she was *different*. And now she was his. He realized that his feelings about her were unique in his experience with women. He would teach her about the world and men. *Aye*, he touched her face softly, *I'll teach you well, wench. I'll teach you what it's like to lie with a real man*.

They rode for a long time through the cold night, he deep in thought and she unconscious as the powerful beast moved beneath them.

Bronwyn returned to consciousness gradually, first cognizant of the towering, black-shadowed trees as they swayed overhead, beckoning hideously to her like emaciated fingers. All too soon she remembered the abduction, her sisters and Harry. At some time while she was unconscious, Warwick had removed the gag. Her mouth was tender and dry as dust. Her face throbbed where he had slapped her; her whole body cried out in pain as the movement of the horse jolted her. Her hair whipped around her sensitive face as if it had a life of its own.

Somehow, he sensed she had awakened and he laid his gloved hand on her shoulder. "Don't you want to know where we're going?" he asked her in an amused voice.

She pretended not to hear him.

"Listen! Do you hear the ravenous wolves out there searching for their next meal? They are hungry. It's been a hard winter." He gathered her closer to him and she stiffened in his arms. "Perhaps, if you cannot speak, I'll leave you here for them to devour. You won't have to worry about the cold with them around. You won't be alone for long." He taunted her cruelly and laid a fevered kiss at the base of her neck. The wind cut like a knife as it swept around them and she huddled lower on the warm beast that carried them.

"Would you like to be their midnight tidbit?" he persisted.

He wouldn't leave her alone until she answered. "*No*," she finally spat. "But I can believe *anything* of such a monster as you. You would leave me out here and laugh as you did it!" Her voice was full of hatred and she wanted to say more, but words wouldn't assuage her grief or satisfy her fury. Only hurting him as he had hurt her would do. But some inner warning told her to say no more. Not now. Not yet. Even though words were her only weapons, she didn't dare to irritate him further until she knew better what to expect of him. He was stronger than she. She was only a woman; therefore she would have to depend on her wits.

"So. Milady finally chooses to speak with me. I'm flattered. That's good. You're learning. Soon, you'll be right where you belong and right where I want you—on your knees." He was deadly serious.

"In that, my lord, you will be proved wrong," she gasped, hating him more than she had ever dreamed possible. "I shall *never* be your slave, though you break every bone in my body and throw what's left of me to those greedy wolves. *I shall never bow to you!*" Despite her resolve, she couldn't seem to stop the hatred from spewing forth. "Your very touch disgusts me. You're an evil, vile devil and I shall hate you always! You had no

136

right to kidnap me, abuse me, and kill that stableman back there at the inn. He only tried to help me," she said through gritted teeth. "*I hate you*!" She stopped, biting her tongue and closing her eyes.

"The wench does have a sharp tongue." He chuckled lazily and slowed the stallion to a soft canter. "But I must tell you that that meddling man back there in the courtyard is most assuredly *not* dead, my sweet," he drawled. "I don't kill unarmed peasants. I'm not that much of a monster, as you so prettily put it. He was in my way and I simply dealt with him; nothing more, nothing less."

"*So . . . you don't kill unarmed peasants*!" Suddenly all her suspicions and terror exploded. "I believe your memory plays you false, my lord?" Her voice was bitter. "Do you not take pleasure in killing innocent men?" She knew this man had great power, not just over her poor battered body, but power that came from his position next to the throne. He was the great Earl of Warwick, leader of Edward's armies, commander of great wealth and power. In England, only the King had more power than this man. And she was, after all, just a common peasant, nameless and worthless. He could do what he wished with her and no one would say a word against it. No one cared. But still her hatred was so virulent that her reasoning deserted her. How she despised him!

"*You are a murderer*!" she hissed.

"*I told you* . . ." She could feel his anger by the tension of his body. "I did not kill that peasant! He's still alive, probably rubbing his bruises in the snow."

She turned to glare at him in the moonlight and her eyes were deadly. "Not just that one," she said. "Do you recall a night two winters ago? A night very much like this one? *Remember* . . . you and a few of your henchmen rode down a group of drunken Lancasters outside an inn and brutally *murdered* all of them! Do you remember a peasant who was getting their horses for them, a thin man with grey hair who walked with a limp, a man who had never done you harm? He was a soldier once for the King, just as you are now. He was wounded in France many years ago.'' Her voice had settled into a lifeless monotone that now rose to a sharpness that cut like a knife. ''That peasant you killed that night out in the snow was *my father*! Do you remember it now? A peasant, a kind and gentle man. *My father!*'' Her whole body was as tense as a bowstring.

His eyes gleamed with sudden recognition. She thought she saw a shadow flit across his stony face. Could it have been guilt, or remorse? No. This killer could have no guilt, because he had no heart.

Staring down at her, he seemed to really see her for the first time. He thought there was something familiar about her—the way she had fought him, her fury in his arms. ''*You!*'' he exclaimed, shocked. ''*You* were that little hellion that attacked me that night and bit me in the leg. *You're* the one. *You!* That little waif?'' Utter disbelief. ''You know, you bit deep. I still bear the scars.''

''Aye. It was I. And if I had had a dagger that night, I would have gladly thrust it into your throat! *Murderer!*'' she screamed, her voice a wail. *And if I could kill you now, I would!*

''If I were you, wench, I'd be careful what I said. You have no idea of what you're talking about. There are circumstances that you know nothing about. You are just an ignorant woman and you don't know whom you are threatening. I don't take threats lightly. I usually kill those who dare accuse me without proof.'' His voice was emotionless and cold.

''You have no conscience nor heart, my lord,'' she whispered, then added, ''and I care not that you are the great Earl of Warwick . . . you are still a foul murderer and nothing can change that. What else could you do to me? You've killed my father, abducted and beaten me and I'm sure you won't stop there.''

He was surprised that she had enough spirit to talk like that to him since she knew his identity. She wasn't afraid of him and it somehow impressed him. Her accusation and the memory of that night she spoke of, no matter what she thought, had shocked and upset him. He was sorry he had killed her father; he hadn't meant to. But he was not the kind of man to apologize for what was already done. The incident was regrettable, but it couldn't be changed. He said, ''I should beat you within an inch of your worthless life for speaking to me like this.''

''No doubt you will!'' she spat. The little alley-cat with the sharp fangs had grown into a panther.

He raised his gloved hand instinctively to slap her, but stopped his hand mid-way. He had killed her father. She had good reason to hate him.

''Go ahead! It seems your style, to kill defenseless old men and to beat women!'' she screamed.

He sighed and lowered his head. He said nothing and she turned away.

There were some things, he brooded as they rode through the night forest, she would never understand. True, he had little conscience, but that was because he was a soldier trained to fight and kill—a conscience was a luxury he couldn't afford. Remorse could drive one mad; he'd seen that happen to many a weaker man. Since he had been a small boy he had been taught to be hard, unfeeling. He was sorry about her father, but he couldn't grieve over it. Neither tears nor accusations could change that now.

But sometimes a small voice nagged at the back of his mind. He heard it more and more frequently these days and during long, sleepless nights when the winds of time and change howled about his head. *He was haunted by the faces of those he had had to kill or maim on the King's business . . . the King's business!* He was just a paid assassin. The girl was right—he was nothing but a murderer! *No.* He mustn't think that! He must never doubt the rightness of what he did. He did it for Edward and for England! He had no time for guilt. Guilt was for weaklings.

As they rode along, he remembered that night more vividly—the way the snow had glimmered iridescently under his stallion's hooves and how hard and crusty its top layer had been, like ice. The bitter cold and the long wait at the edge of the woods outside the inn until the drunken Lancasters had emerged; then the slaughter, like so many times before—except for that skinny brat sinking her teeth into his leg, cursing him as he rode away. Ah, he did remember. He had tried to forget. He rubbed a gloved hand across his aching brow. What was wrong with him? Why now, of all times, was doubt stabbing at him? Why was he no longer sure?

He gazed down thoughtfully at the girl's fair head and lightly stroked her loose hair. He rested his shaggy head silently on hers. He wished he could tell her he was sorry. But he felt her stiffen at his touch and knew that she hated him too much for that. There was a wall between them and he had put it there. It wasn't in his proud nature to let anyone get the better of him, especially not a woman-child like this beautiful peasant. She was nothing—and yet, she had a hold on him that couldn't be assuaged any other way but by possessing her, body and soul. She had bewitched him! That slut at the inn had been right about the girl, she was a witch! For no other reason than that, she deserved everything she got! Aye, she was a witch . . .

A witch whom Edward also craved. He smiled then as he thought of Edward. By God, he had succeeded in snatching the girl from right under his nose! He would have loved to have seen Edward's face when he found the girl was gone. Warwick recognized lust when he saw it! He gloated—and then, like a thorn in his side, an unwanted image crowded into his mind of a glorious day in March of '61.

He and Edward riding proudly into London to claim Edward's throne. Together. It had been a memorable battle, winning the city back from insane Henry and his bitch-wife Margaret, but it had been far easier than either had anticipated. The city hadn't been properly defended; any army could have marched in and taken it from those incompetent fools! And they, he and his cousin Edward together, had laughed as Henry and his foolish queen had run off like beaten dogs with their scraggly tails between their legs. That woman who had always fancied herself a man had been as much a coward as any of them in the end. *Ah, God, Edward*, he moaned inwardly at all the bittersweet memories of that day, *what a time that was! The best time of his life. What had happened?*

That day had been so much more special because of all the hard, hopelessly lean years of fighting that came before it. He remembered Wakefield in the bloody winter of '60. *Wakefield . . . where he had nearly died for Edward and England. His beloved England.* He ruminated darkly on those hopeless days in St. Albans when, after they had tasted how bitter defeat could be, Edward had cried like a child over their great losses. Bloody St. Albans, where Warwick's own good father, the great Duke, had died as well as so many other brave men on the gory battlefield for the white rose and the House of York.

In the good times and in the worst times, he and Edward had stood shoulder to shoulder all these years. Until now. He couldn't fathom when the change had begun, or why. When had he first felt the shift in Edward's favor? Even more puzzling, when had he begun to mistrust and then eventually to hate Edward? *Edward, whom he had always loved like his own son!* Suddenly they were no longer on the same path together, no longer going the same direction. He suspected that Edward felt the same way about him. Why? He still remembered Yorkshire where he bravely told Edward not to worry over the obstinate Lancaster forces who had yet again gathered their armies. He had told the frightened Edward, *It makes no difference how strong they are. We shall fight them again! And win! Have no fear, Edward.* And they *had* fought. With just a tiny rag-tag army they had trounced their enemies and finally (or so they had thought at the time in the heady flush of their great triumph) sent them fleeing for good and all to the cold sanctuary of Scotland. *Palm Sunday.* But those stinking Lancasters never gave up! They were even now sniffing at England again . . . scheming.

But now, what difference did it make? Edward mistrusted him more every day, Warwick grieved silently. Edward no longer needed him; no longer confided in him. Warwick felt sure that even this mission was like a small bone thrown to an old, faithful dog, for past services well done. *Edward, you insolent pup!*

Those glorious days were gone. They would never come again, he accepted sadly. *Never.*

Something occurred to him then. "Wench, I never thought to ask . . . you do have a name, don't you?"

She gave a small, scornful laugh. "It's really very funny. You've been too busy abusing me to have bothered with such mundane pleasantries as names. Don't you find that funny? I do."

He grunted. Apparently he didn't. "Well?"

She sighed wearily. "It's Bronwyn, my lord. Bronwyn Rouet. I'm a peasant, and so was my father and his father before him."

"The name is French," he said. Was he trying to make polite conversation now, after all he had done? It almost made her laugh.

"Yes, it is. We are of Norman stock," she said proudly.

Yet she was tired, so very tired. Her ordeal had exhausted her—she felt so heavy she could hardly move; her mind was becoming confused. Even her anger had evaporated. She was so weary; everything seemed muddled, lost in a mist, even her beloved sisters. At the thought of her sisters, she moaned. Surely, she reasoned with a heavy heart, Martha would take care of her poor abandoned poppets?

They kept on riding. Some time during the night, she dropped off to sleep, and when she opened her eyes, the sun was glowing over the black rim of the distant hills. She had no idea where they might be or where they were going.

The stallion had stopped, the reins slack across its neck. Warwick was sleeping behind her—she could tell by his even breathing. She focused her eyes on the reins that lay across her thighs. She was so cold, she was sure her legs were frozen. Cautiously she stole a glance back at her abductor. His eyes were closed.

There was probably a small dagger in a sheath at his waist under the cloak. It wasn't so far away from her . . .

She stealthily maneuvered her stiff body to where she could touch the hilt of the dagger with her teeth. It was difficult and painful because her hands were so firmly tied to the pommel and her teeth kept wanting to chatter from the cold. Her lips were cracked and bleeding from the bitter wind and when she lowered them to the dagger's hilt, she felt blood ooze from the cracks. Her body cried out in protest and her hands, bound too tightly, were numb.

After what seemed an eternity, she had it! Bringing the dagger to where she could drop it into one of her bound hands, she grasped it and started hacking at her bonds. Once or twice her numb fingers almost dropped the knife, but finally the ropes slid to the ground and she smiled as she rubbed some feeling back into her hands and wrists. The returning blood made them tingle painfully.

143

She studied the land around them—woods and deep gullies filled with snow. Nothing else in sight for miles. She had an important decision to make. Run or fight? She wondered if there were farms or a town near by. She could slip from the saddle and run into the woods to hide—or she could stab him, take his horse and leave him behind to die in the snow, just as he had left her father that infamous night. She could go back the way they had come, following the horse's tracks.

If she hid in the forest, she wouldn't stand much chance of survival, not with the wolves and all the other hungry animals that roamed there. She had no warm clothes or food. If she ran away, he'd only chase her down until he found and caught her. She knew him well enough to know that he wouldn't give up easily.

But as much as she hated him, she thought, staring down at his bent head as he slept, she knew that she couldn't kill him. She was a healer. It would be a sin to betray what she was. If she merely wounded him, he would hunt until he found and punished her. There was no place in the land safe enough to hide from the powerful Earl of Warwick.

She had never felt so helpless and alone before. What should she do? There wasn't much time. *Hurry. Hurry*! If he awoke now the evidence would damn her—the knife, her cut bonds. His eyelids fluttered and she sucked in her breath in mortal fear. If he awakened now and she found herself staring into those black eyes, all hope of escape would be gone forever. The dagger glittered in her red hands.

She braced herself against the pommel of the saddle and with a strong shove, she threw all the weight of her slight body against his as he slept. The sheer force of it as well as the surprise sent him tumbling off the horse into the snow. His eyes flew open in disbelief and he yelled as he hit the ground.

She positioned herself in the saddle and grabbed the reins, slapping the horse's warm sides wildly with her frozen feet and urging him into a gallop. The stallion, startled, balked at first but then did as she wanted.

Warwick bellowed like an angry bull behind her as she galloped away into the woods. *"What the hell! Wench . . . come back here! Do you hear, you little scheming . . ."* was all she heard clearly as she fought to control the huge spirited beast under her. He was nothing like the gentle mare she had ridden the other day under Harry's care. This was a fierce warhorse. She slid around in the saddle, barely able to stay seated and she felt her tenuous control of the monstrous beast slipping.

"*Bronwyn*!" She heard Warwick scream at her from far away. "Bring that horse back here now! *Damn* . . . wait until I get my hands on you!" His anger was so strong she could almost feel it washing over her like a huge wave. The horse was prancing sideways and yanking at the bit in a frenzy, unused to such little weight on his back and such inexperienced hands on the reins.

As she rode farther away from her abductor, Bronwyn felt suddenly so relieved that she began to laugh. *Faster. Faster*! She kicked the stallion's sides harder. Her laughter rang through the woods, bouncing against the trees and echoing away into the air. She had showed him! She had tricked him again!

But she wasn't the only one laughing . . . she could hear a man's laughter far behind her and her heart seemed to stop as she realized it was Warwick. Warwick was laughing at her! She had bested him, and left him on foot alone in the woods, and *he* was laughing at *her*! It made no sense.

"You'll regret this." A faint threat so far behind her. He couldn't hurt her now; he couldn't catch her or beat her. She was free!

Then she heard a sharp whistle, then two, then three. In

horror she found herself clinging for her life to the beast's arched neck as it abruptly reared and snorted to a dead stop, quivering. It rolled its eyes wildly and flickered its sensitive ears, snorting and pawing the snow as she struggled to make it go on. Her heart in her throat, she clung as the stallion reared again. When it couldn't dislodge her, it spun about and stood ground, refusing to move another inch, no matter what she did.

Another whistle.

The stallion whinnied and galloped towards its master, who was waiting for them, standing there like stone, a scowl on his dark face. The stallion stopped dead at Warwick's boots and he calmly patted its shiny neck, the horse nuzzled him.

"No!" Bronwyn screamed as a wickedly smiling Warwick yanked the reins casually from her trembling hands. In one swift movement, he had pulled her from the saddle and tossed her roughly to the ground at his feet where he towered over her, laughing.

"Devil, my horse, is well-trained, don't you agree?" he said as he glared down into her pale face. The blanket had fallen away and she clutched it, shivering, at his feet.

"And you, my sweet, will pay for that little escapade. Believe me, you will. You will learn to obey me and stop trying to escape. It will do you no good."

He's going to kill me! She looked into his angry eyes and she knew it.

He reached down for her then, but she dodged his hands and scrambled to her feet, turned and began to run barefoot through the trees, clutching the blanket around her, the dagger forgotten in her hands.

But it did not good. He tackled her a second later and brought her down to the ground beneath him. She raised the knife to strike him and with one swing he knocked it from her hand.

He pinned her down on the hard ground, his piercing

eyes full of anger and lust. "You stupid, foolish girl . . . don't you know that you can't get away from me? *You're mine*. It's time I claimed you." His smile mocked her struggles as he lowered his lips to hers and kissed her so hard and hungrily that she couldn't breathe. He laughed then. "But I must admit that you amaze me! You can ride, somewhat. Staying on Devil is not easy—he usually lets no one but me near him. Aye, it was something to see, from the beginning when you woke up and took the knife; imagine, you really thought you could trick me and escape. Clever. So very clever of you. Even if you didn't succeed, it was an admirable try."

Her eyes narrowed. "So you were awake all the time . . . you taunted me with a taste of freedom. Was it so you could further humiliate and torture me?"

"No." He replied lazily, looking down at her flushed face. She was so pretty, so desirable. "To teach you a lesson."

Something snapped in her then and she went berserk, fighting like a mad woman, snarling, biting and kicking at him in a mindless fury like an animal. Laughing, he struggled with her and they rolled over and over together in a deadly embrace on the ground.

He finally succeeded in dragging her to her feet and took both her wrists into one of his large hands. He whistled for his stallion and took a blanket from his saddlebag, still holding her tight. He threw it down upon a pile of dry leaves and shoved her down upon it, then dropped down beside her. Everything she feared most was in his eyes as he held her down and kissed her.

"*Now*," he told her. "You will have your first real lesson in obedience, wench. And you will submit to me or I will beat you and leave you out here to die alone in the woods and you'll never see those sisters of yours again. In fact, if you don't behave yourself, I can arrange that no one ever sees them again." He held her hands high above her head and lowered his body heavily over hers. He could feel her warmth under him and his desire grew. She tried to bite him and he threw her an amused glance, then slapped her until she was so weak and hurt that when he stood up to undress, she was beyond caring or fighting. It was so cold that she could see his breath as he stood above her.

"*No*," was all she could whimper when he lay down next to her and his rough hands tore the thin chemise from her body, then demandingly explored every inch of her. As she shivered and tried not to cry out, he spread her thighs. His hands were strong and cruel. She had never been touched that way before. She had never known that it would be like this, so humiliating and painful. Still she fought him. Her nose was bleeding and her body ached . . . all she could think about was getting away from him. It was like a nightmare, but it was happening. His teeth tore hungrily at her nipples and she arched her body in revulsion and, finally, panic. Then he entered her cruelly. His love-making was hard and fast and the throbbing shaft inside her seemed to be splitting her in two. That was the only time she cried out, in shame and horror at his violation of her body. Tears coursed down her cold cheeks. She knew this happened to many women, but it was small comfort to her as she closed her eyes and bore it until the end, in silent agony.

When he finished with her and had shuddered in completion, he held her frail, shaking body next to his, covering them both with her blanket. He held her for a while in his arms, not letting her push him away. "Ssssh, don't cry any more. You are finally a woman. Sooner or later, it would have happened," he whispered, his steel arms about her like a vise. She *had* actually been a virgin, he thought in awe. She really had been pure. It had been a long time since he had had a virgin. He almost felt guilty.

Yes, it would have happened eventually—*but not by*

148

the murderer of my father . . . not brutally taken against my will like a whore! she thought miserably to herself. There wasn't an inch of her body that didn't ache, as well as her heart. He had taken something very precious. Now she was what he had called her—a whore, bought and paid for.

"You're beautiful . . . and you are mine." Could he want her again so soon? she thought with fear. Did he think his paltry compliments would alter what he had just done to her, could change the past? She shuddered uncontrollably and turned her wet face away from his. Now she hated him! But she said nothing; there was nothing to say. There was no way on earth to regain her lost virginity. All she craved now was for him to leave her in peace. Like a wounded cat, she only wished to be allowed to slink off to some dark place alone where she could lick her wounds and mourn. But he wouldn't even give her that.

"Don't turn away from me," he told her, his voice oddly gentle, tilting her face back to look into her eyes. "Someday you will desire me so much that you'll beg me to take you! It will not always be like this." She wondered what he meant. He was ready to take her again and this time she was too tired and beaten to resist. She just prayed that he would get it over with quickly.

"*No . . . you're wrong. I'll never beg you for anything! Never,*" she whispered as he entered her again. Her eyes, that had been glazed and distant, suddenly blazed into his with a little of the old spark as he moved within her. *I hate you*, they said. *I will always hate you!*

But then the spark faded and she felt detached from all reality; the man using her body, even the penetrating cold seemed to fade away. The only thing she could think about was this man had killed her father and had ravished her, and she knew that someday she would have to kill him . . . to be free of him at last.

As though from far away she heard him speaking. "You

liked it, didn't you? Ha! All wenches fight it at first, but in the end, they crave it. I'll never understand women . . . why fight it then?'' He didn't wait for an answer but shoved her away from him into the snow and turned his back on her while he stood up and hurriedly rearranged his clothing. She had no way of knowing that his apparent anger was his way of hiding his guilt and anger at himself. She scrambled for her torn shift and the blanket to cover her nakedness.

Her chemise was barely wearable, torn, wet and dirty, but it was all she had, and she put it on and then silently wrapped the blanket around her shivering body as he finished dressing and strapped on his sword under his cloak. The shame of what had happened enveloped her like a shroud and she felt as if she were going to be sick. She scooped up a handful of snow and washed the tears, dirt and blood from her bruised face and arms. Her tangled hair hung in long, dirty strands about her face. She could hardly stand, she was so weak. There was pain where he had intimately used her and she hobbled over to crouch by the tethered black horse, waiting for what was to come next. Would he kill her now?

He sauntered over and grinned down at her, then untied the reins of his mount and turned it around. ''You are a picture, wench. You should see yourself!'' He raised a mocking eyebrow and then swung himself up into the saddle and started to ride away from her. She stood up slowly, watching him, then followed behind his horse, walking faster as he quickened his pace. Her face went white and her bloodless lips quivered as she began to run beside him. ''It's cold,'' she stuttered, staring up into his glittering eyes, trying to hide her growing fear. For a terrible moment, she thought; *He's going to leave me out here alone in the woods! He's going to leave me to freeze to death*! Was he really going to desert her, or was he merely teaching her another of his ''lessons''? He urged his mount forward and she ran faster to keep up. When she looked up at him, he was smiling as if he had just been told something quite amusing. He laughed loudly and spurred his horse into a dead gallop, leaving her quickly behind. She stood there like a statue, watching him go.

No! She told herself. She wouldn't cry; she wouldn't grovel or beg . . . she wouldn't!

But when he was completely out of sight over the hill, she crumpled to the ground and let the tears come. What would she do? She was cold, beaten, hungry and unarmed. Which way to go; what to do? Did it really make any difference? She would die, either from exposure or as the victim of the ravening wolves.

She'd never see her sisters again. Or Martha. She put her head in her hands and her sobs shook her entire body.

Suddenly she heard laughter. Startled, she looked up to see Warwick watching her in amusement some distance away. Her heart stopped in mid-beat and a great feeling of relief rushed over her, quickly followed by anger.

"You bastard!" She jumped up and yelled at him, clenching her fists.

He leisurely trotted over to where she was standing, shaking with fury and cold, and with one expert move he scooped her up into the saddle before him, still chuckling.

"Well, wench. How did you like being left alone? That should teach you." He squeezed her tightly, burying his face in her bedraggled hair. His dark face became serious as he looked down at her. "Did you really believe that I'd give you up after all I've gone through to get you, to find you again? No. You will never escape me again. But now, let us hope, you know better than to cross me, little witch. You won't win."

Bronwyn hung her head and closed her eyes, defeated. She was so tired. Oh, to be able to sleep and forget everything!

They rode for a short while and then he said, "I think

we should stop for awhile and warm ourselves over a fire. I'll trap a rabbit or something and you can cook it. Are you as hungry as I?''

She wouldn't have believed it after all she had gone through, but she found she was hungry. Ravenously hungry. She nodded.

"Ah," he said. "I might even have some tea in my saddlebags as well. You'd like a cup, wouldn't you?" She wasn't sure but she thought she could detect concern in his gruff voice.

But that was impossible.

"Aye, tea sounds good," she mumbled. A steaming cup of strong tea! It was a wonder how sometimes the simplest pleasures could mean so much. She was so cold and weary. She would have done almost anything to know what he was thinking now; what he had in mind for her and where they were going. But she couldn't bring herself to ask.

They stopped and made a make-shift camp. He built a fire and piling leaves nearby, he laid a spare blanket over them and told her she could rest there until he came back with some meat. Without another word, he tied her wrists with a long length of rope and then looped the other end over a nearby branch.

She glared up at him for a moment, hatred alive again in her eyes. But she was really too tired to care. She sighed. He marched into the woods then. "Don't go away, wench. I won't be gone long."

She supposed he was gone only a short time, though she couldn't be sure. She had immediately curled up on the blanket, tucking part of it over her along with the blanket she'd had wrapped around her, and slept. She awoke to feel the toe of his boot prodding her side.

"Wake up, wench. Here's lunch." He looked down at her. She was so disheveled and sleepy-eyed. He thought she looked like a child staring up at him. "Here." He dropped the bloody rabbit down next to her, then knelt to untie her hands. "Clean it and cook it," he ordered, then went to check his mount and get some things from his saddlebags. She watched in anticipation as he withdrew cheese and a hunk of brown bread, a flask and various smaller packages.

Crouched over the rabbit she was cleaning with the same knife she had used earlier to cut her bonds she said to him, "You seem to have come prepared for anything. Are you planning a long journey?" He ignored her. "You wouldn't also happen to have some warm clothes in one of those saddlebags for me, would you?"

"I might. If you behave yourself—and don't burn the meat." He rummaged around in the other saddlebag. "I always carry a change of clothing for myself, an old tunic and a few other things, in case I should need them. They'll no doubt be much too large for you, but at least they will be warmer than the rag you've got on, and that blanket."

"*Anything* would be warmer than what I have on," she replied curtly. She finished cleaning the animal and rammed a sharpened stick through the meat. She carefully made a crude spit over the now blazing fire and laid the meat across the licking flames. The fire felt so good, she thought, spreading her frozen hands over it. She turned back to see him standing a short distance from her, studying her. Inwardly she felt herself cringe. He couldn't want her again, could he? The thought terrified her and it must have shown in her face because he looked away.

"Before we do another thing, perhaps we should clothe you better. Like that, you distract me far too much. We have a long way to go before dark and we can't dally. It would be better if I'm not tempted thus every foot of the way, or we might never get there." He contemplated her lithe, partially clad body and threw her a bundle of clothes. "Here—put these on, before I am tempted beyond endurance." He grinned at her red face.

She turned her back, but didn't really bother to try to hide her nakedness or ask him to look away—he'd seen it all already, hadn't he? She stripped off her soiled, ragged chemise and slipped on a shirt and an old woolen tunic. On him it was probably only calf-long, on her it fell almost to her ankles.

"Do you have something I can use for a belt?" she asked softly, afraid to meet his brooding dark eyes.

He tossed her a piece of rope and she wrapped it around her slender middle. "Thank you. This is much better. I was so cold," she said in a dead voice as she knelt down before the fire and turned the sizzling meat on the spit. It smelled good. She was very hungry.

"Before we go, I'll fashion you some kind of footwear. It won't be much more than scraps of cloth, but it will be better than nothing," he said, glancing at her feet which she had endeavored to wrap in one of the blankets.

She gazed down, too. Her feet were scratched and cut and so cold that she couldn't even feel them. When she looked back up at him, her eyes were great and sad. "I wonder why you care. You beat me and rape me, yet you worry about my feet. I don't understand you!"

He closed the distance between them in a second and pulled her to a standing position. There was a look on his face she couldn't read. With one hand he brushed her tangled hair back from her bruised face. He had done that to her. *He.* If only he could convince her that he hadn't meant to hurt her. If only . . . "Why shouldn't I care about the well-being of something that belongs to me?" He hated himself for saying that, but he couldn't show any weakness, not now. He must not let this little witch see how strongly she affected him. "You'll see, in time, that I take very good care of what is mine. And if you behave, wench, you'll learn to appreciate my finer qualities." His hand around her wrist was as strong as a steel band and his eyes were black ice under his shaggy eyebrows. There was no doubt in her mind that she was nothing but his prisoner and would remain so unless she could somehow escape. Whatever else he thought of her or any other reasons she could see for his obsession with her, did it really matter?

She would have been astonished to know that at that very moment he was thinking of only how beautiful she was. Even battered and dirty, her spirit shone through like a diamond. Not even the bulky, masculine clothes could hide that beauty.

They sat and ate in silence, his eyes never leaving her as if he feared that if he glanced away for a second, she would disappear. She crammed her portion of cooked rabbit into her mouth still steaming, and drank the hot tea she had made in quick suspicious gulps as if she feared someone would snatch it all away from her.

She was a pitiful sight, he thought with a stab of guilt, with her bloody face and her swollen eyes.

"Do you want some wine?" He offered her the flask he had taken from his saddle, then added, "It will take the chill from your bones."

At first, she was going to refuse, but then she abruptly reached for it and took a few long, greedy swallows. It would be better if she were a little drunk. Maybe it would blur where she was and with whom she was and all that had gone before. It burned going down, but it created a welcome tingling spot of warmth in the pit of her stomach.

When they had finished eating, they cleaned their greasy hands in melted snow. The shadows were lengthening and it was even colder than before.

Warwick towered above her, working his thick leather gloves on and staring up at the sky. Dark, ugly clouds were coming in; there was a heaviness he knew well in the air. It had suddenly grown so dark, it might have been evening and not just mid-afternoon. "We'd best be going, wench," he said, swinging up into his saddle and riding over to her with outstretched hand. "Come. We have a long way to go before nightfall."

She instinctively shrank away from his hand and a frown of impatience settled on his grim face. She never wanted to get back up on that horse with that man, touching her, so near her again. Her emotions must have been reflected in her eyes because, scowling, he finally captured her wrist and yanked her up into the saddle before him as if she were a misbehaving child.

"We're wasting precious time. A storm is in the air, I can sense it coming. I prefer to be somewhere warm and dry before it hits." He spurred his mount and they galloped through the trees in the descending gloom.

She was relieved when he didn't automatically retie her hands as she had feared he would. There were already rope burns around her wrists. Perhaps he thought that she had suffered enough for one day; there was always tomorrow.

As they rode, each wrapped in their own silence, the sky darkened and the wind began to tear at them with vengeful teeth. There was a pinkish glow everywhere as the sun's rays were screened from the earth. It made Bronwyn feel as if she were in a dream.

"We will arrive at our destination, I trust, by evening," he informed her at one point.

She nodded. She didn't really care.

Warwick scowled. He had wasted too much time on the wench as it was. If he missed the rendezvous with his men, he would have a lot of explaining to do to the King. And he didn't want Edward to have any further reason to doubt his loyalty. Not now.

Much later, as the wind howled bitterly around them and the swirling flakes of snow plagued their passage, he offered her more wine. She nodded and as she gulped it down, he suggested teasingly that if she kept going like that she would get drunk. He didn't think she was used to it.

"I'd welcome being drunk, my lord," she said acidly, staring away into the distance. "Maybe then I could forget what you have done to me; what you did to my father." She gulped a few more hearty swallows and then reluctantly gave the flask back to him. Soon the wine began to affect her, as exhausted as she was, and she felt light-headed and very drowsy. She closed her eyes and went to sleep . . .

CHAPTER VI

IT WAS night and pitch black when they finally rode into Croydon. During the last part of the journey Bronwyn had been dozing fitfully, covered by Warwick's large cloak. The storm was almost at its peak when he woke her. At first, disoriented, she wasn't sure where she was; then as the awful memories crowded in again, she closed her eyes briefly, not wanting to face whatever was to come. They made their slow way, plodding through the snow, down the dingy streets of a small town. Faint light seeped from cracks in the shutters of the houses; dark, huddled shapes slithered past them seeking to find shelter from the storm. She wondered how many of them had homes to go to. She fancied she could hear bodiless voices and haunting laughter wafting on the night wind like homeless banshees, and her soul as well as her body shivered. There were people nearby, but she knew none would lift a hand to help her. Even here, she was still alone. This man behind her was a warrior and no one would stand up against him for the sake of a woman they did not know.

Warwick brought his stallion to a halt and dismounted before what she took to be some kind of tavern. He tied

Devil's reins securely to a post before a squat building. She could hear noise inside. *People. Food.*

"Here there will be a warm fire and mulled cider to warm our frozen bones," he told her as he lifted her from the saddle. He didn't seem nearly as weary as she, though he must be every bit as tired and cold. She was unaware that this was the meeting place which they had been traveling to for so long, and he was anxious to take care of the business at hand. He knew he had been unwise to bring her along, yet he had had no choice. Now he wanted to accomplish his task and spirit her away somewhere safe where he could be sure no one could interfere.

He held her back for a second, though, and said, "Tie your hair back with this piece of cord." He handed her a piece of rope. "Then tuck it down into your shirt."

She looked up into his face inquiringly but didn't say anything as she obeyed his command.

"We soldiers usually share our women," he explained, a grimace on his dark face. "Especially the pretty ones. But I don't intend to share you with anyone. So it will be better all around if you don't look particularly fetching. My men won't bother you if they don't think you're worth the trouble." He inspected her and sighed. Even with her bruised, dirty face and her lovely hair tied back; even in the shapeless men's clothing, she was still attractive. She was much too pretty to expose to the vultures that sometimes frequented this place. But she was also about to collapse at his feet from exhaustion, so he had no other choice but to bring her inside. There wasn't any other place where he could take her. Irritated that just gazing at her sorrowful face could inspire the softer feelings in him, he dragged her into the gloomy tavern by one arm, as if she were nothing more than a prisoner and carelessly shoved her into a corner before the blazing fire. When Bronwyn's abused body hit the floor, she moaned softly in pain and curled up right where she had landed, uncaring. Warwick turned and left her without a word.

The fire was warm on her icy skin and she huddled before it, pulling her knees up to her chin and spreading her cold hands towards it. She didn't know where they were or why. She cared about nothing but escaping from this monster and returning to her sisters. Like a beacon, the inn and her sisters beckoned her. She must not give up hope! She fought to keep her eyes open and looked about her. She must always be alert for means to her end—escape.

Warwick had been welcomed to a corner table where two men in dark cloaks sat drinking ale. They turned now to stare at her and one smiled, laughed suggestively, and was just as swiftly sobered by an angry word from Warwick. The man's head snapped back towards Warwick and Bronwyn heard an argument ensue. Over her? She smiled ironically, turning her head away. She must resemble a wounded bird that the cat had dragged in. She explored her misshapen, tender face, then shook her head and lowered it to her knees, closing her eyes. What did it matter?

The men huddled at the table were indeed discussing her. "A pretty little piece of baggage you've brought along, my lord," commented the man with the scraggly beard and a scar across his right cheek. He'd noted Warwick's intense possessiveness. "But she's quite a mess. I can see by the way she looks that she must have put up a hell of a fight—a real she-devil, eh, my friend?" His voice was as coarse as sandpaper. Warwick knew him to be a lecher, though he called him friend. Not too long ago the man had fought a jealous husband and had fared none too well. His throat had been slashed neatly almost from ear to ear. He'd been unable to talk or move for months; now his beard concealed the scars because he was a vain man. But

161

he'd killed the husband before it was over. It was a miracle that the lout was still alive at all, he had so many scars to show from all his miscalculated escapades.

"You could say that. But, to be absolutely truthful, the wench is quite mad. She fancies herself a cat at times; at times she thinks she is a horse . . . wants to eat grass. Ah, she's a strange one. I'm delivering her to a friend of mine along the way. She's even too crazy for *me!*" He laughed and made a circling gesture near his ear and shook his shaggy head. He looked back at Bronwyn huddled in front of the fire and then leaned over to whisper to the man conspiratorially, "*She hates men,* I've been warned—all men. Rumor has it that she's killed a few and hid their bodies out in the woods. They even say that once—" here his eyes widened in mock horror for his friend's benefit, "they say she took a sharp dagger and cut off his . . ."

His two comrades turned and stared at the girl in open horror. "*Jesus Christ!*" the bearded man muttered.

The other, a smallish balding man with sandy hair, whistled in astonishment. He then looked at Warwick with an amused twinkle in his eyes. He was a great deal wiser than the other man and Warwick didn't think he'd fooled him as easily. "Hum," he said with a smile. "She is dressed strangely, too. Does she always dress like a man?" He nudged Warwick in the side and chuckled. He knew what the old wolf was up to. "It seems to me that, crazy or not, you've tried her out already. It was a long, lonely journey, hey, my friend?" he whispered and then, in an even lower whisper, added, "And who's to say, my lord, that we can't handle the murderous little she-devil as well ourselves." Warwick glared at him and replied, "You will not have the opportunity." The man's eyebrows shot up, but he only smiled and nodded, while the scar-faced one, still believing the story, turned to stare at Bronwyn again.

The other man said no more. He would cross any other man but the Earl of Warwick. The man was a vicious fighter, and he held the King of England in the palm of his hand . . . he was not one to anger. And he was no fool, either. *Though,* he wondered, *why such a fuss over that*? He, too, turned to look again at the girl in front of the fire. It was strange. She didn't look like much of a prize—more like what was left for the loser.

"As you say, then, my lord." He accepted easily enough. Salisbury, for that was his name, knew that maybe later . . . Warwick usually tired of his women soon enough, and Salisbury was not too proud to take Warwick's leavings. Then, stealing another glance at the wench, he said to himself that he'd seen better in the dock's whorehouses. He really didn't want her anyway.

Bronwyn knew they were talking about her and gawking at her. Her ears burned, yet she kept her back turned to them, dismissing them as if they did not exist. She wondered, though, what Warwick was telling them about her. Would he give her to them now, now that he was done with her? She cringed and tried to ignore their muffled voices and their crude glances. The way they studied her was obscene. She looked back just a second and caught the bearded one smiling hungrily at her. How she hated them all! Slowly, for the lecher's benefit, she drew her finger across her throat and grinned viciously back at him. The look on his face! How she would have loved to twist a dagger deep into his gullet!

She stopped her thoughts in horror. What was she thinking? What had she become? An animal, like him? She hung her head and told herself she mustn't let this change her. She must keep hatred out of her life or it would cloud her mind so that nothing good could ever dwell there. There wasn't room in her heart for so much hate.

The man with the scar was the Earl of March, and he was smarter than Warwick gave him credit for. He'd already realized that Warwick was infatuated with the bedraggled little urchin huddling there before the fire. He'd known that from the very beginning; crazy or not, heaven help the stupid clod who bothered Warwick's wench. And like Salisbury, he knew that Warwick wasn't one to cross, especially over a mere woman—it wasn't worth it.

Besides, they had an important mission to accomplish. The Earl of March thought it strange that Lord Warwick would bring a wench along in the first place. He'd known Warwick for a long time, and this wasn't like him. He thought about it as he watched the girl and listened at the same time to Warwick detail their clandestine sortie into the freezing night. *Damn!* Why did these blasted things always take place at night, in the cold or rain, or snow?

The Earl of March didn't miss the way Warwick's dark brooding eyes covertly kept glancing over at the girl as he outlined the steps of their mission.

Warwick didn't trust the little vixen. He didn't trust his two comrades, either. That was the saddest thing about being who he was—it seemed he couldn't trust anyone anymore.

At one point in his narrative, Warwick's eyes encountered Bronwyn's across the dim, smoky room and he was shocked at the intense hatred that flickered between them. *Why had he abused her so?* he sighed to himself. *Why?*

Salisbury was speaking and Warwick reluctantly returned his full attention back to the matter at hand. Murder. A political execution, as Edward would refer to it. "I know exactly where Duncan and his worthless brother are hiding," said Salisbury.

"Good," Warwick replied, forgetting the woman entirely for the moment. "The sooner the deed is done, the better. I'm sick of butchering. I have little stomach these days for such grisly business . . . I'm getting too old for all this riding and killing in the dead of night." He rubbed his heavy-lidded eyes and looked over to where Bronwyn was miserably huddled and thought of her father. "I want to accomplish the deed with all haste.

"But first I need to feed myself and the girl. We have been riding all day and night. The sooner we finish our business, the better. The girl is about to collapse."

Warwick showing concern over a mere woman! That was unusual, Salisbury mused.

"Food and drink are easy enough to take care of, my friend." Salisbury waved his hand at the innkeeper. "Food and drink for my comrade here, proprietor . . . and more ale!" He laughed, slapping Warwick affectionately on his broad back.

A few minutes later Warwick was gulping wine and tearing hot roasted chicken hungrily from the bones with a contented sigh, his long legs stretched out under the table. Soon, the feast was added to by trenchers of steaming potatoes and slabs of tender ham, fat loaves of bread and fresh butter. The delicious smell was everywhere. Warwick thought of the girl, but to cater to her too much would only call attention to his interest in her, so he waited until he had eaten his fill and then turned to her. She had been staring at the feast like a starved kitten who wasn't allowed to beg at the table. "Come here, wench," he bellowed out across the room and she blushed in humiliation at being treated so.

To hide her anger, she came across to him with demurely downcast eyes, her hands tightly clenched at her sides. As hungry and tired as she was, she couldn't bring herself to beg for food. These men were his friends. They were snickering at her as if they knew what he had done to her . . . as if she had a flaming *W* across her breast for *Whore* . . .

"Yes, my lord?" she whispered obediently, hating both herself and them. Suddenly, realizing that subservience would be just what he wanted, she lifted her eyes to his. She held her chin high. Damn them! She wasn't broken yet!

"What, no smile for your master?" Warwick taunted. The others were staring at her.

She simply stared coldly back at them.

Salisbury was startled by the haunting quality of the waif before them—the defiant way she looked at them, her chin held high. There was something about her . . . Suddenly he knew why Warwick had lied about the girl and why he wouldn't share her. Under the bruises and baggy clothes, she was indeed a prize.

"Here, wench. You may eat this," Warwick told her coldly. "You must keep up your strength. It will be a long night." He winked openly at her and he reached up to cup one firm buttock. At the same time his other hand shoved a hunk of meat and a thick slice of bread at her as if he were doing her a great favor by throwing her these crumbs from their table. He watched with a raised eyebrow as she silently took the meat and bread into her trembling hands and, wrenching herself away from his roaming hand, scurried back to the safety of the hearth, as far away from all of them as she could possibly get. Her eyes had been full of hatred and not one of the men, including Warwick, had missed it. She turned her back as the snickers and whispers began and when she ate, the food stuck in her throat. But she had to eat; she had to be strong to fight if she were to survive.

When she had devoured the food and wiped the grease from her mouth, she found just how tired she really was and crumpling down next to the fire, she tried to get as comfortable as she could. She thought longingly of her sisters and Martha at the Red Boar right before sleep claimed her. How worried about her they must be, not knowing if she were alive or dead. When she fell asleep, she dreamed of women being dragged screaming out into the cold night, beaten, and raped in the snow over and over by a black-eyed hairy beast that resembled Warwick, yet was a demon from Hell with a huge ice-cold member . . .

It seemed she had slept only seconds when she looked up to see him bending over her, shaking her. For a terrible second it was as if she were still dreaming. She cringed away from him, her face livid with fear. Something flickered in his eyes, but all he said was, "I've let you sleep as long as I can. Now we must go." He pulled her unceremoniously to her unsteady legs and she could see that her nearness was affecting him. He was a little drunk. His eyes were red and there was a smell of ale on his breath as he bent over and suddenly kissed her. In instant retaliation, she dragged her nails down the side of his face and when he pushed her away there were vivid red scratches on his cheeks and his eyes were blazing. But he didn't say a word or raise a hand against her.

"Go? Where are we going this time of night?" she asked belligerently. The man was crazy. Why couldn't he just let her sleep? Bronwyn was wide awake now, but it was as though she'd passed from one nightmare to another.

After he had explored the new scratches, he nearly yanked her arm off, and twisted it until her eyes filled with pain, then said. "Never question me again, harlot!" He turned and dragged her along behind him, a little unsteady on his feet.

His two comrades were waiting at the door, dressed in heavy cloaks and hoods, swords ready at their sides. They looked like they were going out to kill someone . . . they had a gleam of murder in their eyes, Bronwyn thought fearfully. Her heart began to rampage in her breast. Where were they going and why?

"Christ, my lord!" The Earl of March growled, staring at the cowering girl in Warwick's grasp. "Do we have to drag her along?"

"Aye," Warwick stated simply and the look in his hard face didn't admit of any argument. He didn't trust her; if he didn't take her, she would find some way to escape him. She was clever, so clever . . . Since the episode in the woods that morning, he would never underestimate the sly wench again.

Salisbury couldn't refrain from saying, "She's dead on her feet, man, can't you see that? Must we take her out into a night like this?" His hidden meaning was clear—*Must we take her along on such a mission?"* She should stay here where it's warm and dry." Then he looked over at the poor creature and added, "Surely she won't run away in the condition she's in. Where would she go on a night like this? My God, man!" Why was he mistreating the girl so? That he—or someone—had already beaten her half to death was clear enough; but dragging her out on a night like this to witness what they were going to do was insane. What had gotten into the man? He wondered if he really knew the great Earl as well as he had thought. Maybe all the killing year after year had driven the poor bastard mad.

Warwick was getting angry. His eyes narrowed. "I have my reasons for what I do, and you, gentlemen, must not question them. She cannot be trusted and she'll stay at my side . . . to Hell and back, if I should decide it!" At the look of indignation in their faces, he added, "But I'll leave her outside. She won't interfere with our work."

Bronwyn knew what he had in mind. He'd bind her up like a trussed turkey or a criminal out in the frigid night. She was so tired, so weary of it all. She would rather die than to go on being treated like this. There was pity, she saw, in the other men's expressions. She smiled tentatively at the man with the reddish hair and Warwick jerked her roughly back behind him.

"Enough! No more delay! We must go. Let us get this *business* over. I'm getting older each moment." *Too old to be running errands for a spoiled boy-king. Too damn old . . .*

He shoved Bronwyn ahead of him and followed her out the door. The Earl of March, feeling pity for the poor shivering maid handed her his cloak right before Warwick tossed her up onto his saddle. She could tell the gesture had angered him, but she didn't care. She was grateful to have it because after the lulling warmth of the tavern, the cold was even harder to bear. She thanked the man in a hoarse whisper and then he, too, mounted his horse and they all galloped off down the snowy street, the others trying their best to keep up with Warwick's furious pace. Bronwyn had a premonition that something terrible was about to occur, and she was being forced into participating in it.

"Will you tie me to the saddle again?" she asked him as they rode along. "I promise I won't try to escape again—tonight," she mumbled, ashamed of how sick she felt, how cowardly, but she couldn't stand the thought of being bound again. Her body and heart cried out to be somewhere warm and safe.

"And what would you say if I told you that I don't trust you?" he asked.

She let out the breath she had been holding painfully and shrugged. "Then there is nothing I can do. I was a fool to believe you would show me even that little kindness." She slumped in the saddle, her mind as numb as her body. She couldn't fight him anymore. He'd finally succeeded in breaking her spirit.

"Granted then, wench!" His voice was strangely sad. Empty. "Just remember that I will not take your promise lightly. If you try to escape, I will kill you." He frightened her. She knew he meant every word.

After what seemed like endless hours, they reined up before a cluster of low wooden buildings. Snow and mud had been splattered all over Bronwyn's clothes by the horses' galloping hooves and she had begun to shiver almost uncontrollably. She felt as if everything was happening in a feverish cloud of unreality.

"They should be here." Salisbury pointed a gloved hand towards the second, brightly lit building. Warwick flashed a malicious smile in the moonlight.

"We must be silent. They must not have a chance to escape," Warwick whispered, tightening his hand about her wrists for a brief second. "John, you go around the back." He turned in the saddle, calming his nervous mount with a steady pressure of his legs. "Martin, stay here and when I call for you, enter." Bronwyn watched as the other two men disappeared like phantoms into the shadows.

"And I, my lord?" she asked. Snow was coming down in large wet flakes and in a growing delirium, Bronwyn stared down at Warwick. One moment he was there in front of her eyes and the next—gone. She shook her head and was suddenly engulfed by a wave of dizziness.

For answer, Warwick reached up and jerked her from the saddle. "I'll take you somewhere safe. There's a stable over there where you can wait for us. Do you *understand* me, wench? Did you hear what I just said?" He met her glazed eyes and shook her until she nodded. He suspected she was becoming ill; he'd been far too rough with her. Yet he feared that perhaps she might be crafty enough to feign illness in order to slip away from him. He looked at her swaying body and felt the fever through her clothes with a twinge of regret that he had treated her so harshly. What if she died?

She didn't resist as he swept her off her feet into his arms and carried her to the stable, depositing her like a sack of meal onto a layer of musty-smelling hay in a corner. "At least here you can sleep and be out of the wind. *Don't try to escape*. I'll be back for you in a short while." He bent down and captured her hot face in his strong hands and made her look at him in the semi-darkness. *"Do you understand?"* he hissed.

"Yes. Yes," she moaned, falling back into the hay when he released her. She was too sick to care what he did or did not do. Her eyes slowly closed and she listened to his retreating footsteps until all was silence. *He was a killer; he had already killed many, many men . . . what did it really matter if he were to kill yet another? She couldn't stop him. No one could. . .*

Minutes sped by . . . no, years. *What was that?* Bronwyn sat up with a startled cry, trembling. She could hear screams everywhere on the midnight air, and heartbreaking sobs, then the sound of men cursing and shouting and the clash of swords. Was it real . . . or was she dreaming? She felt so sleepy. She touched her cheek. It was blazing with heat.

Another scream rent the air, a cry of such horror and pain that Bronwyn could feel the terror. She was so weak she could hardly move, yet she dragged herself to her shaking legs and made her trembling way to the door. For a second, the dim hay-smelling stable spun around her, and she grabbed onto the wall so she wouldn't fall; she couldn't remember where she was or what she had been trying to do. Then the blood-curdling howls brought her to herself again and drew her forward as if in a trance.

Outside . . . then to the building from which the screams originated . . . to the half-open door from which light streamed . . . Bronwyn halted on the threshold of the place and with blurry, horror-filled eyes she gazed at a hellish scene.

Bodies lay sprawled on the floor of the room. She was aware of lanterns swinging as the icy wind swept past her through the open door. She hugged the cloak closely around her body as if it could protect her from what she was seeing. She was haunted then by the images of other dead men on a winter night over two years ago. There was a sickening odor of whiskey, burnt food and the cloying scent of blood and death. A woman with long straggly black hair was keening in agony over one of the bodies, blood all over her hands and across her cheek as if she had touched the wounds and then brought her hands to her face in horror. She turned to Bronwyn and lifted her bloodstained hands imploringly. "*Help me!*" the woman wailed.

"*Dear God! What has happened here?*" Bronwyn gasped as she leaned dizzily against the door frame. Her head was pounding and her body ached with a pulsating fury.

The woman was screeching, "*Them devils killed 'em. Killed em! All of 'em.* Didn't even give them a chance to say a dying prayer before they sent 'em to their maker *Bastards!* Why did they do this, can you tell me, girl? *Why?* We weren't harming no one. We never did anyone any harm." The woman was wringing her bloody hands and wailing in a high-pitched sing-song.

"*Them?*" Bronwyn repeated. *Warwick. The others . . . where were they?* Her heart cold as ice, she looked about the room, behind her. There was no one except herself and the sobbing woman . . . and the bodies.

The woman leaped up and grabbed Bronwyn as if she were clinging for her life, as if she knew she might be next. "*Don't leave me alone! Don't let 'em kill me,*" she begged in a horrified whine that pierced through Bronwyn's heart like a knife. "I didn't do *nothing* . . ." She pushed herself away far enough to stare into Bronwyn's white face. "They called Duncan a traitor to the King . . . they said he was a traitor!" She shook her head wildly, her hair flying. "*Jesus!* They weren't no more traitors than I be! Aye, they were spoiled, proud men, Duncan and his brother, and sometimes they spoke too loudly. They say the King has ears everywhere. But I swear to the blessed Virgin, they'd never dishonor their country or betray the crown, nor spy for that crazy witch Queen Margaret . . . *I swear it! They weren't traitors!*" The woman was pleading with Bronwyn as though Bronwyn had the power to save her, kissing her hand and weeping; then, rolling her eyes like a terrified animal, she whispered into Bronwyn's ear. "T'was their money they killed 'em for, I'd bet my soul upon it! The King wanted their land and their wealth and if a man dies a traitor's death, the crown can claim all that was his. That's why they were killed!" The woman was hysterically clawing at her and Bronwyn had to struggle to push her away or she would have pulled Bronwyn down to the floor with her. "Help me!" she sobbed. "Now, any second, they'll come back for me. I hid, but I know they're out there looking for me!" The woman was on her knees.

Bronwyn could hardly stay conscious, her head was spinning so fast. The woman kept fading away, all except her wailing.

Then as if from out of nowhere someone came up behind them and Bronwyn was thrown aside. When she landed on the floor she found herself looking up into Warwick's savage eyes. He shoved her back against the wall and turned on the weeping woman cowering at his feet. She grabbed his legs, begging for mercy instead of trying to get away. It was her fatal mistake. Too late, she saw the sword raised above her head and though she tried to scramble away from its descending blade, she was not quick enough. She screamed just once, more in surprise than in pain, and then collapsed on the floor, silent forever.

Bronwyn hid her face in her hands in horror and then, mercifully, fainted. The next thing she was aware of was Warwick lifting her up into his saddle. As he spurred his horse out into the night ahead of the other two men, she could smell smoke everywhere. She glanced back just once and saw the buildings burning, yellow flames licking against the black velvet sky. The moaning and cracking of burning, collapsing timbers echoed in the still air above the sounds of their horses' thumping hooves. She heard Warwick say to her, "*I told you not to follow . . . I told you to stay there!*"

She felt every fiber of her being, as sick as she was, cringe in revulsion.

Bronwyn said nothing. Strange, she couldn't feel the cold anymore. But she would be haunted by that poor woman's face for the rest of her life. She hadn't been able to help her. She couldn't even help herself. What good was she to anyone?

Warwick drove his mount as if the very devil were behind them. *He is running from his own devils*, she thought dazedly, *as if he fears the spirits of the men he has butchered will come after him for revenge—he must outdistance them . . .*

Warwick's horse was foaming at the bit and its eyes were rolling crazily. It, too, sensed its master's black mood. It would drop dead beneath them, she thought fuzzily, if he didn't ease off . . .

Bronwyn remembered little of that wild flight. Later, she would recall only vague snatches of it and thank God for her benumbed state, else she too might have been driven insane by the knowledge of Warwick's foul deeds. Insane, as the Earl of Warwick himself must be.

So dazed was Warwick with the killing fever that when they rode up to the tavern, he didn't notice the other horses tethered there. He leaped from the saddle, tired and stiff, and pulled a half-conscious Bronwyn into his arms.

It came as a shocking jolt when he burst through the tavern door with Bronwyn in his arms and found himself face to face with a grim Edward.

"*Sire!*" Warwick nearly choked on the word, his dark

face flushing. "Why are you here?" For one of the only times in his life, he was all but speechless.

Edward's handsome face wore a black scowl as his flashing blue eyes rested on Bronwyn and narrowed to slits of fury. He stepped up to Lord Warwick, staring at the seemingly lifeless bundle in his cousin's arms.

"*Sweet Christ, Warwick! What have you done to the poor maid*? She's been beaten!" Edward's voice was deadly. He touched Bronwyn's still feverish face where it was cut and bruised. He glared up into his cousin's eyes with hatred. "What exactly did you do to her, my lord? Drag her behind your horse through the woods? Is she dead?" His eyes filled with intense pain as he snatched the girl's body from Warwick's grasp and rushed with her to the fireplace to have a closer look at her. Trembling, he cradled her tenderly in his arms in the firelight and gazed down into her feverish face. He touched her lips and traced the cuts along one cheek. *How could anyone have done this to her? She had been so beautiful, so innocent*.

"You did this to her!" Edward looked back at a stone-faced Warwick. Edward couldn't see the fury boiling in the other man's eyes or see his hand poised dangerously near the hilt of his sword. "If she dies, cousin, I shall never forgive nor forget your hand in it," he spat.

"*Wait . . . Sire . . . let me explain . . .*" Warwick tried to interject, but Edward had turned his back in disgust and was intently searching Bronwyn's countenance for any sign of life.

"*Damnation*! So I was right . . . *you did abduct the girl*! I couldn't believe it of you at first. I kept telling myself that you wouldn't have committed such a heinous act against me, your cousin and your King, not when you must have known that I fancied her for myself. Can you not see that this girl is not like other girls? And this is how you treat such a rare prize!" He was shaking with rage. "Are you such a deranged fiend that you abduct and torture innocent young women? Or is it that you cannot abide beauty and goodness and take some perverse pleasure in destroying it? *Tell me! I want to know*!'' His voice rose. ''*Or*,'' and Edward's tone was chilling though his eyes flamed, ''. . . did you take the girl *because* I fancied her?''

Warwick fell back a step, unable to meet his King's demanding gaze. It was enough to confirm Edward's worst suspicions.

He carefully set Bronwyn down upon the rug and standing up to face his taller cousin, he said, ''You go too far, my lord! I want you out of my sight! Get you gone, before I do something we both shall regret.''

The two men stood measuring each other, Edward with a strange fire in his usually cool eyes. Five of his soldiers stood alert and ready for any order he would give them if Warwick should resist. It would have taken only a gesture or a word. Among Edward's closest men there had always been distrust and jealousy of Lord Warwick's power, wealth and the favoritism always shown him by the young King. There were many who longed to see him in disfavor or banished.

For awhile the two locked eyes in a war of wills, Warwick's hand hovering near his sword. Then suddenly he lowered his eyes, and smiling servilely, he bowed his head before his King. ''Sire, forgive me. I honestly did not know how you felt about the maid,'' he said smoothly. ''I never suspected that you would have designs on a mere peasant. She is so beneath you. After all, Sire, she isn't even particularly pretty. Too thin, for one thing. Not your type at all. So forgive me, if I have offended you. It was not my intention.'' He had no other choice. He was outnumbered and he knew it. When he would finally face Edward, it must be on his own terms, not Edward's.

He sensed Edward weighing his apology. He knew Edward was wavering; he had no choice, either . . . he needed Warwick's power and wealth. The persistent Scots, goaded by the deposed Henry and his bitch were even now threatening England's borders again. No, Edward had no choice but to forgive his lusty cousin.

They both understood as they glared at each other over the girl's huddled form that their bond must not be severed over a mere peasant girl. They needed each other . . . and England needed them both.

Knowing this, and knowing that Warwick knew it as well, Edward let out an explosive sigh of frustration and spun away from his cousin to kneel again by the girl's side, taking her cold hand in his.

As if he were talking to himself, Edward murmured, "After all the commotion had died down, I went in search of her. I wanted to know how she had healed my wound. She did, you know—healed it as if it had never been. She touched it and it healed." He smiled down gently at Bronwyn. "*She has a great gift,*" he whispered.

Ah, 'tis a pity she can't heal her own wounds then! Warwick thought cynically. Though he himself had witnessed the feat, his eyes must have deceived him or they had all been tricked! If she had indeed healed Edward with her touch, it was witch's work. And the wench had bewitched himself as well as the poor King.

But Warwick refrained from speaking his thoughts aloud.

When Edward smoothed the hair from Bronwyn's feverish brow, her eyelids fluttered open and slowly her eyes opened to gaze into his concerned face. "Sire . . ." She smiled softly and then fell instantly back into unconsciousness.

"Norbert, take the maid—gently, she is hurt—up to the room I have taken for the night," Edward told his personal attendant, and then stood up and watched as the servant lifted the girl as easily as a feather into his strong arms and took her upstairs to where a warm bed had already been prepared. Only when she was out of his sight did he turn back to Warwick.

"I will spare nothing, no cost, until she is well again, until she is as lovely and happy as when I last saw her. Well, cousin, you have not answered me concerning her condition."

Warwick was not used to being questioned in such a brusque manner, and practically stuttered over his lie. "She fell from my horse, Sire, trying to escape last night." He was anxious that Edward believe he had neither intended nor caused harm to the girl. "She is only exhausted from our ride in the cold night air."

Edward turned his back on his cousin. He didn't want the man to see the doubt and disgust he felt. Edward did not believe Warwick was telling the truth; intuition told him there was a lot more to the story. But he couldn't afford to make an enemy of the man. So he merely paced the floor and asked Warwick curt questions about their flight and the girl herself. On his mind, too, was the delicate question of the maid's honor, but Edward would not discuss such a thing with the man. He was greatly relieved that he had found the girl alive. More harsh treatment, and she might not have been alive much longer. *The bastard*!

The King was a romantic and a private man; there were questions he couldn't bear to ask if the answers were what he feared they would be. It was better not to know. He had found the girl and that was all that mattered. Staring at Warwick's familiar smile and warming eyes, he couldn't bring himself to shatter the illusions he'd cherished about his great cousin. He had loved Warwick like a second father . . . he couldn't stand the thought that he could have been so cruel and brutal, that the man was a monster.

"I took her, aye. Is it so hard to understand? I am only a man, Sire, after all." Warwick spread his hands and shrugged. "She lured me by . . . *witchcraft*!" As if that were reason enough for what he had done—the allure of a pretty wench and her spells. "Why, the girl is strange. She is surely in league with the devil. She bewitched me! I swear it!"

A tiny-prick of fear chilled Edward at the mention of the word *witch*. He, too, for a brief second the other night had thought that perhaps her gift might come from Satan. Then, remembering the maid's innocent, guileless face and simple manners, he called his thought a foolish one indeed. He said to Warwick, "Nay! She's no witch. She has a gift for healing, a gift she herself may not even know she possesses. And the only spell she casts, I think, is the spell of love." Edward thought of the girl upstairs and knew that she wasn't evil. She could not be.

"Enough of accusations and this foolish talk of witch-craft, my Lord Warwick." Edward sat at the wooden table where they all been seated earlier. He was weary beyond words, and starving. He'd ridden through the night in the cold and he ached all over. The only thing that kept him from collapse was the sweet joy of knowing the girl was his again, and safe. "Let us sit down and eat . . . talk. There are things we need to discuss." His eyebrow went up and his hand patted the bench besides him. "Was your mission successful?" His young face had turned serious and somehow old. He hated what he had ordered done that night. But he must be a strong King and quell any treachery before it spread. He had known Duncan well and his death, and the reason for it, saddened him. He abhorred killing, but there were times a King must go against his conscience for the good of the realm. His people depended on him. He dare not be weak. So he and Warwick sat together as they ate, discussing the success of the night's assignment and what Warwick must tend to now. "We must start gathering our forces. It is time." Edward rubbed his tired eyes. "Henry has finally gotten Scotland's support . . . they are even now preparing to attack. We have much work to do if we are to vanquish them. Our men are scattered, gone home to their families. How I hate calling them back to battle so soon. Damn those blood-thirsty Scots! Damn them to hell!''

The two talked far into the night, making plans and gradually rebuilding their bond of friendship, or so Edward imagined, little knowing that Warwick hated and envied him and coveted everything he had, including the wench . . .

When the two finally parted, right before dawn, Edward went upstairs with dragging steps to check on the girl. He stood pensively in the doorway and watched Bronwyn as she slept. The fire had died down to embers and, not wanting to disturb her by summoning a servant, he fed the fire himself, then went over and sat on the edge of the bed. When he looked down at her, battered and frail, he still saw her as she had looked the first time he had ever seen her that morning in the Red Boar, and that same night. He smiled, remembering the way her lively green eyes had flashed and how soft and beautiful her voice had been, the way she walked and the sweetness of her laughter . . .

Staring at her now, he could have wept. He was overwhelmed by guilt. *He should have protected her from this.*

Bronwyn opened her puffy eyes and her first response was one of fear. She tried to sit up, but he shook his head and gently forced her back onto the pillow, then tucked the blankets closer around her shivering body. He would take good care of her now.

''There. See, I've built up the fire for you. It will be warmer soon. I'm so glad to see you awake. When I first came, I was afraid that you were very sick. I wouldn't want that. You must get well.'' His smile was warm, his arrogance gone. She seemed to realize who he was then, and her eyes opened wide. They were completely alone.

She looked at his tired face and saw how drawn it was, yet how happy he was to see her again.

"*Warwick?*" she whispered, terror in her voice, rubbing her eyes with trembling fingers. Her little bruised face was pathetic and his heart contracted in sympathy. "*Is he gone?*" she asked.

"Yes. I sent him away." Edward let go of her hand and, standing up, with a tired groan he walked over to the fire. Leaning over it, he stared into the flames, his back to her. At that moment he couldn't bear to look any longer at that pitiful face. *He* had done that to her! He never should have left her alone, not for a second. He looked over his shoulder at her and there was poignant suffering in his face. "I promise you, my little flower-face," the term of endearment filled him with sorrow, looking at her now, "no one shall ever hurt you again. I promise you that! You have nothing to fear." He clenched his fists against the mantel and said through gritted teeth, To mistreat a woman is a crime in my eyes. And my cousin shall pay for it. Accept my deepest apologies for his cruelty. He is a heartless brute and I am ashamed to call him kin. He is a warrior who only knows killing and death, not tenderness." Edward was melancholy. Tonight he had seen a side of his cousin that he had never known existed. Why had he stolen the girl, only to beat her, and then lied about it? Not to mention all the other lies . . . all the other suspicions. How could he ever trust the man again? True, Warwick had swiftly and expertly carried out the repugnant task Edward had set him that night, yet Edward still suspected Warwick's loyalty.

The girl moaned.

In a second he was at her side and took her cold hands in his.

"Oh, my poor little kitten!" he murmured, laying his head on the pillow next to hers. "No one will harm you again, I swear." He looked up and brushed the tangled hair back from her forehead. His gentle touch was enough to break the dam of her resistance, and tears began to trickle down her cheeks. She couldn't help herself—she had been so frightened and now Warwick was gone. She was safe! He took her into his arms and rocked her back and forth as he would a hurt child. Her tears, unlike other women's, wrenched at his heart. He knew she was not the kind of woman to play on men's emotions with her tears.

Bronwyn said softly, her voice trembling, "*He beat me* . . . I think he hates me for some reason. Don't send me back to him, please, Sire!" Her tear-stained face pleaded with him and her tears became a flood. "I would rather die!" she moaned. There were so many things about Warwick she couldn't tell the man, would never talk about to anyone.

"No. No," he soothed her. "*You're safe*."

Then she thought of something and gasped, not looking him in the face. "You came after me. Why?"

"Because I have discovered a great tenderness here . . ." He touched his breast above his heart. "Since I first laid eyes on you, I have been unable to forget you. Then you healed my wound, and when I realized you were in trouble, I was compelled to follow and make sure you were all right. I had to see you again." He tilted her swollen face up to his and shook his head gently when she tried to turn away.

"I'm so . . . *ugly*," she whispered, sobbing.

"*No*! To me you are beautiful. I see beyond the bruises and I see . . . *you*," he said softly. "Here—I have brought you something I found, I think it is yours." He reached into the pouch that hung at his belt, pulled out something thin and golden and dropped it into her open hand.

It was the necklace that Martha had given Bronwyn that night in the kitchen—Johnnie's necklace. It seemed years since that moment when Martha had clasped the pretty thing about her neck and wished her luck.

"Where did you find it?" she asked, touched by his kindness.

"In the snow outside the kitchen door. The door had been left open and the firelight caught its sparkle. For some reason, I thought it might be yours, little one." He smiled, pleased to see her answering smile through her tears. She lowered her eyes so he wouldn't see how much his kindness had affected her. She was so tired, and everything seemed unreal. Maybe this was just another dream . . .

"Thank you," she said weakly.

"One good turn deserves another. You healed my wound the other night just by touching it. *How did you do that*?" His eyes were curious, yet reverent.

She stared at him, fear in her face. But he reassured her. "It's all right to talk about it. I believe your power is a gift from God, no matter what others may say. I am the King, and I promise, no one will harm you because of it. I will protect you."

She relaxed then, slipping from his grasp and falling back on the pillow. What difference did it make if she confessed it all now? She really believed he cared for her and that he would not hurt her. He was not like Warwick. "I've always been able to heal . . . since I was a child. It is as if I had been born with the knowledge . . . I know the healing properties of herbs and how to heal some sicknesses—sometimes. I cannot heal everyone. It's strange—I can't heal those I love most, and I can't heal myself." She smiled faintly. "A gift from God. My father always said it was and that I was only to use it to help people and ease suffering. Sometimes, when I touch a wound . . . it heals. But it drains me, too. Sometimes it makes me sick . . ." Her voice faltered. "I'm so tired, my

183

Lord." Her eyes closed, but the smile lingered like a pale shadow on her cracked lips.

"You are special . . . yes, I sensed it from the first time I looked into your beautiful eyes. There is something about you . . ." He studied her as she lay there. He knew he was losing her to sleep but he didn't want to let go just yet. He had so many things to tell her . . .

He beats me . . . she had said. Edward experienced such fury at his cruel cousin that if the man had still been within his reach, he would gladly have had him flogged and damn the consequences!

"Do you want revenge for what he did to you?" The King's voice was as hard as crystal. Bronwyn's eyes sprung open, eyes full of pain and sadness.

"No," she said in a tiny, thoughtful sigh of a voice. She knew who Warwick was and his relationship to Edward. She didn't belong in their glittering world . . . *why didn't they set her free?* "I only want to be left alone. I only want to be allowed to go back to the Red Boar, to Martha and my two little sisters."

"Sisters?" he echoed stupidly. "I assumed from what you said that you had a husband and two young children!" He held his breath until she answered.

She shook her head on the pillow, the firelight soft on her bruised face, and laughed weakly. "No, Sire . . . why did you think that? I have no husband, no babes; just two younger sisters whom I've cared for since our parents died. That's why I was working at the Red Boar, to earn our living. They are there now. They needed a safe, warm place to live. Ah, and my poor little Mary is so sick . . ." The memory of her sisters had made her come awake again and she searched his eyes. "Are they all right? Do you know if all is well?" she asked anxiously.

"I didn't know they existed until this second. I thought the two you talked of were your children; that you were married!" He laughed then, his face alive with relief.

"And all this time, I thought you belonged to another." He shook his head and chuckled again. So she was free. No husband, no babes. As if that would have made a difference, he realized. If there *had* been a husband, Edward thought, he would have found some way to win her. Now he knew he would never let her go again. She had a gift. She was meant to be his, and he was convinced that God had sent her to him for some as yet unknown reason.

"They must think I am dead by now," she sighed.

Edward smiled down at her. "At first light, I shall dispatch a messenger to put their minds at rest! To let them know you are well and will be returning to them soon." He was rewarded by another faint smile.

"Again . . . thank you, Sire," she replied, drowsiness pulling heavily on her eyelids again.

"And I myself will escort you back to them," he informed her.

"You honor me, Your Majesty," she murmured, yet even as she spoke, she was sure that this was all a beautiful dream. In real life, peasant girls didn't speak to kings, and kings did not put themselves at the disposal of their subjects.

How could he tell her that he would do anything and everything she asked except set her free? Edward mused. But he would keep that to himself for a while, until she was fully recovered.

"Sleep, *my little flower*. You must rest and grow strong again, to smile and to sing for me," he whispered gently as he smoothed the blankets and brushed her lips with a feathery kiss. Looking at her as she drifted off into blessed sleep, he knew he must first win her complete trust and then her love. Then she would never leave him. Somehow, he would make her love him as he was beginning to love her.

She looked so vulnerable and young as she slept. He longed to take her in his arms. When he was sure she was

185

really deeply asleep, he lay down beside her and tenderly gathered her poor battered body close to him. He could feel her heart beating next to his and the feel of her was so right, so comforting. It was as if a great burden had been lifted from his shoulders, now that she was safe in his embrace. Gazing down into her face, he knew that in Bronwyn he had found a part of himself that had always been missing, though he had not known it until now.

He was King, supposedly omnipotent and all-knowing. Hah! He could have any woman he desired, but they came to his bed only to wheedle and cajole money and favors, to gain power and prestige at court. He had never found a woman with a true heart who would love him for himself. They had all loved his glittering crown and the fame it might bring them.

"But you," he whispered to the sleeping maid in his arms, ". . . you will someday love me for myself. It was destined that we should meet and love each other. I feel it. I need you. If I ever lived before, some other place or time . . . it must have been you I loved. I have found you again and I will take care of you and love you dearly, little songbird."

He tried to imagine life without her, and failed. She filled his heart and his soul. It was a miracle.

He held her. A child—she was little more than a child with a magic gift of healing. Aye, she had healed his wound and filled his heart. He needed her as he had never needed anyone before. "You shall be my Merlin, my lover, my friend. Together we can stand against the world!" he whispered to the sleeping girl. Then, lulled by the warmth of her body next to his, he too closed his eyes and slept for the first time in three days.

CHAPTER VII

BRIGHT DAYLIGHT playing across her face awoke Bronwyn; rubbing her sleep-filled eyes, she propped herself shakily up on one elbow and studied the handsome face beside her on the pillow. Then it had not been a dream, all the loving words he had spoken, the gentle touch of his hands. The King of England had actually taken her under his protection. The King of England, lay beside her, peacefully sleeping.

Her moving roused him and a moment later she found herself in his arms and he was kissing her tenderly. But gentle as he was, her mind was flooded by dreadful memories of what Warwick had done to her in the woods and she panicked and pushed him away. He did not persist, merely watched her with sleepy eyes as she moved to the far end of the bed, cowering in fear.

"Don't touch me!" she whimpered in a tiny voice full of pain.

His heart went out to her and he reached out and softly touched her cheek. "Don't worry—I won't hurt you, little one," he promised, agonized by her wan haggardness. Her manner was like that of a beaten animal. Whatever that bastard Warwick had done to her had broken her spirit. Edward wondered if she would ever be the same again. She was shivering and Edward glanced at the fire which had burned down to cold cinders and black ashes. He would have to build it up again. Smiling reassuringly at her, he swung his stiff, sore body slowly off the bed and went to tend to it. There was a stack of wood next to the hearth and he pulled out the smallest pieces for kindling, then struck sparks from the tinder. In a few minutes there was a roaring fire. The warmth felt good. Bronwyn eyed him warily when he came back and sat down across from her on the bed. "Does it still hurt?" he asked, looking at the bruises on her face and the black eye that was now turning vivid purple and bright red. He didn't have the heart to tell her that it looked much worse in the daylight than it had the night before. She shook her head.

His look of intense concern and his gentle manner began to calm her fears. For the first time in days, she felt that perhaps the nightmare was over. She knew that in time, her bruised body and even her wounded pride would heal. As for her virginity . . . well, what was gone was gone and tears would not restore it. She must go on. It was a lesson she had learned many times in her short life. She raised her hands to her swollen face, fretting over how she must look. Vanity—such a silly thing, yet she was ashamed. The tears began again and she turned her ravaged face away from his piercing eyes. Until now, she had never really thought much about her looks or worried if she were pretty or not. *Beauty is in the heart, my child. Beauty is in the soul*, her father had always told her. But for some reason, for this man before her, not for Edward the King, she wanted more than anything to be pretty and she knew that at this moment she was far from it.

But he turned her back around to face him and wiped her fresh tears away. "Nay, maid, 'tis not so bad as all that! Indeed, you look much better this morning," he fibbed, feeling the welcome warmth of the fire on his back. Aye, her cuts and the bruises would heal, but what of her wounded spirit? He longed to ask her if Lord Warwick had done more than beat her, but he so feared the answer that he couldn't bring himself to ask. When she tried again to hide her face in her hands, he tugged them away and smiled up into her clouded eyes. "In a few days, your loveliness will be fully restored, believe me." Though she resisted, he firmly but gently drew her back into his arms and pressed a soft kiss on her brow. Her skin was very hot against his lips and he realized that she was still feverish. He decided then and there that as soon as they returned to London he would take her to his private apartments and have his personal physician attend to her. He was worried about her. She seemed so frail, like a leaf in a storm. She was still shivering in his arms.

But Bronwyn shivered not only from her illness, but because she was thinking about the Earl of Warwick and remembering how brutally he had used her . . . remembering the bodies in that burning house and the terrified eyes of that poor woman just before he had struck her down. Those eyes would haunt her the rest of her life. The memory triggered another, and she suddenly gasped. "*Harry!* The stableman back at the Inn . . . Warwick trampled him into the snow when he took me!" She was horrified that she could have forgotten all about Harry. He had tried to save her and it was her fault if he were dead. "Is he still . . . alive?" she asked.

Edward smiled. "Aye, he lives. A few broken bones, I heard. But he will mend after a long rest in bed and Martha's care. It was he who alerted me to your fate. If not for him, I never would have known where to look for you." Edward hadn't wanted to believe that his cousin would have done such a thing, but he had followed the tracks of Warwick's horse and had known it was true long before he faced Warwick with Bronwyn in his arms.

"Thank God he's alive!" she cried. "I was so afraid he

had died!'' She sighed and then, shuddering, she pulled away from Edward's embrace and crumpled back upon the pillow. She was still so very tired . . . She closed her eyes and opened them only when she felt Edward's cool hand brush the tangled hair back from her hot face.

Was it a second later, or hours when she heard him speak?

"I've sent for some food and a tub and hot water so we both can wash." He had thought that a hot bath might soothe her bruised, tired body as well. "I've also ordered some clothes more suitable for a lady." He frowned at the filthy, over-sized man's clothing she was wearing. "Those rags don't do you justice. Where did you get them?" he asked.

"My Lord Warwick gave them to me," she whispered, glancing down.

Edward said no more.

She was amazed that a man such as Edward, a King, was concerned about her welfare and what she was wearing. What did he want from her? All men wanted something . . . She looked up into his smiling eyes and realized that his desires were far different from Lord Warwick's. He had wanted to own her, to possess her body and quell her spirit. But Edward . . . what was he seeking? He had not taken her by force as Warwick had, and his every gesture and word was full of consideration and tenderness. He had spent the whole night beside her and had done nothing but embrace her. It was all quite beyond her understanding. Maybe, she thought this was still a dream and she had never really awoken; perhaps she was still up in the loft above the inn, her two sisters sleeping next to her. If only that were true! She sighed deeply.

"Such a sorrowful sound," he said. "Such a serious wench you are. I've never known such a serious wench as you. Do you never laugh?"

"Aye, Sire, now and again. When I have something to

laugh about," she shot back. He was teasing her. She felt she could trust him. She had never known anyone like him.

There was a loud knocking at the door and Bronwyn threw the covers over her head and hid. She heard Edward laugh and give orders to the servant as to the placement of the tub and the buckets of hot water. When she was sure the servant had gone, she peeked out to see the King of England pouring water into a large wooden tub. "There," he said when he was done. "It's all ready for your ablutions." He made a low, sweeping bow and grinned at her. "Come, before the water gets cold."

Bronwyn waited for him to leave and when he didn't move, she said hesitantly, "Thank you, Your Majesty." She blushed, then faltered, "You *are* leaving, aren't you?"

He came over to the bed and smiled down at her. "As soon as I see that you can take care of yourself. Last night you could hardly stand."

"Well, I'm sure I can bathe myself, Sire," she said testily. Though she knew he would go or stay as he chose, she still hoped that he meant her no harm. But the thought of another man ogling her naked body renewed her terror of Warwick's attack. She would show him how well she could manage on her own. She swung her legs over the edge of the bed and started to stand up. The room immediately dissolved into blackness and when she came to, she was in Edward's arms on the floor. His face was worried and his arms were strong around her. He feared she was a great deal sicker than she realized.

"What did I tell you, you stubborn child!" His voice was teasing, masking his real concern. She leaned her head against his chest and looked longingly at the tub of hot water. "Oh, I so want to be clean again!" *I so want to wash Warwick's very touch from my body, to wash all the filth away with clean hot water*!

Edward smiled at her, knowing what she must be thinking. "It's all right, my little modest one. I'll help you, but I promise not to look. A hot bath is just what you need and you're going to have it. If there were a woman to help you I would call her, but there isn't one in this whole God-forsaken place; I've already asked. So I'm afraid I will have to play lady's maid. I will help you over to the tub and turn my back. If you need assistance, you have only to speak."

Bronwyn trembled. She owed this man her very life, and yet the thought of being naked before him repulsed her. "Sire, if you could only help me over to the tub and then leave, I'm sure I could handle it myself." It was just crossing the room that was the difficult part. Nodding, Edward lifted her in his strong arms and deposited her next to the tub. He handed her a clean towel and a bar of perfumed soap. Bronwyn had never seen such a thing before. It smelled delicious. She glanced at the door and he made a mocking bow. "Call me if you have need of me, my sweet. I'll be right outside."

The door closed behind him and Bronwyn waited a few minutes to see if he would go back on his word and come back in. When he didn't, she untied the rope around her waist and painfully slipped out of her clothing, dropping it in a heap by the tub. Even though the fire was blazing, she shivered, then gingerly stepped into the water with a contented sigh. She listened for a second longer and hearing no one at the door she debated only a brief moment before lowering her head under the water to let the clean water soak her filthy hair. She soaped her hair and rinsed it hurriedly and then washed the rest of her body. Then, feeling she shouldn't tarry too long in such a vulnerable condition, she stood up in the glow of the crackling fire and reached for the towel. The dizzy spell came upon her suddenly and she only had time to cry out once before she collapsed back into the tub, barely conscious. The next thing she was aware of was Edward carrying her wet, naked body to the bed, drying her off and tucking her under the covers, reprimanding her all the while for being so foolish.

"I feared you were still too weak to bathe yourself," he told her. "And if you can't take care of yourself, you must be taken care of. If I had let you drown, my wild, painful chase through the snow in pursuit of you would have all been for nought! Since I've found you at last, do you think I'd lose you in such a foolish manner, little one? If I hadn't been listening at the door so closely . . ." he continued as he stood up and began to shed his own clothes, "who knows what might have befallen you?" She gaped open-mouthed at him in shocked surprise. He didn't seem self-conscious at all as he stripped off first his outer tunic and then his undergarments. He didn't even turn his back.

"You mean . . . you were right outside the door listening all the time?" she exclaimed.

"Aye." He looked into her embarrassed eyes and smiled. "I was tempted to peek through the keyhole as well . . . just to be sure you were all right, but I refrained." His smile broadened. "May I say, that you are as beautiful as I had anticipated you would be. You are lovely!" He pulled off the last of his clothes and Bronwyn once again buried her head under the covers to hide her embarrassment.

"Now it's my turn. A bath will feel wonderful. It's a shame you didn't let me share yours. Well, all in good time." He laughed at the lump that was Bronwyn under the blankets and, tugging the covers from her face, he bent over and kissed her reddened face before she snatched them back and re-covered her head as she stepped into the tub.

She could hear him splashing as he scrubbed, humming to himself. His behavior left a lot to be desired! Perhaps, she thought, kings had no modesty as other people did.

What did she know of the ways of kings? She closed her eyes tighter and pretended he wasn't just a few feet away, naked, in a tub of water. But the bed was soft and warm and in her weakened condition she had to fight to stay awake.

" 'Tis a shame you're unwell," she heard him say a while later, but by the tone of his voice she could tell he was teasing her. "Or I'd have you scrub my back. Unlike you, I am unused to bathing without assistance." He chuckled. Bronwyn said nothing.

"I had my man bring you a gown to wear, my little songbird," she heard Edward say next. "I think he put it on the bed. It isn't particularly attractive, but it is far beter than what you had on."

A gown? Bronwyn peeked out from under the covers, careful not to look at Edward who was still in his bath, and her eyes searched the top of the bed and lit upon a pale blue gown. Her hand crept out and snatched it into her lair. It looked a little large, but it was of warm wool. "Thank you, my lord," she mumbled as she maneuvered her sore body into the gown. There was even under-clothing, she discovered, and was awed that the King had been so considerate of her needs.

"Does it fit?" Edward asked. His voice was suddenly very near, so near that when he pulled the covers off, Bronwyn gasped in astonishment. Edward stood before her completely dressed, laughing at the look on her face. He was wearing an apricot tunic trimmed in white fur and hose of a russet hue. A leather belt girded his slim hips and held a small dagger. He sat down on the edge of the bed and began to pull on a pair of leather boots. He looked at Bronwyn closely, noting the fit of the gown and how lovely she looked, bruises and all, now that she was clean. "The gown becomes you, little one, but it is far too simple to set off your beauty. When we get to London, I will buy you so many beautiful gowns you won't know which to wear first.

And jewels, and furs to keep you warm . . ." He was smiling as he spoke. She blushed beneath his intent gaze. Her hair, though still damp, framed her face perfectly. Even battered as she was, when she smiled shyly as she was doing right now, she was poignantly appealing.

Then her face grew troubled and she shook her head, pushing his hand away when he tried to capture hers. "No!" she said firmly. "I don't want silken gowns or furs and jewels . . . you don't understand. This gown will do nicely. I don't want you to buy me anything." How could she make him understand that after all that had happened to her in the past two years, beginning with her father's death, she was no innocent, silly girl who yearned for fine clothes and other fripperies and would allow herself to be bought with promises of jewels? Jewels and silks were not for her. It was as if she knew now what she must do and it was not becoming his kept woman. God had punished her, she felt, for concealing and denying her precious gift. She was a healer. It was time she stopped trying to run away from what she was. It was time she realized *who* she was . . . and she knew she wasn't meant to be a rich man's mistress, even though he be a king. "No," she reiterated softly. "I don't want silken gowns and diamonds on my fingers. I am better off as I am."

He looked at her solemn, battered face and her sad eyes. He had never known a woman who hadn't begged for what she had just rejected. Now, faced with this girl who wanted nothing to do with them, he was at a loss for words. Was it all an act, or was she really as genuinely humble as she seemed? Something in her eyes told him she meant every word. He reached over and lightly touched her hair, then followed the strand all the way to the end near her waist. Their eyes locked for a second and, again, he was overcome by the same protective, tender feelings he had experienced the night before. It occurred to him then, as the firelight caressed her lithe figure and

195

her intense face, that she was different now, different even from the girl who had so entranced him at the Red Boar three days ago. Her abduction, her ill treatment at Warwick's hands, had left their mark. She did not trust him, Edward—did not trust any man, and small wonder. He must convince her that she need not fear him, that nothing could harm her now.

"You need not be afraid of me," he assured her and he gently took her into his arms. He could feel her trembling and when their lips met, he restrained his ardor with great effort. He held her like that, her damp hair against his cheek, for a long time in total silence. Her skin was still very hot, he noticed, and when he looked into her eyes, there was fever blazing in their depths. "I will not hurt you, I promise," he murmured. *I only want to love you.*

"I know, Sire." Her voice was a raspy whisper and when he laid her gently down upon the pillow and she smiled at him, he smiled too, knowing that he had overcome the first hurdle. But he must be patient. He must give her time.

"I'll leave you here to rest a little longer before we begin our journey. It seems to me that you are still not fit to travel." He wished he could let her remain in bed a few days more, but he had urgent business to attend to in London; even now he was late. Though he cared about her health and welfare, he was first of all a King and he had duties to attend to, duties that couldn't wait even for her. And he was determined that he would not let her out of his sight, lest harm befall her. She would ride to London with him.

"I'll be back in a few hours to fetch you. So rest, my sweet, until then." He bent over and pressed one more soft kiss on her lips and tucked the covers around her. But already she was half asleep and she merely favored him with a shadow of a smile as she drifted off. He tip-toed across the room, standing in the doorway watching her for a few seconds until he was sure she was really asleep, and then he left, closing the door silently behind him. There were many things to be taken care of before their departure. He knew his men were curious as to why they had come so far and who the wench was. He also knew they were anxious to get back to the city and their families. The journey would take most of the day; Edward could only let Bronwyn sleep a short while.

There was a knock at the door to Bronwyn's room and she bade them enter.

"His majesty is ready, miss." The man, tall and thin with white hair and sharp brown eyes, bowed slightly. "He sent me to bring you down. We're ready to ride. We must be in London tonight if possible." They should have started at dawn, he thought, but he understood that this girl with the pretty, bruised face was one reason for the delay. He, like most of the other men, wondered why his master had gone off into the night in pursuit of the wench. But he said nothing, only handed her the heavy cloak he had been given for her and led her downstairs through the now empty tavern out into bright sunlight. He watched her as she pulled up the hood to hide her face from curious stares and he almost felt sorry for her. She seemed unsteady on her feet and he caught her when she wavered on the steps, raising a hand to shade her eyes. The girl looked as though she had been beaten within an inch of her life. He wondered who had done that to her. He turned and bowed as the King came up behind them and when he looked the fair young man in the eye, he hoped it hadn't been he who had done such a despicable thing.

Edward took Bronwyn's arm and smiled down at her as he escorted her to where a tall white stallion pawed the hard ground. The hood hid her expression from prying eyes as she was lifted up into the saddle. The King sprang into the saddle behind her and gathered up the reins.

"I'm sorry, but there were no other mounts to be had, so you must ride with me. Just as well—you're not really well enough to ride alone, little one," he said with concern. He could feel her shiver in his embrace and worried that the long, cold ride ahead of them might further debilitate her.

Bronwyn didn't utter a single word as he draped his cloak over hers to keep out the wind. She sat rigid in the saddle before him, as if she were afraid to relax. Was she afraid of him? It would pain him deeply if she were.

Bronwyn silently watched the scenery as they rode along. All the things she had only glimpsed in the dark the night before under such terrible circumstances now took on form and substance. The snow-laden trees were beautiful. And the man behind her was so different from Lord Warwick. He was a good man, she was sure of it. He had said that her healing powers were a special gift from God; he respected her. For the first time in her life, she marveled, she didn't need to hide her gift. Edward understood.

"Are you hungry, my pretty songbird?" he asked as they cantered down the icy road, his entourage keeping at a respectful distance behind them.

"Yes, Sire," she admitted and was surprised when Edward opened a pouch slung from his saddle bow and produced something wrapped in oiled paper, which he handed to her with a boyish grin. "I had this made especially for you before we left."

Awkwardly because of the horse's jolting gait, she unwrapped the parcel. It contained a piece of roast fowl of some kind, duck perhaps, and it was still warm. There was also a thick slab of coarse bread, and then Edward handed her a flask. "Wine," he explained. Bronwyn thanked him and eagerly consumed the food and wine. She hadn't realized how hungry she was. In fact, she couldn't remember when she had last eaten. When she had finished and had handed the flask back to him, she asked, "We are on our way to London, then, Sire?"

"Aye, London. Important business awaits me there."

He thought of Warwick, his growing doubts. Edward scowled. What was he to do about the man? He raised his gloved hand and pounded it on his thigh as he dug his heels viciously into his horse's sides and urged him to a gallop. Why did he seem so suddenly angry? Bronwyn wondered apprehensively. Was it something she had done? But she had done nothing! The temper of a king was surely unpredictable. Yet he had promised to take her to her sisters . . . Waves of dizziness suddenly washed over her, and when she slipped into unconsciousness, Edward wasn't aware of it until he spoke to her on some matter and she didn't respond. He reined up his mount in despair and would have returned immediately to the inn if possible. But it was not possible, and he also realized, looking down at the girl's white face, that she needed a physician and a warm bed and both could be found at his royal residence in London. He turned to his men and urged them to make haste.

It was nearly dark when they galloped up the high ground on the southeast side of the city and made their way along the north bank of the River Thames towards the nearest entrance past St. Thomas's Tower. The only other entrance to the great fortress and garrison was at the southwest corner, through the Middle Tower.

Edward gazed in relief at the sprawling old Roman walls that enclosed the thirteen acres, with its six towers and two bastions in its inner wall and thirteen towers in the very heart of the fortress. He often chose to stay inside the great armed garrison, especially in troubled times—there was no better protected castle in the whole of England than the great Tower with all its fortifications, inner and other wards and the huge moat that surrounded it.

The cavalcade thundered through the second wall and reined before the White Tower that stood forbiddingly in the central part of the enclosure. Its whitewashed Caen stone shone eerily in the fading dusk as the black ravens, who had made their home here as far back as anyone could remember, swooped through the air, screeching and calling to one another.

As the King swept Bronwyn from the saddle and carried her into the keep, his eyes glanced to his left, towards the Tower Green. If ghosts walked this place, it was surely there they roamed in the moonlight on silent nights. Many good men had laid their heads on the block there. He handed his mount's reins to a tired looking lad who then led the lathered beast swiftly away for a rubdown and a warm stall. Edward, in fear for Bronwyn's very life, had nearly run the poor animal to death in his determination to provide shelter and care for her. He never should have taken her out into the cold again so soon after her ordeal at Warwick's hands. *If she dies*, he worried, gazing down into her still face as he laid her carefully on the bed in his private apartments, *it will be both Warwick's fault and my own*. A heavy dread weighed upon his heart and he covered the girl's slight body with a fur coverlet and touched her burning face. He spoke her name, but she didn't answer. What had he done? He should have left her at the tavern with a protector and sent for her later when she was recovered. Why had he taken her with him when he knew she was ill? If she died, he would never forgive himself!

He turned to one of his companions who had dutifully followed him and ordered, "March, fetch my physician. Drag the old goat from his soft feather bed, be he alone or not. Bring him here immediately!" March was a good man. He'd followed his liege into many a battle and Edward knew he was thoroughly dependable. When March had bowed and left to seek out the royal physician,

Edward slumped down into a high-backed ornately carved chair that faced the empty grate of the great hearth while servants hurried to provide him with hot food and to build a fire. Edward watched them with tired eyes and said nothing. His thoughts were far away as he gazed at the frail girl in his lavish bed. Thick scarlet velvet draperies hung from the bed's canopy. He had partially closed the curtains to keep drafts from her. *If she dies*, he pondered, his eyes rapt on Bronwyn's face, *how shall I go on without that special light that has so recently entered my dark life?* To have just a taste of such joy, and then to have it so cruelly wrested from him was something he couldn't bear to dwell upon. *If she dies, I'll kill that bastard Warwick*, he swore, then buried his face in his hands.

Exhausted, he fell into a deep sleep before the flickering fire. It was thus that his personal physician, La Rouel found him when he stumbled in sometime later.

"Your Majesty!" The old man stood before him, bowing, an expression of concern on his sharp, intelligent face. "You sent for me?"

Edward sighed, stretching in the chair, and suddenly his eyes flooded with memory and he looked towards the bed in alarm. How long had he been asleep? He sprang up from his chair, almost knocking down the surprised physician. The elderly man eyed the King, astonished. "Sire, what is it?"

The King went to stand before the bed without a word and nodded toward where Bronwyn lay. "The maid is very sick, I fear. I sent for you because I know you alone can help her, my friend." Edward was more humble than La Rouel had ever remembered seeing the young King. He was usually so confident and devil-may-care. This was a change, indeed. The physician's gaze took in the girl at one glance and he walked over purposefully and bent over her, laying his thin, white hand on her hot brow, clucking all the while.

"Where have you been?" The King demanded as he hovered right behind him, not so humble now. "I sent for you hours ago." But his voice was only mildly angry. La Rouel had been his friend and physician for most of his life. He was truly fond of the old man, and respected his knowledge.

The physician looked over his narrow shoulder at the young King with a stern glint in his black eyes and one bushy white eyebrow arched high. "Sire, I am truly sorry, but I was attending to a patient. She was an old friend in dire need or I would have been here sooner. When your man found me, I came as swiftly as possible under the circumstances."

When the King began to speak, La Rouel silenced him with a few words, unsmiling. "She died. I came as soon as I could."

Ashamed at his curt manner and the grief the old man must be feeling about his friend's death, Edward merely nodded and rubbed his eyes. "Forgive my ill humor," he said, contrite.

"No need to be sorry, Sire," La Rouel muttered as he started to examine the girl. "She was an old woman who had suffered long. I was glad death finally came to claim her. She was prepared." He spoke as only a physician could who had long ago learned that death was sometimes a welcome visitor. He turned again to look at the King. "How long has she been in this condition?"

Edward replied, "For the better part of the day. As we were riding here, she became unconscious. I was unable to rouse her. Will she recover?"

"You rode with her in this weather?" La Rouel exclaimed in a shocked voice and then looked back down at his patient. Who was she? More important, what was she to the young King? By his manner, La Rouel had already surmised she was something very special.

Edward avoided the question. "I had to bring her here," he said firmly.

The older man grunted and stood up. Facing his young liege, he stated, "Sire, she is a very sick girl. If you would please leave the room so I may examine her fully, I will see what I can do." He pointed a long slender finger towards the door and his owlish eyes glinted intelligently in the firelight, then he bowed slightly to the King.

Edward looked longingly at Bronwyn, and seemed to hesitate until he saw the look on his physician's face. The old man smiled then, recognizing the unusual concern in the young King's expression and manner. He was in love with the maid—or thought he was. Ha, it was so simple to see; it was all over the young man's face. "Do not worry about the girl, my Lord; tis a high fever she has, and I think she suffers from exhaustion. How did she get all those cuts and bruises?" he asked, raising his bushy white eyebrows. He was a formidable figure, almost grotesquely tall and thin, far taller than Edward. And his eccentric habit of always dressing in long black flowing robes, and the large silver medallion he always wore suspended from a heavy chain around his neck gave added fuel to rumors that he dabbled in the black arts and that he knew much magic. His eyes were piercing and dark, and his long straggly beard silver-white like his hair. But no matter how he looked or what people thought of him, Edward knew he was the finest physician in England. It made no difference that the ignorant called him wizard or warlock. He was brilliant, and the King trusted him time and time again with his very life. Edward, young as he was, had fought in many battles and often been wounded. La Rouel had always nursed him back to health.

Now Edward's face flushed. " 'Twas not I who misused her so, physician. It was told me that she fell from her horse. What the truth of the matter is, I cannot say." He knew that the actual story was best kept quiet, especially since it concerned Warwick. "Will she recover?" His abrupt manner left no doubt in the physician's mind that he would receive no other information.

"My Lord, I'm sure proper care and rest will bring her around. Now, will you please leave? Don't worry, I'll treat her as I would my own daughter. Sire, trust me . . . I can see how much she means to you."

"Aye, she means a great deal to me," Edward confessed. Then his eyes grew serious and he said, "There's something you should know about the maid . . . she is a healer."

The physician raised his eyebrows so high, they nearly left his face, and his head cocked attentively to one side as he stroked his beard with thin, gnarled fingers. "She can *heal*?" he asked incredulously. He'd known some who claimed the power, but had never met one who actually possessed it, certainly never a maid so young.

"By the touch of her hands," Edward said. "It's a pity she cannot heal herself."

La Rouel turned to look at Bronwyn's pale face again. "That is often the case. They can heal others, sometimes, but not themselves. As for myself," he ruminated aloud, "I've never known a true healer. How do you know for certain that she has this gift?"

"She healed a deep cut on my hand a few days ago merely by laying her hand over it. I was amazed, but it's true."

La Rouel's eyes seemed to take on an unusual shine as he took a leather pouch from the girdle about his waist and set it down on the bed. It contained medicinal herbs and his surgical instruments as well as other necessities of his profession.

"My, my," he mumbled. "That is a great gift . . . but a dangerous one, Sire, these days." He gently dried the perspiration on the girl's hot brow with a clean white cloth he had taken from the bag.

Edward sighed and reluctantly moved to the door. "Physician, I shall be back later. I have let affairs of state wait far too long. If there is anything you require, don't hesitate to inform the servants; they will provide them. Good night to you." Edward paused at the door, waiting for a response, but the doctor was busy with his patient and, Edward, knowing she was in good hands, left the room. His steps were weary and heavy as he followed the dark narrow stairs down to the entrance of the White Tower and stepped out into the freezing night. As tired as he was, and worried over the girl, he had duties to attend to; orders to give; a mountain of papers and documents to peruse and sign and messengers to dispatch into the cold night, before he could rest himself. At least, he thought as his men fell in behind him as he strode toward the fresh horse that awaited him, mounted and led the way from the Tower's grounds, she was in good hands. Perhaps by the time he returned from his meeting with the archbishop in a few days, she would be fully recovered.

As Edward jumped from his horse and stood on the wharf in the cold night, his cloak blowing about his slender figure, he thought about the girl up in the Tower. Here she was safe from everyone, even Warwick.

He heard the water lapping almost at his feet at the end of the wharf, then he saw the lights of the boat in the distance and then, while his men stood silently by, he heard the shouts of oarsmen skimming over the water from the opposite shore. He wished he could stay until she recovered, if only to see her smile again; but the archbishop had been waiting far too long and since he was the man who held the pursestrings, Edward must see him as soon as he could. Then he must make a detour to Trent where they were burning more Lollard heretics, a distasteful and distressing duty, to be followed by one almost as unsettling. His vast holdings in Hauinalt were under seige by a band of lawless scavengers. He must ride in with support troops, as many as he could muster in so short a time. Any prisoners would have the choice of death or being impressed into his armies.

The boat docked and he stepped into it, his eyes raised toward the faint outlines of the receding Tower walls until they were only shadows in the distance. He wrapped his cloak around him, trying to escape the bitter wind, and get a little sleep. He hated to leave her . . .

The boat moved silently down the river into the night as the city slept.

Bronwyn awoke weak as a kitten, and, puzzled, surveyed her opulent surroundings. The bright colored silk and velvet hangings around the huge canopied bed made her head swim. Her eyes painfully swept around the large chambers, taking in only briefly the glowing hearth and the brocaded chairs. At that moment, the question of where she was was only a vague curiosity. She felt as if she had been away for a long, long time and that there was something important she had to do. She weakly tried to rise from the warm bed, feeling as if there were somewhere she had to go—someone who needed her, but her legs wouldn't hold her and the room spun. Then everything blurred again and she drifted back into a deep sleep.

Later, she wasn't sure, but she thought someone—a towering black-robed specter with a white haze about his head—had hovered at her bedside. In her delirium she thought he was surely death come to claim her. Her cracked lips parted to emit a frightened protest but darkness reclaimed her before she could utter a sound.

Later, when she finally came to again, the spirit was gone and she was alone, though she could hear voices just outside the large wooden doors. Slowly, she opened her eyes. Though she was awake completely this time and she did feel better, her limbs were weak and her lips and mouth so parched she could hardly talk. This time there was only a little dizziness when she tried to sit up. She stretched painfully and then, rubbing her aching eyes and pushing her tangled hair from her puffy face, she tried to remember where she was. What had happened? Then she slowly began to remember . . .

She peered at the walls covered with tapestries depicting forest scenes and the shelves on one wall which appeared to contain manuscripts and precious books. Only the wealthiest of noblemen had such libraries. Weapons, long-bows and glittering swords hung on the wall above the fireplace and there were bright rugs and animal pelts stewn on the cold stone floors. A long, gleaming oak table stood along one wall, covered with charts and all sort of strange instruments—she had no idea what most of the things were. The heavy wooden furniture in the room was beautifully crafted and carved with animals and flowers and maidens in relief, the carved wood so highly polished that it shone like glass. Velvet chairs stood before the fireplace, one upholstered in gold and the other in peacock blue velvet. A elaborately carved chess set and board of shimmering ivory and ebony sat on a small table between the two chairs.

Bronwyn gazed up at the gold and crimson canopy above her head. It was all so breathtakingly beautiful! She suddenly wanted to smile, but her head ached so that she groaned instead.

The sound brought La Rouel back into the room and to her side, a benign smile on his wrinkled face. For a moment, Bronwyn was taken aback by the tall dark-robed figure that loomed above her, but when she saw the look in his intelligent, sympathetic eyes, she knew he meant her no harm.

''Ah, sleeping beauty finally awakens! It is about time. I

gave you a potent dose of my remedies, but for a while I feared you would never awaken. I'm glad to see you are back in the land of the living . . . it revives my faith in myself."

"Who are you, Sir?" she whispered, her throat so dry and swollen she had difficulty in forming the words. He handed her a cup of water and watched as she gulped it thirstily down. She handed it back to him with a whispered, "Thank you."

He nodded and sat down next to her, eying her as though she were an object of great interest. She realized then that he must have been the figure that had haunted her fevered dreams.

"I'm the King's physician, maid. And you've been very ill." He patted her cold hands and then laid a bony hand on her brow. He pursed his thin lips, his beard quivering, and announced, "Ah, good! The fever is almost gone. You will be as good as new in no time." The long, gaunt face almost broke into a smile. "I've done a commendable job curing you, if I do say so myself!"

Arrogant, she thought; but something in the way he was watching her and the way he was smiling suddenly made her realize that he was only teasing her. He stood up and Bronwyn's head tilted back to look at him. He was so *far* above her!

"Sick . . . how long have I been here?" she asked, propping herself up on her elbows as he arranged her pillows so she could sit up. "I'm grateful for all you've done for me," she added, awed by the knowledge that she was only a peasant and he was a King's physician. It was a wonder he had treated her at all. She ran her fingers self-consciously through her tangled hair. "How long?" she repeated softly.

"Nearly three days, maid." He expelled a sharp breath. "As I said, you were very sick. It's been three days since His Majesty brought you here."

"Where is 'here'?" She looked around her and then back to him.

"The King's private apartments in the Tower."

Bronwyn was astonished. "His—private apartments?" she echoed incredulously.

"His Majesty wanted you in a safe and comfortable place so I could tend to you until you were well," the man assured her. "You seem much better this morning."

Bronwyn smiled shyly at him. "Aye, I feel a lot better. 'Twould seem I have slept the days away. I owe you a great debt for caring for me. Thank you."

"It was nothing. I do what the King commands. My name is La Rouel, and I am at your service." He bowed deeply to her and smiled again. He wasn't so very frightening, she thought, when he smiled.

She put her hands up to her throbbing temples. She suddenly felt very tired again. La Rouel regarded her knowingly and handed her a small pewter cup, bidding her drink of its contents. "This draught will make you sleep again. You are still weak and need rest. Drink it slowly, otherwise it might make you nauseous," he warned as she lifted the cup to her lips and drank slowly. "I know it is bitter."

"Aye. Though the mixture is a weak one, henbane is always bitter. I would know it anywhere." Her eyebrows arched and she wiped her lips with a slight grimace. A large dose of the herb could be lethal, while a small dose brought on healing sleep.

La Rouel's clever eyes acknowledged her wisdom in the art of medicinal herbs. "You know the forest's healing herbs very well. Edward told me you were a healer." Bronwyn saw compassion and acceptance in the old man's eyes and she knew he understood. He was a healer too. Yet her eyes evaded his as she spoke.

"Aye. I can heal. I've been able to heal since I was a small child . . . and it has been a curse to me ever since."

There was sorrow in her voice, and something else he couldn't quite identify. Perhaps fear . . .

" 'Tis a great gift," he reminded her, "if you use it wisely. Do you?"

She watched him suspiciously from under lowered lashes and sighed. "I have never used it any other way, Sir. I cannot stand to see someone suffer, if I can be of help. But it has made my life so much harder . . ." Her voice faded away. She shouldn't be pitying herself and she shouldn't be telling all this to a stranger. She gazed up at him. "Sometimes I wish I didn't have it."

He understood exactly what she was talking about. "I know. Even though I haven't the healing gift myself, my interest in medicine as well as my desire to find cures for people's sickness has made me a target of vicious rumors. Many people are ignorant—they spurn the hand that tries to help them . . . it is human nature, to destroy what one cannot understand. But in all my long years, my child," he said kindly, "I have learned that it is far better to help others and to be true to whatever gifts one has. 'Tis a crime to deny what God has given one."

"Some say 'tis the Devil's work—the laying on of hands," she whispered. "They've called me witch . . ." She shut her eyes, the drug was beginning to take effect. Le Rouel could sense a great sadness in her. He also sensed an uncanny bond between them, as thin and delicate as a spider's web floating in the air.

"Hush, little one. You are no witch. You are far too pretty and kind to be a witch." He chuckled softly. "I have great respect for anyone who can help another human being. Though I have never before known a true healer, I know they exist . . . and if you are one of them, I envy you. There are so many sick in this world; so many who need help. We must talk later about your healing gift. I would like to know more about it. There are many things you could teach me," he said gravely, patting her head as he would a little child.

She nodded and then whispered, "Aye, and no doubt there is much *you* could teach *me*." She smiled as he tucked the covers up to her chin.

"Later. Now hush, and sleep. We shall talk later." He stood guard over her peaceful form for a long time, thinking about what she had said. There was much he could teach her, though he was sure she knew more of the forest herbs and cures than he. Peasants passed down that precious knowledge from generation to generation, lore that was not to be found in books. His expertise was limited, but she had the gift of healing while he was a mere chemist. He both envied and pitied her. She seemed so vulnerable, so young. Life could be so cruel . . .

He ambled away from the bedside, grumbling to himself about the unfairness of it all. To give such a great gift to such a helpless child and expect her to withstand the world's censure was almost a sin. He followed the stairs from the chamber where Bronwyn lay down into the bowels of the Tower where he kept his laboratory. Here he experimented and brewed strange concoctions from herbs and roots. It was a little room lined with dusty shelves filled with strange bottles, some filled with things he couldn't even remember. Papers covered with his peculiar scratchings littered the tables. Sometimes, squinting at them in the candlelight, he couldn't even read them himself. He looked around and set his lantern in a clear space. He never seemed to have enough time for his experiments. Caring for patients and the demands it made upon his strength and time overwhelmed him lately. Battles. *Fighting. Fighting. Fighting.* Was there nothing but war and death these days? He tried . . . but he was no longer a young man. The sands were running out in the hourglass of his life. He slumped down in the hard chair and ran his fingers lightly over the dusty bottles lined up before him like so many tiny, silent soldiers. He smiled into the gloom beyond the lantern's glow, thinking of the girl, her youth and her gift. She would make a fine pupil, if she would accept her gift and learn what he had to teach her. He had waited a long time for such a pupil to come . . . years, so long he had all but given up hope that he would ever find such a one. Ah, he had much to teach her . . .

And teach her he would.

Bronwyn awoke the next morning and for the first time she felt as if she were among the living again. She slipped from the bed and slowly walked about the room, exploring the beautiful things in it with her eyes and her careful fingers. She had never seen such a lovely room. So this was how a King lived? Amazing! Just one of these items—a chair, that rare leather-bound book, or even that bed—would buy food for a poor family for a year! What extravagance, what waste! And yet . . . she let her small hands linger lovingly on the soft velvet of one chair, to live among such beautiful objects would be heaven. Though not for her; never for her, she thought heavily, going back to the bed and lying back down. She must have drowsed for a short while. Then, opening her eyes again and growing restless, she got back up and strolled back to the chair before the blazing fire. It seemed to invite her to share its warmth, which she did gladly, settling herself into the chair with its high brocaded back, her face towards the soothing flames. It was then she saw the large tub of water on the other side of the chair, close to the fire. Going over to it, she was surprised to see it was full of water; a towel and bar of that sweet-scented soap lay on a table next to it. There was also a bundle on the end of the bed, she noticed, that looked as if it might be a gown. Were there elves or fairies about? she wondered. Things kept being done for her and she had seen no one but that strange black-robed physician. She shook her head, bemused by the whole situation. Then she touched the water in the tub. It was warm.

As weak as she still was, she didn't think twice as she shrugged out of the nightshift she had been wearing—she did ponder a second on who had put it on her—and lowered herself into the tub. She remembered the last time she had had a bath. Where was the King now? More important, when would he be back and what exactly would he expect from her? She frowned. After she had washed and rinsed her hair, she lounged in the water, sighing. The warmth of the water and the raging fire did more for her than any medicinal cure. She felt her very bones warming and she sat there for a long time, thinking, fretting over what was to become of her now and wondering how her sisters were faring. What did the King want from a worthless peasant? The events of the last few days were blurred in her memory, as if her heart and mind were trying completely to block out something horrible that lurked on the fringe of her consciousness . . . *he wanted her gift*, she suddenly thought. No, she was furious with herself to think of such a vile thing. Perhaps he wanted her to perform magic to amuse him? No! That she would never do! She moaned and clutched her aching head in her wet hands. She shivered then and rose from the water, picking up the towel and rubbing herself dry, then drying her hair as best she could. She found the gown left for her, a woolen gown of a soft tan. Edward must have remembered what she had told him about not liking fancy clothes, for the gown was simple, yet soft and lovely. She pulled it on and sat in the chair before the hearth again, where she tucked her bare legs under her, and spread her long, still damp hair across her shoulders to dry. Her thoughts kept spinning in circles.

She was lonely for her sisters. She prayed they were safe and that they knew she was, too. Now she remembered everything that had happened with that beast Warwick, but she refused to dwell on any of it. Yet she was fearful that he would come and fetch her, kidnap her again. She worried that she was a prisoner. If she tried to leave now, would someone stop her? She was sure they would. The King had wanted her to be safe and comfortable and he had wanted her to remain here until he came back for her. And he had saved her from Warwick. It was all so confusing! What did Edward want of her? Everything seemed shrouded in mystery and there was no one to answer her questions.

Oh, how she missed her sisters!

How, she mused as she watched the fire dancing, had she so lost control of her own life?

A little while later, she heard a noise behind her and cautiously looked over her shoulder. A small, plump woman bustled over to her, her hands loaded down with a tray of tea things. "Ma'am, I heard you moving about. 'Tis right glad I be that ye are feeling better, so I brought ye these tea cakes, some soup and a pot of good hot tea to warm your stomach and give you strength. Ye haven't eaten much o' anything since ye were brought here." The woman kept her eyes down as she fussed with the tray, setting it down on the little table, after moving the elaborate chess set to another table. "Must keep up your strength, miss." She dropped a small curtsy and was gone before Bronwyn had a chance to thank her.

Keep up my strength? For what? she sighed, shakily pouring a cup of sweet smelling tea and practically gulping it down. Suddenly, she was very thirsty, and hungry. But she knew she shouldn't eat too much at first. It might make her ill again.

She ate a little of the soup and a few bites of the cakes, and found it took very little to fill her up. Then she gazed into the fire and thought about her life so far, trying to imagine what was in store for her. She had always tried to do right and where had it gotten her? Raped and mauled, half-dead in the snow. She'd helplessly watched her innocent father murdered and her reputation as a healer had done nothing but set her apart from the rest of humanity. She had always been good to others and in return she had been shunned and beaten, chased and threatened. Pursing her lips and feeling her still swollen eye, she feared there was no place in the world for someone like her; she must change—grow strong. She thought once again that she had been *wrong* to be ashamed of her gift; perhaps God had punished her for her cowardice. *She was a healer*, and if she wouldn't help people, then what good was she? She didn't possess wealth, a title or great beauty, but she did possess one gift and she should use it. A tiny smile touched the corners of her lips. Hadn't the worst happened already? What else did she have to fear? What else could happen to her?

So deep in her own thoughts was she that she didn't hear the door creaking open or the light footsteps of someone coming up behind her.

"So, my little songbird . . . you are mended." Edward was kneeling down beside her chair, his voice a husky whisper.

Startled, she put her hand to her throat and gasped, "Your Majesty! I didn't hear you come in!" She tried to rise to curtsy, but he gently pushed her back into the chair and took her hand. She looked down into his smiling eyes, noticing how tired and worn he looked. There were lines around his eyes and his face and clothes were dusty with travel. He must have come straight to her the moment he arrived. The weariness in his expression and the tenderness in his blue eyes touched her heart. She felt sorry for him. Did they never let him rest?

"Nay. Stay where you are, maid. You make a pretty picture in front of the fire, with your hair loose and spread about you, your face aglow with warmth and your eyes shining." He squeezed her hands and smiled at her. "I am so relieved to see you thus! I have had nightmares since I left." He sighed and sank down on the fur rug at her feet, leaned his blond head against the arm of her chair and stared into the fire, his face troubled. She looked at his profile for a while before she said, "I have just today gotten out of bed. It would seem that I have slept the last four days away. But, aye, I am better." He turned his face up her and his adoring expression made her relax and smile in return. "Thanks to you, Sire. If not for you, I would most likely be lying out in the woods somewhere, meat for the hungry wolves. Have I thanked you yet for saving me from that monster?" She knew that perhaps she shouldn't have said such a thing about the King's great cousin, but she didn't care. The man had killed her father and had brutalized her, and she had nothing but loathing for him; she couldn't hide it from Edward.

"I am sorry for that." Edward looked away, misery in his face. "I am ashamed of Richard and what he did to you . . . I cannot beg forgiveness enough. But I swear, I will try to make it all up to you. Anything you want—you have only to ask and it shall be yours." His shoulders drooped and the pain in his voice was so hard to bear, Bronwyn laid her hand lightly upon his shoulder. *It is all right. I understand*.

"But Your Majesty, it was not your fault—what happened," she declared. "If nothing else, it was my foolishness alone that got me into such a fix. I thought that I could handle any man . . ." She broke off and when the King looked at her with a question in his eyes, she laughed faintly. It was strange, that she could laugh about it, but only because she had cried enough when it had happened and if she didn't laugh now, she just might cry again.

"The Earl of Warwick is not *any* man." Edward said,

closing his eyes and leaning his head against the back of the chair.

"That I know. He is my enemy. I hate him more than any man I have ever known," she breathed in a hoarse murmur and her eyes as they looked at the flickering flames were full of that hatred. "He killed my father." She said this last in a chilling tone.

Shocked, Edward moaned aloud and rubbed his eyes. Now he understood that the maid had double reason to detest Warwick and now, he might also have the key to why Richard had abducted her and beaten her. "Bronwyn . . . I am sorry," he said, but he knew all the words in the world wouldn't assuage her grief. The Earl of Warwick could be a deadly, vicious man when thwarted. Edward wondered why he had murdered her father. Surely he hadn't been anyone of importance. Guilt hit Edward like a hammer. He prayed that Bronwyn's father hadn't met his death by his own order! If so, she would never forgive him, either.

"He killed your father?" Edward spoke carefully, his eyes still shut and his body now tense against the chair.

"Aye. Two years ago on a winter's night. By accident, as he put it, when he sought to kill a group of traitorous Lancasters. My father was in his way and he cut him down as one would a dog in his path." Bronwyn suddenly didn't want to talk about it all and she said softly, "But it is all past now and done with; nothing can change the past. I must accept it and go on. What is done is done." Edward knew she was referring to much more than her father's death.

"I know what it is to lose one you love. I lost my father, too, just a short time ago . . . in battle." Edward said sadly. "Like your father, he was a good man. A loving man."

Bronwyn gazed at the tired, begrimed man at her feet

and was amazed that a place was forming for him in her heart. She had almost forgotten that he was a King. At that moment, his handsome but now haggard face was familiar and comforting to her, like that of the man in her dreams. The warm fire and the late hour were almost lulling her to sleep again. It felt so right, so safe to be here with him. He hadn't made any move toward her and for that she was grateful. There was a special feeling for him in her heart, but she realized that the worst possible thing that could happen was for her to fall in love with someone as unobtainable as he.

"You look tired, my lord," she said. "Have you ridden far?" She was curious as to where he had been these last days and what he had done.

Edward stared into the fire, brooding. Perhaps, Bronwyn thought, he didn't want to talk about it, or perhaps it involved great state secrets that a mere peasant like herself had no right to ask about. When he didn't reply after a few minutes, she felt foolish for presuming he might share his thoughts with her. She was surprised when he abruptly began to let the words flow; they started as a trickle and soon became a river. He talked on and on about the wretched Lollards that the church was accusing and sending to the stake.

"God's blood, I must stand by and watch as they condemn the poor misfits! I hear them screaming in my nightmares. And I can do nothing!"

"Can't you have it stopped?" Bronwyn gasped, horrified. She wrung her hands and suddenly she could almost see the poor friars being dragged to the stakes, their flesh feeding the fire. She, of all people, knew what it was to fear the flames . . .

Edward groaned and looked up into her flashing eyes, his own full of agony and helplessness. "I cannot speak out against the Church, little one. I am very vulnerable at this time. I dare not oppose their policies. They would just

218

as soon as declare me a heretic as well than brook any dissension in religious matters. I need the Church more now than it needs me. Without the funds the Church can give me, my crown is in jeopardy. There will soon be another confrontation with the stubborn Lancasters and I need wealth to equip my armies. Without them, I will lose everything. Not even mighty Warwick would stand by me, if Mother Church should cast me aside.''

Bronwyn knew what he was saying was true. The Church was the most powerful force in the land and to oppose it or its doctrines was to court disaster. 'Twas the greatest folly any monarch could commit—to lose the support of the Church. She remained silent. There were things he *could* do, she thought, but it was something he must decide for himself. There was always a way to help innocent people. He just had to care enough about his subjects. She couldn't tell him what to do. She had no right.

"If I could only stop the burnings . . ." he agonized aloud, as if to himself. He sighed and stretched; then, seeing the tea tray behind him, he poured a cup of tea and proceeded to eat all the rest of the food on the tray.

"I can have more food brought, Sire," she said, ashamed that she hadn't thought to offer sooner. He must be starved!

"Nay, I'll order it myself." He jumped up and strode to the door. "You have been sick, and I will not hear of you waiting on me," he said as he called to the servants waiting outside.

Bronwyn was touched by his thoughtfulness. He was so very different from Warwick, or from any man she had ever known, that she didn't know what to say. She sat back then and let him bring another tray laden with food and wine into the room and watched him as he ate, talking a mile a minute about things he had seen and done during the last few days, telling her about the duties of a King. He laughed at a lot of the stories, but she could tell that underneath it all, he was unhappy. Lonely. It was a shock for her to realize that. And yet, it also made him seem more human, more like an ordinary man.

A while later, as he sat satisfied on the fur rug at her feet and after he had built the fire up again, she found herself asking him about his family, his life. Soon she got up the courage to ask him what his plans were for her.

He smiled and patted her hand, holding it so she couldn't move away from him. "I have never admitted this to anyone, my little songbird, but I have not been a good king these last years." There was guilt in his voice. "I have played the spoiled child while I let others run my kingdom . . . and, now, it seems, I shall pay dearly for it."

Bronwyn waited and he went on.

"I will not trouble your pretty head over things you don't understand, but I have decided it is time for me to take control of my own destiny. I want to be a good, righteous King. I know I have a lot to learn, but I am trying. I want to know the hearts of my people."

"Is that why you have saved me? Is that why I am here? You want to see one of your subjects up close and see how we think?" Bronwyn asked. "Inspect me like an insect in your hand?"

"Nay, nay!" Edward laughed and pulled her down to his level just long enough to plant a swift but sweet kiss on her lips. He could see the tiny golden flecks in her deep green eyes and he could also see what was left of the bruises on her face. Soon they would be completely healed and she would be even more beautiful than she had been before. He so longed to tell her that in that moment after the kiss as they looked into each other's eyes, but he feared it would bring all she had suffered back to mind and he didn't want to hurt her again. "I followed you through the desolate woods and saved you because . . . I cannot stay away from you. I think of you constantly. I see your smile, hear your sweet voice; I long for your touch almost every waking moment. When I sleep, I dream of you. I think I am in love with you. It matters not who or what you are. I need you near me, need to know that you will always be at my side.'' Bronwyn's heart softened.

He kissed her again, longer this time, and when they drew apart, a taunting voice she alone could hear whispered viciously, *Nothing can come of this love. Nothing! He is a king and you are nothing! It is not meant to be. When he tires of you he will cast you aside like all the others. It is hopeless. Do not give away your heart, for you shall never reclaim it whole again!*

Edward must have known what she was thinking, for his smile faded and he caressed her face, looking deep into her eyes, as if any second he might lose her again and wanted to remember her always. But neither said a word of their fears. It was enough that they were together now and they both understood that they could ask for nothing more. They existed in two separate worlds. It would never change. Someday Bronwyn would have to return to the world she knew, and he would have a state arranged marriage and produce royal heirs. *Someday they would have to part . . .*

Someday, Bronwyn kept telling herself, it would end and become one of the dearest memories of her life, one she would wonder over and cherish when she was an old lady somewhere with grandchildren tugging at her skirts. Whether they were to be friends or lovers, she would never forget this beautiful man with the blue eyes who had first come to her in a dream.

They sat and talked through the night until the first tentative rays of light began to filter through the mullioned windows, holding hands and laughing at times. He never forgot that she had been ill and he tried many times to urge her to go back to bed. But she had slept too much already these last few days, she told him with a light laugh, and so they had kept on talking learning about each other. She asked him what it was like to be a King and he told her. With pained eyes she sadly told him about her childhood and her parents' deaths, about what had brought her to the Red Boar that fateful morning when he had first spied her. In the end, she told him everything—everything but that the Earl of Warwick had succeeded in taking her virtue that day in the woods. That she would never tell anyone. It was better if she forgot it; she forebade herself to think of it.

And when the dawn was full and the sun was shining in on them, Edward leaned against her knee; her hand resting on his broad shoulder, and peaceful sleep claimed them both.

It could have been hours later, for all she knew, when she awoke. The first image to cross her mind was that of Edward, and she opened her eyes, yawning and stretching like a great cat. But when she looked down, the King was gone. She smiled softly to herself as she let her mind wander back over all they had said the night before. She wasn't afraid he wouldn't come back; her heart told her that he would.

She stood up and stretched again, rising up on her toes. For the first time in a long time, perhaps since that fateful night when her poor father had been so brutally cut down, she was truly happy. There was something laughing and smiling again deep inside her. There were no more tears. She laughed and twirled around, lightly dancing on the soft rug on the floor beneath her. She strolled over to a small table by the bed and picked up a hair brush and, humming a tune, she brushed her long hair until it rippled and crackled under the brush and fell in shining waves to her waist. When she had first been brought here, Edward had sent someone to fetch her personal belongings from the Red Boar and had sent a message to her sisters and Martha, telling them she was alive and well. Last night he had told her that she could go and see them whenever she desired when she was well enough to travel. The Red Boar wasn't far from the Tower and he would send one of his best men as an escort to see that no one bothered her and she returned safely.

They had discussed that, too. The King needed her. He begged her to come back, but he had not ordered it. That was what had made her decide she *would* come back. Her sisters were well, he had told her. They missed her, but they were happy with Martha, and Mary was completely recovered from her illness. Bronwyn was sure it was all true, though she was determined to go today to see for herself. She could well understand how they could have come to love Martha. She was so much like their own mother had been. Bronwyn shook her head and her long hair swayed about her waist. She caught half of it up and by force of habit began to plait it.

"No, my little songbird—do not imprison your lovely hair like that! Let it swing soft and free. It is so pretty about your face."

Bronwyn turned and smiled at Edward as he entered the room remembering the night they had just spent together. "If that is your will, my lord, I will leave it this way for a while." She was amused at the way he cared about even the little things.

"Thank you." He took her hand and slowly bent his head to kiss her. She didn't turn away and he didn't press her for more than she could give. He still saw fear in her eyes. He must give her more time. She was just starting to trust him.

"I wondered how long you would sleep," he said, still holding her hand and walking over to the window. "I had business to attend to and couldn't bear waking you to say goodbye. It was only for a few hours . . . did you miss me?" he asked, his eyes laughing down at her. Her bruises were almost gone now and there was a sparkle in her eyes again and life back in her smile. He was so relieved that she was better and almost happy again.

Bronwyn laughed. "No, Sire, I didn't have time to miss you. I only just now awoke." Then her eyes lit up. "Could I see my sisters today?"

His eyebrow raised as if he meant to be stern with her. "Are you well enough to travel, do you think? Perhaps, you should rest another day?"

"Nay! *Please*, Sire! I am fine. I just want to see them for a short while . . . I miss them so and they must miss me as well. We've never been apart so long, not ever." Her eyes pleaded and for a second she was afraid he might refuse.

Instead he chuckled and pulled her gently into his arms, laying her head on his strong shoulder. "Aye, you may go if you want to so much. I cannot refuse you anything. I know how much you love them." He still smiled when he thought of Bronwyn's little sisters and what he had believed before—that they were her children. It was funny now when he thought of it, but at the time, it hadn't been funny at all. "You may go, my heart, but you must promise to be very careful." He looked down into her happy eyes and there was a sudden strain in his voice. "You will come back to me, won't you? My little dove, you won't fly away from me, will you?"

She gazed up at him and shook her head. "Nay, Sire. I will return if you want me to, if you need me." Her voice was barely a whisper. Her face flushed and she turned away from him and stood apart, but then flashed him a great smile. "I can't wait to see them again! They must have been frantic when I left as I did . . ." There was a moment of silence as the memory of Warwick crossed both their minds like a black raven. Bronwyn broke the spell by asking, "Might I perhaps have something to eat?"

Good—if her appetite was returning she must surely be recovered, Edward thought. It pleased him that she was beginning to look and act like the proud, happy girl he had first met; he never wanted to see her suffer again.

"Well," he laughed, "I suggest we breakfast together before you set off on your journey. I have my rounds to make as well and the sooner I accomplish what has to be done, the sooner I can come back to you. If you're as hungry as I am, you'll be glad to know that I have ordered our meal to be brought up immediately."

"My Lord, you think of everything," said Bronwyn. For the first time in many days she looked forward to food with her old relish.

He took her hand and led her to the fire and before they could say another word, the food was brought in on great trays and arranged on a table. Bronwyn was amazed at the abundance and variety of dishes, as well as their delicious aromas. It made her head spin. The King bowed and led her to the chair as two servants, trying to hide their overwhelming curiosity as to who she was and what she was doing there, scurried out at a look from the King giggling and whispering. Bronwyn smiled behind her hand until they were gone and then, unable to help herself, burst out laughing.

"They don't know what to make of me," she told the King as they began to eat the delicious oat cakes smothered in honey, tender slabs of ham, eggs prepared three different ways and buns drenched in fresh butter and cinnamon. She had never eaten such wonderful food; she had never tasted anything so good. Edward watched her innocent delight in the fare and it made him enjoy his even more. He had never before given much thought to all the luxuries to which his royal birth entitled him, had never asked why he was served ten courses at every meal while the poor in the city starved. Now, looking at his captive sparrow, he was beginning to understand what it must be to be poor, not to have food when you were hungry or a warm bed and a fire when you were tired and cold. Imagine, not having anyone cater to your every whim and having to wear rags, live in filth and in fear of other men with more power than you. For the first time in his life, Edward's eyes were beginning to open and he wasn't sure he liked this new vision of the world he was being shown through Bronwyn's eyes. On the other hand, he couldn't pity her. She had more courage and inner strength than any other woman he had ever met.

He regaled her as they ate with stories of his family, and his remarks made her laugh at times and at others look searchingly into his eyes, as if she were trying to see what sort of man he really was—as if she were looking into his soul and heart to see if they were pure, judging him. All he knew was that in this intimate meeting of their hearts, he didn't want to be found lacking in her eyes. He cared what she thought of him and that was unusual.

"One of my brothers, Edmund, died three years ago at Wakefield Green," he had begun brusquely, as if he didn't really wish to discuss it further. "He was only seventeen . . . And then there's Richard, the youngest." His face brightened. "He's twelve—about the age of your sister Samantha, I believe." She nodded and he went on, "Though he's but a lad, he can best any other boy his age at the quintain and on the practice fields . . . aye, and he has a military mind, that one. Brave and fearless, a warrior . . . but also a scholar, my Dickon. That's what we call him. Though he is slight of build and not fair like the rest of us, he is by far the most loyal to me and no one tries harder than he." He laughed. "The whelp can beat me at chess or tables every time and takes great pleasure in doing so!" Edward smiled when he talked of his youngest brother and Bronwyn could see that he loved him well.

"And our dear mother, why, she's the bravest and truest of us all. She is strong as rock and always there for us. Thirteen children did she give our father," he said wistfully, "and five did she bury still in swadling clothes.

My father's death was hard for her to accept, but she is a strong woman."

"They say you have another brother," she recalled.

"Ah, George, the Duke of Clarence . . ." A frown darkened his countenance but disappeared so swiftly she wasn't sure if she had seen it or not. "George is a good lad too, in his own way. Just a bird of another feather. A peacock, I might say, even at fourteen. Well, almost fifteen. But his appetites are very—developed for his tender age." His look was thoughtful as if there was more about his other brother he would not or could not divulge. "Oh, I love him well enough. It's just that the Duke of Clarence is not much of a fighter. He already prefers to court the women and taste of the grape. His mind does not travel the same path as Richard's or mine. Yet he is an affable sort of fellow and can make one laugh over anything. He can make *me* laugh when no one else can. I love him well." he repeated. "You shall meet them all one day," Edward told Bronwyn as he refilled their mugs with ale.

"Meet your brothers?" she gasped. She didn't want to hurt his feelings or offend him, but that was impossible. "I *cannot* meet your brothers, Your Majesty!"

He leveled his piercing blue gaze at her. "Why not, pray tell? I am not ashamed of you."

Bronwyn lowered her eyes, unsure how to express the way she felt. She had been a peasant, poor and unnoticed all her life. How could she ever hope to mingle with his people in their exalted noble world? They would laugh at her—and at him for forcing her upon them. But she only said meekly, "You do not need more enemies or gossip now, my Lord . . ." She looked up at him and her eyes were huge and sad. "They would talk about you and . . . *your witch*."

It took him a second to understand what she meant and

then he exploded. "No one questions what I do or whom I care about! I am King, and no one dares to malign those under my protection!" He stood up and pounded the table, his eyes flashing and his jaw tight. Here was power, here was the real King, Bronwyn thought in awe and, even though she knew his rage was not directed at her, she couldn't help feeling a little afraid. God grant that this all powerful monarch might never be enraged at her. In his words and his anger she could almost hear the cell doors slamming shut . . . smell the flames, see the gleam of the wicked blade above her slim neck. This was Edward the Fourth, monarch of all Britain, a warrior and great scholar. This man could be a powerful enemy. But, she thought as she saw him smile sheepishly and sit back down, sorry for his outburst, this man was kind and good. He did not crave power for power's sake; he wanted to be a good King. Then he took her hand and said, "Forgive me. I must learn to control my temper. It is a grievous fault." He sighed and stood up again. "But, trust me, no one shall ever speak ill of you as long as I draw breath. Don't worry, I shall protect you." She knew he meant it. He was a man of his word, and a King's word was sacred.

She nodded and smiled up at him as he slung his fur cloak over his shoulders and then bent down to brush her lips lightly with a kiss. "But now, I'm afraid I must leave you yet again. My ministers await me, and affairs of state cannot be postponed, not even for love. I travel to Salisbury and I won't be back until tomorrow morning. I shall miss you." He pulled her up into his arms and held her close, so close she could smell his manly scent and feel the softness of his silk tunic, hear his heart pounding rapidly in his breast under her ear. "Will you be here when I return?" He tilted her face up towards him. His eyes mesmerized her with the growing love she saw mirrored in them and she answered, "*Yes. Yes!*"

She was very sad that he had to go, but she didn't ask

him what his business was. The feelings she was experiencing were as yet too fragile to question. "God be with you, my Lord," she whispered and then stood up on tip-toe and astonished him by returning his kiss.

"And with you," he breathed into her fragrant hair. "I pray He will bring me safely back to your arms." Then he added, "And you, my little one, be careful as well. I have assigned a guard to escort you when you visit your sisters. There is a leather pouch in the top drawer of my desk behind you; if you look inside, you'll find it is full of marchpane. All children love candy." He grinned, planted one last kiss on her cheek and left.

Bronwyn walked to the windows and stood silently watching as he called for his horse and his men in the courtyard below. She wished she could follow him down and wish him Godspeed once more before he rode away, but she was afraid she might cry. She smiled as he and his retinue rode through the gates, and waved when he looked back up towards the windows where she stood . . . she would miss him, too, if only for a day.

CHAPTER VIII

BRONWYN'S SISTERS were ecstatic upon her arrival. It was strange going back to the Red Boar after all that had happened to her. Was it really less than a week ago that Warwick had carried her off? It seemed like years. Bronwyn was not the same girl as she had been then. She cried as she held the girls in her arms and kissed them over and over. She couldn't remember ever seeing Mary healthier or happier than she was today. It was easy to see why. Martha had practically adopted them. It was amazing; Martha even stood up to Jack when it came to the girls. Mary especially had become Martha's pet and and couldn't do enough for her new "mother." She took Bronwyn by the hand and showed her where, up in an old storeroom that Martha had turned into a tiny closet-sized sewing room, she was mending and fixing the inn's linens and making new gowns for herself and her older sister. Ah, she always was the nimble-fingered little elf! Bronwyn laughed and hugged her as she proudly displayed what she was making at the moment—a thick, tasseled shawl for Samantha in a pretty red wool. It almost made Bronwyn a little melancholy, watching the two girls with a smiling Martha. They didn't need her anymore, not as they had before when she had taken care of them in that hovel they had called home. But Bronwyn didn't begrudge them their happiness. Indeed, she was delighted for them. They had found a place where someone cared for them, where there was plenty of good food and warm beds. They belong here, she realized.

Samantha had taken over Bronwyn's job, waiting on tables and helping Martha with the cooking. She enjoyed it, she told Bronwyn as they ate the delicious meal Martha set before them, but her smile was touched with guilt because it was plain to see that neither girl wanted to leave Martha and the inn. They didn't want to hurt the sister they loved, the sister who had taken care of them for so long and loved them, but they had found a home at last. So Bronwyn was prepared when they asked, a little sheepishly, if they could be allowed to stay with Martha. She *needed* them so!

"Sister!" Mary piped up, her tiny face alive and glowing, as she took Bronwyn's hand. "You could come back and stay, too. Martha wants you to. And as for old Jack . . ." She giggled behind her little hand and her eyes squinted up with mirth. "He'll not say a word against it. Martha can handle *that* old windbag!"

Martha threw her a stern but affectionate glance. Some kind of silent communication had been given. The girls had grown so close to the plump, loving woman . . .

Bronwyn looked down into her little sister's hopeful, anxious face and she felt a pang of loss. They didn't need her. No one needed her . . . *except the King*. It was a hard decision to make as she gazed at their excited faces and slowly shook her head. They couldn't leave the Inn now, and she couldn't stay. Not after what had happened to her there.

She could never come back. She looked up helplessly into Martha's understanding eyes, and Martha stepped in when she couldn't seem to be able to utter the words.

"Nay, children, methinks your older sister has a quest to perform first . . . she cannot come home yet. But she will visit us, won't ye, my child?"

"Often, I promise," Bronwyn told them as they snuggled in her arms. They would miss her and they didn't want her to go, but Martha was the one they needed and clung to now. Bronwyn knew she could never take the girls away from that lonely woman without breaking her heart. Her love for them was plain to see. Martha needed those small poppets as much as they needed her.

Bronwyn couldn't hurt any of them. "We aren't far apart, really; my lord says I can visit any time and stay as long as I wish."

Samantha gave her a questioning look but asked nothing. Mary didn't seem to care what was going on. She was so content at the inn that nothing else mattered.

Martha walked with Bronwyn to the door later as she was getting ready to leave and they talked about the strange turn of fate that had placed Bronwyn under the King's protection.

"He is good to me, Martha," Bronwyn whispered with a timorous smile. "He wants nothing from me but to remain with him. He has asked for nothing I am unprepared to give. He wants to be a good King to his people."

Martha gave her a searching look and then, smiling too, she nodded and hugged her close. "Aye, I know what he did for ye. He sent a messenger to tell us all was well. It seems impossible that a King should care about the likes of us . . . but, then, I knew ye were special the moment I laid eyes on ye! I can see where any man—even a King—would be proud to have you for his lady. There are rumors, though . . ." Her grey eyes were troubled as she spoke and she seemed embarrassed. "They say the King has a new paramour—they say she has *bewitched* him. 'Tis ye they speak of, is it not?"

Bronwyn felt a sadness deep inside. Wherever she went, whatever she did, gossip and accusations always followed her like hungry dogs on her trail, seeking to tear her flesh to bring her to the ground and trample her into the mud. Witch. *Witch.* Would she never be free of that dreaded name?

She looked up into the older woman's face and replied wearily, "The gossips waste little time in weaving their juicy little stories." She sighed and fastened the rabbit fur cloak, a gift from the King, around her shoulders. "But fear not, good friend, I am being cautious. As cautious as I can be when I have done nothing. As to being the King's paramour, that too is untrue. But he is my protector and I can ask for no better." She smiled then and gave Martha one more farewell hug before she left. It felt strange, leaving her sweet poppets with someone else and riding back through the crowded streets to her new home—if home was what the Tower could be called. Home was where the heart was, was it not? In that case, Bronwyn had two homes—here with her sisters; and with Edward.

As she rode, the King's guard at her side, she recalled something that had been bothering her during her visit. She had not seen Molly the whole time she had been at the Red Boar and she briefly wondered why. But it was a small matter and it left her thoughts almost as soon as it had entered. Hateful Molly with the painted face. What had happened to the woman? She would have to ask Martha the next time she came, aye, that she would.

Bronwyn's thoughts returned to her sisters, so healthy and happy, with new gowns and glowing faces. How different they had looked today, nothing like the empty-eyed starving waifs she remembered from such a short time ago. Even though her heart longed for them, she knew they were content; so she must be as well.

As the sun was sinking, Bronwyn and her guard entered

the Tower's courtyard. The burly, silent soldier to whom Edward had entrusted her, dismounted and then helped her down. They had spoken but little on the journey to the Red Boar and back again. It was as if the man were afraid of her, or contemptuous of her position as mistress to the King. After a while, sighing, she had stopped trying to make conversation. No doubt he resented the privileges accorded one who was of no higher birth than he himself. He escorted her to the doors of her chambers and with a curt bow, was gone.

She was glad to see a big fire blazing. She sat before the fire in the same chair as last night, when the King had held her hand and talked to her. Images and snatches of their conversation kept coming back to her and she smiled wistfully, still wrapped in her fur cloak.

She must have been sitting there staring into the fire for a long time when she heard a knock at the door behind her and got up to let her visitor in. She had suddenly become lonely, thinking of the King and her absent sisters, and she was pleased to see the white-haired old physician standing on the threshold.

"What brings you out on such a cold night, sir?" She asked with a welcoming smile and led him to the other chair before the warming fire. He looked as if he needed a warm place to perch, he was all wet and shivering. She helped him off with his black outer cloak and spread it on the fender to dry. "You are wet!" she admonished him as if he were a child.

"Of course. 'Tis raining buckets outside, my little lady!" he huffed back at her, his bushy white eyebrows arched in annoyance. "I wasn't sure if my horse and I were swimming or trotting the last few miles. I came to see how my patient was faring. The King bade me keep an eye on you for a while longer. You look fit, I must say. Have you been taking the medicine I prescribed for you? Have you been resting? Have you kept warm?" His questions came one right after the other; she had to put her hands up to stop them.

"Aye, physician. You are right; I am better." She was glad he hadn't arrived any sooner, or he would have caught her coming back in and been upset that she had gone out at all. But she wouldn't mention her little journey. "You know your craft well. But there was no need for you to come out on such a night just for me," she added humbly. "You will fall ill yourself."

He peered at her from the other chair, rubbing his cold hands before the fire to warm them. "I came in response to my leige's orders. Don't want me beheaded, do you?" There was a glint of humor in his sharp old eyes.

Bronwyn leaned back in her chair, folded her hands in her lap and smiled back at the old man. "Nay—who then would take care of His Majesty if he became sick?"

His eyebrow cocked at that. "You, of course," he threw back. "That's another reason why I've come. I wanted to talk to you about your healing knowledge. The last time we spoke of it, as I recall, you weren't quite yourself."

Instantly Bronwyn steeled herself and her chin raised in defiance as it so often did when she was confronted with knowledge of her secret. "There is not much to say," she hedged, unused to speaking openly about her gift. How could it suddenly be permissible to talk about something that she had always been forced to hide, something that people needed, yet shunned her for providing?

La Rouel shook his head, exasperated with her stubborness. "My dear, you do not have to be afraid of me. I respect that talent God has seen fit to bestow upon you I only wish I myself had the power. All the pain and suffering I could cure . . . I have seen so much terrible suffering in my long life. If I could whisk it all away, I would and be glad of it!" Still she looked at him with veiled eyes.

"Ahh, I see." He turned his head away with an audible

sigh and stared into the fire. "You still don't trust me, child. I understand what you are feeling; I know why you refuse to talk of this gift of yours." He shook his head, propping it in his left hand. "But I will tell you this. I need someone like you . . . I have been seeking just such a one for a lifetime. I am an old man, as you see. I have gleaned much skill and knowledge over the years as a physician and I have always hoped I could hand it all down someday to one who would use it as wisely as I have tried to do. I thought that *you* might be that pupil."

Now Bronwyn turned and looked into his earnest old eyes. She saw compassion and wisdom. He only wanted to give her a part of himself. He only wanted to help others, as she did.

She closed her eyes and let her body relax again as a hundred images flashed through her mind—visions of those she had helped, mended or cared for in the last years, followed rapidly by all those who had then tried to harm or accuse her. For a second, the visions were at war in her mind and when she opened her eyes, she merely nodded, and he understood.

"You want to teach me what you know?" Something deep inside her was beginning to awaken. She was born to heal. That was what God wanted her to do—to help people. If she could combine her healing power with the old sage's knowledge, she could be even more effective.

"And you can teach me what *you* know," the old man said.

They smiled at each other.

He asked her then about her childhood, about her life and her sisters. They sat and talked for a long while, and then La Rouel changed the subject to the young King. Bronwyn brightened at the mention of him and her eyes shone.

"He's a headstrong pup, that one," La Rouel sighed as he rose to take his leave. He had some distance to travel before he lay his head down upon a pillow and it was already late. God should never have created the night, he thought sardonically, if it was not His intention that His creatures take their rest. There were so many sick people . . . "But, mark my words," the old man continued, "he shall someday be known as a great King. Until now, he's been like a spoiled child, without compassion for those less fortunate than he." He stared straight at her as he spoke. "Until now. You are good for him, child. He has learned a great deal from you already. 'Tis time he grew up and stopped wasting his talents. It is time he takes control from those other influences that are leading England into danger."

They both knew he meant the Earl of Warwick, though neither mentioned the name. "It is best to avoid taking sides, though, child. It is best not to get involved with politics. *To be safe.*"

As he was ready to leave, he gave her one further admonition. "Care for the King as best you can. He needs someone like you now. But do not fall too deeply in love with him. There are rumors that a certain person is even now hopeful of making an advantageous French match between Edward and King Louis's sister-in-law, Bona of Savoy, to end the strife between England and France once and for all. Now, with the Lancasters rallying under the battle flag again, he will be more eager than ever to seal the bargain and bring France to our side. If Warwick has his way, it will happen soon." There was pity in his voice for the young girl before him. Her face was drained and pinched at his unexpected news.

But Bronwyn was glad he had told her, reminding her of who she was and who Edward was, and of the vast difference in their stations. "I am no fool. I will never ask the King for what he cannot give," she answered in a low, husky voice. She knew that Edward could never be completely hers, but she had decided in that very instant that she would accept whatever he was able to offer and never ask for more. She must be content with that. "Indeed, I have not asked for what he has already given me." She looked around at the luxurious room, and then back to La Rouel's grim face. "So do not worry, physician. I shall never be a millstone around his neck. I shall stay only as long as he needs me."

La Rouel nodded and squeezed her hand. He had a feeling about Edward and the girl. He believed that they were already falling in love and he hoped, for both their sakes, that neither heart would be wounded too deeply when they had to part. La Rouel knew that Warwick would eventually succeed in arranging the French marriage for Edward, and that Edward would do what was best for his country. A French alliance would bring a much longed for peace. The marriage was inevitable. It was best she knew that from the start.

"Get yourself to bed, girl," he sternly advised her on his way out the door. "You're not well, yet. I shall stop by to see you again soon."

She stood by the door a long time after he had left. *The King was to marry a French Princess. The King was to be married . . . soon.* She shrugged her thin shoulders impatiently as if to convince herself she didn't really care. After all, a week ago she had never even met him, except in her dreams and fantasies, so why should it make such a difference to her if she lost what she had never really had? She told herself that over and over as she prepared for bed and yet again as she vainly tried to capture sleep.

"Bronwyn . . . Bronwyn?" The deep voice penetrated her consciousness until she opened her eyes and saw the King bending over her. She sat up, clutching the covers about her, her hair in disarray and her eyes still sleepy.

"Your Majesty!" She shook her head, trying to wake up. She had been dreaming and the sudden shock of seeing Edward standing before her had confused her at first. "You've returned!"

"Aye, sweetling. I just arrived . . . but, alas, I must soon leave again, I fear." His face was as tired as it had been the other day and full of woe. "I just couldn't leave without saying hello." He sat down on the edge of the bed close to her.

"And goodbye?" she asked softly.

" 'Tis not by choice that I ride away again, little one." He sighed. "Today the burden of Kingship bears heavily down on me." She detected real melancholy in his words, and reached out a hand to touch his. He smiled tiredly at her. "But seeing your lovely face has brightened my day. I can leave with my heart a little lighter, though I go for a sad enough reason."

Fully awake by now, Bronwyn noted the anguish in his voice. "Can I help in any way, Sire?" she asked.

"Nay, pretty one. No one can help me in this matter. And I had so looked forward to spending more time with you. All the way here I could hardly wait to see you, talk to you as we did the other night and hold you in my arms." He slapped his riding gloves against his thigh in agitation. "I had barely reached the Tower's gates when a messenger caught up with me . . . *damn all blood-thirsty clerics*! If I had my way I'd send all those fat, lazy clergymen to the flames and have done with them all!" He muttered this last in a vicious inflection.

Bronwyn had guessed what he was talking of. "The Lollards?"

The King jumped up and started to pace the room. "That they dare to go against my expressed wishes—that's what I can't believe. I did what they asked of me, and now they dare to disobey my orders! Sweet Mother of Mercy . . . they burned three hundred of the poor miserable wretches last week in Lincolnshire alone. That I could hardly stomach, but this—! How shall I stop it now?

They have tortured and beaten, starved and burned them, rounded them up in droves and now I am informed by one of my loyal spies that they plan to burn as many again tomorrow in Kent!'' He spun about and faced her, his anguish clearly visible. ''The other night we spoke of these poor people, and you asked me if there was nothing I could do to stop the burnings. I have been going over and over in my mind if it is right for the Church to punish heresy in this matter. I am questioning so many things I have always taken for granted . . .'' He stared at her with affection and awe in his blue eyes. ''Suddenly I am seeing so many things—but 'tis not all my fault . . . I have grown hard these last years, inured to suffering I had never seen before. The burning of these hapless Lollards appalls me!'' Shame replaced his anger then and he walked over to her and took her hand. ''They have done no harm to anyone. They hurt no one, attack no one. They only want to be left alone to do God's will as they understand it, and to care for the poor, as they prefer to be themselves. Unlike the greedy churchmen!'' His eyes were flashing with disgust. ''The clerics not only wring every possible farthing from the people, but against God's laws they take mistresses and concubines into their rich houses. Have I been wrong, Bronwyn, in being ruled by the Church in this matter? Have I sent innocent men to the stake for nought but other men's avarice and arrogance?''

''Do you really want me to answer that, my Lord?'' Bronwyn had been completely taken aback by Edward's impassioned words. She was nearly speechless that the King was asking her opinion. Who was she to tell a King what was right or wrong? She knew nothing about such matters other than what she felt in her heart. What did he expect her to say?

''Aye. What would you do if you were I?'' He was serious, she saw.

And Bronwyn knew then why fate had sent her to the

King. She feared that her immortal soul would be damned if she kept silent when she could perhaps help those poor creatures who would die tomorrow unless the King stepped in. "If I were King . . ." her face glowed and her eyes were shining, "I would stop *all* the burnings—at least until I was sure what purpose was really being served by their deaths—God's or the greedy Churchmen." Her voice was soft, but filled with intensity. "If I were King, I would rule my kingdom according to my conscience rather than dancing to someone else's tune. I have seen the poor friars among the people, and they do nought but good. Why must good men die because the Church feels threatened by them?"

Edward's face had slowly turned crimson and he rose from the bed to stand tall and straight above her. For a terrifying moment she feared she had dreadfully overstepped her bounds and now she would feel his wrath. But her eyes held his, though she trembled.

He was angry, but not at her. He nodded in silence and began to put on his gloves. "Then I know what I must do. I only regret having to leave you again so soon."

She didn't know what possessed her at that moment, but the words came before she even knew she had voiced them and then it was too late to take them back. "Let me go with you, my Lord!" she pleaded, and there was a longing in her voice that touched him deeply. "I could talk to them and hear their side. I am one of them. They'd trust me."

"You mean, they wouldn't trust me?"

"You are a *King*. You represent the Church. They *couldn't* trust you. 'Tis common knowledge they would rather go to the flames than recant their beliefs. Perhaps, I could talk to them . . . and . . ." She paused, her heart wrenching at the thought of what they must have already gone through. "The Church uses torture freely. Perhaps some might need my care."

Edward turned away and said, "I care for *you*, Bronwyn, and you have been so ill. I would never forgive myself if you were to fall ill again because of my folly. I could not stand to lose you now," he whispered. He had already lost so much these last few years—a brother, a father, a beloved uncle and many, many others . . .

Bronwyn steeled her reserve. "I am fine. I went out yesterday and I am none the worse for it. And Kent is not very far away, my Lord. I want to come. Please let me?"

She was right, he noted. The journey to the debtor's prison in Kent where the Lollards were awaiting their fate was but a few hours' ride. The bitter cold had abated and the sun was warming the land, though it was only the end of March. And, he had to admit, that looking at her this morning, with the roses back in her cheeks and her emerald green eyes flashing, she seemed herself again.

She was to be his friend, his lover . . . his Merlin. He remembered how she had touched his wound and it had healed. He remembered the way she had looked when he had found her with Warwick that terrible night. He loved her courage, her spirit, the flame he could even see burning in the depths of her compassionate green eyes.

He put out his hand to her. "If you are coming with me, you had best get up and get dressed." Then his face dissolved into a smile. "Swiftly!"

Bronwyn was delighted. There *was* something she could do to help! There *was* a reason for all that had happened to her; and, thus, perhaps a reason for her very existence.

"Aye, Sire . . . as soon as you leave me, I shall get dressed," she said demurely. She glanced at the door behind him and with a rolling of his eyes to the ceiling, he spun on his bootheel and walked out, throwing back at her one last reminder.

"Be sure to wear something warm and simple, and a hooded cloak to cover your face. You are far too pretty to be ogled by passersby. I would keep you to myself as long as I possibly can.''

The door closed behind him, and as he walked down the corridor, he frowned. Edward still was not sure if taking Bronwyn with him was the right thing to do, but he had given her his word. Besides, she was right—there might be those who would have need of her skills. Just the thought that it could be possible made him flinch. He had never condoned the Church's methods of gaining confessions from those whom it accused. It seemed to him that if a human being is subjected to enough torture, he would say anything, confess to anything, just to stop the pain. Until now, Edward had always been uneasy about the whole thing, but had never questioned it. He, who never thought twice when it came to killing on the battlefield, cared about his people. Aye, Bronwyn had changed all that. She had taught him that the poor were worthy of consideration, and that knowledge was changing everything for him. She was forcing him to care for his fellow man, after so many bitter years of battle, death and carnage, betrayel and pain.

When he returned a few minutes later to tap at her door, she opened it smiling, fully dressed in a simple forest green gown of heavy wool. Her hair was pulled back into a long, loose plait that hung almost to her waist. He never ceased to be amazed at how lovely she looked, dressed so simply. Her smile and her brilliant eyes were all the embellishment she needed. There was only a tiny cut along her right cheek and a faint shadow under her eye to remind him of what she had looked like when he had rescued her from Warwick.

"There, Your Majesty.'' She executed a perfect curtsy and smiled up at him. "Was I swift enough?'' She twirled around and then slipped her old cloak over her shoulders and pulled up the dark hood. "And like this, I don't think I shall call too much attention to myself." Then her mirth fled from her manner as Edward nodded, taking her hand in his. They must hurry. The sooner this business was over, the better.

His men were waiting in the courtyard when Edward stepped out with Bronwyn at his side. He gave an order to one of the waiting grooms and the lad, a slight youth of about thirteen, with short blond hair and freckles, ran off to the stables and returned a few minutes later with a small bay mare.

The King handed Bronwyn the reins and said, "Chelsea is a sweet-tempered mare. She belongs to you now." The groom helped Bronwyn into the saddle, and she stared down at the King's handsome face. "You mean she's *mine*?" She couldn't believe it. A horse of her very own! And such a beautiful horse! Bronwyn stroked the mare's silken withers and the horse nickered and arched its graceful neck, then turned to look back at the girl sitting so lightly on her back, nickering again. "I think she knows she belongs to me, Sire," Bronwyn laughed and stroked the mare's neck. "You are a beauty, my girl," she whispered in the mare's alert ear as Edward mounted and gave the order to set forth.

"Thank you," Bronwyn whispered as she gathered the reins and urged the mare forward alongside the King's stallion. "I've never received such a wonderful gift before. But I can't keep her, Your Majesty," she continued with real regret in her voice. " 'Tis too much. But may I pretend she's mine and ride her sometimes?"

Edward laughed so loudly, that Bronwyn stole an apprehensive glance back at the soldiers who were watching them intently. The King shook his shaggy blond head and whispered back to her conspiratorially, "And then, I shall just *pretend* you didn't give her back to me and we shall be even."

Bronwyn blushed, unaccustomed to being teased. He would have it his way in the end no matter what she did or said. After all, he was the King.

"I have many horses in my stables and I shan't miss one little mare. I thought that you might like a horse of your own to ride when I am away. I cannot take you with me all the time. I want you to be happy here."

Again she was amazed that such a man could care how she felt. She could think of nothing else to say so they rode along together in the sunlight. Unwillingly, her thoughts returned to the Lollards. She had no way of knowing that the King, too, was thinking of them. In the last few years he had seen so much bloodshed and savagery, that he had become accustomed to the atrocities he witnessed. For a second his bright blue eyes clouded as they rode, stirrup to stirrup, and he was haunted by the gory visions he carried with him always these days. The contest to win and keep his throne had been a terrible one. He'd seen friends and followers fall beneath the sword in pools of their own blood, heard the agonizing death groans of many good men on the battlefields of Towton and Mortimer's Cross, and he'd known sorrow that swiftly hardened into vengeful rage on the day he had stared in horror at the bloodied heads impaled upon spikes outside the town of York—his father, the great Duke of York, his sweet brother Edmund and his uncle, the Earl of Salisbury, his cousin Richard's father. That vile French-born witch Queen Margaret had been to blame for that. Aye, those crimes and many, many more. The Lancaster horde, the Scottish border rats and mercenaries and any other criminals she could gather beneath her banners had, in the end, become a plague that ravaged England, pillaging, butchering and raping, until even those loyal to poor Harry and the Lancaster cause had cringed with fear and hatred. Her army's viciousness and thirst for blood had finally been her downfall. Relieved, a frightened London had gladly opened welcoming arms to him and Warwick in February of 1461 and had crowned him King. Momentarily beaten, she had fled to Scotland to lick her wounds. Her best man, Somerset, had been captured on the battlefield of Towton, as well as Clifford and Trollope, who had been a traitor to the house of York. Edward had been sure that was the end of her and the Lancasters, but he had been mistaken . . . for even now she was gathering another army to recapture the realm for her insane, pious husband and small son.

Edward himself had not been innocent of savagery and bloodshed . . . and yet, when he looked at the pale girl riding next to him, and remembered the peaceful, happy days before he had donned his armour and raised his sword, he felt a great sense and loss. He had always sought peace, yet found himself time and time again wading in a river of blood across yet another battlefield. Now after years of killing, fleeing, fighting and attacking, he longed for a respite, a brief moment of happiness before Margaret's forces came sweeping down from the north once more into his poor, bruised England. He looked over at Bronwyn and the sight of her brought not only a smile on his lips, but joy to his heart. Aye, he had grown cold and hard these last grueling years, there was no denying it. But he could try to help those who had already suffered far too much. They had been trampled beneath the armies of red rose and white, helpless. Even in his childhood home at Ludlow, Queen Margaret had not spared any of those hapless villagers in October of 1459, when the ill-prepared Yorkist army had fled to regroup their forces. His mother, Cecily, Duchess of York, and his two youngest brothers, Richard and George, had been left to the tender mercies of the Lancasters. Edward would never forget the heartless way the French witch had treated his mother and brothers. It was as if the world had gone mad these last few years, as if all chivalry and human kindness had died.

It was time he began to show mercy to those who could

not defend themselves. But for the Lancasters there could be no mercy. They deserved none, for they had shown none.

They entered the gates of the town, the royal standard whipping above their heads in the brisk breeze. The party then proceeded onward, past the town pillory where stakes had already been erected, each centered in a pile of wood and straw awaiting the victims and the flames.

With her heart in her throat and her eyes averted, Bronwyn rode by the gruesome sight in heavy silence, as did Edward. How could God-fearing men be so eager to hurt each other so? How could any man have the right to burn the flesh of another in God's name? That was more heresy than any poor friar had ever committed.

Sensing the turmoil in her and the fear, Edward leaned over in his saddle and laid a calming hand upon her cheek for a moment, smiling encouragingly. "Fear not, little one, I will put a stop to this, I swear."

They pulled rein before the prison's gates and were eventually let into the inner ward. A page helped Bronwyn to dismount. The cold stone building loomed around them and her eyes dismally swept upwards over its forbidding walls and took note of the long, narrow barred slits that served as windows. Little light filtered through such arrow-slits. She shuddered.

"Little one," Edward whispered in her ear, "You don't have to stay. I can have you taken to the Abbey and there you can wait for me until this hateful business is finished. This is painful to you, I can see it, and I don't want you to suffer." He recognized the horror in her eyes as she stared at the prison. It had been a mistake, Edward thought now, to have permitted her to come. He had been taught to respect women and to deal with them gently at all times, always to protect them from the harsh realities of the world. He was accustomed to riding with his squires, his knights and his lords; he was used to cold steel and chain mail, the shout of soldiers as they rode into battle. Men, not women. Women were meant to be protected and kept safe within strong walls along with the children. Yet, he had allowed this woman-child with the intense eyes to persuade him to let her ride at his side to this dreadful place. It was as though she had some strange power over him. Was her coming an omen like the three suns that appeared over the battlefield of Mortimer's Cross two years ago and prophesied his first great victory over the Lancasters when all had been thought lost?

She shook her head. "Nay, Sire. I must go with you . . . there may be some I can help. At least, some might talk to me and I might listen to their grievances." She turned large, frightened eyes up to him and said, "I am safe with *you*, your Grace." She looked down at the hand he still held in his. "I'm not afraid." Yet for a moment she was overwhelmed with melancholy and a feeling of helplessness. So many times she couldn't help or heal no matter how hard she tried. It was the curse of her gift and she could never find a reason for her failures. Yet always, the painful empathy she felt toward her patients, especially those in agony of body or of mind, emotionally and physically drained her, often leaving her weak and sick as if she had taken on some of their suffering just by touching them. The King would never understand, though, that she never had a choice. She did what she did because she *had* to, not because she wanted to. She was a healer and must try to help those who needed her.

Touching the cold stone of the prison as they were let through the first barred door, it was as if the evil and suffering of the place transmitted itself through her trembling fingertips and flew straight to her heart and her whole body went as taut as a pulled bowstring, overwhelmed by the inner sorrow of the hideous place. Her eyes were vacant and her lips a grim slash in her white face. This was the place of her nightmare . . .

"Sire, I can feel the anguish within these walls," she quavered. There was no turning back now, though she knew that for the people lodged behind those bleak walls she had little hope to offer. Herbs, roots and medicinal teas would not help those within. Many of them were doomed and would never step outside these walls again, except perhaps on their way to the stake, or the block. Some would die in prison at the torturer's hands or of starvation or sickness. These walls spoke silently of human misery and Bronwyn's heart was a cold lump in her breast as they traveled hurriedly down narrow stone passageways to where the condemned friars were quartered.

The King held her arm, keeping her from tripping on the slimy stairs that wound their way steeply down into the very bowels of the prison and the strength of that arm reassured her. The flustered prison guards escorted them in a stony silence, unsure why this royal personage was entering such a place—and with a woman. They knew it boded no good to have the King poking his nose into Church affairs. Like the other inhabitants of the town, they, too, had been eagerly anticipating the morrow's entertainment. A mass burning like this one was always a cause for celebration. Already the word had spread concerning the spectacle and people had been pouring into town for days from miles away to watch the entertainment.

Bronwyn recoiled at the filth and the stench as they passed the tiny cells and her ears were assaulted by the cries and moans of the poor souls within. She held the King's arm tightly and prayed that he might succeed in his mission of mercy. A burly guard halted before a small wooden door and put a key into the lock, grumbling when, at first, it wouldn't turn. Then, with a coarse oath under his breath, he twisted it roughly to one side and the door finally opened with a loud grating noise as it scraped the damp stone floor. "They be in 'ere, your Grace." He bowed to the King and stood back nervously. "Are ye sure you want the lady here to go in, your Grace?" the guard was brave enough to ask, as he stood back from the open door. " 'Tis not a pretty sight." He frowned then, afraid he had overstepped his bounds by saying such a thing. But he couldn't help wondering what reason there could be for subjecting a woman to such a scene. He was a hard man, but the sight of her white face touched even him.

Gazing into the dark cell, Bronwyn instinctively clutched Edward's hand in mortal terror. Inside she could hear shufflings and moans, the heavy breathing of frightened men reduced almost to the status of animals. The smell was like that of putrid flesh or of things long dead . . . she covered her mouth and nose with a fold of her cloak, forcing down the nausea that rose in her throat. Her eyes, glazed and pained, flew to Edward's seemingly calm face. It hadn't affected him, she saw with astonishment. There was no way she could have known that his familiarity with blood-soaked battlefields littered with the dead and dying had long since hardened him to such sights. At least, these men were living.

But when he stared into her horror-filled eyes, it came to him that once upon a time this scene would have turned his stomach as well. Ah, how he envied her innocence and tender caring.

"My sweet," he whispered urgently as he held her back from the yawning portal, "you do not have to involve yourself in this matter. Go back up into the sunshine and let me question the good brothers alone."

"Nay, your Grace . . . I must go in. I must help them if I can. We both must do what we have to do. I am a healer." Her face was set and there was a fire in her that he had seen a few times before. She was right, he thought, as a low, keening wail from somewhere within raked at them. They both had to go where their destiny led and do whatever that destiny bade them, no matter how painful that

251

path might be. She was as much a healer as he was a king. Neither had a choice.

"I will attend those who need my help and I will talk to them to see how they were brought so low," she said. Stepping across the threshold into the dank cell she was once again forcibly reminded of her nightmares. She turned to give one last tender look at the tall man behind her. Yet if this was the place of her nightmares, he was the man of her dreams . . . the man wearing the golden crown, who comforted her . . . and then she peered through the dimness and saw what appeared to be bodiless white faces floating before her inside the large cell. The brothers were clustered all around the cell in their dark cowled habits. Most were kneeling in prayer, murmuring their benedictions on a world that had treated them so shamefully. It shocked her to realize that they probably thought her entrance signaled that they had finally been sent for to feed the hungry flames. Of course, she thought, sharing their agony, they had no way to tell day from night in here. They thought it was their time to die and die they would for their beliefs. She walked across the slippery stone floor to a man with bent head who gripped a cross to his breast and feverishly whispered his prayers. Her eyes had become accustomed to the gloom, and she could see that his hood had fallen back from his tonsured head and his habit was stained and torn. She marked that he had lost his rope girdle and the hands that held the cross were bloody. She shrank deep inside herself but walked up to him and touched his shoulder gently. "Brother, what crime have you committed that they have done this to you?" Her voice was soft, her gaze compassionate. The men about her continued to pray and only a few looked up. The friar she had spoken to raised his head, revealing empty, burnt sockets and Bronwyn gasped in horror and compassion as she realized that the man had been blinded. With a cry of sympathy she touched his face. A tear slid

252

down her face as she knelt before him and took one of his bloody hands in hers. "What have you done to deserve this?" she whispered.

He turned his head away and his whole body stiffened as he answered her. "Have you come to further taunt or torture us? I say, *enough*! We have already confessed to the crimes Mother Church has accused us of . . . preaching heresy and speaking out against her greediness and daring to condemn her to the people she has wronged. We will not lie and protest our innocence to these charges. *We are ready to die*. Have the fires been lit? Is it time?" His voice and manner were of unearthly resignation.

"I haven't come to accuse you or taunt you, brother," she assured him, her heart breaking for all he and the others had had to endure. Her voice was soft and caressing. "I've come with someone who might help you win your freedom. I've come to *help* . . ."

"No one can help us. Not now!" He pushed her hand away and tried to stand, but swayed back against the wet grey wall, his robes swishing over the filthy wet straw under his sandaled feet. "The bishop desires our deaths so his justice can be served and our properties confiscated," he rasped. Then the anger dissipated as swiftly as it had arisen and he moaned, lifting his bloody hand to the place where his eyes had been. His cry of pain cut through her and she repeated, "Who did this to you?"

"Why, the Bishop's men, of course. They say if one is led by God, one will not feel the pain of the fire . . ." His voice died away. Her heart wept for him as she slowly rose and stared down at his bent head. He said only one last thing: "*I am prepared to die. We are all prepared to die.*"

She turned and cried to them all, "I want to help you. All of you. Do you *all* want to die?" They were like sheep ready for the slaughter. They actually *wanted* to die. For their beliefs, for their God. They acted like dead men already! But what good would their deaths do for the poor who remained, those the friars had attempted to help?

From the doorway, the King had listened and waited, his eyes following the girl as she moved among the robed figures. He could hardly keep his stomach, the stench was so terrible. The smells of blood, human waste and death were everywhere. Stupid fools, he thought angrily. They didn't care if they burnt; didn't care if they were tortured and beaten. They wanted to die for their faith, to become martyrs. It was the main reason why he had never been roused to come to their defense. The Lollards were religious fanatics who seemed to desire nothing less than the final glory of flames. Well, so be it! Let them burn!

"Little one, come. They do not want your help. There is nothing you can do for these men. With their own words they have sentenced themselves to the flames. Come," he called out to her and started to make his way to her through the kneeling friars who fell back from his passage as if he were the devil himself.

But Bronwyn hadn't heard him. She stooped down to the blinded friar and, not even realizing what she was doing, laid her small cold hands over the man's empty eyes. Something deep inside her soul cried out in pity for this poor, tortured creature. When she pulled her hands away, the man cried out, "What did you do? *There is no more pain! Sweet Jesus . . . a miracle. A miracle!"* The friar lurched to his feet and threw his arms about her. "Brothers! The maid touched my face and now there is no more pain!" Then he collapsed to the stones again and began to pray, tears streaming down his face. She could never return his sight, but the pain she could heal. *"Thank you,"* he whispered and kissed her hand as the other robed figures all rushed to her and tore her from his grasp. They milled around her, crying, *"Touch me . . . help me . . . You healed him, heal me!"*

Bronwyn was overpowered and slid to her knees on the matted straw as they swarmed over her. None of them wished her harm, yet all clamored for her aid. Bloodied hands and broken limbs were thrust at her; they fought to touch her skirt or have her lay a finger on their wounds. Their cries and pleas for attention became a roar and, aghast, Edward shoved his way through the mob that had just a few seconds before been a group of gentle, pious men and now threatened to trample the poor girl in their frenzy to touch her.

"Bronwyn!" he called above the din and their eyes met for just a fraction of a second and she smiled sadly back at him before the pitiful, groping creatures closed in about her figure once more.

Infuriated, he tossed the dirty scarecrows away and fought through to her side, calling for her. His men moved in around him and cleared a path. The friars clawed at him with bloody fingers or stumps and as he looked into their hungry eyes and battered faces he saw such looks of suffering that he nearly ordered his men to stop abusing them—but he didn't. He was too frantic to rescue Bronwyn and they wouldn't get out of his way unless he used force. Lord Christ! They had all been beaten and broken, bloodied and scourged . . . little wonder they prayed for the release that death would finally grant them! The King felt his great wave of fury transfer itself as he saw the Church's handiwork. He would see justice done or he was not King!

With an angry bellow, he finally reached Bronwyn and pulled her from their grasping midst, only to lose her again and when he next looked down, there she was crouched on the stone floor, her eyes staring blankly and her lips trembling as she rocked back and forth, a man's head resting in her lap. The others fell away then and silence fell upon them all.

"Look . . . he smiles at her . . . we had left him for dead and, look he is healed!" There was awe in the voice that spoke. No one moved for a second as she looked up

with unseeing eyes at Edward and then he gently lifted her up and into his arms to take her away from that horrible place.

He said not a word, but kissed her hot forehead as he carried her back up through the passageways of the dark prison, leaving curt orders behind them that none of the friars were to be again misused or abused on penalty of death until their case could be reviewed by a secular court. The King was determined, as he took the girl out into the sunlight, that he would see true justice done.

"My Lord," she muttered faintly and then closing her eyes, fainted in his arms. She seemed to be in a trancelike state and he feared that she had been hurt. He never should have let her do such an insane thing! He should never have allowed it! He swore an angry oath as he laid her down on his own cloak under a nearby tree and called for a page to bring some wine. At last she roused sufficiently to drink, and she opened her eyes. "I helped them, didn't I, Sire? I helped them . . ." She closed her eyes and drifted off again, a faint smile on her pale lips. He sighed aloud with relief and began issuing orders in preparation for their departure in a few hours. Then, after seeing that Bronwyn was carried to a nearby Inn to rest, he remounted and set off to visit the guilty Bishop. He would see this matter solved and then he would take Bronwyn back to London. There would be no burnings tomorrow. No one would have sport the next day at these good friars' expense. Though he himself felt little sympathy for their attitude, for Bronwyn's sake he would save them.

As the King rode away, he kept seeing her there moving among the brothers—her gentle smile. He was astounded at what she had done even though he had known she could heal . . . until now, he had never known the true power of her gift.

She had healed so many of them, and he had seen it with his own eyes. Yet, as he spurred his mount onward, there lingered a doubt, a budding fear that what he had begun with this girl was growing out of his control. He feared for her. He feared for what other people would say and do to her if her powers were common knowledge. With a grim smile upon his tight lips, he rode off to save the poor wretches in the dungeon from the flames, but his thoughts were on the girl. And they were uneasy thoughts. *The French, after all, had burned Joan of Arc . . .*

CHAPTER IX

"IF ONLY I didn't have to go again so soon, little one."

The King stood gazing at Bronwyn with a faraway look in his eyes. She could see that he was preoccupied. Since that morning when she had visited the friars in their cell, he had been unusually quiet. When he wasn't aware of it, she caught him staring at her as if she were a stranger. But she believed it was more than what had happened that morning, much more. There was something deeply bothering the King and she sensed that he was unsure how to broach the subject.

They had ridden back to the Tower with hardly a word said. Bronwyn had still felt weak after the episode in the prison and she had been exultant when the King had told her that the friars would not die the next morning; that he had given orders to set them free. The Bishop had been furious, of course; Edward was defying the Church's mandates in this matter, but he had stood firm, he told her later with a half-smile, and gotten clemency for them. They were to be exiled from Kent and warned never to show their faces again, on penalty of immediate death.

"For you, my little songbird, I did that . . . for what you did for them this morning and for what I feel for you.

God's blood, though," he swore, "they don't deserve it, fanatics that they are! Did you not see that they wanted to die? That they didn't care one way or another?" He shook his head in the fading sunlight as they rode leisurely towards London. "To care so little for one's life, as these Lollards do, it is beyond my understanding. I've seen men mortally wounded on the battlefield, bloody and beaten to a pulp who, though one might think death would be a welcome relief from their pain, held on tenaciously to the spark of life. Aye, and I've seen men beg shamelessly for their lives, as I've seen others fight like demons against unbelievable odds to ward off the approach of death. But these Lollards and their kind, I cannnot understand nor condone."

He looked over to where Bronwyn rode beside him, silently listening, her face still pale and drawn from her healing deep in the bowels of that filthy prison and then took her hand gently. He feared for her. He cared for her in a way he had never cared for anyone else. He had promised that he would permit nothing to hurt her again, and this morning had shaken him far more than he would ever reveal. "These men do not cherish the lives the good Lord gave them . . . and, little one," he whispered with serious eyes, "if not for you, I would have let them burn."

Bronwyn nodded, her face etched with weariness. "I owe Your Grace a great debt."

She meant it in all sincerity, and Edward smiled, attempting to appear his usual cheerful self. He replied in a light-hearted fashion that brought a faint answering smile to her lips, "Aye, a debt that I shall collect one day, you may be sure of it." His gaze was warm and Bronwyn felt herself blush.

Edward, weary in body and mind, had never been so glad to see the walls of the great Tower loom up before them as he was that evening.

Yes, Bronwyn was right. There was something on the

King's mind. All through their supper of roasted eel, sturgeon baked in a sweet sauce of cinnamon, raisins and ginger, and malmsey wine, the King watched her and at one moment, in the firelight from the blazing hearth behind them, she saw a look of sadness lingering on his handsome face. When the servants had finally left the room, she touched his hand, and looked him straight in the eye, waiting for him to speak. But rather than reveal his true thoughts, he said, " 'Tis the weight of my duties that bear me down so, my sweet. To keep my men paid and prepare for yet another scrimmage with Margaret d'Anjou I must needs call a special Council at Westminister to ask the lords for yet another loan, and even that will not be enough. So I must ask the Lord Mayor of London and some of his most affluent merchants for private funds, as well, for I dare not ask Parliament to levy yet another tax to equip another battle force. It seems that begging is all I have done since I ascended the throne."

"But . . ." She hesitated for a moment, then plunged ahead. "They do say that the Nevilles are wealthy beyond counting. Can you not depend on their aid in this matter?" She meant the Earl of Warwick, but she couldn't bring herself to mention his name, and the King marked that.

She had struck a raw nerve and the King scowled. "Oh, 'tis true the Nevilles are wealthy enough . . . as we Yorks were once wealthy. But, my naive little one, you have no conception of how much gold is needed to run a country and to wage its wars." He laughed bitterly as he stood up and came over to her. She looked up into his earnest face, the face of a very troubled young man—he couldn't be more than twenty or so. So much responsibility for one so young. "Ha! I am a King and yet I am a pauper. Damn that Lancaster witch and her daft husband! The Lancasters have drained the blood from our fair England and turned its King into a penniless beggar!" His countenance was stormy. "As for my Lord Warwick." He looked away from her so she wouldn't see the distress that consumed him over his cousin's straying loyalties. "It is true he would give me whatever I desire if I will be privy to his grand schemes. He wants me to marry King Louis's sister-in-law, Bona of Savoy, but such a marriage is abhorrent to me. France has been forever England's most hated and bitter enemy. That wily old Spider King must weave a finer web if he hopes to entangle me. Yet he already seems to have convinced my greedy cousin that he only desires peace. I, however am *not* convinced that there is not some deeper, more nefarious motive behind his actions. It would not surprise me to learn that he intends the English to fight his battles with Charles of Burgundy, since at this moment France has neither the money nor the men to fight himself, and the Burgundian has long been a thorn in his side. To my mind, Richard has become far too thick with that devious French King. I do not trust him. A French alliance would hardly prevent Louis from invading English lands should he so choose. I am not a prize to award to the highest bidder! I'll not be forced into marrying some plump, ugly Frenchwoman, someone I have not chosen myself. Warwick be damned, cousin or no! I will marry when and whom I please." His eyes flashed. "If Warwick wants a French match so badly, why, let him marry one of his brothers off to the woman! I'm sure John would agree to such a notion, as much as he *loves* the French." Bronwyn was sure by his sarcastic tone that his cousin's brother had as little affection for England's age-old enemy as Edward himself.

But she had heard gossip about the French King. "They say Louis loves his people, though . . . that he goes out among them to find out at first hand their needs and desires. Is that true, Your Grace?" she asked, fearing to let him see how his mention of a French marriage had upset her. For one brief moment she felt a terrible sense of loss and sorrow that she could never be his wife, never his equal. Their worlds were so far apart that one day some other lucky woman would love him and give him sons and stand beside him as he ruled England, not she. Never she.

She let her eyes roam over the remains of their splendid feast on the table before her. Once she would have been overjoyed just to have coarse-grained ravel bread baked of unbolted flour, or boiled cabbage and roasted turnips. Her eyes lingered on the golden plates they had eaten from and suddenly she wanted to both laugh and cry. One day she was a starving beggar, and now she dined with a King! In her wildest daydreams and fancies she never would have imagined such a thing. And now she fretted because she could never be a King's wife. Her lips trembled. No, she could not laugh, not when he smiled down at her with those brilliant blue eyes that seemed to read her very heart and soul, and laid a caressing hand upon her slender shoulder. *I am in love with him . . . in love with this great King!* The terrible truth made her want to weep because such a love was so hopeless. A sigh escaped her lips as Edward gently pulled her to her feet and encircled her with strong arms.

"Aye, I have heard that, too," he said. "In truth, I have him to thank for finding you, my sweet songbird. I was persuaded to follow his example and travel incognito among my subjects." He looked deeply into her wide green eyes with such tenderness that against her will and despite her common sense, her heart began to sing. What did it mattered if she could never be his wife? She loved him and she suddenly knew that it was as true and pure a love as she would ever know. No matter what he did or where their separate paths would lead, she would always love him from this day forth. He had won her heart completely.

He drew her yet closer to him, so close that she could lean her head against his broad chest and hear the wild beating of his heart. She had never been this close to a man . . . except for Warwick. Her body froze at the memory of that monster and she would have pushed Edward away in terror at that moment if it had not been for the soothing, gentle hands that stroked her hair and the soft voice that was asking, "What do they say of me, little one? What do my subjects say of Edward of York? Do they hate me or love me?" He was so earnest that it touched a part of her that she thought had died long ago. She, along with most of the common people, had learned to hate and fear all noblemen, Lancaster and York alike. The war between those two great houses had impoverished and beaten them all. The great lords not only slaughtered each other in their bloody feuding, but trampled the English people under their destriers' hooves as well. Queen Margaret promised her mercenaries and the lords who fought under her banner plunder in lieu of pay, and they had times without number these last years past cut a wide swath through England, slaughtering, pillaging and raping. If a town was unlucky enough to open its gates to the wrong army at the wrong time, its citizens were branded traitors by the other side and woe to them when the tide turned. Was it any wonder that they cursed York and Lancaster alike? The warring armies were like great, hungry plagues of locusts, destroying everything in their path. Soldiers must be billeted and fed, and so must the knights and lords who led them, and on whose shoulders did such burdens fall but those of the merchants and peoples of the towns and hamlets? They were sick of war, for no one paid more heavily, in the end, than they. A fleeting image of her poor father's broken body on the snowy ground rose to haunt her and her heart stopped a second. He had died because of York's hate for Lancaster.

But as she tilted her head up to meet Edward's inquiring gaze and answer his question, she also recalled what was being said in the streets and taverns of London about this great golden lion of a King . . . about the mercy he had often shown to the common soldier as well as to the common men . . . about his desire for peace in England, even if he must win it with a strong and bloody sword . . . how the people who had seen him upon his great warhorse claimed he looked like a young god come to save them. *Aye, those who had seen the young King did love him*.

"Well, what do my people say of me? Have you no answer?" he repeated.

His hand began to caress her back and his nearness as he held her set fires raging in her blood, yet gave her a sense of total peace and belonging. His arms seemed the sweetest place she had ever been. For the first time since she was a child upon her father's knee, she felt truly safe. And for the first time in her woman's life she felt truly alive . . . as if being with this man completed her and made her whole. Was this then what being in love was like, this bittersweet aching that engulfed her whole being? Yet she forced herself to concentrate and answer his question.

"Sire, those who have seen you upon the battlefield swear you are as courageous as a lion and those you have vanquished say you are merciful. The people pray that you will end this civil strife and bring peace. They want peace and a strong, fair King to lead them. That I know to be true," she whispered.

"I, too, want peace, finally and forever. England has been torn asunder long enough." When he spoke she could feel the heated sincerity of his beliefs and her heart ached for him. It would not be easy for him to raise England from her knees; it would cost him dearly. It might cost him his life. The Lancasters would sell their black souls to see his bloodied head upon a spike at Micklegate, where many of his kin had already been impaled. The thought of this man who held her in his arms dying such a wasteful, cruel death cut her like a knife and she clung to him as if he were already being dragged from her embrace.

Edward buried his face in her soft, gleaming hair so warm from the blazing fire. He was wise enough to know that as much as he wanted this woman in his arms, and as easily as he could have taken her, he must wait until she came to him for the love he so longed to give. He knew that love given freely was much the sweeter and he also strongly suspected that his brutal cousin had abused the girl in the woods that day, and that she had not yet fully recovered. He had to give her time. He had never had to be so patient with a woman before; on the contrary, he'd always had to fight them off. He kissed her back, almost overpowered by his desire for her. But he would wait. He had never felt this way before. When he was with her, he was happy for no other reason than that he could see her shy smile and hold her close. He looked at Bronwyn in the firelight and his hunger for her flared like quicksilver. They stood, slightly apart and breathless now, watching each other in the flickering light and there were no more words to say.

It was Bronwyn who made the first move. She smiled that strange half-childlike, half-womanly smile and her eyes were glowing as she reached up and caressed his cheek. Where her hand touched so lovingly, he felt fire. He cautiously took that hand in his and brought it to his lips and then drew her into his arms once again. She seemed to stiffen for just a second, so he paused and just held her closely, as closely as he could, his breath warm on her ear. For a long time they stood there locked in each other's arms, neither daring to move lest they break the spell their mutual desire had woven between them.

Then Edward pressed his warm lips to hers in a deep, lingering kiss full of urgency and longing, and this time she didn't stiffen or pull away but returned his kiss with gentle hunger. She encircled his neck with her arms and stretched up on her toes as he lifted her from the ground, cradling her in his arms, his heart racing so furiously that he could hardly breathe.

"Sweetheart. Sweetheart," he murmured as he carried her to the furs in front of the crackling fire and lowered her to their silkiness, dropping down beside her. She turned and gazed dreamily into his eyes as he put his arms around her again and drew her near. "I do not know why, little nightingale, but I do love you, love you so much it fairly bursts my heart. I cannot get enough of you, cannot touch or see your sweet smile enough to cure me of this ache." He placed her hand over his pounding heart. "From the moment I first saw you, I wanted—nay, *needed* you. Not your body alone, but your heart. Nothing less than that will I accept. I love you." He kissed her again and then, taking her braided hair into his hands, he carefully unbraided it and spread it loose and free about her shoulders as she continued to stare into his eyes, her expression both fearful and loving. "Your hair is so beautiful . . . like you, my love. Beautiful." He wrapped a long silken strand about his finger and used it to draw her toward him. He kissed her again. Her heart was beating crazily like the wing of a captured bird and he knew she was afraid.

Taking her face in his hands, he told her, "Do not be afraid of me. I will never hurt you, I have promised. If you wish, I will leave you . . ." His eyes reflected pain even as he said the words. His body cried out for release and fulfillment, yet he meant every word he spoke. She sensed it and, shaking her head, eyes wide and hands trembling, she drew him back to her.

He undressed her gently and then stood up to take off his tunic as she watched in fascination. She had never seen a man more beautiful to look upon than he. She gasped when she saw his manhood, large and swollen with need of her. Where Warwick had been hairy and chisled like stone, all sharp, hard angles, Edward was graceful and

267

smooth, yet strong, so strong she soon found, when he knelt next to her and pulled her into his embrace, his muscles rippling like silk-clad steel under her hands. He was like a great furred cat . . . golden fur across his broad chest and down his long, strongly muscled legs. And she soon found out he was nothing like Warwick. Nothing.

When he started to caress her full, naked breasts and then her waist and smooth thighs, he did so with a gentle and practiced touch as if he desired to give her as much pleasure as she was giving him. Soon, her fear and nervousness faded away and her body began to glow and yearn for his. He kissed her breasts as she shuddered, then ran his hands down her inner thighs and smiled when she trembled and closed her eyes, losing herself in the rapture of his touch.

When he finally entered her, careful not to hurt her, she moaned in ecstasy and clung to him as he moved. Slowly, with endless thrilling kisses that caused her to arch beneath him as her passion grew, he showed her what making love was meant to be.

So this is what it's supposed to be like, she thought giddily. This is what birds sing of and women talk of when they claim love is a hunger. This is what men fight for and crave so. This . . . treasure, this painful, aching ecstasy that is carnal love! It had been so different in the woods that day with that rutting beast, Warwick. Nothing like this. Where Warwick had been cruel and hurt her, had crushed her spirit and abused her body, this lovemaking brought her back to life. Her whole body glowed, pulsed with heat and she cried out with joy when he filled her. She wasn't ashamed or miserable. Her ecstasy mounted and she cried out with joy as he stroked her and murmured loving endearments. She returned his kisses with equal ardor, moving under him faster and faster, arching up to meet his powerful thrusts and still craving more . . .

more. He rode her, his eyes closed and the veins of his neck tensed in a frenzy that soon claimed her as well. *Faster, harder. Faster* . . . until, with a wild cry she exploded into a million little fragments of joy. It was as though her body had melted into his until she felt him shudder above her and, gasping, they finally collapsed in each other's arms, content yet frightened at the intensity and the sweetness of their union.

"*I love you! I love you, little green-eyed cat*! I never thought to find a love like this. I sometimes thought that I had loved but until you, I didn't know the meaning of it, the sweetness. I *need* you, Bronwyn, more than any woman I have ever known. *I need you*," he whispered and drew her tenderly against his naked body.

"*And I love you*," she replied, so softly that he felt the words rather than hearing them. He kissed the top of her head and covered them both with one of the furs, a large grey wolf skin that had been cured and rubbed into a supple softness.

Bronwyn never wanted to leave the haven of his arms. This was where she belonged, no matter what the future held in store. They were together now. It was all she could ask of life. Edward felt the same. Too often had he faced death on the battlefield and miraculously evaded it not to know the value of this perfect moment. He had her in his arms now, kissing her and laughing with her, and that was the only thing he cared about.

They curled up together after they had talked about trivial things that meant nothing except to lovers such as they, and as the embers of the fire sputtered and died, they fell asleep in each other's arms.

In the morning the streaming sunlight woke them and, their passion renewed, they made slow gentle love again.

They ate then still naked, bathed in the glow that

belongs only to lovers and they were happy. When Edward rose at last with a deep heartfelt sigh and began to dress, Bronwyn felt a great sadness.

"Do you have to depart now?" she asked.

"Aye, I have stayed too long already, little one," he said regretfully as he stood over her stroking her wild, tangled hair and bestowing tiny kisses on her upturned face. "My mother awaits me at Baynard Castle with messages from my brother George. He has been in York these last few weeks on the trail of Scottish rebels who are inciting rebellion up in Yorkshire. There is a chance I may have to travel there myself to bring reinforcements. I have tarried far too long. My brother's well-being may depend on my speed. So, beloved, do not forget me when I am gone. Keep your love for me strong in your heart until I return."

Fully dressed now, he buckled on his sword and dagger. Bronwyn feared that she would not see him again for some time, since after he had seen the Duchess of York, he would be off to join his forces with those of George, Duke of Clarence. There was a somber look in his eyes and a tension in his manner that told her he harbored the same fear.

"My mother sent word just this morning that she awaits me forthwith, for she is preparing even now to leave for Berkhampstead." Edward sheathed his sword and picked up his helmet, an expression of yearning on his handsome face as his eyes devoured her one more time. *As if he were never going to see me again,* she thought unhappily.

They had discussed the night before what she would do while he was gone. He had tried to warn her that he might be gone a long time, and had told her she could stay in her chambers in the Tower or visit her sisters and Martha at the inn. But no matter what she did or where she went, at all times she was to leave word with one of his men to where she was.

"I want to know where you can be found at any time of the day or night when I return, my dearest," he had said, punctuating his words with kisses. "I don't want to have to look for you, but have you close by so you will be back in my arms the sooner."

Edward was glad that the Earl of Warwick would be with him on this campaign. He would know where the man was every minute or, as he had sworn to her, he would never consider leaving her alone again. But with his cousin under his watchful eye, he would know she was safe. She had nothing to fear. She would be well guarded and provided for. He wanted to leave her money, but she would not take it. He merely shook his head and told her that he would leave a purse of gold in his squire's care if she should ever have need of it. One look at her stubbornly set chin told him clearly enough that she would not touch it, but he was adamant.

So he took his leave of her that bright April morning and she watched him from the courtyard as he climbed upon his white stallion and, with a grim look upon his face, set spurs to its snowy flanks. His retinue galloped behind him through the outer bailey, passed through the barbican and out of sight. It was a warm morning for early April and Bronwyn shaded her eyes as she watched the horses disappear from sight, straining her eyes for one last glimpse of the man she loved. She had no thought that morning save one: Would she ever see him again?

Then she went with heavy steps back into the Tower's shadow and after a while, made her way back up to the chambers where only a short time ago she had lain with her Kingly lover. It seemed suddenly like a misty but beautiful fleeting dream, not reality.

She smiled to herself as she touched the place where they had lain together the night before and made such sweet love. Already she missed him.

CHAPTER X

April 1464

BRONWYN PUSHED tendrils of hair back from her flushed face and continued to stir the thickening Gauncele sauce. It was *too* thick—probably too much flour and not enough milk. She splashed a little more milk into the heavy brass pot and then, with a tiny frown, tossed in another clove of garlic. There, that should just about do it.

Martha didn't like to see her working so hard, she well knew, but with Edward away so long, she couldn't bear to sit around like a fine court lady and do nothing while the days dragged by. Her chamber in the Tower was lonely indeed when he was not there. Over the past year during his many absences she had been drawn back to the warmth and friendliness of the inn. Since Molly had been sent away as soon as her involvement with Warwick in Bronwyn's abduction had been brought to light, the Red Boar was a safe retreat, a place where she could be herself with the other three people in the world that she loved, her sisters and Martha, who had become like a mother to them all.

In the last year Mary had blossomed into a healthy, plump eight-year-old, her illness only a memory; and Samantha at twelve had started showing hints of the beautiful woman she would become. Mary had become Martha's pet and Samantha was her right hand, and a fair cook as well, Martha swore often. Her sisters were healthy and happy and Bronwyn was happy for them as well. What a difference a year could make!

She wiped her hands on the coarse apron that covered her homespun gown. The gown was blue and made of wool frieze; not pretty to look upon, she had to admit, smiling as she lifted the finished gravy from the fire and set it aside to cool, but while she was at the inn she dressed like all the other girls who worked there. Though she refused to be treated any differently, it was common knowledge that she was the King's paramour (how she hated that word!) and the other girls regarded her with respect and a great deal of awe. She hated that part of loving Edward, that, and endlessly waiting for him, uncertain that he would return to her every time he rode away. Rumors were everywhere that soon there would be a major confrontation with Margaret and her Beaufort and Scottish allies . . . it was only a matter of time, they said.

It struck fear into Bronwyn's heart when she heard people talking of their King's prowess in battle as she shopped in the open marketplace. It was her lover they spoke of and she feared that one day she would hear that King Edward had been slain on some bloody battlefield in some God-forsaken place she had never heard of. She'd almost gotten to hate going to market, her basket on her arm, because of all the endless rumors and gossip about the King, Warwick and the Lancasters. There were reports of various armed scuffles in Bamburgh and then Carlisle and then, months later after a silence that was maddening, stories of scrimmages along the Scottish border. It seemed that all the malcontents in the north were flocking to muster below the accursed Lancaster banner. It was rumored, too, that the Scots were whole-heartedly backing Margaret d'Anjou and the former king, Henry, on promise

274

of an alliance to be brought about by a marriage between Margaret's twelve-year-old son and the Scottish Queen's young daughter.

So the long months dragged on and Bronwyn tried to pick up the threads of her old life. But it is never easy to pick up where one leaves off, especially when something has occurred that will change that person's life forever afterwards. Bronwyn went back to the inn because her sisters and Martha begged her to while the King was away. She lived in two different, conflicting worlds. Half the time she spent at the inn with her sisters, working when the worry and the waiting became unbearable; the rest of the time she stayed in her rooms in the Tower or rode the mare Edward had given her across its vast acreage. While she was there, she spoke to no one and no one spoke to her, with the exception of La Rouel, the old physician. It was as though she were invisible. And always, she was lonely for Edward. In her rooms and out on those acres within the inner bailey of the fortress she felt closer to him when he was gone, yet always that very loneliness would drive her back to the inn.

Edward had been gone for nearly three months. There were many moments when Bronwyn thought that everything that had happened between them was all just a fantasy; that their love was a dream. Then she would go back to visit La Rouel at the Tower, and being back in the place where she and Edward had first found love, the truth would come flooding back. It was the old physician who listened to her doubts and her worries for the future. She came to trust the old man and he, her. As he had suggested, she became his apprentice and eagerly learned all he had to teach her about the healing arts. He had seen much in his long life and had studied with the most famous surgeons in France. On a lovely spring night, as they went to visit one of his patients who had become quite fond of the girl he had begun to refer to as his daughter, he told her that as a young man he had traveled with the old Duke of York's army as their surgeon during battles, but sitting a horse for days on end and sleeping on the hard ground under leaky tents was far too taxing on his brittle old bones.

After they had left his patient's house that night and headed back to the inn where she was staying at the time, he continued, "That was when I was in my prime, my child. My surgical skills were well respected. But now . . ." he stared down in the twilight at his old gnarled hands lightly holding the reins of the horse he rode, "these old hands tremble and refuse to do what I tell them to do. 'Tis a pity I never had a son to carry on after me. All I have is you, daughter. All I have is you." His words touched her heart. She had grown very fond of the old man. La Rouel, she had discovered, was a very lonely man. His wife had died years ago and they had never had any children. The old Duke of York, Edward's dead father, had been like a son to him, and he regarded Edward and his brothers almost like his grandchildren. It was La Rouel who satisfied Bronwyn's curiosity about the King and his family. She asked him once about how Edward's brother, Edmund, and his father, the late Duke of York had met their deaths, and he had told her about that bitter December of 1460 when the doomed Edmund, Earl of Rutland, Edward's third brother, had been ambushed outside Sandal Castle by the vicious Lancasters, and at only seventeen years of age, been run through with a Lancastrian sword as he stood bound and defenseless. La Rouel also related how after the battle of Wakefield Green, Queen Margaret and Henry Beaufort, Lord Somerset—who thanks be to God, resided in hell—had ordered the execution of the Earl of Salisbury, Warwick's father, and had commanded that his son, Thomas Neville, be beheaded and his head, along with that of the Duke of York who had been killed on the battlefield that day, be placed on spikes atop Micklegate Bar in York City for all to see.

"Neither Edward nor his mighty cousin Richard, Earl of Warwick, has forgiven the Frenchwoman—nor forgotten," La Rouel said. "When the King rode into York after the Lancastrian forces had fled to free John Neville, Warwick's other brother, they do say he nearly went wild with grief and fury at the pitiful sight of those two heads rotting upon those spikes."

Bronwyn shuddered. "No wonder the King hates them so," she murmured.

La Rouel became her only friend at the Tower. Under his guidance she learned things that no woman before her had been allowed to do. Her healing gift was useful to him, though he never abused her ability, having learned its limitations as she had long ago. Her gift was not always at her command. When her ability deserted her, his knowledge and experience or her familiarity with medicinal herbs and treatments took over. La Rouel accepted her just as she was, a woman with a unique gift, a caring heart, and an alert, questioning mind, whose strong, steady hands could often do what his trembling ones no longer could. He had found a jewel and he knew it. By no means did she have a faint, womanish heart and he admired that. *Oh, if only she had been born a man*, he wished so many, many times as he watched her with the sick. What he wouldn't have given to have had such an assistant years ago! A pity she was but a woman. But it made little difference, after all, he decided . . .

Bronwyn turned when Martha came bustling in, her arms loaded down with fresh linen she had just dried outside after scrubbing them clean in a wooden trough filled with a solution of wood ashes and caustic soda. Her eyes were sparkling as she dumped her burden on the end of the trestle table. Bronwyn knew immediately that there was something the older woman had to tell her. Her heart started to thump and before Martha could mutter a word, Bronwyn let out a little excited cry and ran past her out the door and into the courtyard. *Edward*! She had heard neighing and clattering on the cobblestones and she knew it must be someone with a message from her lover. After all these months, she had sometimes doubted that he would send for her once he had come back to London. His troops had been straggling home for days now, she knew, because of the soldiers and archers who had been steadily filtering into the inn and the tales they had to relate. She had been on tenterhooks for days . . . If only it was a message for her from the King!

The courier was one of the body squires that attended Edward. He recognized Bronwyn on sight. He had reined up a hard-breathing palfrey caparisoned in the York colors of murrey and blue, and on the man's doublet was a badge that sported the falcon with a fetterlock and the white rose. He jumped from the horse's back to the ground and Bronwyn ran to meet him with a radiant smile.

"Mistress, His Majesty has sent me to fetch you—if you would come?" He was a frail looking lad with very long black hair and sad black eyes. Though young, he was trustworthy and he knew of Edward's affection for this beautiful peasant. He didn't seem to condemn her for loving the King, and every time they had met, he was as polite as if she were a high-born lady.

Bronwyn's face was wreathed in delighted smiles and she clapped her hands in glee. Then those same hands flew to her dirty face and she gasped, "*Now*? This minute?" Her face—her hair—her clothes!

The squire's name was James and he took in the girl's predicament at a glance, saying, "Nay, mistress. I shall wait until you change your gown." He took his mount's reins and after checking the palfrey's lathered flanks and running a practiced hand down his wet legs to check them after the hard run, he led the horse around to the water trough on the other side of the courtyard. As Bronwyn spun on her toes and started to run back to the inn, she heard James call after her, "But make haste. My master impatiently awaits us. He bade me return with all speed."

Bronwyn nodded happily and continued into the Inn still at top speed. From across the courtyard, James watched her disappear inside. A handsome wench, to be sure, not a common doxy. It was strange, though, the rumors he had heard about her. He was frowning as he checked his mount's girth and then stirrups. They said she was a witch, that she cast evil spells . . . how ridiculous! he thought, as he went in search of the maid's mare. Harry, the stableman, was nowhere in sight. But James knew which stall the little mare was kept in.

With a baffled sigh, he ordered a stable boy to saddle the mare and had it brought out to where his own mount was tethered. James shadowed his eyes and peered up at the clouded sky. He could smell rain coming. Soon there would be a real downpour and it would be nice to be in the warmth of the Tower's garrison before a blazing fire, drinking ale with that buxom little serving maid, Mary, on his arm. He gazed impatiently at the door to the inn. Nay, he couldn't believe what they were saying of Bronwyn, that she was a witch and a sorceress. She seemed so *good*, pure and sweet, with always a kind word for him. Yet the rumors were gathering strength and viciousness. There were those who did swear they saw her in the forest at night consorting with the wood spirits, and those who said they had seen her casting spells and sacrificing small animals to the Devil. Some said she had made a pact with Satan himself so the King would love her. He tied her mount next to his and then, shrugging off these unwelcome thoughts, he patted his palfrey lovingly and strode with brisk steps to the inn. Suddenly he was very thirsty and he was sure he could coax the Innkeeper's wife into giving him a tankard of ale. She always did if he asked her sweetly enough . . .

Bronwyn was up in the loft, putting the finishing touches on her appearance. She had scrubbed her face and hands and was glad she had taken her weekly bath just the night before. She had hurriedly slipped on one of the few gowns she had permitted Edward to bestow upon her. It was his favorite, a light blue gown with a tight-fitting blue cotte and a gold-bordered surcoat that Edward had given her the last time they had been together. She had not worn it since. Her fingers trembled as she twisted her thick hair into a roll at the nape of her neck and worked a gold filigree caul around it, tucking in any stray hairs with trembling fingers. When she had finished, she stood staring into the steel mirror above her little washing stand. It had been so long since she had last seen Edward! And she wanted to look absolutely beautiful for the man she loved. The woman who gazed back at her from the mirror smiled hesitantly, her expression full of love. Her eyes were nice, Bronwyn thought. But perhaps her nose could have been a little longer . . . She almost laughed at her foolishness, but she couldn't help it. She was on her way to see Edward! Edward whom she had missed so sorely, Edward whom she dreamed of and thought of constantly . . . Edward whom she adored. She grabbed her old cloak and threw it about her shoulders, and ran down the steps, laughing when she saw James openly charming Martha and a rapt Samantha. Bronwyn couldn't help but notice how her sister was staring at James. There was a lovelorn look in her pretty blue eyes that belied her tender age. Yet she was almost thirteen. Bronwyn would have thought her far too young to fall in love, but Samantha had always seemed older than her age, as Bronwyn had always been; and hadn't she herself been just thirteen when their father's murder had forced her to fend for all three of them?

Bronwyn walked over to James and he bowed to her, open admiration in his eyes. Bronwyn saw a look of jealousy flicker ever so briefly in her sister's eyes, and the glance of exasperation Martha threw at her. Bronwyn put her arms about Samantha and whispered something in her ear that made the girl smile and steal a glance at James under her thick lashes.

James held his arm out for Bronwyn. "Come, mistress . . . we are waited upon, and it grows late. I fear a storm may be brewing." After thanking both Martha and Samantha for their hospitality, he ushered Bronwyn out into the courtyard where their horses were pawing restlessly.

As James helped Bronwyn into her saddle and then leaped into his own, he didn't notice the young blond girl watching him from the doorway, a tender expression on her pretty face. He was only concerned with prodding their mounts out into the street and on their way.

Bronwyn had become a proficient rider over the last year and as she rode at a brisk canter behind James, she sat up sure and straight in the saddle, her hands firm but light on the reins. The overcast sky had cleared somewhat, and many people were out enjoying the mild April evening. Bronwyn watched them all milling about her and wondered where this one or that one was heading. Ah, that young couple strolling there before the chandler's shop . . . they acted as if they were in love, she mused. A group of archers, their bows slung across their backs, were heading for the tavern at the corner, laughing and singing war songs. She saw drovers and peasant farmers in their homespun tunics and chausses, in town for their weekly pleasures away from the fields. Merchants were hawking their wares in stalls along the street and artisans were displaying their crafts. Weavers unrolled bolts of their finest cloths for their customers to view, and apprentices were hurrying to their masters' shops before they were found missing and boxed about the ears. And there were soldiers everywhere, all of them dressed in York murrey and blue or Neville crimson. The troops were home with their King, she thought happily. Edward! In a short while she would be in his arms! Would any of these heedless passersby believe it if they were told that the girl who rode so rapidly through the narrow cobbled streets was the beloved of their King?

James helped her down once they had passed into the Tower's inner bailey and escorted her to the door of the King's apartments where he took leave of her with a gallant bow. She paused for a moment, unsure of what she was supposed to do once she heard voices behind the door. Apparently Edward wasn't alone. She bit her lip and then, taking her courage in her trembling hands, she knocked on the chamber door ever so softly. When no one answered, she knocked again a little louder. It took her breath away when the door was thrown wide open and she stood facing the King himself. Their eyes met and before his face lit up with delight at seeing her, she saw intense weariness and impatience mirrored in his bright blue eyes—but just for a brief moment. And then he rushed forward with a brilliant smile to embrace her in his strong arms.

"My little songbird! How I missed you! I have thought of you constantly, these long weeks and months!" He spun her around and laughed like a lad before he set her down and held her at arm's length, devouring her with his eyes. "God's truth, my love, you are more beautiful each time I see you!"

Bronwyn was about to reply, when she saw two gentlemen standing behind the King.

Edward took her hand and pulled her into his chamber where a multitude of candles and wick lamps made it seem as bright as day, though the sun was beginning to set. A table was set before the hearth and a lavish dinner had been prepared. It looked as if they were all getting ready to sit down to eat. Bronwyn had interrupted their meal and she felt like an intruder. She blushed and held back, but Edward laughed and set her in front of him facing the other two men, his hands firm on her shoulders. "Dickon, George . . . this is the woman I've told you about. One of the two nodded his head while the other, a boy of about thirteen or so, studied her with much interest. "This is Bronwyn Rouet," Edward said softly, as he encircled her waist with his arms and then placed a kiss upon the top of her head. "You look so lovely, my sweet," he whispered in her ear as a brief glance passed between the other two.

"Bronwyn, this is my brother, George, Duke of Clarence . . . and this is my youngest brother, Richard, Duke of Gloucester—Dickon," Edward said of the younger boy with the dark, straight hair and the thin, brooding face. He was willow thin, and his coloring the exact opposite of his two brothers. His eyes were also a much deeper blue, almost blue-black, and when he reached out to take her hand and kiss it as she curtsied, he grinned down at her like a child. It was then that his whole face and manner changed. His smile brightened his serious face and his eyes twinkled. "My lady, this is a pleasure. Ned has told us so much about you." In his friendly eyes she saw acceptance and humor. So this was the Dickon that Edward had spoken of, the brother that he so loved, the one who was to be a great warrior someday.

The other brother, as she turned to him and curtsied, also kissed her hand, but his lips were cool and quickly taken away. When she looked up into his insolent blue eyes, almost the exact shade as Edward's, she almost gasped at how like the King he was—tall, with blond hair the color of ripe wheat. But she also noticed, that he had sauntered up to her and kissed her hand mockingly. He cocked a blond eyebrow and looked over at Edward with a jaded grin. "Dear Ned, she's far more ravishing than you led us to believe!" Then he turned his gaze back to Bronwyn. "It's true, he did rave on and on about how good and kind you are, but nary a word of your great beauty." The blue eyes so like Edward's flashed at her. Yet they were not really like Edward's, for Bronwyn glimpsed a touch of envy and malice in their beautiful depths before he looked away from her and laughed affectedly.

Bronwyn was usually a good judge of character, and this man, she sensed, was not what he seemed. Though he smiled and chatted with her about her life before she had met Edward and though he was completely polite and attentive, she knew he didn't like her. After they were all seated at the table, he continued to inspect her, his eyes hungry, and she felt decidedly uncomfortable. She remembered what Edward had said about the Duke of Clarence—that he was a real charmer, a ladies' man. Once Edward had laughingly called him a peacock. Though Edward loved both of his brothers, she could see why he favored the younger.

"We must teach you how to play chess, sweeting," Edward said later after they had eaten. "Dickon here plays a good game already though he's but a lad."

"Aye, Ned, but I am far better at tables or hazard," Richard retorted, his whole face alive with open admiration for his older brother.

"I prefer Merelles to them both," George added and stifled a yawn.

Though they had spoken of unimportant topics all evening, there was a definite undertone of strain and Bronwyn wondered why. After the servants had cleared away the food, poured the wine and then departed she realized just how weary the King was. Edward lounged against the mantel, and now the subject changed to the coming battle with the Lancastrians and the Scots. He had given command of one of his armies to his most able commander aside from the Earl of Warwick, Warwick's younger brother John Neville, Duke of Bedford. At that very moment Bedford's knights and men were marching toward Hexham to rout the growing forces gathering under King Henry and Queen Margaret; Edward himself and George were preparing to leave within the next day or so for York with their men and those of the Earl of Warwicks.

At the mention of Warwick's name, Bronwyn cringed inside and Edward turned a gentle look upon her frightened face and, knowing what she was thinking, laid a soothing hand upon her shoulder. *It will be all right*, his eyes seemed to say silently. But it wasn't only the mention of the hated name that upset her but also the fact that Edward was leaving again so soon.

"Ned?" It was Richard. "What chance do we have against the Lancasters? It is said that she has gathered a large army including a host of Scottish mercenaries. You know the Scots are ferocious and deadly in battle. They give no quarter and our men know that only too well." Richard's eyes were troubled. He was worried for Edward too. He had begged Edward to allow him to fight at his side, but Edward had steadfastly refused. He was to stay behind with their mother. It galled the boy that he must be left to wait and worry with the women. As for George, it was common knowledge that he preferred to leave the actual fighting to his older brother and their cousin Warwick. His victories were won in the bed chamber under the sheets.

"I believe we will trounce them smartly." Edward slapped his hand down heavily upon the mantel and his tone was positive. "If it is God's will that I keep this crown he has given me, we will win. And the Lancastrian forces are divided as always in their loyalties. They have their weak links. Margaret's English knights hate their Scottish allies almost as much as they hate the house of York. Need I say more? And time is on our side . . . they do say that Henry is out of his head again and must be kept in his chambers and chained to his bed at night or he would wander about like a child, empty of mind. He seems to care only about his daily prayers. He desires to be left alone, poor wretch." Edward shook his head. He felt great pity for this pious yet deranged man. "But, it is not daft Harry we will face, but Queen Margaret, the Duke of Somerset and the Beaufort clan . . . and the Scots." He drummed his fingers against the stone. "They are a force to be reckoned with even with Warwick and the Nevilles behind us. We are outnumbered in men and mounts," he declared anxiously. He strolled over to where George was standing. Bored with the whole subject, he was fussing with the tawny velvet of his slashed sleeves. His doublet was also of tawny velvet and jewel-studdied in the latest, most extravagant fashion. To Bronwyn's eyes he himself sparkled like a large gaudy jewel, so beautiful, yet so shallow. How different the three brothers were, she thought, and yawned surreptitiously into her hand so Edward would not see how tired she was. He was so busy discussing military stategy that he seemed to have totally forgotten her existence as she sat quietly by. These men were so far above her, so unlike her or anyone she had ever known; their world both fascinated and repelled her. Politics and battles, titles and wealth were something the poor had little time to consider while they were desperately trying to find food for their empty bellies or coins to pay the high taxes, coins that they would not have if their crops failed or their produce didn't sell in the market. To Bronwyn, these three noble lords were like three gods deciding the fate of mere mortals. It excited yet awed her at the same time. In spite of her absorption, she yawned again. She had risen at dawn and helped Martha make lye soap most of the morning. She stared at her reddened, work-roughened hands and felt the weariness seep deep into her bones. The chair she sat in was soft and she had to keep fighting off sleep. What would Edward think if she were to fall asleep the first night they were together after all these months apart?

She came to with a start at the sound of Warwick's name.

"True, Lord Warwick does strike fear into our enemies' hearts. I think the French witch does hate him far more than she hates me." Edward was chuckling, but when he saw the look in Bronwyn's eyes, he strode over to her and took her cold hands in his warm ones, cursing himself for talking about the man she so hated in her hearing.

The Duke of Clarence roused himself at that moment. "Yet, brother, I fear the outcome of this battle. I am heartily sick of Margaret and her stinking traitor following. Why can they not just accept you as England's rightful King and have done with it? The people are learning to love you, Ned, and no one wants that crazy monk back on the throne . . . why, he cannot find the privy by himself, much less rule a country! Why this endless bloodletting for a crown that will never rest firmly on that idiot's head? Don't they know how badly the people crave peace? Damn those dog Lancasters and their endless plotting and scheming! Damn them all to hell!"

His vehemence stunned Bronwyn. She would never have thought by his previous languid manner that he had any strong feelings one way or the other.

That his older brother and Warwick could keep the crown firmly on Edward's fair head, George had no doubt, but he felt some expression of loyal concern was expected. He was perfectly willing to leave it all in their capable hands. Ned could handle it. Ned could handle anything, George thought.

"Why?" Edward repeated. "For Margaret's son, Edward. That's why she perseveres! It isn't Holy Harry she seeks to put on the throne, but his young son. She's a lioness fighting for her cub; that's why she is so ruthless and merciless. She would sell her soul to win the throne for him by offering her armies the only payment she can give . . . and the booty, she has no trouble raising fresh troops. And they are like devils when they smell plunder to be had right under their very boots, unlike our men who must wait for their pay."

Bronwyn saw disgust cloud George's handsome face. He loathed bloodshed and the deadly gleam of polished steel, the stench of human carrion rotting on the bloody battlefield. He looked upon Dickon's eager, yearning face and Edward's hard one with incredulous eyes. He wondered again how he came to be their brother. They were born to be warriors, not he. Never he.

Then George said something that stung Bronwyn to the very marrow of her bones. He had been casting sidelong glances at her all night and now he looked directly at her and said, "If it's victory we crave so much, why not just ask your little witch to cast a spell? Mayhap her magic can overcome the Lancastrians. I'm sure she has the power to tell us what the future holds. What say you, little witch? Can you conjure up a great victory? I daresay we shall need either a miracle to win over the forces of Lancaster, or a spell to keep them from raising their weapons! Weave us a great magic to protect our soldiers! According to Edward there seems nothing you cannot accomplish, once you set your mind to it!" His voice was sweet, yet sharp, like a dagger dipped in honey.

Richard was smiling, shrugging off his brother's strange sense of humor, for which he was well known. But Edward turned red of face and his eyes were angry as they glowered at George.

Bronwyn had gone completely white. Her heart was in

her throat. What had the King said of her that the Duke of Clarence should jibe at her so?

"My lord . . . She finally broke the heavy silence that had fallen, addressing the Duke herself. He had directed his query to her, after all. "I am *not* a witch. I can neither foresee the future nor change what is to happen. Only God has that power, my lord." She had lowered her eyes and spoke humbly, though she trembled inwardly.

"What a pity! You do not read tea leaves or palms?" She shook her head, trying to smile but having a difficult time of it. He was purposely goading and teasing her. " 'Tis a shame. I had looked forward to a little entertainment after our long journey." He sighed elaborately, refilling his wine cup with malmsey. "Then what is it that you do that is so unusual? What are those powers you possess of which my brother had told me?"

"I am a healer. I aid the sick. I know the properties of herbs and I have a soothing way with those in pain . . ." Her voice trailed off softly. What use was it to explain to one such as the Duke of Clarence? It was easy to see that she was only boring him.

Edward came to her rescue. "What Bronwyn says is true. It is He who will give us a victory over the Lancasters, George, and none other. Now, it is very late. I hadn't thought to keep you both so long tonight. Accept my apologies . . . it has been a long week, and I am anxious to lay my weary body down upon a featherbed this night. Sleeping on the hard, cold ground or on the Abbeys' lumpy beds has done little for my disposition. Since tomorrow we must prepare to march, I think it's best if we part now." Edward came over to Bronwyn and reached for her hand. Richard slung on his cloak with a flourish and strapped his sword back on. He was so young, Bronwyn thought, watching him. So young to carry a sword and yearn for battles to fight! But he was the King's brother and thus no ordinary lad.

The Duke of Clarence had hastily swallowed another cup of malmsey and when he stood up, he wobbled ever so slightly.

"Ha, brother, you cannot fool me!" George winked slyly at Edward. "I know why you are thrusting us into the night." His hot eyes raked Bronwyn's body. "I, too, would want to be alone with such a wench if she were to warm my bed this night."

Bronwyn flushed with anger and humiliation, wishing she could slap his handsome face, but he was Edward's brother, and drunk as well. So she said nothing though her heart turned cold with shame. What he said and thought was true. She was the King's paramour, his harlot, his mistress. No matter how much they loved each other, she was only that and nothing more. The shame was something she must be prepared to deal with. She had brought it upon herself.

Edward's expression was grim, but sent George out the door with a brotherly pat on the back and warmly hugged his younger brother.

Only when they were gone, and Edward and she were alone, did his face brighten as he turned to smile down at her. But he still looked exhausted. Immediately she ran to him and threw her arms around him. Against her shining hair, he muttered, "Do not mind my brother George's waspish tongue, my sweet. It is his way. I cannot account for it, nor can any of us. He is a coward and a boastful fool at times, especially when he is in his cups, which is more often than not of late. He loves wine, wenches and fine clothes far more than a coat of mail. But he is my brother, for all his faults, and he means no harm by his loose words. Will you forgive his sharp tongue for my sake?"

"For you, my love, would I forgive anything." She smiled, her cheek against his chest, so happy was she to have him back in her arms. There would come a time when she could no longer hold him thus, and that bitter truth softened her heart to his every whim.

"I truly like your youngest brother, Richard. He seems a pleasant youth. But he is so young to crave going to war," she added wistfully.

"He wants only to please me. He cannot wait until he is allowed to ride into battle at my side. He longs to protect me from a Lancaster's deadly blade and that he cannot do unless he is with me. But for my part, I would keep him a child as long as I can. I have not forgotten the tragic death of my other brother, Edmund. I do fear for Dickon. Loyal and fearless as he is, he will probably set himself right between me and another's sword, given the chance. George . . ." as he spoke he was loosening and setting her hair free of the caul "will take care of his own precious skin well enough, I daresay."

Then he crushed her to him and kissed her until, breathless, she gasped for him to stop. "Give me air before I faint, Sire!" she laughed. He picked her up then and carried her to the great bed and threw her onto its softness. He closed the velvet curtains around it, creating their own private world, then lay down next to her and held her close.

"God's blood! How I've missed you, my little sweeting!" he whispered as he undressed her, savoring every second.

"And I you," She tried to see his expression, but it was too dark. Instead she cupped his face in her hands and brought his lips down to her lips in the shadows.

He continued to caress her body in intimate places, stroking and fondling her, and suddenly his need and hers were so urgent that in moments he was moving into her and she was clinging to his strong body as if she would never let go. She rained kisses on his face, his neck, his shoulders and chest and moved her hips under him to match his deep thrusts. Making love with Edward seemed so natural that the shame that had assailed her before melted completely away. She loved this man and could deny him nothing, especially not her body. Herself and her love were all she had to offer and she yielded to him fully and with a singing heart.

When it was over and they lay entwined together, satisfied and content, he felt tears coursing down her cheeks. "Have I hurt you, then?" he murmured. "Oh, my sweet, please forgive me if I was too abrupt with you. But I couldn't restrain myself. I've wanted you so these last terrible weeks and my desires couldn't wait." He wiped away her tears and held her close, his face buried between her breasts.

"Is is not that, my love," she exclaimed and held him tighter. "You have *never* hurt me! It's just that I am sad it must all end so soon . . . you are leaving again tomorrow. I'm frightened that you may never return . . ."

"Alive?" He finished the thought for her in a dry voice. She could hear his heart beating faster. So he was afraid, too? Even Kings were afraid to die.

He pulled open one of the heavy curtains and the moonlight from the high oriel windows shimmered through and spread its pearly glow over her lovely, troubled face and silken body. He stroked her soft thigh and cupped her full breasts. How she delighted him! She gave him all her love and never asked for anything in return unlike the other women he had brought to his bed. They demanded jewels and furs and privileges. He had grown so weary of them all, yet he was not the kind of man to go for long without a woman in his bed. He had seen too many men die not to know how precious were life's fleeting pleasures. But the joy he knew with Bronwyn was far from fleeting. It filled his heart and soul, lingering even when they were apart. She was the one person in the world whom he loved and trusted completely. Yet there were those whom he had once trusted and loved who were even now trying to betray him, those who would betray him for their own greedy gain. Of all of them, his cousin Warwick was the one he most feared and the one he had loved best . . . No, he would not think on it tonight. He would not torment himself, as he had done so much these last few months, with the fear that he might one day be forced to brand him a traitor and send him to the ax. He prayed every night that he would never have to do that. He had once loved Warwick as he had loved his own dear father. God help him!

He had touched Bronwyn's cheek in the moonlight then, his heart and mind suddenly so heavy that all he wanted was to drown in her love and forget everything else.

"My little songbird, do not worry about me. Nothing will happen to me. Don't they say I am the luckiest man on earth? All I want is to be a good King and to bring peace to our land . . . surely God will support me in that and protect me." He would have added, but did not, that he had no choice but to do what he had to do. His life meant little compared to the welfare of England. His destiny was clear. Too many good men had died to help him achieve his crown and too many looked to him for protection. He would gladly lay down his life if necessary. Yet he was afraid of dying. Only fools pretended they had no fear.

"My Lord, God is with you, I'm sure. But still I fear for you this time more than ever before. Now that I love you so deeply, I'm afraid you will be taken away from me." *Like her parents. Like everyone she had ever cared for. Even Samantha and Mary were gone in a way. They didn't need her. They were happier at the inn with Martha than she had ever seen them.* "I dread seeing you ride away tomorrow, my sweet lord. I wish I could go with you . . ." she moaned, pressing close to him. Her heart pounded

293

and she considered her words carefully before she spoke. "Sire? Could I? Perhaps, this one time . . . could I come with you?"

He started to shake his head, but she went on in an excited whisper. "I am free, you know. My sisters no longer need me. I belong to no one save you. And La Rouel has taught me so much—why, I could assist the surgeons! I am a healer and, you cannot say I would be of no use after the battle . . ." She was sitting up now, her hands lightly resting on his shoulders as he lay beneath her. He could see the hopeful smile spreading across her face, heard the yearning in her voice. "I can help!"

He was about to refuse, and then something fell into place in his mind and he lay gazing at her in the moonlight. She was right—there was no father or brother or husband to prevent her from going with him. She could be useful with her special skills and most important . . . Christ, how he wanted her with him, now of all times! If ever he needed a talisman—a Merlin—it was now. Yet how could he subject the woman he loved to the discomfort and rigors of war? They both knew that if he had been gone three months this time, the next time he would be away just as long or longer. One night together and then months until they could be together again . . . He peered at her loving face misted by moonlight and could not bear the thought that he might not see her again for months.

"Are you sure?" he said softly. Perhaps she had only said it to show him how much she loved him and would do for him, not thinking he would take her seriously . . .

"Yes, my love, I am sure," she whispered, sinking down next to him and wrapping her slender arms around his neck. "Wherever you go, so shall I follow! Always. I promise I will not hinder you in any way! I shall wear the plainest clothes and ride back with the other women or with the supply carts, and I shall not bother you unless you summon me or need my services. Just to be near you, I would do anything!'' If only she had thought of this before! All these months of idle, useless, lonely waiting would never have had to be. Then she stopped herself. No, these lonely months had not all been wasted, for La Rouel had taught her the skills that would enable her to care for wounded men after battle. So it had not been in vain after all.

"Little one, it might be possible." He spoke hesitantly, thinking the whole while. "You *could* be of help . . ." He paused, then continued, "If—*if*, mind you, I were to bring you with me, I would not allow you to ride with the camp followers. They are whores that follow after my army like stray dogs begging for bones after the meal is done; you could not stay with them. My men would fight to buy your favors—or take them. Nay, there must be a better way . . ."

"What way, my lord?" she asked softly. She would gladly have done anything he suggested if only she were allowed to go with him. She could hardly grasp it. It was like a dream come true.

"When I rescued you from Warwick, you were dressed in men's clothing, your hair tied back. You looked like a lad, sure enough—an awfully pretty one, yet a lad all the same. If I hadn't known who you were, I would have been fooled." He stroked her warm naked, shoulder and ran his hand over one taut nipple, then leaned towards her in the dark and set a kiss upon her parted lips.

She would have preferred not to remember that time or the beast who had abused her, yet she instantly understood what Edward meant. "It was a good disguise, at that." She shivered, for time had not dulled her pain or humiliation. She didn't think a lifetime would erase it. "I could dress as a boy again . . .

"Aye! You could be my page, and an apprentice to one of the surgeons." Edward laid his head upon her breast and suddenly laughed aloud. "Ye gods, what a joke on the others! A beautiful woman riding with me and no one but I the wiser!''

"And I have been practicing not only my healing arts, Sire, but my riding. I can ride as well as any man! '' she blurted out proudly. It would not be easy, pretending to be a boy, but she could do it if it meant being with Edward.

"I warn you of one thing, though, my love." His tone had become grave and he closed steel fingers about her bare arms. For a moment she saw the intense glitter of his eyes in the moon's light. "You must not speak to anyone. Pretend to be mute if you need to. Talk to no one but me and the doctor—I will take him into my confidence. And when we come to arms against the Scots you must promise me you will stay out of sight and far away from the fighting. Promise me that you will do what I tell you, and if anything should happen to me . . '' her heart almost stopped at the thought ''. . . you must flee! Run as far and as fast as you can. I will make sure you have money and a horse. It is my only fear in taking you along. Do you promise me that you will *not linger, nor try to find me* if we are beaten and I am slain? Promise me on the love you bear me that you will return here forthwith!'' He forced her head back to stare into her wide eyes and would not release her until she promised.

If something were to happen to him, Bronwyn thought, nothing else would matter. Without him her life would be empty, meaningless. She might as well be dead if he died. She couldn't remember what her life had been like before she had loved him and she couldn't conceive of what it would become if she lost him. Some day she would be forced to lose him to another woman, a princess or a noble-woman, and she was prepared for that. But if death claimed him, she would not want to live.

"Then it is settled.'' He let a great sigh escape him as he sank down on the soft feather pillows. Bronwyn knew how tired he was and she snuggled down next to him, savoring his nearness after so many months alone. "I'll find suitable clothes in the morning, something loose and drab to conceal your charms, my lovely. Though I daresay it shan't be as easy to disguise them as last year when you were but a scarecrow-thin waif. You have filled out nicely. You will make a pretty lad—mayhap too pretty! I shall have to guard you well to make sure no one discovers your true identity." He found her waiting lips and tired as he was, the months of wanting her stirred him again. Yet even as they kissed, he was reminded that there was another marching with him tomorrow who might see through her disguise—Warwick. He thought it best that he not mention that right now. He resolutely banished the thought of Warwick from his mind, and his hunger for Bronwyn flared anew. Soon they were making love again, but this time he was tender and brought her to her pleasure first before he took his own and then he slept in her arms, sated and content.

Long after he fell asleep, Bronwyn lay in his embrace, her thoughts darting this way and that, remembering the last time she had worn men's clothing, remembering Warwick and the smell of blood fresh on a drawn sword. She shivered in his arms and convinced herself that what she was doing was right. The King needed her. And yet she feared it was her own stubbornness that had worn him down at last, and that her presence on the battlefield might prove distracting, even dangerous to the man she loved so dearly. At last she too slept, knowing that nothing on this earth would keep her from his side.

The next morning dawned black and stormy above the companies of knights and archers and the heavily laden supply wagons that mustered in the Tower's grounds. There were thousands or more, Bronwyn calculated, scanning them with wide eyes as she sat astride her horse waiting like the others for the command that would send them surging out of the gates on their way to battle. More thousands would join as they marched through the towns and hamlets towards York, flocking to the white rose banner and the young King in shining armor astride a huge white stallion. She was dressed in a page's nondescript green jerkin with a hood that hid most of her hair, which she had drawn back from her face and secured in a knot at the back of her head. To make her disguise more convincing she had cut her hair in front and combed it down over her brow and ears as a lad would have worn his shorter hair. It helped to hide her expressive eyes and some of the soft contours of her face. Over her loose jerkin and hose she wore a heavy woolen cloak that also concealed a long, sharp dagger in a sheath and a small pouch for the money Edward had insisted she take in case things went against York. Atop her hood she sported a feathered cap that tilted low over her forehead and almost covered her eyes when she lowered her head. She wore heavy leather gauntlets and tall soft leather boots to her knees to hide the frailty of her hands and legs. She was covered so well and the rain was falling so heavily that even Edward didn't recognize her at first when he rode near her at their appointed meeting place where she sat waiting patiently on the large roan horse he had provided for her.

When she considered that he had fretted and worried enough waiting for her, she urged her mount up next to his and tugged at his sleeve, humming a few bars of a popular song she had sung so often for him. He laughed then, gaping at her in the rain and with an acknowledging nod, motioning his pretty young page to follow, he swung his mount around and lifted his gauntleted hand to signal to his men that he was ready to move out.

Warwick and his men would join them, at Middleham, Warwick's castle about three days' ride from London.

Edward had just received word by a breathless courier that his cousin would await His Grace there instead of coming to meet him along the way. Warwick was still gathering his forces and felt that he should remain there until King Edward's army arrived. Edward had been relieved for several reasons, chief among them being the doubts that assailed him concerning his dark cousin's true loyalties. Whenever they met lately, Edward could see anger in the older man's eyes. Yet he needed Warwick and the Nevilles; they were the fiercest warriors under his banner.

Edward lowered the visor of his helmet and eyeing the columns of knights, squires, archers, and foot soldiers, he gave the command to march forward. The trumpets sounded, and the cavalcade began to move.

Only once that morning did the King turn and glance back at the slim figure that stiffly sat the bony roan horse. Bronwyn was a good rider, her short legs gripping the roan's flanks firmly, her cloak flapping behind her in the rain. He smiled, but made no other sign, fearful of calling attention to them both. Edward needed no rumors concerning him and a pretty boy on this campaign. He had troubles enough. His battle captains were already feuding among themselves and his lords were grumbling about his orders to bivouack at Barnet for the night. Some wanted to move ahead and camp out in the open while others desired the comforts of a billet in town. Edward cared not how his men would disperse and fill their gullets with wine and their beds with whores; but on the other hand the weather was atrocious and to set up camp in the muddy, wet fields would be hard on them. Bad weather could discourage and rout an army faster than any enemy, he'd always found, and he wanted them to be in fighting trim when they joined forces with Warwick and headed for the Scottish border. Then, too, the King frowned under his helm, his brother George would sleep nowhere but in a soft feather bed if he could help it and Edward really wasn't in a mood to argue with him. They would bilet the troops at Barnet tonight.

At that precise moment, his brother George was thinking of him as well. Riding back with the Duke of Norfolk, Sir John Howard and Lord Hastings, George watched with eagle eyes the slim frame of the mysterious lad who rode close behind Edward. He had seen through the clever ruse barely minutes after he had caught Edward's glance back towards the boy. From then on he had been curious about the lad and had asked questions until the truth dawned on him and he laughed aloud, slapping his thigh as he realized who the "lad" really was. He marveled at the blatant audacity of the whole scheme. Later, he maneuvered his dappled stallion to his brother's side, leaned over and said nonchalantly, "That lad back there?" He cocked a thumb back towards Bronwyn. "Too pretty to be safe among our men, don't you think, Ned? I've never seen such pretty green eyes on a boy, have you?" Behind his lowered visor, George smiled roguishly. "Rides his horse like a woman, I'd say." Then he laughed and Edward threw him a warning glare.

George then whispered, "Good God, Edward, a pretty boy has as much to fear at times among soldiers as does a pretty woman. You don't need to be reminded of these minor details, surely?"

He sent a thoughtful stare back towards Bronwyn and, feeling the Duke of Clarence's eyes fully on her, she blushed and turned her head nervously aside.

"He blushes like a woman as well," George chuckled, and added, "he is much too pretty, Edward. Take care."

Edward merely grunted and shifted uncomfortably in his saddle. The rain was chilling his bones and the half-armor he was wearing was heavy besides, he wasn't in the mood for George's japes. He turned in the saddle and threw George a warning glare. "Aye, he may be too pretty

300

to some eyes. But those who dare to scrutinize the boy too closely . . . will feel the edge of my blade.''

"Forgive me, brother, for mentioning such a delicate matter.'' George bowed slightly in his saddle, his eyes looking up to meet Edward's. After a moment, Edward sighed, realizing he could not fool his lusty brother.

"You are forgiven. It is hard to forget her once you have seen her. I of all men should know that. But do not call attention to her in any way. *He* is one of my pages and a young apprentice to Rutledge, one of our surgeons. And *he* makes a potent sleeping draught that I have found to be very soothing," Edward said quietly as they cantered along. He looked behind him at the city walls that were receding into the morning mist and rain. "You know how poorly I sleep the night before a battle."

"I'm sure he will comfort you well enough." George spoke suggestively and stole one more quick glance back at the "lad" in question. "Don't worry about me, Ned. I shall keep your secret to my grave." He laid a hand dramatically on his breast above his heart, then set spurs to his horse and turned the huge beast around in an elaborate dance, galloping back to rejoin his companions.

Bronwyn stretched in her saddle, sore from the unaccustomed jolting gait of the bony roan and from riding astride. She wished for about the tenth time that she were riding her little mare, but that would have destroyed her disguise. She wiped her face with the edge of her cloak and prodded her horse along the muddy road. What did it matter? She was happy. She set her eyes on Edward's broad back up ahead and forgot both the rain and her discomfort. She was with the man she loved. What more could she ask?

They stopped that night in the village of Barnet and while the men dispersed to find their own billets and settle down for the night, Bronwyn went with Edward to the Abbey and was given a pallet outside Edward's chambers.

No one noticed when the young page entered the King's rooms later that night and the pallet remained empty until dawn.

For three days they traveled through towns and villages toward Warwick's stronghold of Middleham, gathering more men and supplies along the way. The people were rallying to Edward's banner. Their ranks were swelling and when she looked behind her, she could see the glint of armor and silken banners trailing out behind them for what seemed like miles into the horizon. Edward spent most of his time conferrring with his battle captains on strategy and mediating the petty squabbles between his lords. It wasn't easy keeping the various factions from killing each other off before a battle could be joined.

On the third afternoon, sore and weary from long hours in the saddle, Bronwyn raised her tired eyes and saw Middleham for the first time. Edward had discussed the meeting that would take place with Warwick and he understood her apprenhensions, but had set her mind at rest. After all, in three days no one but George had seen through her disguise. Why should Warwick? He had warned her to stay away from the man and all would be well. But as Bronwyn shaded her eyes from the bright sun and scanned the massive outer walls and the grey stone gatehouse that faced the village sprawled about those walls, she made the sign of the cross in a silent plea that Warwick would never penetrate her disguise. She only wondered how she would keep from running away should his hawkish black eyes rest on her. How could she keep him from seeing the hatred that still burned deep within her.

As they rode up the southern slopes of Wensleydale and onto the moors, then across the castle's drawbridge over the brackish moat and clattered into the quadrangular castle's bailey, Bronwyn could feel the hair on the back of her neck bristling like a cat cornered by a pack of snarling dogs. Most of the main body of the army had camped out around the castle and in the village as they were staying the night. They would head for Durham at dawn where they would pitch their main encampment to prepare for the battle that would surely follow once the Scots and Queen Margaret's Lancastrian forces realized they were there.

She rode into the castle's inner courtyard behind Edward, her head tilted down and her cloak tightly around her, even though the beautiful afternoon in early May was warm. Edward nodded back towards her just once with a brief encouraging smile as he dismounted and was welcomed by his tall, dark cousin before the towering limestone Norman keep that was the mainstay of the whole fortress.

From a distance, Bronwyn observed her enemy with hooded eyes. He looked much older and heavier than she remembered, and his acquiline features were haggard. Then he happened to glance at someone past her and in that second, she glimpsed the anger lurking in his feral eyes when next he looked at his kingly cousin. There was hatred and frustration hidden behind his smile as he and Edward strolled into the great hall of the castle. Bronwyn's heart pounded with fear and loathing. It was apparent that Warwick hated Edward and begrudged him his power and the adoration of his people. He was a threat to the man she loved, as well as to herself.

The night was an agony for her. Sitting at one of the lower tables, Bronwyn's eyes were glued to Edward at the high table discussing battle tactics with Warwick. She pretended to all around her that she was mute, listening to the gossip and the ribald jesting that soldiers indulge in when they are with their comrades. There was something else that bothered her as well. Edward had told her that his brother George knew who she was and at times she saw him watching her with amused eyes. He thought this whole escapade outrageous, yet tremendously interesting, especially after he had learned from Edward about her previous involvement with Warwick. He had found it all fascinating. So the wench had once been Warwick's? It was food for thought. The whole situation was highly intriguing.

Unlike Edward, George got on extremely well with his cousin Warwick. In fact, if all his plans went right, he would soon be Warwick's son-in-law as well since he hoped that Warwick's daughter Isabel would be his wife. She was one of the richest women in England, and lovely, too, but Edward was vehemently against the match and it had set the two brothers at odds. George could see no connection between Edward's doubts about their cousin's loyalty and George's projected marriage to a very impressive fortune.

It would serve him right, George thought at the table as he gripped his wine cup and watched Bronwyn closely, if he revealed the girl's identity to Warwick. At least, it would make for an interesting night. But then he recalled with a frown how fond his brother was of the little witch and how angry Edward would if he learned of George's betrayal. George laughed then as he stuffed more cold venison into his mouth and washed it down with wine. No, he'd bide his time until the proper moment, when Edward would never be able to connect the indiscretion to his younger brother . . .

In the meantime the feast went on—succulent rissoles of pork and tender pike roe, venison cut in large slabs and smothered in gravy, heaping plates of rice cakes, oat cakes and apple fritters crisp and brown that melted in one's mouth, and baked partridge with cold herbed jelly. Then after the main meal, the servants brought in candied quinces, dried figs, Brie tarts and beautiful sugar sculptures in the shapes of swans and roses in honor of the King's visit. While they dined, minstrels in their bright garb sang their songs. Most of them were vagabonds or traveling gypsies that stopped at manor houses and castles along their route and offered their services. The jugglers and dancers, too, were quite good, George thought, but he had seen the way the girl seemed mesmerized by the gypsy troubadours in their flashing jewelry and vivid silks. He was halfway in his cups by then and remembered that Edward had bragged incessantly about the girl's lovely voice. He was just about to call out to her to sing for them all and had already captured her eye and gestured, when he realized his error. For a brief second, he saw panic flood her pale face and turn it crimson and then, with a small startled cry that was lost in the general clamor, she jumped from her seat and fled the room. George sighed and shook his head groggily, reaching out for his wine goblet as his glassy eyes met Edward's angry ones over the crowd. George gave him his most engaging grin and shrugged his shoulders as if to say, *Ah, it was only a slip . . . a mistake. No harm done.*

Edward made a swift excuse of being weary from the long march and, politely taking leave of his cousin and their guests, went in search of Bronwyn. Silently cursing his brother and the trouble it had almost caused, he found her exactly where he thought she would be, huddled in the stable by her roan as it stood munching hay.

"My poor sweetheart!" He gathered her into his arms. "I know how difficult this has been for you. You're trembling like a leaf in a storm. My brother is a fool when he is in his cups. But rest assured, my cousin Warwick is in precisely the same condition and did not notice that ill-judged piece of byplay. Never fear, sweet Bronwyn. Your secret is safe."

She gazed up into his loving face with troubled eyes. "Yes, but for how long? What if your brother calls attention to me again? If my lord Warwick finds out who I am . . ." Her voice trailed off into a whisper.

Edward soothed her with gentle kisses and then, his arm about her thin shoulders, he guided her to his chamber. They were unobserved since everyone was still carousing in the castle's great hall.

Later that night in the privacy of Edward's huge bed, the velvet hangings drawn against the night air, Bronwyn lay naked in his arms and watched him as he slept. How innocent and gentle he seemed, sleeping like that. How she did love him! Yet, even after their passionate love-making, all she could think of was Warwick's feral smile as he had raped her. She could still feel his brutal hands punishing her soft flesh, and sleep eluded her that night because she lay under the same roof as the man she loathed. How long would she be able to continue this dangerous masquerade? If Warwick saw through her disguise, what would he do? Both she and Edward had pierced his vanity and wounded his great pride. He would surely seek revenge on them both.

She had had no idea that just seeing him again would do this to her. No idea at all.

The next morning, though she had had very little sleep, she sat her roan stoically, her cap tipped low over her face and her manner outwardly calm. Edward had decided that as long as Warwick was riding with them, she should ride in the rear with George for the next day or so, until they reached Durham. George had apologized profusely for his lapse the previous night, and had promised to guard Bronwyn well. Once they had set up camp outside of Durham and Warwick was busy requisitioning mounts, ordering supplies and conferring with the other lords, he would be far too busy to notice one small page. And Edward would be sure that he was kept away from her until the opposing forces met on the battlefield. Even now couriers were galloping in every few hours, giving the location of the approaching armies which were fully armed and ready for the fray.

They clattered into the village of Durham two days later. Bronwyn had hardly seen Edward since that night at Middleham, except from a distance. He was completely absorbed in making plans for the coming battle and had spent the entire night in conference with his lords and lieutenants. The soldiers began to pitch the tents, and had already staked out the horse parks, where the great warhorses would be enclosed. Bronwyn watched in fascination as the camp buzzed and hummed with life—pages running errands for their masters, meat being set upon spits for roasting, squires scurrying here and there cleaning their knights armor with sand and vinegar, and the archers sitting before the campfires bragging of past campaigns and victories as they checked their longbows and trimmed the feathers on their arrows. The activity both fascinated and repulsed her. All this preparation for maiming and butchering other men, not inspired by personal animosity against the enemy but as though fighting and killing were a job like any other. And yet, she mused sadly as she let her eyes travel over the bustling scene around her, it was the common foot soldier that would suffer the greatest losses. How many would never go home again? How many good men, husbands, and perhaps fathers, would never see another day? How many children, wives, sweethearts would have empty arms when this campaign was over? How many young knights would be grievously wounded? She remembered her father and how his old war wound had ruined his life. She looked about her and wished she hadn't come. Edward had been right; healer or no, a woman didn't belong on a battlefield. Her gaze swept the fields, so tenderly green and fragrant under the May sun, and she listened to the birds singing in the trees, then turned her face up to feel the warm breeze that kissed her cheeks. Yet all she could see was the battlefield that in a day or two would run with blood. Why had she been foolish enough to come?

For Edward, she answered herself. For love of the man who had saved her life and given her cause to live and laugh again. But she didn't feel like laughing now. It wasn't until she came up to the tent with the royal banner waving before it in the soft breeze and saw a smiling Edward come forward to give orders to his "page" that she was able to relax somewhat. She followed him sedately into his tent where he laughed and pulled her to him, and she felt the doubt and melancholy lift from her heart. She was here for Edward's sake, because she loved him and her life was empty and meaningless without him. Because she loved him. That was reason enough.

CHAPTER XI

May 1464

IT WAS STRANGE, sleeping on a straw pallet again, Bronwyn thought, amused. She had never slept in a tent, especially not in a King's tent on the eve of battle. She had slept comfortably on a fat mattress stuffed with straw at the foot of Edward's camp bed, ostensibly his devoted young page. When they were alone, they acted like the lovers they were, but when others were about, which was most of the time, she once more played the part of a shy, silent lad.

Late in the morning of the next day, which promised to be beautiful and sunny, Bronwyn was bending over the coffer that held some of Edward's clothes when she heard the guards in front of the tent coming noisily to attention and the unmistakable sound of horses approaching. She knew immediately that it was someone of great importance and her blood froze in her veins when she heard the Earl of Warwick requesting an audience with the King. The devil himself come to visit! she thought, panic-stricken.

She lingered in the shadows, hoping he wouldn't notice her lurking there like a truant child. The Earl of Warwick came striding in, dressed in full armor. He made a hurried obeisance to his royal cousin, removing the helmet from his shaggy head. He looked tired and nervous. Bronwyn almost felt a touch of pity stirring in her breast for a moment, and then he smiled that wicked grin she remembered so well causing her to tremble. He was facing Edward, telling him that he had just ridden from where the Lancastrian and Scottish armies were camped after spying on them to gauge their strengths and weaknesses. "They are more than we bargained for, Your Grace," he said. "I estimate perhaps two or three thousand men. I could make out the Duke of Somerset's banners and the Scots are everywhere. Christ, there be a river of them out across the fields on the other side of the wooded corpse! My spies say, however, that Margaret will not lead her army into battle, not after the disastrous beating they received last time she was foolish enough to take the field with her men; but she is close by they tell me, in Carlston Abbey, where she awaits the outcome. They have far more archers than we expected . . ." He went on in that deep voice that grated upon Bronwyn's raw nerves as he listed those knights and Lords whose banners and colors he had recognized. Edward bade him sit and ordered wine for him to drink and a basin of water so he might wash his travel-stained hands and face. He was sweating in his armor and as one of Edward's squires helped him take it off, his piercing eyes returned to Bronwyn again and again, and she shivered deep inside. He seemed to sense that something was disturbing Edward's new young page. She didn't need to lift her eyes and meet his dark, evil ones to know he was now openly staring at her.

She could feel his eyes boring through her and she turned abruptly away and made a pretense of straightening out Edward's garments in the large wooden chest. Warwick still watched her as she worked.

"They are even now sending in more Scots from the fortress of Berwick and if we don't strike soon, Edward," Warwick crashed his huge clenched fist down upon the table at which he and Edward were sitting, "we will be hopelessly outnumbered! The time to strike is now! We dare not delay another day."

The mention of Berwick had deepened the frown upon Edward's already grim face. It had been an English fortress and port for many years until Margaret had given it over to the Scots in payment for their assistance against the house of York. She had no right to dispose of that property and it had galled Edward as much as it did Warwick.

The King stared into nowhere, thinking deeply. Finally he leaned back in his chair and sighed, nodding his bright head. "You are right, cousin. We dare not delay any longer."

Warwick looked into Edward's blue eyes and smiled. He threw one more searching glance towards the back of the tent. Something about that youth was familiar, but he couldn't for the life of him place the lad. He rubbed his tired eyes and slumped in his chair, resting for the first time in days. He shook his head and took a long swallow of wine as he turned back to Edward. "There are rumors about that the Scots are fearful of this battle. They fear the York rose and the Neville bear." He laughed sharply. "The Scottish lords are feuding with their Lancastrian allies, I hear tell. There's little trust on either side. They are awaiting reinforcements . . ." and here Warwick leaned over and tapped the table with his large rough fingers, ". . . that may never arrive. There is a deep concern over it. 'Tis the Beauforts they are depending upon but they fear they may not come as they had promised." Warwick's smile was cunning. "We should strike at dawn. My spies have informed me that Beaufort's men have been delayed by sickness. We should attack before their arrival and that of the rest of the Scots."

Edward's grim face brightened. He knew they had made excellent time marching from London, but he had had no idea that they would actually beat Beaufort to Durham.

"When are they expected?"

"Perhaps in two days. And without Beaufort, Margaret's forces do not stand a chance in hell."

Edward laughed then, a laugh of relief. Warwick had found the Lancasters' fatal flaw. None of the Lancasters trusted anyone . . . not even other Lancasters. Some Lancastrian knights and lords changed their loyalties as often as they changed their clothes, more often, in fact, always wanting to be on the winning side.

Warwick glanced over at the mysterious lad again. He'd never have thought Edward the type to like pretty boys. He scratched his sweaty neck, puzzled, and continued to stare at the youth as Edward plied him with endless questions concerning the preparations for battle.

"You shall command the vanguard, cousin," Edward was saying as he took a sip of wine. "Suffolk shall take the center and Buckingham shall command the rearward. I shall stay with my knights and come to the aid of whoever needs me."

Bronwyn knew how dangerous this would be, since the King's banner of scarlet and blue with the *Rose en Soleil* was known to all and the first standard the enemy would seek to destroy, as well as the men who rode beneath it. It would be safer if the King did not enter the fray at all, she thought, but stayed behind the lines, ordering the campaign and letting his men fight for him. What good would it do if the battle was won, but Edward lay dead on the battlefield? Yet he always insisted on fighting with his men, knowing that he could give no greater encouragement than to risk his life as they did, ready to shed his royal blood for England.

Bronwyn watched Warwick from under her tilted cap, wondering as Edward did how far he could be trusted. Was he only tired of all the bloodletting in the King's name, or did he seek to seize the crown for himself? She studied his face and listened to him speak, and, much as she herself distrusted and feared the man, his fervent words almost convinced her that he and Edward had the same goal—peace. It was unsettling to look at that man she remembered as being bloodthirsty and ruthless, and realize that he, too, sought the end of bloodshed. But it was possible. Anything was possible. Perhaps he and Edward had come to an agreement since that time in the wintry wood when she had heard him damn Edward. Perhaps he had at last forgotten his own personal grievances.

"Good!" Edward was saying. "But I have given strict orders that if Henry is with them—and he may be—they do drag him about at times as if he were their private mascot, he is *not* to be harmed in any way . . . I want him a prisoner."

Warwick stood up violently from the table, almost causing the platters of cold meat and cheese to slide off, and glared at Edward.

"Surely you can't mean that!" His voice was incredulous. "After all the bloodshed and intrigue that idiot has caused you are simply going to imprison him and let him rot while the Lancasters rally round his cause and a thousand more rebellions take root and blossom in his name? Sire, I thought you had learned your lesson better than this!" His whole body vibrated with anger and disbelief. He leaned down close to Edward and spat the next words in a hoarse voice. "*Have done with it*! Kill the wretch! 'Twould be doing the poor fellow a favor, I'd think. He knows not what time of day it is, they say, and wants only to be left alone with his prayers and his holy beads. Send him to Heaven where he longs to be. Simpleminded though he may be and blameless of the uprisings in his name, *we dare not allow him to live*! You know that as well as I! For as long as he lives, the cursed Lancasters will keep plotting to sieze the throne, and England will drown in rivers of blood!" He slammed his fist down on the table and his black eyes locked with Edward's cool blue ones.

Edward stood up then and with a nonchalance that Bronwyn could see was feigned, he said in deadly tones, "We *dare not* kill him now. When he has been in the Tower under our good and kind care for awhile, even the Lancastrians must see how fair and merciful we have been to a poor lunatic. He will be a prisoner of state under our control. For in truth, my good cousin, it would be far more dangerous to kill him and gain the hatred of the people for murdering such a helpless, harmless soul. Henry was once King of England, anointed by God. The people do not take that lightly, my lord. *Do you*?"

"I think you are making a terrible mistake and one you will live to regret one day, my young liege," Warwick growled.

"Then that will be on my own head. It is my decision. We shall take him alive and treat him gently. In the end, mercy will gain us far more." The matter was closed. Edward would hear no more of it.

Warwick cursed Edward's stubborness under his breath. The young whelp was as headstrong as ever! He was King, after all, and he meant never to let Warwick forget it. No matter that it was Warwick himself who had set that glittering crown upon his golden head. Why wouldn't the man listen to him? As long as Henry lived, there would be rebellion and more bloodshed. Warwick's narrowed eyes were as black as slate as he studied the man before him. Edward was too merciful, too kind to be a king. A monarch must be heartless and give no quarter when it came to his bitterest enemies, or they would stab him in the back the first chance they got. Was he still so naive that he didn't see this?

But the Earl of Warwick said nothing. After a moment of strained silence he slumped back down upon his chair and rubbed his eyes wearily. "Edward, excuse my rashness. The decision is indeed yours to make." He looked towards the slit of fading light that was stealing in through the open tent flap. Soon it would be night. Would it be their last night alive? He wondered. "I must see to my men and the horses, with your leave, Sire." Warwick snapped his fingers and his squire ran about gathering his discarded armor.

"You are right, cousin. It grows late and we both have much to do this night before we rest. I will summon my battle captains at dawn. Tell them we fight tomorrow at first light." Edward stood up and accompanied Warwick outside the tent. Bronwyn couldn't hear what was discussed for their words were muffled by distance and the noises of the camp preparing to bed down for the night.

When Edward came back in, she breathed a huge sigh of relief and smiled tremendously at the King. "I'm so glad he's gone!" She shuddered. "I was so afraid he would discover who I am. Even though I know how important he is to you and your cause, I do not trust him." She half expected to be reprimanded, but Edward was staring away into space deep in thought, as if he hadn't heard a word she had said. She reached out and touched his cold hand.

Edward smiled down at her then, his gaze clearing. "Rest assured, he did not recognize you." He stroked her hair as she still knelt on the ground by the chest, and drew her up into his arms. He had given the guards outside his tent strict orders that he wasn't to be disturbed for the next hour. He was bone-weary and his heart was disquieted. His smile as he held her close was shadowed by concern about the coming fray. "I imagine he thinks I've changed my tastes somewhat," he continued, "and that now I am partial to pretty boys!"

Bronwyn laughed softly and returned his passionate kiss.

After they made love, tenderly and with all the fervor of

315

lovers who fear it may be for the last time, they lay in each other's arms and talked about what would happen the next morning. He made it clear to her once more that she was not to tarry if York lost the battle, and Bronwyn, her heart suddenly filled with dread, agreed.

The knights and soldiers, too, were thinking of the morrow and wondering if they would live to see another sunset as rare and lovely as this one.

When Bronwyn had fallen asleep, Edward got up quietly from the bed and dressed in a simple gray tunic. He looked at all the other men crouching over their campfires, telling stories to each other to lift their spirits and keep their minds off what they would face tomorrow. Edward left the tent and walked out among them under the clear, black star-studded sky.

He felt a need to be out among his men tonight, to talk and laugh with them as an equal and not as their almighty King. He was a man of flesh and blood, with hopes and dreams just like any one of them. One of the camp's wolfhounds came up to him and sniffed his hand, then loped beside him as he mingled with the others. He was glad of its company. Though he was in a huge crowd, he was very much alone. His knights recognized him; most of his men did not. They accepted him as one of them and he, too, squatted before a roaring fire and listened to the glorious tales of past victories from the older veterans. He laughed at the ribald jokes and traded pleasantries with the lusty wenches who were out plying their trade that night. For a few hours he was only a man, afraid to die, afraid to be alone the night before a battle. He observed the archers testing their bows, the priests shriving the men of their sins, knights exploring new tactics they would try in the field in the morning, and heard hushed whispers of fears and hopes.

Hours later after he had made his rounds, he returned to the tent and, still dressed, lay down next to a dreaming

Bronwyn. He pulled her into his arms and for a long while stared into the darkness, his mind years and miles away. He looked down into the face of the girl in his arms and thought of what the soldiers had talked of—wives, homes, children . . . He rested his cheek against Bronwyn's warm flesh. He loved this woman, but she could never be his wife. If he survived this battle, he must marry a woman who would bring him closer to his ultimate goal—peace in his troubled realm. He needed a wife; he needed heirs to his throne.

Tomorrow, if he died, he would leave no heirs, and Lancaster would triumph.

"*God, don't let me die tomorrow*," he prayed in a whisper, holding Bronwyn so tightly that she moved in his arms; he had awakened her. He felt her eyes on him. She blinked away the sleep and reached up to bring his face down to her lips. A soft rain pattered on the tent, and she could hear a soldier singing a mournful lovesong somewhere, singing of a woman far away, one he might never see again. It brought tears to her eyes and dread to her heart. She was so afraid . . .

"You will not die, my sweet love," she said in a husky manner.

"No one but God knows that for sure, my love. What will be, will be." His voice mingled with the gentle sound of the rain. "There is so much I have yet to do. If I should die, what is to become of those I leave behind—my mother, my brothers, my friends. My country and its poor, suffering people . . ."

"*You shall not die*! I could not live without you, my Lord!" Bronwyn cried and when he kissed her feverish cheek he felt the wetness of her tears.

"You cannot stop living because the one you love dies—or leaves." His voice was so serious that it frightened her. "Anyone can live without another. You must be strong. There is so much ahead of you, sweet Bronwyn. Do

317

not reject it because of me. Life is beautiful and one must live it to the fullest." His voice then took on a light teasing tone she knew well and it made her smile faintly in the dark. "Besides, if I die, my ghost would surely haunt your steps . . . you would never be rid of me then!" He hugged and kissed her.

No, she thought, the memories of their love would never die, and therefore, Edward would never die because she would always have those. She would never lose him. He would always be with her, always.

They made wild, passionate love again to the rhythm of the rain outside and the pounding of their frightened hearts, their ecstasy taking them far away from reality. Her warm breasts pressed against his naked chest and their lips melted together, and when he filled her yearning body, neither was conscious of anything other than this love they shared . . .

Bronwyn trembled in her saddle, the chill of early morning penetrating to her very bones. Her face was bloodless as she turned toward the terrifying sounds of the battle raging below her in the fields surrounding Durham and beyond. The Scots had raided before dawn and left many dead where they slept. Edward had mustered his troops immediately and pursued them, into the trap the Lancasters had prepared in the fields below. There was furious hand-to-hand fighting in the center and on the left flank; under York's banner the line was faltering even now as she stared. Soldiers were throwing down their weapons and fleeing in panic. The Earl of Warwick's men were fighting to the far right and she could see the glint of upraised shields and flying lances. The archers of the white rose were nowhere to be seen and, wringing her hands in agony for the hundredth time, she wondered why they weren't sending their arrows to their enemies' black hearts. There was the stench of death and blood in the air.

She could no longer see Edward's great white warhorse nor the white gleam of his Flemish armor. Arrows could penetrate plate armor and the finely linked mail shirt beneath like a hot knife through butter, she had heard a soldier say. And the forces of Lancaster had archers, too. Bronwyn shuddered at the thought.

The trap had been so swiftly and cleverly sprung, she thought, watching in horror, the fighting below. The small band of Scots had led Edward's troops right into the ambush on the edge of the woods where their archers had been positioned sometime in the night, unseen and unexpected. And they had sent their arrows singing through the air as Edward's men had ridden into the field. The air had been full of screams and wails of agony. Bronwyn had covered her ears and moaned in anguish at the waste of men's lives and dreams in pools of blood mingling with the ripening grass, heather and bracken.

A fog was moving in and it swirled around Edward's rear flank as they fought. From far off she heard a trumpet fanfare and then another. Someone was in trouble, calling for reinforcements. Even from this great distance on top of the grassy hill Bronwyn could see a poleaxe plunging downward, hear a horse scream in agony and topple, unseating its rider. A sword flashed in the gray mist, and another man died. Horses galloped in all directions, their reins trailing and their bloody saddles empty. Edward's men were suffering great losses. *Where were the reserves? Edward . . . where was her King?*

She groaned, covering her eyes, but she could still hear the moans of the dying and the voices of the maimed crying for pity, for mercy. But the Scots gave no quarter, killing every Yorkist they came upon without exception. The only way she knew the King must still live was because if he had fallen, there would have been a shout that would rend the heavens.

"*God help them all!*" She slid from her saddle and,

leaning up against the roan, she rested her forehead against its warm neck, dampening it with her tears. She had heard much in her short life of the Devil and of Hell, and the carnage going on below seemed like Hell itself. It must be the Devil that had inspired such tragic butchery! War was the Devil's handiwork. She wept, clutching her horse's reins as if she were preparing to get back into the saddle and ride away, escape the madness below. But she remained motionless, paralyzed by something much stronger than her own will. She couldn't escape, she couldn't ride away; she had to know how her lover fared.

Her horror-filled eyes continued their frantic search for the white helmet with the white plumes floating in the breeze, for the royal banner flapping in the misty air, for the man she loved. As if they had a morbid will of their own, her eyes searched the melée of milling soldiers, knights and horseflesh. At last she found the York banner that was moving ever closer to the pitiful creature astride a horse under the blood-red standard with the three golden lions of Lancaster proudly clawing at the air. He didn't seem to see the battle raging about him, nor hear the cries of the dying. His ears were hearing voices from another world, perhaps. They had decked Henry out in bright raiment as if he were a king indeed, yet the tide of battle swept around him, never touching him, as if he weren't there at all. His knights guarded him and encircled him. Bronwyn's heart went out to the poor man—a King who did not know he was a King. A child sent out to battle as though it were a game, but he didn't know the rules. *Poor Henry.* Poor pitiful man. At times she swore she could hear him . . . *singing!* That men were dying to seat him on a throne he knew nought of was a mystery to her.

Mare screams rent the air and Bronwyn cringed again. She wished she were a man and could ride into battle and fight beside Edward, then shook her head sadly, knowing that she could never bring herself to shed another's blood.

Killing was a shameful sin against the will of God.

The fog had crept up on the hill and was swirling thickly around her and her mount making the beast nervous. He pranced skittishly, snorting and nickering, and she tried to soothe him with her hands and soft voice. Did he sense something she couldn't? Bronwyn apprehensively scanned the silent swaying trees behind her and to her left, but all she could see was the thickening mist. She saw no one else anywhere around her. But was she really alone? The King had warned her to stay in his tent, waiting until a messenger brought news of the progress of the battle, but she had disobeyed him, brooding and fretting as the trumpets blared and Edward's army had ridden forth. She had paced back and forth in the tent for what seemed like hours wringing her hands until they ached. When she could wait no longer she had slipped away while the guard wasn't looking. She had run until she found her horse and she had fetched the saddle and bridle, struggling to put them on her mount without assistance. Astride at last, she had urged the roan into a wild gallop up the nearest hill overlooking the battlefield.

Suddenly Bronwyn heard a shout rippling down the lines. "*Loose!*" It was the order that commanded Edward's archers to speed their arrows to their targets. She hid her eyes when she saw men, arrow shafts protruding from their bodies, fall to the bloody ground where they lay motionless or were trampled beneath the chargers' hooves. Now the Yorkist forces forged ahead with mace, sword and halberd, crying "*A York! A York!*," sweeping the Scots and the Lancastrian army closer to a ravine. Soon they were tumbling into the deep gully; Edward's knights pursued them, on the offensive at last, putting the enemy to rout. Bronwyn heard the screams of dying men mingled with shouts of triumph and the clash of sword on sword. The day was won by York, but at such great cost of human suffering and loss of lives!

The tide had turned and the Scots deserted the field, leaving their Lancastrian allies to the Yorks' mercy. Throwing their weapons to the ground, or dropping their armor as a sign of surrender, they fled like rats from a sinking ship. The Yorkist archers sent more flights of arrows across the field and now it was the forces of Lancasters that were in retreat as well, the Yorkist army right behind them, driving them into the woods where they were slaughtered as they ran among the trees, trying to escape the deadly swords.

The mist was lifting now, and Bronwyn cried out with relief and joy to see Edward's great white stallion rearing and plunging in the melee. She saw the glint of his sword rise and fall again and again and he moved ever closer to the pathetic figure of poor King Henry, who had been deserted and left to fend for himself. Finally a company of Edward's knights surrounded him and escorted him off the field, a King without a kingdom.

For a second she thought Edward had accompanied him to safety. Then she saw his white stallion again back in the midst of the fray, and Edward slashing at stragglers and rounding up what was left of the fleeing Scots. Then suddenly a giant of a man in silver armor on a dappled grey stallion with black and silver trappings charged full tilt toward the King, his wicked claymore swinging in wide arcs as his warhorse rammed into Edward's. Both horses stumbled and Edward's stallion fell to its knees with a great piercing cry. The knight in gray whirled his warhorse about and charged at the King, still brandishing the claymore high over his head.

Bronwyn screamed then, screamed for Edward to turn about and defend himself before it was too late, though she knew he could not possibly hear her.

It was Warwick, galloping between them upon his great black, whose gleaming sword pierced the gray knight's throat. Warwick who, with a gallant salute to his King as he spun his warhorse around, plunged back into the midst of the battle, his sword now red with the gray knight's blood. Warwick had saved Edward's life!

Bronwyn watched with tears of relief pouring down her face as Edward, his steed having lunged to its feet unharmed, joined his cousin as the last of the enemy forces were driven off the field. Trumpets blared in triumph, announcing the victory of the house of York.

Dazed with joy, Bronwyn dug her heels into the roan's flanks and galloped down the hill, heading back to camp, where she knew Edward and Warwick would soon return. Edward was alive and York had won the day! Her heart overflowed with gratitude—and she had her enemy the Earl of Warwick to thank. How ironic, that the man she hated above all others had just saved the life of the man she loved above all others!

The camp was swarming with knights, lords, archers and soldiers, all concerned about the King's safety. Rumors were everywhere—*the King was wounded! The King was unscratched! The King was dead*! And Warwick—what of Warwick? *Dead . . . wounded . . . unharmed . . .*

Bronwyn slid down from her horse, tossed the reins to a startled young soldier and ran to the tent, but the crowd clustered outside was so dense that she couldn't get close until one of the guards posted before the tent saw her and cleared a path, recognizing her as the King's favorite young page. Breathless, she burst into the tent and the first thing she saw was Edward, hale and hearty. The second thing she perceived was a bedraggled man crouched in a corner on the ground, his hands bound and his lank brown hair falling over his face. *King Henry.* He was being totally ignored by the others in the tent whose entire attention was focused on a wounded knight who was being tended by the surgeon, Rutledge. The King was standing by, his expression tense and grim, his eyes never leaving the wounded man. He did not notice Bronwyn's entrance, nor did anyone else. As the battle-weary knights jostled one another for a glimpse of their fallen comrade, Bronwyn nearly stumbled over the man in the corner, England's former King. He stared up at her, his eyes empty, and then he smiled surprisingly sweetly. She had an overwhelming urge to curtsy to him, but remembered just in time where she was and who she was supposed to be. Poor man! He huddled at her feet like a captive bird with tarnished golden feathers, one of the spoils of war for the victorious Yorks. Poor King Henry! But she realized that he didn't need pity; he was unaware of where he was and that he was a prisoner.

She heard a muffled groan and turned around, to see Rutledge bending over the wounded man. The mud-caked straps and buckles that crossed his cuirass had been unfastened and the knight's bloody breastplate lay on the floor. The surgeon was now stripping away the rerebraces that protected the man's upper arms. She heard Edward gasp as if he himself were in pain and she moved closer to see who the wounded knight was, but the other men's bodies blocked her view. Seized by a sudden impulse, she made her way to the small chest that contained her few belongings and took out her bag of medicinal herbs. As Rutledge continued to minister to the unknown knight, she quickly prepared a drink of agrimony in herb tea and managed to make her way to the surgeon's side.

"Give him this drink," she said in a low voice. The patient's head was turned away and her eyes met the doctor's over the man's prostrate form. "It will ease the pain," she explained quietly. He nodded, for Edward had informed him of this young lad's knowledge of the healing arts, took the cup and supported his patient as he drank. Bronwyn turned away then, and at last caught Edward's eye. He seemed startled to see her, yet relieved, but his worried expression lightened only for a moment and then he turned his attention back to the surgeon and his patient. Who was the man? Bronwyn wondered yet again. Surely he must be some great lord, one whom Edward valued greatly.

"Sire! I can't stop the bleeding!" Rutledge's voice pierced through the muted murmur of voices in the tent. "It is far worse than I had thought . . . he has been slashed to the bone."

Bronwyn could see instantly that the man was dying. As though in a trance, she stepped around the surgeon and knelt beside the pallet where the wounded man lay. She saw blood streaming from a deep gash in his chest and heedless of anything but the need to save a life, she laid her hands over the wound. She closed her eyes and bowed her head, praying silently as the blood trickled down her arms and dripped into the rushes strewn on the tent floor.

It seemed ages later that she became aware of total silence in the tent as she awoke from her trance. She stared down at the healing wound beneath her bloody hands. Her patient stirred. He lifted his head and looked at her for the first time with glazed, pain-filled black eyes that slowly focused on her face. Bronwyn's own eyes filled with regognition and she drew back in shock and fear. *It was Warwick!* Warwick, whose thin lips weakly twisted into an evil grin, Warwick's cold black eyes that devoured her face. His hands reached up and pulled her closer to him with surprising strength. His face was drawn, pale and full of pain and though his eyelids were heavy, his gaze was sharp and clear.

It took every ounce of courage and restraint Bronwyn possessed not to cry out at his touch and give herself away. Already everyone was gawking at her and whispering over what they had seen.

It stopped bleeding . . . Look! The wound has healed!

Bronwyn's head spun and she reeled back trying to free herself from Warwick's grasp, but to no avail.

"Christ! 'Tis you! It *is* you, wench!" The Earl of

Warwick muttered weakly. His eyes were now as she remembered them, hard, glittering and mocking. He laughed ironically, then glanced at his wound. She felt a shudder go through his strong body and when he raised his eyes to her white face, there was astonishment reflected in their depths. "Sweet Merciful Jesú! Edward was right . . . you *are* a witch! You *can* heal by touching . . ." he whispered in a stunned voice that only she could hear.

Her eyes widened with fright and she pulled away from him, easily this time for he was still so weak. She stared at him, speechless; then he shook his shaggy dark head. "Fret not, wench, I will not give you away." Closing his eyes, he sank back onto the pallet, drained both physically and emotionally.

The King had been standing behind Bronwyn all the while, watching what had just transpired between them. It had happened so swiftly that, like most of the others in the tent, he was at a loss to understand what was happening at the time. But unlike the others he knew her secret and realized immediately what had occured. Edward sent his lords and knights from the tent with a curt order. When they had all gone, he turned and walked back to Bronwyn. Taking her hands in his he said, "You saved my cousin's life. For that I thank you, my love." He knew how she hated the man, yet she had overcome her personal animosity in order to heal his wound.

"I would have let him die . . ." she raised loving eyes to his, "but I remembered . . . on the battlefield . . . he did save your life."

"Aye, that he did, and as a consequence he was wounded. The blow he took was also meant for me, so it is twice he stepped between me and certain death." He enfolded her in his aching arms and she noticed for the first time sweat and blood staining his tunic. "You are not wounded, my lord?" she asked anxiously.

Edward shook his head. "Mere scratches—nothing of any importance, thanks to my brave cousin."

"Thank God," Bronwyn whispered, tightening her arms around his neck.

"I shall have Lord Warwick removed to his own tent where he may recover in peace and quiet," said the King, looking over at where the warrior lay in exhausted slumber, and his thoughts were in turmoil. This was the man whose loyalty he so often questioned, yet Warwick had saved his life twice. Could it be that he had been wrong about his dark cousin? Could it be that he had seen treachery where there was none? Was he incapable of distinguishing his friends from his enemies?

Over the next few days, Edward periodically visited Warwick's tent and found him rapidly regaining strength. Neither spoke about Bronwyn and how she had healed him, but Edward noticed an unusual thoughtfulness about his cousin that he had never seen before. Edward was aware that the camp was buzzing with speculation about what had actually happened, but the men would fall silent whenever he came upon them unexpectedly. The rumors and the sidelong glances worried him but he was so busy helping to identify and prepare the dead for burial after the battle as well as ordering the diposition of his prisoners that he had precious little time to spend in dwelling on the matter. Stragglers and Lancastrian deserters needed to be rounded up as well, and negotiations must be made with the Scots and the captured forces of Lancaster. The Scots were eager now to make peace and Edward determined to be lenient in hopes that the border raids would halt and the Scots no longer foment rebellion. Edward was especially eager to settle the situation as soon as possible for there were reports that another large Lancastrian force was gathering at Hexham and he had sent the Earl of Warwick's younger brother John Neville with an army to subdue them. The infamous Edmund Beaufort, Duke of Somerset and Queen Margaret's leading defender, was leading that advancing force, and Edward wanted to leave Durham and march for Hexham in support of Neville. Somerset was a formidable opponent and Margaret had realized that breaking up her main force and fighting on two fronts might gain at least one victory for Lancaster. Where would Margaret strike next, Edward wondered. No doubt she would turn to King Louis of France and try to enlist his support now that the Scots were out of the picture. *Dear God, will the woman never give up?* Edward thought.

Meanwhile, Bronwyn stayed in the tent and did her best to stay out of everyone's sight. When she ventured outside, the men would point at her and whisper. It made her uneasy.

One morning when Edward was gone, she made her cautious way down to the stream on the edge of the camp to refill the water skins; she lowered her head and spoke to no one and was returning to the safety of the tent when a figure loomed in front of her, blocking her path. With startled eyes she looked up to see the Earl of Warwick staring down at her.

"So we meet again, my pretty *lad*," he said. His voice was itself again, harsh and cold as his black eyes bored into hers. "I've waited all these days for you. Sooner or later I knew you'd have to come out of hiding. I am on my way to see the King . . . I have news to impart, news which he will want to hear. I'm sure." He reached out to touch her arm and she instinctively stepped back to escape his grasp. He laughed.

"You still hate me so much, eh, little witch?" This time when he reached out, she could not elude him and he soon had her arm firmly pinned against his side. His eyes were as stormy and cruel as she had remembered them and his grasp like iron. She struggled with all her strength, but to no avail.

"The King will be back any minute, my Lord," she said through clenched teeth, glaring up at him with flashing eyes. "Please, sir, let me pass." She tried to speak politely, but it was hard with his sharp face hovering above hers. It was a face she had seen many times in her nightmares and it was all she could do not to scream and lash out at him. Yet she wasn't afraid of him any longer. She was under Edward's protection and if Warwick harmed her in any way, he would answer to Edward.

He stood there studying her as if she were some wild animal he had caught in a trap. He smiled that wicked grin and her blood went cold.

"My Lord, I ask you please to let me go!" Her voice rose.

"I wanted to thank you for saving my life." He touched her cheek, still smiling. Then he bent down close to her and his eyes glittered like black diamonds. "I couldn't ride off without expressing my gratitude. My wound is almost completely healed. *How did you do it, witch? How?*"

"I did nothing, my Lord. It was nothing!" she said in a tiny voice. Her eyes searched beyond his towering bulk for a sign of the King returning. She could hear horses coming from a distance and with a sigh of relief she said, "I think the King is coming now, my lord, so you can deliver the news you spoke of." He wouldn't dare harass her once Edward rode back into camp.

Suddenly his whole manner changed. His eyes grew calculating and his voice intimate. "I will say what I have to say to you first. Then I will let you go. I don't know what you did a few days ago or how you did it. I'm not a religious man. I do not believe in either miracles or witchcraft, unlike most of my peers. But many people do." He emphasized the words by saying them in a slow, biting drawl; his grip on her arm was so tight that she almost whimpered. The approaching horsemen were galloping into the heart of the camp now and she saw the King among them.

"But," he continued, fully aware that their conversation must soon come to a hurried conclusion, "I would not be your friend if I did not warn you." Bronwyn's heart was beating frantically. "Warn me of what, my lord?"

"What is being said of you and Edward. There are those who have seen through your disguise, as well as those who merely whisper about your healing powers. Do you realize how dangerous you have become to the King? All over London they say you have bewitched him. I've even heard it said that it is your witchery that has brought Edward this victory. They fear that Edward has sold his soul to the devil and you are the Devil's agent." Each ugly word bit like a fanged viper and Bronwyn cringed, speechless. She shook her head, denying what he was saying but all the while knowing in her heart that it must be so. All her life her healing gift had been more a curse than a blessing and now it was tainting Edward's life as well. She shut her eyes, the pulse in her slender throat beating rapidly. Oh, God, God! What should she do?

There were tears gathering at the corners of her angry eyes and she pulled one more time to free herself, but without success. "*Let me go!*" She suddenly lashed out in desperation and in a mindless fury, stamped her boot down upon his foot as hard as she could. For a second she was afraid he was going to strike her. Then abruptly he let her go and she almost toppled back into the dust.

The King had arrived at his tent and dismounting, he did not immediately notice them.

"*Take care, witch!*" Warwick hissed. "I have not forgotten what I owe you. I promise you someday when he tires of you—if you don't go to the stake first!—I shall pay you back in full. *In full*!'' Then, like the changing wind, he spun on his booted heel and bowed to Edward who had just come up to them. She couldn't believe how quickly his expression changed when he was facing Edward. All smiles and obeisance, as if their conversation had consisted of pleasant trivialities instead of evil threats. Warwick, Bronwyn realized, hadn't changed at all.

"Sire!" Warwick was beaming now. "I have great news! A courier from my brother John has just arrived. You will be most interested in the message."

"And what did it say, my Lord Warwick?" Edward's smile was faint, yet his blue eyes rested warmly on his cousin. After all, he did owe Warwick his life.

"Our men led by my brother John, did gain us a great victory on the banks of the Devilswater near Hexham two days ago! Many were killed on the battlefield and the rest were routed. They are still running for their worthless lives, no doubt." Warwick laughed and the King after a few seconds of stunned disbelief joined in.

"God's blood! Another victory, so soon! God he praised!" Edward cried, slapping Warwick happily upon his broad back while Bronwyn stood by, unnoticed.

"And what of Somerset, then?" Edward's face turned serious, the sun shining on his bright golden hair and his eyes a deep, clear blue.

"Captured on the battlefield along with many more of Margaret's knights."

"Aye," Edward replied gravely, "and not long to keep their heads. This time, I have learned my lesson. I pardoned Somerset three years ago after Towton and he swore he would stay true to York. I will show no mercy. All traitors will feel the executioner's axe. I'll spare them being drawn and quartered . . . I am not a monster and they are high lords. I'll give them a swift death, but death it shall be. See to it, my lord," the King ordered and Warwick merely nodded, his black eyes unreadable.

Edward threw Bronwyn a glance and she scurried into the tent. Their conversation had given her gooseflesh. So easily did a King send a man to the block! Once again she was reminded of who she was in love with and of how insignificant she was. It seemed the longer Edward reigned, the more inflexible he became. Perhaps it was due to the endless plotting and betrayals he saw around him day after day. He could never be sure who was a true friend and who were his enemies. He'd become suspicious and cold. In the last months he had changed a great deal, she hadn't seen it until lately, especially since the battle. He was still loving and considerate of her and they still found ecstasy in each other's arms, but the King of late had a distant yearning in his eyes and he often grew impatient, as if something was troubling him. It puzzled and distressed her that there was something on his mind which he wasn't sharing with her. She could feel him drifting away from her and she was at a loss to understand why. Sometimes she felt it might be better if she just disappeared one night and never came back . . .

A few days later, they rode back to London. Bronwyn saw little of the King on the journey. He was busy with Warwick planning their next move. She knew he'd signed the Bills of Attainder that would toll the death kneel for the teacherous Somerset and the others. Somerset, she'd heard, had been beheaded in the marketplace of Hexham before a jeering crowd and had, they said, died a less than noble death. The rest were to be beheaded before the week was out. Her heart was heavy in spite of the great victory they had won. Sometimes she rode near poor, pitiful King Henry, who slumped in his saddle, and sang tuneless little songs. She tried to befriend him and made sure he was fed regularly, as no one else seemed to give a fig for the poor man. But Henry seemed to exist in another world most of the time, far away from the ignominious

332

present, where everyone had deserted him and left him alone in the midst of his enemies. She even begged Edward to keep the gawkers and whores away from the poor creature, for they loved to taunt him and make fun of him. He cared not, but she did.

"King Henry, I know, is not to blame for all this," Edward told her one night. "And I will treat him fairly. I will put him in Wakefield Tower where he will be treated with respect and decency. But I cannot give him his freedom. He is too valuable a hostage for that, even though he is useless to Margaret. She seeks the crown for her young son. My sweet, he shall be treated well, I promise you."

The King was true to his word. Henry was put in the best apartments of the Wakefield Tower and treated with the consideration due his royal birth. Bronwyn visited him from time to time to make sure he was being well cared for. She pitied him so . . .

Once back in London Bronwyn's heavy heart was full of foreboding. Edward had ridden away almost immediately, and as she watched him gallop off, she had a premonition that it would be a long time before she saw him again, if ever. She sensed a strange reserve in him and her heart wept to know that whatever was coming between them was something she could neither change nor halt.

CHAPTER XII

August 1464

THE BEAUTIFUL spring turned into a long and sweltering summer that Bronwyn thought would never end.

After a few weeks she could no longer abide the loneliness of her chambers in the Tower and went to stay awhile with Martha and her sisters at the Red Boar. The visit that was to have lasted only a short while grew into weeks and then months, and she heard no word from Edward. The suspicion grew deep in her heart that something fragile and undefinable had changed between herself and Edward, and as the summer dragged by and with no summons or message from him, she suffered in silence. Then in late August the city was flooded with rumors that King Edward had secretly married. Confused and hurt, Bronwyn refused to believe it. Then one hot afternoon as she was baking the last of the bread for that night's supper in the inn, she heard a rider gallop up. She continued to knead the large mound of dough, her sister Mary at her side. There were always men and carriages coming and going all day long, and since Jack had persuaded her to sing on Friday and Saturday nights, the business had picked up even more. Bronwyn sighed. Her hair was pulled back and covered with a plain linen wimple that kept her hair from falling in her eyes. She wiped her hand across her perspiring face, leaving a faint trail of flour across one cheek, and Mary giggled.

"You'd best go wash up for supper, Mary," Bronwyn said sternly. "Your face could use some attention, too." The little girl would have lingered for the first batch of warm bread to come out of the oven (she loved to eat it hot with melted butter, and always turned up when it was baking), but Bronwyn leveled an unsmiling gaze at her. "Now," she said. They'd spent the day at Leadenhall Market buying fresh fish and meat for the night's fare, and Bronwyn was very tired. She had been feeling ill and unusually sleepy now for weeks and Martha, mother hen that she was, kept hovering over her, concern in her grey eyes.

Now Martha came bustling into the kitchen, her face tight and her eyes troubled, wringing her hands as Bronwyn had seen her do many times when Jack was giving her trouble. "Bronwyn . . . there be someone here to see you," Martha said nervously. "He wouldn't come in . . . he wants to see you outside in the courtyard."

Bronwyn's eyes lit up and her face was transformed by a radiant smile. It had to be a messenger from the King! She wiped her sticky hands on her apron and, tearing the wimple from her head, she shook her hair free. It fell loose and shining down to her waist. "Where is he?" She was already moving towards the door, her step brisk and bouncy.

"The courtyard . . . 'tis James, child." Martha stepped directly in front of her and touched her arm. "Wait, Bronwyn! I would tell you now so it will not be such a shock . . ." Martha looked down at her clenched hands, as if she were trying to find the proper words. Then, squaring her plump shoulders and taking a deep breath, she forged ahead, though she couldn't look Bronwyn in the eye. "He has a message for you from the King . . . and by the look on his face it is not good news." Martha forced herself to raise her eyes, and saw Bronwyn's smile crumple and her face suddenly turn pale. It was as if she knew what Martha had to stay before the words were spoken.

"You know what they've been saying these last weeks about the King, do you not?" Martha continued gently.

Bronwyn's eyes flashed and then filled with tears as she nodded, speechless. Aye, she knew. She knew all too well and had tried to tell herself that she must face it if it were true. She had no claim on the King. She had always known she was incredibly fortunate to have his love at all, no matter for how brief a time; it was more than most people have in a lifetime. She would always love him, and she had always known he could never belong to her. And yet . . .

Martha went on, "I have heard other things about this matter . . ." Martha couldn't bring herself to say the word *marriage*, but Bronwyn knew exactly what she was talking about. "Whatever the courier has to tell you, my child, remember you have friends and family here that love and care for you. You aren't alone." Martha's eyes were wet and Bronwyn knew she meant every word.

"Thank you, Martha. Now I must find out what the message is." Bronwyn eased past her friend and like a sleepwalker went outside into the courtyard to find James. A million thoughts echoed through her mind and a tiny hope flickered faintly that what he had to tell her wasn't what she feared—that the King was married and would no longer be able to see her, never again. Never again to see his smile. Never again to feel his strong arms about her as they lay abed together . . . Savagely, she pushed the thoughts away and walked up to where James sat his prancing horse near the big maple tree. The horse was lathered as if he had been running for hours in the endless heat. The young man's eyes followed her until she stood below him, his hands lax on the reins and his face covered with the dirt and sweat of his long ride. He leaned down and without a word handed her a rolled parchment with the King's seal upon it.

"You won't stop to quench your thirst, sir?" she asked as she clutched the message from Edward in her trembling hands. "You are welcome to come inside and rest awhile where it is cooler and have a cup of cold ale or cider." It was so hot that she could feel the underkirtle of her light gown clinging to her skin and beads of sweat trickling down her face. Her hair was sticking to her neck, damp and heavy—as heavy as her heart as she saw reflected in his eyes regret at the news he had brought her.

"Nay, mistress. I have orders to ride directly back." He looked solemnly down at her from atop his tall mount and bowed slightly in his saddle. He couldn't help but feel sorry for the poor maid. Of all Edward's many women, this one had always seemed like a sweet maid, not like the rest of them. She was so pretty. He had heard the rumors about her having bewitched the King, and about what had happened at Durham that spring, but he hadn't believed any of that nonsense. She seemed a good woman, and he feared she would be heartbroken by the King's message. Edward was riding toward London even now and soon there would be great festivities. He could not tarry, nor did he want to stay and watch the girl read that note.

"Then I thank you, sir, for bringing this to me." Her chin was held high and he admired her beauty and courage. Suddenly he had the feeling that she was the kind of girl who could take anything in her stride. She was strong, no doubt of that.

Bronwyn stood there and watched as he rode away, her fingers tightly gripping the parchment. Then she turned and looked around at her familiar surroundings, and remembered that terrible night when Warwick had abducted her and Edward had followed and rescued her. She thought of how patient and loving he had been, and of how for her sake he had saved the poor priests from burning at the stake. She thought of many things in those few seconds before she broke the parchment's wax seal and slowly read the words he had written in his sprawling script. She smiled faintly. He always wrote simply for her in large letters so she would be able to read his messages. She wasn't very good at reading and writing, though her mother had taught her as best she could. She found little use for either in her everyday life.

When she had finished the letter, tears were pouring down her white face and as she turned blindly to make her way back to the inn and Martha, who had been standing in the doorway all this time watching her like a hawk, her steps faltered and without a cry or a word, she collapsed to the cobblestones. Martha let out a startled cry and ran to her side.

"Oh, Martha, Martha . . . he *is* married," Bronwyn whispered. "It is all true, everything they say. He married a Lancastrian widow, Elizabeth Grey Woodville! Months ago at a place called Grafton Manor somewhere in Northamptonshire." She wept miserably in Martha's arms.

Martha would never forget Bronwyn's pitiful face, that sad little face stained with tears as she cradled the girl in her arms that summer afternoon. She would remember Bronwyn's heartbreak all her life.

"Who is Elizabeth Grey Woodville?" Martha asked, not knowing what else to say. Being older and wiser in the ways of the world, Martha had always known it would come to this—this lovely child crying over a man she was never destined to possess. Oh, yes, she had always known, and so had Bronwyn. A peasant could never hope to marry a King, 'Twas a simple rule of life. It had to end this way.

Bronwyn moaned and between onslaughts of fresh tears, she gulped, "Edward wrote to tell me that he has taken a widow to be his Queen. She has children and is five years his senior. He writes that she . . . reminds him of me—fair hair and cat's eyes." She tried to laugh but failed miserably. "He could never marry me, but he has married this noble lady who looks so like me . . . He says that because she is a Lancastrian, she will help to bring the two rival factions together and stop the bloodshed between the houses of York and Lancaster. He always told me that one of his greatest wishes was to bring peace to England . . ." Bronwyn broke down again and Martha merely held her and let her weep.

"Hush, hush, child. It will be all right," she soothed. "It is the will of God. You knew it could not last. You've told me so many times, remember?" Martha lifted Bronwyn's wet face up to look at her. "You had what many women dream of and can never have. It is better to have loved and lost, than never to have loved at all. He did love you, child. Perhaps, he still does. But he is a King and Kings must marry their own kind."

Bronwyn closed her eyes knowing that Martha was right. "Aye, Martha, I know it is true. I know. Yet knowing does not ease the pain in my heart when I think of him married to another. I accept it, I do . . . it's just that it hurts far more than I had ever thought it would! It is as though someone had plucked my heart right from my breast and trampled it underfoot. Knowing that I shall never see him again, touch him, nor hear his laughter, leaves such an emptiness that I feel I shall die of it! I miss him so sometimes. I miss him so it hurts! Just to see him again . . . but I know I never shall. And he shall never see our child . . . never . . ."

Martha stared at her, open-mouthed and whispered in astonishment, "You are with child?"

Bronwyn blinked up at her, her eyes red and tear filled. The words had just slipped out. It was Edward she had hoped to tell, Edward she had dreamed of informing with great happiness and love. For weeks she had known she was breeding. How she had longed to tell the King! A son.

340

A son with blond hair and green eyes. And now he had married a beautiful widow who would give him the royal heirs he craved . . . and he would never know about the child she carried. She started to sob again and through her tears she saw Martha smiling with joy.

"But you will have his child . . . a part of him, at least!"

Bronwyn touched her stomach gently, and for the first time since she had read his letter, a misty smile touched her lips. It was true—she still had a part of the man she loved. She would bear his child and no one, nothing, could take that away from her. She would give Edward's child the love she could no longer lavish on the father.

"Well, well!" Martha crooned, her eyebrow arching and her hands on her ample hips as she studied the girl before her. "I wondered why you be so sick of late and now I know!" She smiled and helped Bronwyn to her feet. "Come. Let's get out of the sun. Too much heat is bad for you and the child."

Bronwyn clutched the crumpled parchment in her hand and as they walked back inside the inn, Bronwyn smoothed it carefully against her skirts and folded it, tucking it into her bodice. The shock was wearing off and only a look of haunted sadness lingered on the girl's pale face.

Bronwyn thought of the last line of the letter and it kept repeating in her mind over and over: *I will always love you, my little nightingale. Please understand that I didn't do this to wound you.* She knew it was true. He did love her and she loved him. Nothing could change that. She dried her tears, but now a new pain seared her heart. Perhaps Edward was also frightened of her gift and what people were saying about her, frightened that his enemies would use it against her and to harm her. After she had healed Lord Warwick, she had seen *that look* in his eyes. The Lancasters had already spread so many untruths about the young King—that he was in actuality a bastard, the byblow of an affair between his noble mother and an English archer, and many other such lies—that the charge of consorting with a witch might literally pull the crown from his head and bring her to the stake in the end. He had no doubt feared for her safety, as well . . .

Once, she recalled, he had thought her his Merlin. Now he knew that his people would only see her as an evil being whose wicked powers could bring great harm to England. And people destroyed what they could not understand.

Inside, Mary and Samantha were waiting for her and she took them into her arms, the tears still wet on her face. Neither asked any questions and Bronwyn offered no explanation. After they had left the room, she turned to Martha and said softly, "If it is a boy, Martha . . . if you don't object . . . I should like to call him Johnny."

Martha replied, "If that is what you want."

"Aye, that is what I want."

Martha nodded, her eyes brimming with tears as well. Johnny it would be.

CHAPTER XIII

February 1468

BRONWYN INDEED did have a boy and she named him Johnny after Martha's dead son. He was a beautiful blond, blue-eyed baby, born right before the middle of February, 1465. He immediately became the love of his young mother's life, and of Martha's, too. Samantha and Mary doted on their little nephew and would take him everywhere with them as they worked about the inn. And not even Jack so much as mentioned the fact that the child was illegitimate. Remembering who the boy's father was, he treated him like a young prince.

Johnny was soon to be three years old and Bronwyn sat and watched him out in the courtyard under Martha's watchful eye one bright February morning, all bundled up in thick woolen clothes that Martha and Mary had made for him. He seemed so tiny and vulnerable seated on Chelsea as a stable boy led the mare around, and he giggled and laughed, his little hands beating at the saddle he was strapped into. He looked so much like his royal father that it nearly took Bronwyn's breath away. He was so precious to her!

It had been over three years since she had last seen the King, but she still thought of him constantly. And why not, since she held his tiny replica in her arms every day? Bronwyn sighed, smoothing her skirts and went back to brewing the hot posset she was making for little Johnny when he came back in.

She had had plenty of suitors these last years, but not one had made her heart race as Edward. And it didn't help to hear of the King and his beautiful Queen, Elizabeth, all the time. London was full of gossip about the feud that had sprung up between Elizabeth's Woodville kin and the Nevilles. The Earl of Warwick was said to hate the woman herself almost as much as he detested her family. *There were as many Woodvilles*, they said, *as there were rabbits in Wales*. And all of them, like Elizabeth, were ambitious and grasping. It was said that the King was greatly in love with his ice-queen, but she was reported to be vain and scheming and disliked by everyone at court. Edward had bestowed great rank and high position on Elizabeth's father, Earl Rivers, and on her many brothers. Her brother, Anthony had been made Governor of the Isle of Wight; and Edward had knighted yet another of her many brothers, and had arranged a marriage for a third to the ancient Duchess of Norfolk. The match was considered preposterous because the Woodvilles had so little of everything while the Duchess was so wealthy and so *old*. Earl Rivers was now Constable of England. They said Warwick was livid over the appointments and the arranged marriages . . . Elizabeth had five unmarried sisters as well! He considered that the King had given the Woodvilles far too much power, late in 1467, when the Earl of Warwick was in France and could neither influence Edward's decision or even speak his own mind, Edward promised his sister, Meg, to Charles of Burgundy—France's most bitter enemy and long-time foe. This enraged Warwick and it was rumored that he and the King had nearly come to blows. It was the last straw for Warwick when Edward removed his brother George Neville's title of Chancellor for refusing to sit in Parliament to approve of the marriage which would strengthen Edward's ties with Charles of Burgundy and end the troublesome Burgundian embargo on English wool. But the price of ending the antagonism between Burgundy and England was antithetical to the peace that Warwick had been seeking for so long with Louis of France. Warwick returned to England, his temper hot and his patience with the strong willed King at the breaking point.

There was talk that Warwick was raising a great force to remove the English crown from Edward's fair head. No one knew where the earl was since he had stormed from Westminister a few months ago in a blind rage.

Bronwyn heard all these stories, and her heart ached for the King. Like the rest of the people of England, she attributed all Edward's problems to his greedy and ambitious Queen. There was the unsettling prospect of civil war everywhere these days and the common people were once more preparing for the worst. They feared that Warwick would align himself with other malcontents or, even worse, with France or Scotland, and rise against the throne. With the great Earl of Warwick and the Nevilles behind him opposing Edward, it would create total havoc—brother against brother, cousin against cousin. The camps were equal in size and strength and the chaos and bloodshed would be great.

It was all anyone ever talked about these days, Bronwyn thought as she poured the posset into mugs and peered out to see what Martha and Johnny were up to. Whether Warwick was in France or in Hell made little difference to her, as long as he wasn't tormenting her and her son. She knew she had been lucky these last few years not to have crossed paths with the man again. Did he even know of little Johnny's existence? Bronwyn fervently hoped not. How could he, when the child's own father was unaware of it?

Her eyes misted over again at these unbidden thoughts of Edward. Her ecstatic months with him all seemed like a dream now, so far away and so long ago. Yet sometimes it seemed just like yesterday, whenever she gazed at her wee Johnny or heard him laugh. He was so like Edward . . .

She stood there in the center of the inn's kitchen lost in thought and memory, a pretty woman of twenty dressed in a simple gown of soft brown with a cream colored kirtle and a high bodice, the sleeves long and tapered snuggly about her slim wrists, her hair severely pulled back into a braided knot at the nape of her neck. Her face was still finely shaped and long, dark lashes set off her sad emerald eyes. There as beauty in this woman, but sorrow as well. It was evident in the way she smiled only with her mouth and not her eyes or her heart, except when she smiled at her Johnny or laughed with him. Then her beauty was overwhelming.

Bronwyn had continued to work at the Inn after her son was born, but she kept to herself. She rarely sang for the customers anymore, except on special occasions. Jack had been angry about that at first because she had begun to draw a crowd, but he had deferred to her wishes in the end. Though he would never admit it, she and her sisters were worth their weight in gold. Samantha was now a lovely lass of sixteen, and waited on the customers as Bronwyn had once done, attracting many a masculine eye. Mary, still fragile and thin at twelve, was an excellent seamstress as well as a fairly good cook. Oh, Jack got his money's worth from the three of them, all right, and he knew it and was content.

Bronwyn had stopped singing in the inn when her pregnancy began to show. She had also stopped practicing her healing. Without the King's protection, she had feared for her babe as well as herself. Even though she knew that Warwick was in France most of the time and had probably not given her a thought, she could take no chances and thought it better to be as inconspicuous as possible. But Samantha loved mingling with the customers and teasing with the soldiers, calming those in their cups and flirting with the younger, wealthy patrons. She'd told Bronwyn many times that she intended to snare a rich husband. And Bronwyn had no doubt she would manage to do just that!

Bronwyn was content, if not happy, as she was. She craved no rich husband; she craved no husband at all. The memory of Edward still haunted her and she felt she no longer had a heart to give to anyone. He had taken it with him when he left her and she had never found it again. A sorrowful smile formed on her lips as she remembered the words and tune of a French song Edward had once taught her as they lay in bed together one morning after making sweet love, and he had sung it over and over until she had memorized it perfectly:

Amors, ge sui en ta baille
an ton demoinne m'as saisie
amors, soëf unpo me moine!
Love, deal gently with me awhile . . . what defense have I against love?

What defense, indeed? The King had stolen her heart and he hadn't dealt gently with her at all. She sighed and her eyes were still misty when a laughing Martha chased her son into the warm kitchen and straight into her arms.

"My pet! How cold you are!" Bronwyn laughed down into her son's blue eyes—Edward's blue eyes. She rubbed her hands vigorously over the icy little hands he held up to her. He always did that when it was cold. He'd offer her his hands and she would massage them until they were warm again. He laughed too and flung his chubby arms around her neck.

"Mama! Cold, Mama!" he cried as she tugged the woolen cap from his head and he buried his head of golden curls in the curve of her shoulder.

Martha came up behind them, a smile on her rosy cheeks. Since Johnny's birth she had been like a different woman. She loved the child as though he was her own, often always teasing Bronwyn that people did think she was his mother, the way she doted on him. "The boy is a natural horseman, Bronwyn. The way he sits his saddle—! He's not afraid of the horse at all, as young and small as he be. Such a big, brave boy is our Johnny!" The older woman ruffled the child's bright curls and tickled him under the chin and he began to giggle. Then he pulled away from Bronwyn's embrace and ran to Martha's open arms, giving her a big kiss on her plump cheek. "More ride . . . more Chessy!" he demanded subbornly. He couldn't quite pronounce the mare's name yet. "Marta . . . more ride, pease?" he begged in his piping little voice. Johnny was a charming little boy, smart, too. All of them agreed to that. Very smart and determined for his tender age.

Already Bronwyn could see hints of the man he would someday grow up to be. He was fiercely loyal, strong-willed and loving. He adored horses and dogs. He learned quickly and he was so . . . *beautiful*! It nearly took her breath away at times.

Whenever she looked at her adorable son, she saw Edward. God, how she wished the King could see the child of their love! He would be so proud! What kind of future would the lad have the way things were? What could he hope to grow up to be? A stableboy or a farm laborer—or, Heaven forbid a soldier like her poor father? A common soldier who would be lured to war by dreams of spoils and great deeds to be done, victories to be won and, in the end, most likely find a bloody, useless death on some foreign battlefield. That is what happened to poor men. They lived and died and no one cared.

And yet *he was a son of a King*! The blood that coursed through his veins was as noble as that of any high Lord.

More. Bronwyn had debated with herself for years about sending a message to the King and informing him that she had borne his son, but she could never bring herself to do it. Johnny was hers, the only part of Edward that remained to her. She was well aware of what Kings often did for their bastards, taking them under their royal wing and bringing them to court where they might be ridiculed and hounded, and considered inferior to the other legitimate children. Johnny would no doubt be sent to the castle of some distant lord, where he would be taught to take his rightful place in the world, first as a page, then squire and then perhaps a knight. He would be taught the ways of war and killing; taught how to be a lord. That was what frightened Bronwyn. She would lose her son then. They would be part of two different worlds, as she and Edward had been. Johnny was all she had and she couldn't stand to lose him as well. So she had remained silent and selfishly kept the child to herself.

Last year the Queen had given Edward their first child, a girl. Bronwyn had thought it ironic that the woman couldn't give Edward a son as she had done. Surely that made her the better woman, did it not? But her gloating hadn't lasted long. Elizabeth's daughter would one day be a princess or a Queen herself. That child would know Edward's love and care, while her poor little Johnny would never know either and would always bear the stigma of his illegitimate birth.

This year the Queen had given birth to yet another child, again a girl. This time Bronwyn didn't gloat. She only looked at her lovely son with Edward's eyes and Edward's golden hair and wanted to weep.

Had Edward completely forgotten her? What would happen if he never sired a son but this one little bastard boy? She frowned at the bitter thought and grieved for the boy who would never be able to claim his birthright. Nothing eased the guilt she felt when she thought of what she was depriving Johnny of. Perhaps she *should* send him to Edward? But would he even want him? There was a time she would have said aye, but now she wasn't sure. She wasn't sure Edward had really loved her at all.

She turned and looked at her son in Martha's arms. Would he love their son, or spurn him?

"Want Mama!" Johnny wailed and Martha grudgingly released the child who dashed back to Bronwyn. He snuggled in her arms again and pulled at her hair, his eyes drooping suddenly with weariness. Moments later, he was asleep in her arms and she carried him up to bed and tucked him in.

"Sleep well, my tiny poppet," she crooned, stroking his baby-fine hair from his warm face. "Sleep well and grow to be a strong, healthy man." Ah, she was so proud of him! She loved him so and he was so precious to her.

Bronwyn walked from the room she shared with Johnny on the top floor, right below the old loft room that she had once shared with her sisters. Now Mary and Samantha slept in the loft room while Johnny and she had their own room. Nothing was too good for the King's mistress, old Jack had thought when he had given her the room three and a half years ago; and when the baby had come, even though she was no longer the King's mistress, Jack had let them keep the larger room with its big bed and the huge coal brazier in the corner that warmed the air. Martha wouldn't let him even think of moving them out now, he knew.

Bronwyn made her way back down to the brightly lit kitchen, listening to the familiar and comforting sounds of the inn coming to life for another evening. This was truly home to her now. Her luxurious chambers in the great Tower might never have existed. What, she sometimes wondered, had become of the kindly old physician, La Rouel? He had been her only friend. Perhaps he was dead now . . .

She spied Jack sipping at a tankard of ale as she passed through the main room, already full of hungry customers. She hurried through the crowd, her eyes downcast. It would be busy tonight, if it was this full already. Jack winked at her as she scurried past him and she nodded. She still didn't like the man very much, but she had to admit he had changed a lot from the old days. He still had his women and he was still greedy and fat, but he had never let another woman rule the roost as old Molly had, and he was more discreet now in his dallying. Besides, he was proud of keeping a former mistress of the King under his own humble roof, not to mention a King's son. So much had happened since Bronwyn had first entered the Red Boar.

She was no longer the scared, skinny lass she had once been. Now Jack treated her with respect. The only thing he regretted was that she refused to sing for his customers. Jack had an eye for a gold coin, and he saw them slipping away when he thought of Bronwyn hiding her beauty and talent in the kitchen. But he left her alone. He had never forced his attentions on her since the time when she had stepped down hard on his foot and pushed him into the water trough in the courtyard, and he had come up sputtering and gasping for air, only to be staring an angry Martha straight in the eye! Martha had screamed at him until his ears must have rung for days.

Martha had changed as well, Bronwyn thought. With Molly gone, she had stepped back into her rightful place and with Bronwyn's support she asserted herself, tightened the reins on Jack, and it had worked. Now Jack thought twice before he crossed his wife.

The night was half gone and Bronwyn had just finished dishing out another platter of roast meat and vegetables when she heard footsteps come softly up behind her. Thinking it was Martha or one of the serving wenches returning for the food, Bronwyn ladled out the last of the potatoes. Flushed from the heat of the great oven, she said, "Just a moment. I will be right with you."

There was no response and when she turned to see who it was, her eyes widened in disbelief and her hand flew to her throat.

She could think of nothing to say. She could only stare at him, drinking in every little detail, so starved she was for the sight of him.

He didn't smile or speak, but his eyes expressed the hunger, the longing, the sorrow for all the pain he had caused her. Love beamed from his blue eyes. He was as handsome as ever, perhaps a little older looking, a little heavier, a little more worn. There were tiny lines about his eyes she never remembered seeing there before. And there was sorrow, too, in those blue eyes as he devoured her with his gaze and reached out his arms in the tender gesture she still saw in her dreams. *Edward*!

With a great gasp of bittersweet joy, she ran into his embrace and felt his heart beating wildly against hers.

She could say nothing, nor could he. They stood there locked in each other's arms for what seemed ages until he looked down into her face and gently wiped the tears from her cheeks as he had done that wintry night so long ago. Then he kissed her as if he were starving for what only she could give him. Bronwyn cared not if what she was doing was right, cared not that he had not seen her in over three years, had not written to her. It was as if she had always known this would happen, that he would someday return to her, no matter what anyone said, no matter how their paths had diverged. *She belonged to him, heart and soul, and she had always known it.* By the look in his eyes and the fierceness of his kiss, she thought he had always known, too.

"Oh, Bronwyn . . . my love . . . it's been so long! I have missed you so!" he whispered in her ear and then looked deeply into her shining eyes. He touched her face tenderly with his hand. "Can you ever forgive me?"

Bronwyn nodded. Holding him close to her, she was filled with happiness for the first time in years.

He had brought back her heart.

"I wanted to send for you, Bronwyn, so many times," the King was saying. "But I was afraid that if once I held you in my arms again, I would not be able to let you go. Ever, my love." His smile was like the sun coming out after a long, dark night.

"Why didn't you?" she couldn't help but ask, then was sorry she had. She had no claim on Edward. These years of separation had put a distance between them and the man who stood before her now, she realized, was little more than a beloved stranger. Yet still she trembled at his touch. He was her only love, and yet she didn't know him at all. He was married, with a wife and children. Above all, he was the King. How could she have presumed to question him? She whispered quickly, "Your Majesty, forgive me!"

The sudden look of pain in his eyes went through her like a knife blade. He took her hand and kissed it and then led her to the stairs. When they reached the first landing he drew her into his arms once more, lost in the sweetness of her. He had taken a great risk in coming to the Red Boar tonight. Long gone were his days of roaming the streets of London incognito. He was no longer so daring, nor so unknown. And he had many more enemies now than he had then, among them, Warwick and his own brother George. His distrust of his cousin Warwick had proved to be warranted, but as for George, he could not understand it. True, he had forbidden him to marry Warwick's daughter Isabel; and George had always been jealous of Edward's power and might, though he had concealed it well. But for George to openly turn against Edward with his new father-in-law Warwick was humiliating as well as dangerous. Edward had no sons yet, and George would inherit the crown if Edward should happen to die. It was a terrible truth to have to face—that his own brother would rejoice to see him dead.

"My love," the King said in the darkness as he sat down on the top step and pulled Bronwyn down onto his lap, "I did not send for you for many reasons. My enemies could hurt me by hurting you. Your gift . . ." He didn't need to explain it any further. They both knew of what he was speaking. There was silence for a second and then he brought his lips down searingly on hers and she wrapped her arms about his neck. "But Christ, I love you still! I never stopped loving you, believe that!" She nestled her head against his shoulder and he stroked her hair as he used to.

"And then there is Elizabeth," he said, and Bronwyn thought she caught a shade of anger—just a little.

"Your Queen," Bronwyn supplied. She stiffened in his arms. This was the stuff of her fantasies all these lonely years, sitting here with Edward, her one great love, and now he was talking about his wife. Her heart seemed to burn within her breast.

"Aye, my Queen. My wife, the mother of my children, the woman I was lured and bedazzled into marrying . . . *the great royal bitch!*" His voice was now openly bitter. "She is the most grasping, ambitious, manipulating woman I have ever known . . . but, Bronwyn, I was ignorant of this in the beginning. She showed me a different side of her nature before I wed her. And it was a match that I thought would benefit the realm. But she has brought me more trouble than any woman since Margaret d'Anjou. Because of her and her conniving Woodville family I have lost the respect of many and the loyalty of my cousin Warwick, as well as that of my own brother! My court is like a bear-baiting. So many hate my inlaws and my Queen that I am constantly busy

354

keeping them all from each other's throats!'' He buried his face in Bronwyn's silken tresses until he had regained his composure, then said, ''Aye, my Queen is an impossible woman, and so too are her kin, but I admit she can be charming when she wants to be.''

She could feel his eyes on her in the dark. ''At first, she reminded me so much of you. She *looks* so like you! It threw me off guard at first. Green eyes like yours, and lovely blonde hair . . . but I soon learned that she was like you only in these outward appearances. Inside she is made of ice or stone. She has not your heart, nor your goodness. She cares for no one but herself and her family. She would destroy anyone or anything in her way. That is the other reason I have never sent for you. She would sense in you a great difference from the others that often warm my bed, and she would strike out at you. She can be vicious when she is threatened. I sought to protect you from her venom.

''And I thought if I put you away from me, I would forget you. I thought that we both would be better for it. I was wrong. There has not been a day I have not yearned for you, my little one. Not a day that I didn't wish you were by my side. I would see your smile in my mind, or remember how you looked when you came to war with me dressed as a lad—remember?''

Was this real? Was he really sitting here on this step with her in the dark, recalling poignant memories? Or was it just another fantasy? No, he was here. It was real!

''You see I did not forget. I have forgotten nothing,'' he whispered as he held her close. He could not stay long. He had eluded his men just to stop and see if the rumors he had been hearing—that she was still at the Red Boar—were true. And there was another reason, one he was afraid to mention. But, in the end, he had no need to; she did.

''Sire, they say you have two little girls?'' she asked, her heart pounding within her breast. She knew now that she couldn't keep the fact of their son from him, not now, just as she could not conceal from him the love she felt.

"That is true. They are beautiful, like their mother. I adore them." He sounded like a proud father and it encouraged her to go on.

"But you wish someday to have a son?" Her voice was very calm, but she felt the King stiffen.

"Someday, pray God, I shall have sons, many of them." He would need sons someday, to fight with him and eventually to rule the country. Perhaps, unlike his brothers and cousins, his sons would stay true to him, he thought. "I would give anything to have a son, anything. Even if he were not Elizabeth's . . ."

He knew! She could feel it! With tears in her eyes, Bronwyn stood up and reached for his hand. "Come. I have something I want to show you. There is someone I want you to meet."

He said not a word but followed her up the dark steps and when she led him into a small sparsely furnished room, he squeezed her hand. She walked over to where a child lay sleeping on a large bed and he silently came up behind her as she lit another candle. Johnny was frightened of the dark and so she always lit a small candle for the boy until he fell asleep. She had not come back up to snuff it out tonight. The two candles brightened the drab room and Edward gazed down at the sleeping child with the golden curls, his small fist pressed up against his plump cheek.

Bronwyn knelt down beside the bed and swept the curls from the boy's peaceful face, so beautiful in the flickering candlelight. She looked up into Edward's stunned eyes with a smile, tears shimmering in her wide green eyes.

"He is mine?" Edward asked in awe, his eyes unable to leave the boy's face. He had been told that there was a blond, blue-eyed child at the inn, but he hadn't been able to believe what his heart whispered to him—that the boy might be his. He had hoped . . . he had prayed . . . but, never, had he really believed that the boy could be his son. Now, as he studied the boy and looked into Bronwyn's shining eyes, he knew.

She nodded, the tears brimming over and running down her face. "Aye, my love, he is your son. *Our* son . . . Johnny."

Edward leaned over the sleeping child and touched his curls gently, and then his warm cheek, and there was a look in his eyes that Bronwyn had never seen before. He stared at the boy a long time and then turned to her. A great smile of joy lit his face and his eyes glowed. He took her into his arms and held her so tightly she could hardly breathe. "Why did you not tell me!" The words were fierce, yet his lips on her neck were warm and loving. "Why did you hide him so long? What were you afraid of?"

She paused, trying to find the right words. "I was afraid you would not want him . . . a bastard!" The word stung even as she uttered it. How she hated that word!

"*God, God*! How could I not want my own flesh and blood? My own son! *Our* son! I care not that he is a bastard. I love you." He looked past her to where their son slept on, unaware that his father was so near. "And he is part of that love. I would have cherished him for that alone, not just for his being a boy-child. *Bastard*! No son of mine shall ever be called a bastard! He is my son!" Edward took Bronwyn's face between his hands and when he spoke, his words were sure and strong. "Both of you belong to me! I will not let you go this time. Elizabeth or no, I will not let you go!"

CHAPTER XIV

July 1469

IT WAS A hot July afternoon like any other. Bronwyn was resting under the maple tree enjoying the shade and watching little Johnny chasing the chickens around the courtyard. He laughed and disappeared around the building and, a second later, he was running up to her and throwing himself into her lap, a struggling chicken clutched under his arm. "Johnny, let the poor beastie go before you break its neck." Her son reluctantly released the chicken and they watched it hurry away with a mad flutter of wings and assorted squawkings at the indignity it had suffered at the boy's hands.

It was another very hot summer and Bronwyn shaded her eyes against the sun's glare. The inn was like an oven this time of day. The mornings weren't so bad, but by late afternoon, when the sun was at its highest, the kitchen was so hot she could barely stand it.

Now there were rumors that the Earl of Warwick had gathered a huge force and was on his way, marching toward London, and that Edward had assembled a mighty army with his younger brother, Richard, who at seventeen was already showing signs of being a great warrior, and was heading south to confront Warwick. Mary knew that

Bronwyn was sick at heart over what might happen to her beloved.

"Nay, sister, I have heard nothing. It's been weeks . . ." Bronwyn sighed. She was frightened for Edward's safety. All England held its breath as the two great warlords traveled to face each other, perhaps on a battlefield if their differences could not be settled. All Bronwyn could do was wait, wait and pray that all would be well.

Johnny was now playing in the water trough; perched on the wooden edge and having disposed of his shoes he was rippling his small feet through the cool water. Bronwyn watched silently and smiled. She would do the same thing on such a day as this if she were a little child. Johnny had made a boat of twigs and leaves and was pushing it across the surface of the water. Then a mischievous look crossed his face as he searched the courtyard to see if Jack were anywhere about and, when he was satisfied that he was not, he plunged into the trough like a fish into the ocean.

Bronwyn jumped up, gathering her skirts, and ran breathlessly to the water trough. "Johnny! Johnny!" she cried, but only half afraid. The water wasn't deep, but it didn't take much to drown a four year old . . . She grasped the edge of the trough and leaned over, reaching for Johnny's hand. But he refused to allow her to help him out splashing water into her face and laughing gleefully, as he clung to the inner edge. The sun shone on his wet blond hair and the blue of his eyes was like sapphires. He was so beautiful, so loving and full of life! And Edward loved him every bit as much as Bronwyn did. The King had offered to establish her and little Johnny in a secluded manor house, and to acknowledge the child as his own, but Bronwyn had steadfastly refused. It was enough to know that Edward loved them both. She insisted on raising their son far from the pitfalls and possible dangers of the royal court where he would be protected from those who might seek to use the boy to further their own ends with the King—or worse, to cause him harm. The Queen and her ambitious kin, Bronwyn feared, would not take kindly to the presence of Edward's only son, bastard or no, and she refused to endanger Johnny's precious life.

Now she looked at him with mock exasperation, and then, her smile lighting up her face, she grabbed him and lifted his wet, wriggling little body from the water and set him down upon the cobbles. "You're a little boy, not a fish, my love," she exclaimed, shaking her head at the sight of him. He looked like a drowned rat! "Where are your shoes? 'Tis time we go inside and dry you off!" She tried to take his hand, but he scampered merrily away in pursuit of a passing mongrel. Johnny dearly loved all animals. He was a happy child, and well he should be—he had enough people to love him. Bronwyn smiled as she walked back to the inn. His father, though he didn't see a lot of the boy, adored him, as did Martha, Samantha and Mary. Everyone loved her Johnny.

"Johnny, come inside now." She looked back over her shoulder, but saw no sign of her little son. Playing hide and seek again, of course. It was his favorite game. With a resigned sigh, she went in search of her rambunctious boy. She wondered if Edward had been the same way as a lad.

"Johnny! That's enough now. Johnny, where are you?" She slapped her hands against her skirts and walked briskly toward the stables. The boy loved horses as much as he loved dogs. In that, he reminded her of her own father . . . or old Harry. Poor Harry, Bronwyn thought as she came around the corner of the low wooden stables. Last winter he had come down with an inflammation of the lungs and Bronwyn had done all she could, burning dried coltsfoot leaves so the smoke could penetrate and aid his breathing, and giving him the strongest comfrey-leaf and chamomile tea she could concoct to help him sleep. But his time had come and God would wait no longer for him.

Bronwyn could do nothing but ease his pain until the end. He had been a good man and she missed him. He had been her friend and he too had loved Johnny, showing him, young as he was, how to handle a horse. Johnny often asked about Harry. He missed him, too.

She finally found the little boy hiding in the hay in Chelsea's stall. She heard his giggles first and then saw the hay quivering. Thinking she'd teach him a lesson, she picked up the pitchfork and strolled over to the source of the giggles. "Oh, my! Johnny is gone," she said loudly. "Well, I'll just clean out Chelsea's stall . . . this old hay is stale and musty." She tried not to give in to laughter as she raised the pitchfork above the giggling hay.

Suddenly, Johnny shot out of his hiding place with a loud squeal and ran for the inn as fast as his little legs could carry him. "*Mama! Mama! Don't stick me! Don't stick me!*" he shrieked.

Bronwyn followed him back into the inn and turned him over to Mary. Her younger sister was almost a woman at thirteen, and was showing signs of longing for a home of her own since Samantha had gotten married in the spring. She was still so thin, Bronwyn mused, looking at her frail, dark haired, dark-eyed sister as she entered the kitchen. Mary's face broke into a radiant smile, and suddenly she was beautiful. Johnny dashed into her arms in the blink of an eye. Mary would be a fine mother one day, Bronwyn thought. As for Samantha, she was expecting her first child. It was one of life's little jokes that Samantha had indeed found herself a husband, but not the rich one she had planned on. He was a scribe's apprentice named Walt Shiever, and nothing like the man Bronwyn would have expected her sister to choose. Walt was a scholar, tall and gaunt, with a thatch of wild dark hair and intelligent hazel eyes that were always filled with humor and tenderness. He was not a particularly handsome man, but he loved Samantha with all his heart. Bronwyn had been surprised and then pleased when they had come to her one day last winter and announced their intention to marry. Bronwyn had been afraid that Samantha would wed one of the soldiers she flirted so casual with each night, or one of the wealthy merchants who always seemed to be courting her. Samantha at seventeen was a blonde beauty with a quick wit and a ready laugh who turned all the men's heads.

Thank God she had fallen for Walt, who would be a true and loving husband to her and a devoted father to their coming babe. He was a dependable man and though they would never be rich, they would live comfortably in his parents' house until he could afford their own modest cottage.

"It looks like he was in the hay again!" Mary laughed, as she hugged Johnny. "And he's soaking wet! Find Martha, poppet—she'll give you nice dry clothes." He squirmed out of her arms and ran in search of Martha. She then turned to Bronwyn and asked, "Have you heard from the King lately?" Mary and Samantha had at first been shocked by their sister's impossible love, but since Johnny's birth and Edward's return they had seen how happy Bronwyn was and approved of it.

A momentary shadow fell across Bronwyn's face. In truth, she had not seen Edward for some time nor heard from him, and it worried her, but she didn't want to talk about it just now. Instead of answering Mary's question, she changed the subject, and Mary was sensitive enough not to pry.

Shortly thereafter, Martha came bustling in and flashed Bronwyn a knowing look. She knew Bronwyn so well that she could tell at a glance if something was wrong and usually, these days, it dealt with the King. She had Johnny's hand in hers. The child was dressed in clean, dry clothing and begging for some of his favorite pudding. She spooned some out of a covered bowl and he sat down to eat with a great smile on his little face.

"It will soon be dark," Martha said. "And the horses need to be fed and watered. With Harry gone, those lazy stable lads can't be trusted to tend to them properly. I suppose I'll have to see to it myself."

Bronwyn stood up and she offered, "I'll do it, Martha. I've wanted to brush Chelsea myself, and this is as good a time as any." She was also looking forward to a little time alone. In the inn, privacy was a precious gift and hard to find.

"I'll not turn that offer down. Thank you, child. I'm not as young as you be. These old bones tire far easier than your young ones," Martha said, then ordered one of the scullery maids to start the fire in the great hearth. It was time to begin preparing the evening meal.

Bronwyn passed her son on the way to the door and tousled his hair affectionately, dropping a kiss on the top of his head before she went outside.

The sun was starting to set but it was still very hot. Bronwyn undid the lacings at the top of her bodice and pulled the cloth away from her warm body. It was dry and dusty; there had been no rain for days and days, and she lifted up her skirts to keep them from trailing on the ground. She could hear Chelsea neighing softly as she entered the stables again. She hadn't given the little mare much attention lately, and Chelsea seemed to be telling her so in plaintive nickers as she walked up to her and hugged her. The horse nuzzled her warmly and nipped at her clothing playfully. Bronwyn laughed.

"So, my beauty, you have missed me, eh?" she crooned as she stroked the silky neck and scratched her behind the ears and under her flowing mane.

"Well, my lovely, perhaps after I've finished grooming you, we can go out for a ride. Would you like that?" She patted the mare on her rump, and could have sworn that the horse understood her. Chelsea went back to eating her hay, content.

Bronwyn searched until she found the three young stable hands taking their ease in the rear courtyard, and sternly ordered them to attend to their duties. Then she returned to her little mare and began to brush her coat to a satiny shine. She loved the horse all the more because it had been Edward's gift to her.

She wondered where he was right now, if he were safe, happy. The Queen had just given birth to another daughter and everywhere there was speculation and gossip about what would happen if she never produced a son. If the King had no male offspring, the Duke of Clarence was next in line for the throne.

The sun was almost gone now and shadows had filled the stables with a warm darkness. Bronwyn strolled to the open doors and leaned against the splintered wood, looking out. A beautiful night. There were already large glimmering stars above, twinkling like candles. A cool breeze was blowing across the courtyard and she let it fan her warm face.

She was in the middle of a daydream about Edward, lost in another world and another time, when she first became aware of someone standing a little distance away, studying her in the dimness. She felt the eyes long before she could distinguish a figure. The moon wasn't out yet so the person was nothing but a silent, formless shape.

Bronwyn felt no fear. She was safe here in the stable. It was probably just a customer taking a stroll after eating a hearty supper, or someone trying to clear his head after too much wine.

"Don't just stand there spying on me from the shadows! Come out and show yourself! I don't like being watched when I cannot see who is watching me," she stated calmly, stepping outside the door. Out of habit, her hand found the hilt of the small dagger she always wore under her kirtle tucked in her belt. Around a place as rowdy as the Red Boar often became late at night when the soldiers had had too much wine, it was best to be cautious. She had never forgotten that the one time she had really needed a weapon, she hadn't had one. Often she had wondered what the outcome might have been that night with Warwick if she had had her dagger.

The man walked up to her then with a purposeful stride and she realized immediately that this was no drunk. In the faint light from a lantern hung by the back door of the inn, she could almost make out his face. She knew him, she thought. He was suddenly familiar . . .

"Bronwyn? Do you know me?" he asked in a husky whisper. She could see him smile at her, a flash of white teeth in the dark, thin face. "Do you remember me after all these years? The King used to call you his little nightingale, I recall. I have never forgotten you. That is why I am here . . . my people are passing through London tonight on our way to Dover. We are to meet our cousins there." He stopped speaking abruptly and took her hand.

After only a second or two of hearing that soft, mellow voice, and when the tiny golden earring in his right ear caught the lantern light, Bronwyn knew for sure who it was.

"Leon?" she whispered, amazed.

"Aye, Leon." He laughed back at her. It was the gypsy boy who had sung with her so long ago on that fateful day when she had first seen Edward. He had been a boy of fourteen or so then. She looked up into his dark face. He was almost her age. She had not seen him since that day. Now he was a man with a strong face, dark curly hair, and a fetching smile. As far as she could see, in the faint light, he was handsome. Tall, very tall and lean.

All gypsies are thieves and liars, wanton, Godless roisterers bent only on tricking respectable people out of their gold, Martha had often said. She thought gypsies were shiftless, lazy thieves who stole babies and anything

366

else they could get their filthy hands upon, and didn't allow them near the inn.

"I wanted to talk to you before we left the city. I wanted no trouble for you so I've come by stealth. Gypsies are never welcome anywhere," he told her. "People fear we will run off with their wives and eat their children!" He laughed but it was a sharp, bitter laugh. "I saw you come out a while ago and wasn't sure it was you. It's been so long . . . You are even more beautiful than on the day I first met you. At first I wasn't sure I should try to speak to you—you might have told me to leave." There was warmth in his voice and his touch on her hand was strangely pleasant. Her heart skipped a beat and it took her aback. She was very aware of his maleness, standing so close to him in the balmy night, her hand in his. He was a handsome, exotic man and there was something in his voice, his manner that made her also aware that she was an unprotected woman, a woman alone and unmarried.

But then she scoffed at her fears. This was Leon, the harmless little gypsy boy with the lute. He would never hurt her. He had loved the King, too.

"I remember you well, Leon." She smiled, recalling the tenderness she had seen in his dark eyes all those years ago. "Do you still play your lute?"

He laughed, a deep, throaty chuckle that sent shivers down her spine. "I do. At all the market fairs and celebrations, and I make a pretty penny at it. We entertain the shoppers, and we sometimes play for the gentry as we travel. It is a good life. A free life. No one tells me what to do or when to do it. And you? Are you happy?" He wanted to ask if she still loved the King, but couldn't. It was after all none of his business, and if it were true, she would be very upset when he told her what he knew. "I was surprised to find you still here," he continued. "I had thought you would be long married with babes of your own."

Bronwyn raised her chin and faced him defiantly.

"I have a son, Johnny. He's four." She pulled her hand away from his. "I might as well tell you, for you'll no doubt find out yourself. For many years I have been the King's mistress." There, it was out. Let him condemn her for it if he would. Why should she care what a gypsy thought?

"I knew that day, that very first day, that he would love you and you, him. It was there in your eyes when you looked at each other. It was your destiny. I knew it even then." There was no condemnation in his voice, only a hint of sadness and that surprised her. "And you have given him a son when his Queen can give him nothing but girls!" He raised his hand and caressed her cheek gently. The gesture said more to her than a thousand words. That little gypsy boy all those years ago had loved her! And what of the man now . . .?

"I still love him, Leon," she said. "I will always love him. It is no one's fault that fate placed us in two different worlds. He is a good man and a great King."

Leon shook his head. "You do not need to defend him to me. I did love him, as well. And you are right. He is a good man and a true King." He almost blurted out his news, but instead he asked, "Do you still sing? Or has being a mother silenced your lovely voice?"

"No," Bronwyn replied softly. "I don't sing any more."

" 'Tis a pity," said Leon.

A moment of silence fell between them, and at last he broke it, saying,

"There is something I must tell you." His voice was strained, and Bronwyn felt a sudden apprehension.

"What is it?" she asked.

"I suppose you have not heard the news," Leon hedged.

"What has happened? *Is the King dead?*" Her voice

trembled and she felt as though her heart had suddenly turned to ice.

"Nay. Not dead," Leon hastened to reassure her. Though it would be better if he were, he thought, knowing how he prized his freedom. "Imprisoned at Warwick Castle, they say, by the Earl of Warwick and the Duke of Clarence."

Bronwyn gasped. "How could that have come to pass?" she cried, horrified. "How could he be taken? I've heard of no battle!" She was clutching his arm now in despair and he could see the glint of fear in her emerald eyes.

"In the village of Olney, Edward was forsaken by the Lords Herbert and Stafford; they saw the great numbers of Warwick's force coming down upon them and fled instead of coming to the King's aid. Edward was alone except for his brother Richard and his friend Will Hastings. They say his men began to desert when they saw that reinforcements weren't coming, so the King surrendered himself to his brother George and Warwick. He was taken to Warwick Castle and there he bides. No one knows what will happen now, but there would be no great astonishment if the King were to suddenly die of an unexplained illness or abdicate and go into exile."

"*No!*" Bronwyn moaned and collapsed into his arms. He helped her over to a fallen tree behind the stable and she sat down. He sat next to her, his arm still about her shoulders. Up above, a moon was rising, shedding a faint pale light. She was silent, brooding for a long while; then she found her voice.

"They are holding him prisoner at Warwick Castle?" she repeated. She knew it was the Earl of Warwick's ancient fortress about two hundred and fifty miles from London. So far away! And there was nothing on earth she or anyone else could do to help the King while he was there. The castle was impregnable. She might never see him alive again!

Bronwyn felt a weakness flooding through her whole body. She felt as she had that day when she had received word from the King that he was married, except this was far worse. This time his life hung in the balance. There was no hope. None at all. She knew only too well how Warwick envied his more fortunate cousin. A King, and a King beloved of his people. Bronwyn knew that Warwick wanted the King dead. It was only a matter of time—and precious little, if she knew Warwick—before the Earl thought of some clever way to rid himself once and for all of his liege. Edward was as good as dead.

"There was a battle of sorts," said Leon. "Warwick had Stafford and Herbert both beheaded at Edgecot. But it wasn't much of a battle, I hear, for the Yorks were out-numbered and without their leaders, they ran from the field like cowards. They say that Warwick and the Duke of Clarence are demanding that Queen Elizabeth's kin surrender as well, and they have branded them all traitors to the state. But they have gone into hiding and no one knows where they be."

Bronwyn turned her face away in disgust. Cowards all! So this was the family Edward had married into! She found herself hating the Woodvilles almost as much as Warwick seemed to hate them.

"The Earl of Warwick is even now on his way to London to proclaim King Henry England's rightful monarch," Leon continued, to Bronwyn's astonishment. "Why does he side with the Lancasters now, when they have always been his bitter foes? There is no reason for it."

But Bronwyn suspected that Warwick had his own crafty, clever reasons. King Henry was a madman who could be easily controled, unlike the headstrong Edward of York, and upon Henry's death, his young son, Edward, would be a helpless puppet for his manipulations. It was nothing less than poor King Henry's death sentence. For the past few years he had lived under Edward's protection in Wakefield Tower, left to his prayerbooks and monkish life. He had been happy there. Now they were going to pull him out into the glare of daylight, sit him on a horse and dress him in velvets to be paraded before the subjects he no longer knew were there. And after the parades and the celebrations, she knew that the poor misfit would simply develop a lingering fatal illness. Then his son would be crowned, and Warwick would be pulling the strings as Lord Protector. Such a clever plan.

How Bronwyn hated Warwick! He had been like a dark shadow lurking on the fringes of her life and destroying her happiness. A terrible thought struck her and she turned to Leon. "You say that the Earl of Warwick is on his way to London?"

"Aye. He will come to the Tower, preparing Henry for his triumphant progress through the city to reclaim his crown at Westminster the day after tomorrow. I shall not tarry here any longer than need be. The Earl and I have never been anything but enemies." His voice was hard. That he hated the man was evident. "My people are camped for the next two nights down beyond Southwark, in a field just past the Southwark Stews. Do you know the place?"

"Aye." Everyone knew that den of thieves and streetwalkers. The dregs of London's poor and crippled lived in those filthy streets.

"It is the only place where gypsies are welcome," Leon said dryly. Bronwyn felt compassion for the dark-skinned gypsy, but her thoughts were elsewhere. If Edward had found her here at the inn, then so too could Warwick. If he desired to find her. If he hadn't long ago forgotten her. But her instincts told her he had not. He had sworn vengeance years ago and she had escaped, shamed him and shunned him. No, he would not have forgotten her.

What would she do if he came for her? Sweet Mother of God, what would he do if he found out she had borne

Edward's son? That he was a bastard and could never be King would not matter to Warwick. He was Edward's son. Johnny and she both belonged to Edward and how better could he hurt the King than to hurt those he loved?

She stared into the night, trembling with fear, hardly able to breathe for the constriction in her throat. If Warwick wanted her, he would come here first. He was a man who never forgot a grudge, real or imaginary. He would not forget her.

She would have to leave. It was as simple as that. She must take Johnny and hide. But where?

Leon took her icy hand in his and pressed it to his lips. He knew little about this girl who had bewitched him all those years ago. He only knew that he felt a great attraction to her; that he wanted to help her, protect her. She was obviously distraught at the news he had given her, and for good reason. She must know that she could do nothing to help her lover, the King. That she was in pain he felt as surely as if she had put it into words. He looked at her lovely face in the moonlight and could see tears falling down her cheeks.

"Don't cry," he whispered, cradling her in his arms. It was as if he had known her forever, as if she were a sister or a beloved friend . . . or more. It startled him then to realize that he had buried his affection for her all these years. They were birds of a feather he thought, the same in heart and soul. Bronwyn was a gypsy in her heart, only she had never known it. He could see her clearly, dressed in bright silks and dancing before a campfire to the music of the tambourines and flutes. He could see her with fire in her eyes, her long hair loose and flowing, golden chains about her throat and wrists, and he could almost hear her singing to the accompaniment of his lute. Their audiences would be enchanted by her beauty! He remembered her voice as pure and sweet enough to charm the birds out of the trees.

Impulsively he touched his lips to hers. That was all, just one kiss, but for Leon, it was a pledge of devotion.

"You could come with us, your son as well. My people would love you, I know it! You are a gypsy in your heart. You could begin a new life. A glorious *free* life . . . and no one would ever hurt you again. Lord Warwick could not follow you or find you if you came with us. We are like the wind—one day here and one day there. We have no roots and seek happiness wherever we can find it." He was looking directly at her, his dark gypsy eyes piercing through her fears and loneliness and seeing so much more than other people ever saw. "Gypsies respect their healers. We are not like others who would use your gift, then condemn your powers. You would be treated like a queen, believe me!"

Bronwyn felt the tears flowing faster now, tears of gratitude and relief. In her short life she had been shunned and hated as Leon had been, and he understood. *You could come with us. Your son as well. Gypsies respect their healers* . . . She was overwhelmed with conflicting emotions. Her heart wanted only Edward—Edward's smile flashing at her, his arms about her, Edward loving her and spending their lives together. She prayed for his safety. She loved him so! But Edward was far away, beyond the reach of her love, and it was up to her to protect what her lover had left her—their son.

But she couldn't make a decision now, not now when her grief was so fresh and shock had left her in a daze. "Leon, let me think upon it," she whispered in a shaky voice.

His broad shoulders slumped a little. "I understand. You need time." He stood up and helped her to her feet. "If you decide to come, you know where to find our camp. We will be there tonight and tomorrow night, but we leave at dawn the next day. Remember, you are a gypsy in your heart!'' He laughed then and for a second she had a fleeting glimpse of what it would be like to go with him and his people. They all seemed to love life so, and she had the feeling she could trust him. Strange, that she should feel that way when she trusted so few in her life.

"I must go now." He gently kissed her once again. The kiss left a warm tingling feeling upon her lips. "Sweet . . . We gypsies stick together. We protect our own."

"Thank you for telling me what no one else would," she said. "Thank you for offering sanctuary to my son and me with your people."

Then he was gone, like smoke dissolving in the air. Had he even been there at all? But the heaviness in her heart told him he had.

Edward a prisoner! Caged like a common criminal or a traitor. Edward, King of all England! She still could hardly believe it. It was a nightmare. And she could almost feel pity for poor betrayed Queen Elizabeth. She was probably hiding in some obscure Abbey somewhere, trembling with fear as to the outcome of all this, her fatherless children clinging to her skirts and her future as dark as theirs if Edward were to die. *Almost* she could pity the woman . . . but Elizabeth Woodville had in part brought this evil upon her own pretty head. It was her kin who had helped to bring Edward so low as well as her ambition and her avarice.

With heavy steps, Bronwyn went back into the inn to tell Martha what she had just learned. She could always trust Martha to tell her what was best to do. She frowned then. Perhaps it would be better *not* to tell Martha. She would heartily disapprove of Bronwyn's so much as talking with a filthy gypsy, much less considering running away with a whole Godless tribe! No, she could not talk to Martha, She could not talk to anyone. If she were to decide to leave, it would be better if no one knew where she was going or with whom. Warwick would have no qualms about torturing a woman if he thought there was anything to learn. Bronwyn could not expose Martha to this danger.

The inn was packed and the customers were noisy and hungry. Bronwyn first went upstairs to check on her sleeping son before she went quietly back into the kitchen to help Martha. The boy was the most precious thing in the world to her, and as she studied him sleeping she feared for Edward and for herself, but for him most of all. He was a helpless, innocent child who depended on her for his safety.

Later that night Bronwyn went upstairs again, to pack a few things into neat bundles in case she decided to flee. Then, annoyed at her cowardice, she tore the bundles apart, tears streaming down her face. How could she leave Martha and Samantha and Mary? Samantha would have her first child in January and Bronwyn longed to be here to hold it in her arms. She didn't want to leave.

At last she wiped the tears away and her face grew calm. She repacked and set them in the corner to await her decision. Warwick had abducted her once; he could try it again. But this time she would be ready. This time he wouldn't have his way!

CHAPTER XV

BRONWYN WALKED around in a trance. Every little noise made her jump with fright; every rider that galloped into the inn's courtyard made her heart pound in fear. She had cried through the whole night next to her sleeping son, her sobs muffled in her pillow as she tried to come to a decision. She was frantic to learn what was happening to the King, but terrified of what she might find out. She clung to Johnny the whole day until Martha took her aside and got the truth out of her in broken words and sobs—about Edward, but not about Leon's offer to take her with the gypsies.

Martha had heard nothing further concerning the King, but promised to let Bronwyn know anything she learned. Bronwyn went upstairs early, complaining of a headache, and spent the rest of the evening in bed, besieged by phantom fears and bittersweet memories.

Sometime later, Bronwyn woke in the dark, her heart pounding like the surf against the shore in wild weather. She knew that as if by instinct something was wrong. Johnny was sleeping fitfully curled up next to her and she was still fully dressed. She heard the commotion in the courtyard even before those in the Inn.

She ran to the one small window and peered out into the warm July night. The moon was very high and bright above and she could see men gathered in the courtyard below, silent now except for the nervous prancing of their steeds. She didn't have to see their badges to know they were of the house of Neville, nor did she have to see the face of the tall, black-cloaked knight on the snorting black stallion to know that it was Warwick.

Bronwyn spun from the window and looked at her son's peaceful face in the moonlight. She hesitated only one instant, then grabbed her cloak and the bundles in the corner.

Quickly she wrote a short note to Martha and her sisters, telling them not to worry, that she would be safe and would send word later. She was trembling with fear as she gathered Johnny up into her arms and flew down the stairs. After checking to make sure no one was about, she slipped through the rear door and headed for the stables. The dark cloak making her almost invisible in the dark, she stole into Chelsea's stall. After she had soothed her fretful son and sat him down in the straw, she saddled the mare with shaking hands, then led her mount to the door and peered out.

She heard shouts and screams, and she crossed herself, breathing a silent prayer that she hadn't waited too long. She wasn't sure but she thought she recognized Warwick's voice somewhere in the Inn.

With her hand over Chelsea's nose to keep the mare quiet, she lifted a half-awake Johnny up on the horse's back, got up behind him, then rode from the stable around the back. The stable yard was deserted, and no one saw them leave. In the eerie moonlight they carefully made their way through the silent streets towards Southwark and the gypsies. When she thought they were far enough away, she urged the mare to a brisk canter and then a full gallop.

It had been such a narrow escape! If Bronwyn hadn't

awakened, Warwick would have trapped them there. Dropping a kiss on the top of her sleeping son's silky head, she rode on, her mind empty, her heart dead. *Was she destined to spend her life running from that fiend? Would he never let her be?*

When Bronwyn finally found the gypsy camp, her heart was fearful that perhaps Leon had changed his mind. Perhaps his people would turn her away. Then where would she and Johnny go?

The campfires were blazing and men and women sprawled about them, full of drink or passed out. Raw-boned horses were tied to the back of their sorry-looking wagons and a wolfhound ran up snarling at her stirrups and snapping at her feet. She shouldn't have come! She sat up straighter and pulled her son closer for protection. She had made a terrible mistake! She didn't know these people! They might beat her and steal her few possessions and her horse. They could use her or sell her . . . take her son away . . . a pitiful cry escaped her trembling lips. Why had she come?

The wolfhound growled, showing wicked fangs, and another thin, scraggly dog padded over and joined him. They began to bark savagely as she whirled her mare around and started to ride away. She didn't know where she was going and she didn't care. She was exhausted and sick at heart. Nothing mattered any more except to keep riding, to get away.

Chelsea reared and Bronwyn screamed, kicking at the dogs ripping at her skirts in a fury, and fighting desperately to keep the mare under control.

Suddenly a tall man appeared at the mare's head, calming her and sending the dogs away with a swift kick and an angry command in a deep voice. Bronwyn began to weep in terror as she stared down through tears into the man's shadowed face.

It wasn't until he pulled her down from the saddle and

held her tightly to his lean body, soothing her with gentle words, that she knew it was Leon.

"I hoped you would come. We leave at dawn," was all he said as he took her sleeping son in his arms and carried the boy tenderly over to the campfire in front of his wagon. He turned and looked at her in the firelight, Johnny cradled against his chest. He was a handsome virile man and there was love in his eyes. "Come. Rest before the fire and after I settle the boy in the wagon, I'll return and we can talk."

She followed him into the firelight. Her face was dirty and stained with her tears and her eyes empty. When she tried to go with her son, Leon stopped her. "Nay, my mother will see to the boy." He smiled then. "She does have a fondness for little boys. And this one she will love, I promise," he said and disappeared into the wagon as Bronwyn crumpled before the fire. The night had turned cooler and the fire was comforting as she spread her shivering hands above it.

A while later she looked up into Leon's dark eyes. He smiled down at her. He would not push her, he told himself. But slowly, he would teach her to love him. Looking into her beautiful, haunted face he felt his heart turn over in his chest. She was so lovely! If she could but give him a fraction of the love she bore the King, he would be a happy man.

Someday, he vowed silently as he touched her face with gentle fingers, *you will love me more than you love Edward. Someday you will be my wife.*

"Welcome to my home." Leon grinned and waved a hand at the ramshackle caravan. "I knew you would come. I knew it!"

Bronwyn turned away from his handsome face and stared into the flickering fire. She could hear an owl some-where, calling to its mate and her heart ached as her tears flowed again. More than anything she wanted Edward.

CHAPTER XVI

September 1469

EDWARD THE KING lay on his bed in his cell and glared at the ceiling. It had been almost three months since he had given himself up without a fight to Warwick, his "good and true" cousin Warwick. What more did the man want of him? He was sick of being caged like a criminal, sick of waiting and hoping and signing those damned papers that Warwick and George kept shoving before him while his country, from what he had learned from some friendly gaolers, was in turmoil. He scowled and rested his head on his folded arms. He knew that his people loved him and were incensed by Warwick's treachery.

Warwick had raised his armies in Edward's name and then had turned on him. England needed a leader, their rightful King, not a babbling idiot. They didn't need an inept King or his green son upon the throne or Queen Margaret's bloodthirsty clan tearing the countryside apart. And they didn't want Warwick as Lord Protector. They wanted Edward.

Warwick knew this too. So why was he keeping Edward prisoner? He didn't dare harm him now. There were too many who would hold him to account. The tide was turning and Warwick was clever enough to see that. But

George, Edward's greedy brother, was a different story altogether. He was afraid of what would happen to him once Edward was free. Edward's face was grim as he reflected on his brother. How he could have betrayed him this way and without a trace of conscience play this cruel charade was more than Edward could understand or forgive.

If George had his way, Edward glumly thought as he let his eyes roam around his prison, Edward would be dead now by some so-called accident. How he must lust for the crown to be willing to betray, even kill his own brother to gain it!

Edward could not fathom it. What wrong had he ever done to George? The answer came immediately. He had been born first.

Edward sat up and looked with dull eyes at the stack of official papers Warwick had just brought him to sign. Lord, not more! Now what did the traitor want? His soul or his head? He laughed mirthlessly. Yet he had to admit that so far, he had been treated with courtesy and respect befitting his rank. His guards were properly deferential, but he could barely tolerate the pity he saw in their eyes when they attended him. He was given everything he desired, up to a certain point—everything but his freedom.

But it wouldn't be long now before Warwick saw the error and folly of his ways. Edward had received a letter from his youngest brother Richard just last week saying that Warwick was already at loggerheads with the new Parliament. They could agree on nothing. At first the lords had supported restoring King Henry to the throne, but that was months ago. Henry was again chained to his bed, subject to deep spells of depression, and Warwick and Margaret were at each other's throats trying to control the government and the heir presumptive, young Edward. Henry's son was proving more intractable than Warwick had ever thought he would be. Apparently he felt little gratitude to Warwick for what he had done. But then, Margaret and her people were never thankful for anything. It would perhaps have been better had Warwick done what his black heart really craved—placed the crown upon his own head. Edward hoped that his cousin's schemes would come to naught. Slowly but surely, Warwick was losing control—over Margaret, over the mistrustful young prince, indeed over the entire country.

He heard the sound of approaching boots and the murmur of voices outside the door. Edward leaped to his feet as the Earl of Warwick came striding in, followed by the Duke of Clarence. Edward could tell by Warwick's stormy expression that he was in a bad humor, and his brother George also had a displeased scowl on his face.

Edward's eyes rested cooly on George. "You're not looking well, Brother," he said, then turned to Warwick. But he could think of no words of greeting. He was choked by bitterness and rage at the thought of being the prisoner of the man he had respected as a second father, the man on whom he had bestowed the titles of Captain of Calais, Lord Admiral of all England, and Great Chamberlain.

George said casually as he walked about Edward's stark chamber, "No doubt after you hear what we have to tell you, you shall not look so well either, Ned."

Edward cringed at the nickname. *Hypocrite!* Then he saw the evil gleam in George's ice-blue eyes and felt his heart sink. He knew that look far too well and it boded nothing good.

He turned and glared at Warwick. "What is it, then? What have you thought of to further torment me?" Edward demanded, his anger coming to the surface as he waited for his cousin to answer. God's blood, let it not be anything too hard to bear—Not one of his children, or Elizabeth or Bronwyn, or his death warrant. He felt real fear then. As long as he was alive there was hope of regaining his crown and his power, his birthright. But if he were dead . . .

Nay! They would not dare to execute him. His blood would cry out to all England for swift revenge.

"My cousin Warwick?" Edward's voice held none of his fears but was cold and steady. "What news have you?"

Warwick stood there, his black eyes narrowed and his lips in a tight smile, studying his Kingly cousin, not deigning to answer immediately. Edward looked poorly, he thought. Confinement didn't agree with him, it seemed. He considered for a moment informing Edward that he had set out after that witch, but since he had not succeeded, it wouldn't have the desired effect. She had slipped away right under his nose that night at the inn. He had been so close, and she had disappeared like mist, and her brat as well—Edward's son, they said. But he wouldn't give up! Even now he had his spies searching the country-side for the little witch. Damn! If he had captured the little slut, perhaps Edward would have been easier to handle all these frustrating months. But he would find the wench sooner or later and take his revenge. Edward would not stop him this time.

"I see you haven't signed the papers I brought you." Warwick's eyes rested on the neat stack of papers which were untouched, unread.

Edward made no reply, and Warwick merely glared at him. "Well, my dear cousin, soon we may not have need of your signature at all. If you are no longer King, your signature will be worthless, *Sire*." He made a mock bow, his eyes fixed on Edward's shocked, pale face, and steeled himself against any feelings. *This was the boy he had first taught to hunt and to joust. This was the man he had loved as a son and fought beside, the man he had set upon the throne. This was the King he had betrayed.*

No, he could not show pity now! He had begun this and

now he must finish it, or his life was worth nothing.

"What are you talking about?" Edward hissed and took a step forward, his face livid. George fell back a step and shot a quick glance at Warwick.

"What I am talking of, my dear *bastard* cousin . . . is that Parliament has been ordered to set your title aside because you are illegitimate. Your mother had an affair many years ago in France and you are . . ."

But he had no chance to finish the blatant lie before Edward struck him across the face, his eyes blazing.

Warwick stood there and stared at him, his dark, sharp face expressionless. "You should not have done that, Edward," he said quietly. Edward spun around to his silent brother. "And you? What do you say to this lie? Do you realize what that makes our mother! You know it is untrue!" he shouted. "You know it is a filthy lie! I am King and nothing can change that! You hear, you traitors? Nothing!"

George turned away and abruptly left the room.

Edward trembled with rage, clenching and unclenching his fists. *Declare him a bastard and his mother a trollop, would he? Warwick was crazier than King Henry!*

"There is something else I have to tell you." Warwick's voice was very even and conversational, and Edward simply glared at him. How could he ever have trusted this man? *But he saved my life at Durham on the battlefield four years ago, not once, but twice. Four years from friend to foe . . .*

"I thought you would like to know that yesterday morning your traitorous father-in-law, Lord Rivers, and your dear brother-in-law, John Grey, were beheaded outside Coventry."

Edward closed his eyes in shock and helplessness. When he looked at Warwick a moment later, his eyes were vicious and deadly. But he said not a word.

Warwick laughed, a terrible hollow sound in the

tomblike room. "Have you nothing to say, *Sire?*" he taunted. He waited, and when Edward still refused to answer, he went on. " 'Tis two less scheming traitors we have among us. They would not swear allegiance to King Henry. It gave me great pleasure to see them die, though I must admit they met their end with more courage than I would have anticipated. Not a cry, not a plea for their lives."

Then Edward said in a cutting voice, "Why should they beg, when they knew so well that you have no mercy in your black and craven heart!"

Warwick just laughed again and left the room, the door slamming loudly behind him. Edward wearily sank into a chair and closed his eyes.

"You *will* sign these papers, Edward!" The Earl of Warwick was tapping the crumpled parchments with strong fingers. He had just picked them up from the floor where a furious Edward had just thrown them. Warwick's face was red with rage and his voice was strained almost to the limit, but the King refused to accept them from his cousin's outstretched hand. He knew quite well why Warwick was so insistent that he sign immediately. He had lost the confidence of the common people. He could not raise the armies he so desperately needed to rout the Scots and he could no longer manipulate the Lancasters. Suddenly Warwick found himself alone among a pack of ravening wolves.

If Edward were out of the way by his own choice, the people would turn to Warwick for leadership rather than to the bloody Lancasters.

The King clenched his jaw, trying to control his temper. "*I will not sign these papers, cousin.* I will not abdicate and hand you my crown like a frightened child afraid of his own shadow. I am an anointed King and so I shall remain until the day I die. You may kill me . . ."

Edward's eyes flashed fire, ". . . but you shall never make me give up the throne. *I am King*, cousin. You, of all people, should remember that, since it was you who helped to set that crown upon my head." Edward had risen to his full height and was glaring eye to eye with his nemesis. "*I will die first!*" His face, Warwick noted, was gray with long months of worry and fatigue, of being deprived of fresh air and sunlight. Two months ago, Warwick had given orders that Edward no longer be allowed to walk the grounds in hopes of breaking his will, but to no avail. Pale and weakened though he was, Edward was still every inch a King.

Warwick said softly, "That could be arranged if you anger me enough . . . or perhaps I could arrange for you to visit the dungeons and see what it is like to be a real prisoner without the special privileges you have so far been allowed to enjoy. Perhaps a few weeks or months in the dungeon chained to a cold stone wall, feeding on bread and water would convince you to change your mind."

Edward forced himself not to show his disgust and fear. *Chained by iron manacles in a dark rat-infested pit like some depraved murderer.* The very thought froze his blood in his veins. You would not dare do that, not to your King, he almost said. Not to me! . . . I was once your friend . . . your comrade . . . the son you never had. *You wouldn't dare!* But one look at his cousin's flat black eyes and firm jaw told him otherwise. Edward realized with dawning hopelessness that this man hated him enough to do just that, hated him enough to torture him or even kill him.

Suddenly something inside Edward seemed to collapse. He slumped down on a chair, trembling. His thoughts were hazy, jumbled. He felt very weak. For days now he had been unable to eat. He was breaking down bit by bit. Edward stared at the abdication paper and it was as if none of it mattered. If he were dead, what difference would it make if he were King or not? If he signed, it would end his misery. God help him if Warwick threw him in the loathesome hell-pits of Warwick Castle!

There were many tortures that could be inflicted on a man's body so he would beg to die . . .

Edward looked up at Warwick in a daze and picked up the quill before him. If he abdicated, he could say it was done under duress; he could say he had never meant to sign . . . he could . . . Then he saw the glowing look of victory that had begun to creep across his enemy's dark face. He turned and threw the quill in his tormentor's face and spat, *"Then I suggest, my dear cousin, that you sign the damn paper yourself, because I'll be damned if I will give in to you!"*

For a long time the two glared at each other, neither one giving ground. Edward was prepared to be dragged into a black, airless cell. He closed his eyes, the world spinning away from him. He didn't care any longer. He found himself floating away back into the past. He could see Bronwyn's sweet smile the night she had first shown him their son, and he could see as well the sadness that would fill her eyes when she learned that he was dead. He saw the faces of his other children, his brother Richard, his mother . . . even beautiful shrewish Elizabeth.

It might have been seconds, minutes, or hours later when he came to himself and looked about the darkening room with blurry eyes.

He was alone.

With a great sigh of grief, he fell upon the bed and fought back tears of hopelessness and anger. How much longer would this go on? What did that fiend Warwick plan for him now? In minutes he had passed into a troubled, feverish sleep, lost somewhere between two worlds. When next he opened his swollen eyes, he found he was too tired to rise and he drifted back into a twilight world that as the days came and went seemed to claim him more and more.

He didn't see or hear Warwick the next time he visited him. He could not rouse himself and he didn't really care to. If he woke up, Warwick would only have him tossed into the dungeon with the rats . . . better never to awake again, than that!

Warwick stood outside the door of Edward's prison chamber for a long time. Anyone watching could see the war that was going on in this tall, brooding man. His face was lined and his dark eyes were far away. He touched the door handle and fought against the memories that were haunting him. Inside that room was a man whom he had once loved as a son and no matter how strong his reasons for what he was doing, guilt was gnawing at him like a vicious dog on a bone.

He was slowly killing Edward and he knew that unless he wanted the man's death on his conscience, he must do something immediately to stop it.

At the sound of a moan coming from inside, he shoved the door open and looked with sad eyes at the King who lay pale and fevered in the great bed. A series of images crossed his mind—of Edward and himself when they were younger . . . of the day he had won the crown for Edward and they had marched victoriously into London. He could still see the handsome, golden young man astride his white stallion leading the joyful procession to Westminster. He saw the day he had saved Edward's life at Durham. The images kept coming like a flood and he put his hands up over his eyes and tried to blot them out. *Was he going mad*?

He had killed so many men. Why was this one any different?

Standing over Edward, he shook the man until the King

looked up at him with reddish, distant eyes and said in a whisper, "My friend Warwick . . ." and smiled as if he did not remember who had brought him to this pitiful state. His smile was warm and trusting and it was that which finally softened Warwick's heart.

"*Edward*!" Warwick said in a loud voice. "Can you hear me? Understand me?"

The King smiled dazedly and clasped his cousin's large hand. "Aye, I can hear you . . ." But his eyes were puzzled. "Is it time for me to die?"

The question stunned Warwick and he swallowed hard. *Edward, Edward! Why have you made me do this? Why could you not have trusted me more? Loved me more? Why did you bring us to this sorry pass?*

"No, Edward. You are not to die," Warwick replied in a gentle voice. He could not let this man die, not now. He rubbed his temples and continued to stare down at his cousin, his mind and heart at odds and his soul in turmoil. He could not go down in history as the murderer of a King. He could not go to his grave with such a sin upon his soul. What had Edward done to deserve this treatment? Nothing but to be what he was—a strong, independent ruler. His own man, just as Warwick was. Was that a crime punishable by death?

No! Warwick was suddenly filled with defeat and guilt. It was Edward England wanted as King, Edward they cried for, even now. *Edward!* The people pitied the poor idiot who now wore the crown, but they loathed Warwick for allowing it to happen and for locking their true, beloved King away. He had tried changing camps but found that Margaret was still his bitterest enemy, George fickle and unreliable, the reins of power still elusive . . . and the young prince, Henry's son, a spoiled brat who would listen to no one, least of all a Neville. Edward's Kingmaker. *No.* Warwick knew at that moment looking at Edward's shadowed face that he had taken the greatest gamble of his career and lost. England didn't want Henry, nor Margaret, nor him. They wanted Edward. There was only one thing for him to do now. Edward must be set free, sent into exile in Burgundy, perhaps, because he would never forget his traitorous cousin. Set free before he died. Maybe that generous gesture would gain Warwick the forgiveness of the English people, and then, in time, perhaps he could again earn their trust so that he could assume more power. If he showed mercy to Edward, perhaps the people would rally round him once again.

"Nay, Edward . . . you are to go free as soon as you are strong enough to travel. You will go to Burgundy," Warwick told him and then abruptly spun on his booted heel and strode from the room.

Edward lay there for a long time, his mind trying to make sense of it all. *He was to go free*. Was this another cruel trick of Warwick's? No. He smiled weakly and his eyes began to clear, his heart thumping wildly in his breast. *Warwick was setting him free*! Even the thought of exile in Burgundy didn't dampen his rising spirits. For the first time in months Edward felt alive and he turned and looked at the window high above him where the fading sunlight appeared like a golden mist. *To be free, to go outside into the green forests again and ride his great stallion, to see people again and to laugh . . . to make love. To be alive again*! His eyes shining, he sat up in bed.

And when he was well, and when the time was right, *he would return to England and reclaim what had been so wrongfully stolen from him! Come back and regain his crown!* His eyes glittered now with a deep hatred. *By God! He would show them all a thing or two.*

And next time, he would not let any of the traitors live.

CHAPTER XVII

July 1469 to January 1471

LIFE AMONG the gypsies was for Bronwyn like living in another world. At first she walked about in a daze, not really caring about where she was or what she was doing. Leon's mother, Lilyan, accepted her immediately as if she were one of them and she soon came to dote on the blond, blue-eyed little boy. Johnny became fond of her as well and soon was calling her Grandmama Lillie. He followed the old lady everywhere and in a few weeks, dressed in colorful castoffs and barefoot like all the rest of the gypsy children, the only thing that set him apart from the others was his sun-colored hair and blue eyes. There were many children in the clan and, like the adults, they were small, thin and swarthy with velvet brown eyes. They played about the wagons, laughing and singing like small forest sprites, free and wild. Johnny had no trouble fitting in, once he had gotten over being homesick for Mary, Samantha and Martha.

Every morning when they got up and she watched him run to the next wagon to seek his new friends, she would smile, her heart a little lighter. Slowly the heavy burdens of the past years slipped away, and she felt once again young and free. Leon had brought her two gowns the next morning after she had come. The bodices were in bright colors and the skirts were patched together from silks and rainbow-colored cottons. When she first put one on, her hair long and free about her shoulders, she felt like a different woman. No longer was she the King's sorrowing mistress or a frightened peasant, but a gypsy. Soon she was wearing a strip of cloth about her head to keep her hair from her face and to please Leon she wore the beautiful jewelry he gave her.

As the days faded into weeks, her fair skin turned brown with the sun. She rode Chelsea sometimes during the day beside Leon's wagon and Leon would tease her affectionately until she would sing as they rode along. He would perch on the wagon next to her and play his lute or sometimes his fiddle, and she quickly learned the gypsy songs that had been passed from generation to generation.

His people were from Hungary and before that his tribe had wandered through India and Persia. They spoke a language of their own, and Leon at first translated everything for her, but soon, like her small son, she could recognize certain words and then whole phrases. Johnny learned much faster than she and after a few months he was teaching her. She'd stand to one side and listen to her son as he talked to the other gypsies in the Romany tongue, and she was amazed at how well he spoke and understood it.

From the beginning, Leon had taken them both under his wing. He took care of them and settled them in his own elaborately carved wagon where he and his old mother lived. "It is big enough for two more!" he had offered that first night as they sat over the fire and talked. "And one so small!" His dark eyes flashed in the firelight as he took Bronwyn's hand. "It is a big wagon." It was, she had to agree. It was a home on wheels. The outside was brightly painted and carved and the inside furnished like a tiny cottage. So she and Johnny stayed in Leon's wagon, sleeping on soft blankets in one corner and cooking their food under the skies over a fire. The gypsies camped by streams or rivers each night so they would have fresh water, and often in the evenings Bronwyn talked to Leon's mother, learning about her life. Lilyan was a seer and a reader of the Tarot cards. She was very old, very wise; and like Leon, she spoke English.

"I had always been told I was an orphan," Leon confided to Bronwyn one night as they listened to the gypsies' music and watched the dancing. The camp was celebrating a birth that night and wine and laughter ran freely. "When Edward gave me my freedom, I set out to find what was left of my people . . . and I found that my mother still lived. I had been taken from her, along with my older sister." His face was sad as he spoke of his sister. "It seems Lord Warwick took a fancy to her. She was sixteen at the time; pretty as a wild rose, with her long black hair and great brown eyes. She could dance like a wood fairy and her skin was the color of ivory, not dark like mine." He sighed and hesitated.

"Leon, what happened to her?" Bronwyn asked, for a moment forgetting her own melancholy at the pain in his face. He had loved his sister very much, she could tell.

Leon turned his dark face away from the firelight; away from her, but there were tears in his voice. "Warwick fancied her and he took her for himself. He took me as well to conceal his intent. I was only a small child, too young to remember anything, when we were taken that day out in the woods. We had been out picking berries . . . I remember my hands were stained red. Warwick took us back to London. I was tied to a saddle and forgotten. My sister—Thesil was her name—he used and beat. I could hear her crying at night. I have never forgotten the sound of her misery. It has haunted me ever since."

"And Thesil?"

"I am not sure because I have no way of really knowing.

I was just a little boy. But I believe she killed herself. One day she was not there, and when I asked for her, I was told she had run away. I couldn't believe that. She would have never left me. I didn't believe it and I listened at night when everyone thought I was sleeping. I heard the servants discussing her one night, saying that she had killed herself to escape that fiend. I cried, but as little as I was, I knew I must never let anyone know that I had found out the truth. They would have killed me, I'm sure."

Bronwyn sighed in the dark, her legs curled up under her. She was keeping an eye on her Johnny who was dancing happily with one of the little gypsy girls. They had given him a beribboned tambourine and he was shaking it above his head, delighted at the sound it made, as he danced about the main fire with the other children. He was so beautiful, it hurt her heart. He was so precious! It made her happy to see how content he was, like a tiny bird let loose from its cage. One of the older men swept him up into his arms and twirled him about until he was laughing wildly. Everyone had grown to love the boy. They protected him as fiercely as if he were one of their own. She wondered what they would say if they found out he was actually a prince. *Edward's son*. She looked back at Leon.

"They did not kill me." His lips twisted into a sardonic smile. "I amused them, so they allowed me to live. My sister had carried a lute with her. She could play it so sweetly. When she was gone, someone gave it to me, saying they had found it. She had been teaching me to play and I showed the man the songs I knew. Even then I had a gift for music. Soon I was playing for my captors. So I survived. As young as I was, I knew I had to please them or I, too, would disappear like poor Thesil." He finally looked directly into her eyes as the music rose to a feverish pitch. "I survived. I went to live at Warwick Castle and it was there, years later, that I met the young King." His face lit up. "He heard me play my lute one night and soon he took me away. I was so glad the day I left my Lord Warwick! I hated him and I still hate him for what he did to my sister and to me. He was a cruel master—an evil man. I have never forgotten, never. But I am also clever enough to know that I am no match for the great Kingmaker. There is no way I can ever hope for revenge. Had I tried," he smiled at Bronwyn, "I would not be alive today and sitting next to the most beautiful woman in the world, the woman I love." His voice was a whisper and she blushed.

But she turned away from his adoring eyes and blinked away her tears. Her heart was wherever Edward was at that moment. It was as though she were dead inside. Leon understood and took her into his arms as she cried, her head upon his shoulder.

"I love you, little nightingale. If I am patient, maybe someday you will love me too." But his words of love only reminded her of Edward and she cried harder. He gathered her up in his arms and took her back to the wagon where his old mother was sleeping, leaving her alone there to cry it out. He walked back to the fire then and sat before it until it was only dying embers, thinking of Bronwyn and what the future might hold for them. He looked up at the full white moon and listened to the wind echoing through the shadowed trees around them, thinking, *Someday she will love me. Someday if I am patient, Someday* . . . Was it not fate, as his mother had said, that he had found the girl after all these years and at such a time? Lilyan had read her Tarot cards and had told her son that someday the girl with the silver voice and her child as well would love him. The last of the gypsy revelers had sought their wagons hours ago; it was almost dawn. The sun was starting to come up and the air about him was still and clear. He stood up and stretched, then went to lie down under his wagon. That was where he slept these days since Bronwyn and her child had come. He would think of her right above him as she slept next to the boy. He would hear her cry out sometimes in her sleep and would resist the urge to climb into the wagon and comfort her. He had loved her from the first moment all those years ago. Now, perhaps, she might learn to love him.

Leon lay down on his blanket and closed his eyes. He did not wish Edward harm. But he had heard rumors that the King was dead and not a prisoner at Warwick Castle at all. It would change everything if it were true. Nay, he did not wish ill for the King. Heaven knew he hated Warwick; hated them all but Edward, who had shown him such kindness. But if Edward were dead then Bronwyn would be free to love another.

"Ah, Bronwyn, how I love you. Need you," he said to the wind that tore at the canvas of the wagon above him.

But he didn't have the heart to tell her what he had heard. He couldn't be the one to tell her that the man she loved might be dead. He would have to wait until he knew more. He did not want to break her heart, not when he longed for that heart whole and intact and loving him.

Oh, he envisioned such a life for them! He had told her that with her gift of healing, knowledge of the forest herbs and sweet voice, they would make an excellent team. It had been years since his band had had a medicine woman of any kind. When he was very young, his mother had told him, there had been a healer among them, a wealthy old hag with many gold coins hidden away in her wagon. Not only did she sell the medicinal herbs she had gathered, she was also well paid for healing the sick and afflicted.

His mother had foretold that another healer, would one day come among them and that she would have fair hair and skin and the voice of an angel. Leon had had no doubt from the very beginning that that woman was Bronwyn, Edward's little nightingale, the girl with cat's eyes and a lilting voice.

Leon slept then, Bronwyn's lovely, sad face haunting all

his dreams. Tomorrow they would reach Salisbury and, a few days later, Exeter. He would speak to Bronwyn about the herbs and the healing. Already she had begun to sing with him in the marketplaces they passed through, decked out in bright gowns, as if she were trying to slough off her old identity. In the last few weeks he had seen changes in her as she blossomed into the beautiful butterfly she was meant to be. She had been born to be a gypsy, free and lovely, not a kept woman hidden away in a tiny, dreary tavern like a rose in a walled garden, where no one could smell its perfume or see its rare beauty . . .

The next morning the wagons broke camp a little later than usual. There had been a grievance filed with the tribunal the night before. Two men had claimed the same horse. That the horse had been stolen in the first place made no difference.

Fascinated, Bronwyn watched the proceedings from the back of Leon's wagon as the chief of the tribe sat in judgment. He was a short, dark-skinned gypsy with a massive build. His muscles rippled under his red tunic and a long, sharp dagger was tucked into his sash. Bronwyn herself had been brought before him when she had first arrived; her remaining with the clan was up to him. She had been terrified of the man with the black eyes and the scarred cheek when she had first seen him. He had eyed her up and down as though she were a mare he was considering buying—or stealing. Then he had flashed his white teeth in an approving smile, stroked his thick mustache, nodded his head, and walked away.

"*It is all right. You stay!*" Leon had cried happily. The chief hated outsiders with a well-known passion, and even though Leon's mother had spoken up for the girl and her son, Leon had been apprehensive that all would not go well. But Lilyan was highly respected and her opinion meant much, since she had the power to curse someone or weave a malignant spell. Leon was relieved that she had taken Bronwyn and Johnny into her heart, and that she had convinced the gypsy chief.

Now Bronwyn watched gypsy justice and thought how fair gypsies could be. If only other people knew them as she did! They were proud, clannish and utterly devoted to their own kind as well as to their age-old customs and traditions. A gypsy might steal, but never from another gypsy. Even this particular case was rare. The horse in question, however, was special, not like the skinny camp ponies. One of the men traded horses at the fairs and needed the stallion to service his mares. Bronwyn looked over to where the stallion was hobbled. It was a beautiful cream-colored horse at least sixteen hands high with a broad chest and long, strong legs. It snorted and glared at any man who came near it. It has spirit, she thought. Any foals it would sire would be worth much gold.

The chief sat silently as he listened to each man's story and quickly made his decision. Soon the horse was tied behind the wagon of one of the contenders and the camp roused itself to move. Water was gathered in water skins from a nearby stream and wagons hitched up to the horses. The women put on their gaudiest gowns and finest jewelry because there was a large fair in Salisbury today which meant much business for them all. And Leon wanted her to sing. She climbed up on Chelsea and waited for Leon to get his team of blacks moving before the wagon. Johnny sat next to Leon and was laughing with him, a carved wooden pony in his hands. Leon had given the little horse to Johnny as a surprise, and now the child was galloping the image across Leon's lap and Leon was laughing, too. He was so good to her son. Johnny had already forgotten his life at the inn, lost in this new wonderful world and all his new friends. It was clear to see he adored Leon and Bronwyn felt grateful to him for loving her son as he did, grateful for the warmth and hospitality all the gypsies had shown to both of them.

Had it really been three months now since that terrible night she had fled from the inn and Warwick? There was a chill in the air and as she prodded Chelsea into a canter next to Leon and the wagon, she felt almost happy. She pulled her cloak tighter about herself, the warm cloak that Leon had given her as a present. He was so good to her, showing in so many ways that he cared for her and Johnny. He was protective of them both and always loving. Though she had not bedded with him, it was as if they were lovers. With his help she had finally begun to come out of her shell and now she looked forward to the fairs and to singing with him among the fair goers. He had taught her much. Her voice was growing stronger every day and the people always loved her whenever they sang together. Bronwyn had even begun to dance for the crowd as she sang, a beribboned tambourine beating time to her dance. And the people were very generous. She already had a large horde of coins tucked away. She no longer rode looking nervously over her shoulder, expecting Warwick to find her and drag her away. She felt safe with the gypsies. They would never let anyone hurt her or her boy.

She was also collecting herbs in order to make her potions again. Perhaps at the next fair she would start to sell them. Powder of geranium root for blood coagulating . . . wolf's bane for bruises . . . foxglove for heart disorders . . . frankincense for cleansing of wounds to fight against infection . . . box, which she often prescribed for rheumatism and could also be boiled into a hair dye that produced an auburn color, while southern-wood helped the hair to grow and also guarded its user against snakes. There were so many uses for all the herbs—La Rouel had taught her well. Ground marigolds were good for ulcers and skin sores, chamomile as a tea was helpful for indigestion. A strongly brewed tea of ele-campane roots quieted a cough. These herbs helped the sick, but many were also used for enhancing a woman's beauty. Bronwyn herself was not vain and had no use for auburn dye or belladonna with which to widen the pupils of her eyes. Yet, the beauty potions did sell as well as the medicinal ones.

She would take Johnny and hand-in-hand they would wander through the woods in search of the herbs. Johnny was quick to learn and young as he was, he soon was a great help to her in discovering them among the dead leaves and under bushes. He had sharp eyes and took delight in finding things Bronwyn herself had missed. It became like a game, and they spent many pleasant afternoons together in the woods.

It was natural that when someone in camp became sick, they would seek her out and ask her to help them. She never refused and as the months went by and she saw how they respected her gift, she was amazed and proud. No one but Edward had ever accepted her in this way without accusations or fear. She saw reverence reflected in their dark eyes and shy smiles. Not only did they respect her but they were as possessive and protective of her as Leon.

Leaning back in the squeaking saddle and guiding Chelsea with a light hand on the reins and little pressure on her flanks, Bronwyn breathed deeply of the fresh crystal clear air. She was beginning to love these people as well as the gypsy life. But the rumors she had been hearing concerning Edward darkened her mood that morning. They said he was dead, that Warwick had had him poisoned. He had not been seen by anyone for months. Her heart was heavy, but she had almost accepted it. She had cried so long, fretted so long, living in a shadowed world of regret and pain. That Edward was gone from her life and Johnnys she had finally been forced to accept. She had loved him and now he was gone. But she was still

alive. She had their son to raise. She smiled sadly back at
Leon as he waved to her over Johnny's bright head. She
belonged to Leon now and his people. *Her people*, she
corrected herself firmly.

Leon had asked her to marry him last night as they lay
under the stars and he had held her, kissing her so sweetly.
Her eyes grew misty and her heart pounded in her breast at
the memory. She could not lie to herself. She had fallen in
love with the gypsy. But how could she have helped it? He
had been so good to her and Johnny. She should marry
him, but she had given him no answer. The thought of Edward still haunted her. Was he really dead? Could it really be
true? She couldn't be sure of anything anymore.

Suddenly Lilyan's white head popped out from the back
of the wagon and in a husky, cackling wisp of a voice she
called to Bronwyn.

Bronwyn manuevered her mare so she could talk to the
old woman.

"Yes, Mother?" Lilyan had insisted that she call her
that and would not take no for an answer. Almost from the
first the two had embraced each other as if Bronwyn were
her lost daughter returned, and in the last weeks Bronwyn
had done as she asked. At first it was hard, but the woman
had been so good to her and Johnny, she could hardly
deny such a simple request. It hurt no one and soon it
might be true . . .

"Child, come in here awhile with me and chat. It must
be chilly out there, and I want to read your cards." The
white head disappeared back into the wagon, leaving
Bronwyn surprised at the woman's request. She exchanged
glances with Leon, who nodded solemnly, and then smiled
at her as he raised his dark eyebrows. For months Bronwyn
had begged the old woman to read her cards. She craved to
know what the future would hold for herself and her son.
She wondered if the cards would tell her if Edward were
alive.

A little anxious, Bronwyn tied the reins to the back of the wagon as soon as Leon halted the team, and gingerly climbed into the back. It was dark inside, like a cave, after the sunlight and Bronwyn had to squint at first until her eyes became accustomed to the dimness.

Lilyan let the back canvas flap open enough to direct a shaft of sunlight across the blanket in front of her where the deck of faded Tarot cards lay. "These cards were painted by my mother's mother long before I was born. They are very beautiful, are they not?" the old woman said in a voice like the dry sound of dead leaves underfoot.

"Aye, they are beautiful."

"Painted so delicately with such vivid images." The old woman pushed the stack of cards at Bronwyn on the blanket. "Touch them with your fingers, child," Lilyan mumbled. She saw the question in the younger girl's eyes and said, "It is the way I read them. When you touch them, it lets the cards know whose fortune is being read."

Bronwyn touched the top card lightly.

The old woman then spread the cards face down before her on the blanket and concentrated on them, every once in awhile looking up at Bronwyn with far-away brown eyes. The old fortuneteller had cataracts so badly that she was all but blind. White wisps of hair stuck out at wild angles from under the cloth that bound her head. She still wore as many gaudy trinkets and as bright colors as she had when she was young and beautiful, though she was now old, wrinkled and stooped. Great circles of gold hung from each withered ear lobe and her smile showed yellowed teeth in her lined face. Leon had told Bronwyn how, when his mother had been young, she had been well known among the gypsies for her power as well as beauty. She had had many suitors and had lived a wild life. Men had fought for her love and some had died for her, so it was not strange that she was still so vain. She still saw herself as that slim enchantress from all those years ago.

"What do you see, old one?" Bronwyn stared at the cards that were being turned over and clucked at one by one. It was a strange sensation to be looking at those scraps of paper, knowing that they would reveal her life-to-be. She knew there were many charlatans that read cards for coins, but she had heard, too, of those rare fortunetellers that had a true gift. There were those who could truly see the future. She shivered. Everyone was in awe of this old woman's abilities. She was very seldom wrong, Leon had assured her.

"*Ah, the Cavalier of Cups* . . ." the old woman hissed and slapped the card with her bird-claw of a hand. "He is a warrior—a great warrior—he will bring you much grief, I can tell. Much grief. But . . ." She stopped and licked her dry thin lips, "you have time yet. It will not affect you for a while yet . . . you will be happy for a while longer." She went on to the next card, her white bushy eyebrows raising, as her fingers touched it. Bronwyn shivered apprehensively, but couldn't help saying, "Go on. Please tell me more!"

"Are you sure you really want to know?" The old lady leveled worried eyes at her. The silence of the wagon cast a pall over them both. It was as if there was no one else in the world but the two of them.

Bronwyn met her gaze and nodded, though her heart almost slowed to a stop.

The second card. "*The falling tower!*" the old fortune-teller gasped. " 'Tis a very bad card. A very evil sign to find so early in the reading, child." Suddenly the old woman began to slap over each of the remaining cards, her face shadowed, unreadable.

She sat there for a long time, eyeing the cards in distress. *How could she tell the girl such an ill-omened future as the cards revealed?*

"Child—if you are brave—I will tell you what I see. If not . . ." She shrugged, her thin shoulder blades sticking up through the worn cloth of her gown like brittle sticks. ". . . I will put the cards away and not another word will be said of them. *It is not good.*" She was shaking her head, and looked up at Bronwyn's troubled eyes in the dim light.

"Go ahead . . . I want to know," Bronwyn said firmly. "What do the cards say?"

"There are those that have called you *witch*, am I not right? You have not had an easy life. I know it is hard at times. I share your afflictions. It is so difficult to be unlike others. You have much courage . . . and soon you will need it," she said in a grave voice. "Believe me, you will need it. There is much trouble ahead for you. *Death.* Aye, it be true, even death. There has been death before?"

"Aye," Bronwyn whispered, mesmerized by the bright cards. "There has been much death." She was thinking now of Edward, the man she loved and the man she feared was dead now, too. *Edward*! Did the cards speak of him, then? Or Johnny, her own beloved child. Surely not Johnny!

"You have more ahead of you, child. The cards say soon. There be pain and heartache in these cards. *See here . . . the Hanged Man.*" She tapped the ugly card of a trussed figure hanging from a wooden beam, stuck through with knives, blood dripping slowly to the ground. "*Betrayal, death . . . heavy chains binding you . . .* Yet you will survive . . ."

"Does it have to be this way? Is there nothing I can do to change it?" Bronwyn cried, terrified now. Wringing her trembling hands, she kept telling herself they were only cards, only scraps of paper! They had no real insight into her future! And yet, she could not convince herself. Her fear increased.

Lilyan sighed, and gathered up all the cards quickly, tucking them into a pouch that hung at her scrawny waist. "No, my child," she said sadly. "You cannot change what is to be. Only be prepared for it. Your fate is foreordained, my little golden bird. We all must accept what the fates decree. There is only one thing I can warn you of. *Beware a black warrior, a powerful evil one who seeks you even now.* Do you know who this could be?'' The old lady touched Bronwyn's hand, concern in her nearly sightless eyes.

Bronwyn murmured, ''Aye, I think I know of whom the cards speak.'' She stared at the old gypsy woman who had befriended her and her son. Suddenly she feared for her, for Leon, for all the gypsies. *Warwick!* The cards warned of Warwick. Was it fair to Leon, who loved her, or to the gypsies, who had been so kind to her, to expose them to the wrath of the tiger? If Warwick was to find her, they would all be in danger.

But where could she and Johnny go now? Weren't they safer with the gypsies than traveling alone? Warwick would never think of looking for her among such people, would he? Bronwyn's mind grappled with the dilemma but could find no solution. How could she leave the gypsies and Leon? Johnny would never forgive her if she dragged him away from his new friends now. He would never understand why they must be constantly on the run, always leaving the people they loved behind.

Bronwyn couldn't lie to the old woman. ''Old one, you know there is someone pursuing us. We fled from London because of him. It is dangerous for us to remain here with you. We could bring harm to your people. Perhaps Johnny and I should go . . .'' Warwick was destroying her happiness again! He had killed her loving father, raped her, had perhaps even been poor Edward's murderer. How she loathed that beast!

''Nay! You and the boy must stay!'' The old woman spat the words as if she were angry. ''You don't think we can take care of our own, little one? Do you think the gypsies are cowards, to abandon someone in need? You are one of us. We can take care of ourselves as well as one young woman and a helpless child!'' She squeezed Bronwyn's cold hands between her own bony ones and her voice was so low Bronwyn could hardly hear. ''I've always known you brought danger with you. The first night I laid eyes on you, I knew it! So you will stay. We will protect you.''

Bronwyn was so thankful she could have cried. But the old lady patted her cheek and continued, ''Fear not. All will be well in the end. The cards say so. If you can overcome the obstacles in your path, they say you will find great happiness. You are special. Great things lie ahead for you, if you are patient.

''And besides, golden one, we need you. You are a true healer . . . and my son does love you beyond all words, I know. Has he asked you to marry him yet?'' she asked, taking a round loaf of hard bread and a slab of cheese from a bag she had tucked behind her. She started to chew, offering Bronwyn a piece.

Bronwyn took it with a sigh of relief. She would be allowed to stay, even if she brought trouble upon the tribe. They wanted her. Now, smiling shyly, she replied. ''Aye, he has.

''Then marry him. He's a good man. With you by his side he will go far. And he loves you, I knew it from the first. I have never seen him so happy. Before you came, he was always restless, seeking something he could never find. Now he's found it.'' The old gypsy's golden earrings tinkled as she bobbed her head up and down. ''He will protect you and the boy with his very life, I do believe. Well? Are you going to marry him?'' she asked.

Bronwyn hesitated. She feared that Edward was dead, but her enemy was still very much alive and would not rest until he had found her. Why, she would never understand. Why did he hate her enough to continue to pursue her? What did he want of her? She had done nothing but hurt his pride . . . and love a man he hated, perhaps. But did that warrant this continual harassment? Would he never let her go?

Bronwyn felt her heart flutter, thinking of kind, loving Leon up ahead, driving the wagon she rode in. She could hear the sound of voices coming from the front of the wagon, heard Johnny's childish laughter. Johnny loved Leon like a father already—he had virtually no memory of his real father, since Edward had played such a minor role in his short life. Leon was so good, so tender. He wanted her to be his wife, and Edward could never have offered her that. Was it fair to the boy to deprive him of a normal family life if his real father were truly dead? And even if Edward were still alive, would he want Bronwyn and Johnny after all that had happened? Leon offered the two of them a new life. Wasn't it time she decided to accept Leon's offer? These last months of unusual happiness and constantly being with Leon, the simple way the gypsies lived and loved had made her yearn to be first in someone's heart, not second best. She was hungry to be no longer alone, hungry to belong to someone.

She nodded at last, and Lilyan must have seen the gesture, for she smiled approvingly. "*About time!*" the older woman grunted. "You are far too pretty to be unmarried. You and the boy need a strong man to take care of you." She pulled the younger woman close to her musty old body that smelled of rosemary and dried herbs, and hugged her mightily.

"Well, you had best tell my son. Off with you, then! Climb up front with him." Lilyan grinned widely. "You two have plans to make. The marriage should be very soon, I'd say, by the way my son has been behaving—moody one minute, high in the clouds the next. *Love! Bah!* I'm glad I'm too old to have to go through all that agony again!" She laughed a cackling laugh.

"But wait." She suddenly remembered something and started to rummage in one of the many old bags that filled the wagon. "I have a gown to give you, aye, a very special gown. I think it will fit you, though I was larger in my younger days." She chuckled again. "My wedding gown . . . ha, here it is!" She pulled a bundle of yellow silk from deep inside a bag she had taken out of a large trunk in the back of the wagon. She laid it out tenderly, smoothing the wrinkles from it with gentle strokes of her clawlike hands. It was a lovely gown, with gay though slightly faded ribbons at the waist and lacing up the low-cut bodice. It was beautiful, Bronwyn thought. "It has a petticoat," the old gypsy said proudly. Most of the dresses the gypsies wore had no underskirts at all. The one she produced from the old trunk was still as white as it must have been when it was first worn. "There! Lovely, isn't it?" The old woman dreamed over the bright gown. "I remember the day I wore it, I loved Leon's father so much. I still miss him . . ." She sighed sadly. "Leon is so like him. You and the boy will never want for anything, Leon will see to that!"

"It is lovely . . . do you think it will fit me, though?" Bronwyn breathed, touching the silk. She was so excited and happy now that she had made her decision that the gypsy's dire predictions were forgotten for the moment.

"Oh, it will. Or I will make it fit, one or the other." The old woman folded the gown and handed it to Bronwyn. "It is yours now." It was like a silent pact between them, Bronwyn knew. Lilyan had given her the wedding gown and in return, she expected that Bronwyn would love her son and be true to him. There were tears glimmering in Bronwyn's eyes as she went to sit with Leon and Johnny.

But in the back of the wagon, as they bumped along over the rutted road, the old woman sighed and shook her head. Her son had found his happiness. She only wished the cards weren't so bad . . .

They were married the next feast day. Bronwyn wore the lovely yellow gown and was attended by a happy Johnny. The gypsies gave the new family their own wagon as a wedding present. It was small, but all theirs. There were gifts and a large celebration the night they were wed by the gypsy chief. Gypsies had their own customs and traditions and their own special wedding ceremony. Bronwyn did not care if they were married in the eyes of the church or not, though to one of her kind, she was still living in sin as she had been when she was Edward's mistress. But she had decided to embrace the gypsy way of life and the love in her new husband's eyes convinced her that what she was doing was right and true. Surely even God could see that and would bless their union, church, priest or no. As she spoke the words and held Leon's warm hand in hers that night under the stars before the blazing fire, Bronwyn truly became his wife. She danced with Leon almost until dawn with the gypsies. They had killed a deer and roasted the venison over the open fire. The gypsy women had all prepared special dishes for the occasion.

And when the festivities were through, Leon led her away to their small wagon and closed the flap. Johnny slept for the next few nights in the bigger wagon that belonged to the old woman, so the newlyweds could be alone.

Leon was gentle and made love to her as if she were made of glass. She pushed her memories of Edward firmly from her mind. Edward was gone, and Leon was here with her and Johnny. She knew she cared for him and that, in time, it would grow into a strong, lasting love.

There was nothing Leon wouldn't do for her. He constantly lavished her with gifts and little tokens of his love. Bronwyn had never had a more constant and devoted lover. They were two of a kind, she thought, laying in his arms one night after they had made love. It had been beautiful and he had been tender, wanting only to please her. She had never known a man like Leon. His whole world revolved around her and her son. For the first time she knew what it felt like to be loved by a simple man, not a man driven by duties or plagued by others' ambition and greed. Even Edward, as much as she had loved him, had not been able to put her first in his life. After all, he was a King, with a wife and state duties to attend to, while Leon's life was her and Johnny.

The time went swiftly after Bronwyn's marriage. She settled down with her devoted husband and her growing son and was almost completely happy. Perhaps, she realized one day as she was preparing the meat for that night's supper, happier than she had ever been. It frightened her. She could never forget that every other time in her life when she had been happy, something had always happened to spoil it, and that thought was like a cloud hanging over her head. How long would she be permitted this happiness? She never forgot what the cards had foretold.

They traveled from town to town, visiting markets and fairs. She sang and danced for the crowds, astonishing the onlookers with her sweet voice and wild beauty. Each day she felt more like a true gypsy, and no one who saw her perform ever forgot the blond wench with the flashing green eyes, or her equally fair, blue-eyed son. Word of her talent and her healing powers spread before her and her reputation lingered long after the gypsies had moved on to another town.

Bronwyn also did a good business selling her herbs and various potions. But she never charged those who could not afford to pay, and was relieved to see that Leon approved. When the poor asked her for help she could not refuse them, for she remembered the agony of being penniless herself. She was generous to a fault, but Leon never said a word.

"You are a good woman, my wife," he whispered fondly one night as they laughed together and made love, seeing only each other and lost in their own loving world. "Aye, my little love, you are a beautiful, loving, giving woman and I love you beyond measure. Do you love me?" he would then ask her, raining kisses on her face and throat, eager to make love again. In time, it was easy to respond with the words he wanted so to hear—"Aye, I love you, husband. I do love you," she'd moan as he covered her naked body with his own and she opened to him. And she meant it. She was, indeed, a fortunate woman. After they had been together over a year, she rarely thought of her old life, or of the frightening future the cards had foretold.

And one day when she learned that the King was not dead at all, but in exile in Burgundy and raising a great force to come back to England and regain what was rightfully his, she felt little. She was happy to hear Edward still lived. She still loved him, but the life they had shared was long ago and far away.

"You will not leave me now?" Leon had asked one night after they had heard the news that Edward was heading back for England's shores. His dark face was ashen and his eyes full of apprehension. He held her tightly that night, as if she would disappear if he let her go.

She laid her cheek against his and whispered softly, "Nay, never, my love. I am your wife and I am happy. All that is behind me now. Edward doesn't need me, and you do. I love you, Leon, and Johnny loves you, too. I will never, never leave you now." Leon sighed with relief, holding her so close that she could hear his heart racing.

"Little sweetheart, he said later, "never leave me. I could not live without you. Life would be meaningless if I lost you and the boy."

She smiled in the dark and reassured him again and again until he finally believed her loving words.

There was no longer any doubt in her mind. After a year and a half, she was Leon's wife and a gypsy. She wanted no other life. Her sisters and Martha were well provided for, she knew. She had no desire to force herself upon them and disrupt their peace.

One morning as she washed her hair in a cold stream, shivering, she stared up at the stormy skies above her. She dried her hair, dressed and went back to the wagon. Leon had said they would have to seek winter shelter. It was nearly January and they had been traveling to their winter quarters for weeks now. Sometimes they stayed on the outskirts of the villages, but the townspeople didn't like having gypsies among them, though they wanted their entertainment and their services—tinkering and wood carving, singing and fortunetelling. They appreciated the horse-shoeing and the magic way the gypsies had with sick animals, and they needed Bronwyn's medicinal herbs and cures for their ailments, but they still mistrusted the gypsies with their free, wild ways and their strange dress. Now the gypsies were headed for some caves up in Yorkshire where they stayed during the coldest part of the winter. The caves offered protection when the snow came and the winter winds howled.

A few more days and they would reach their destination. Bronwyn was cleaning the rabbits Leon and Johnny had caught next to the fire outside her wagon. Smiling, she kept seeing Johnny's glowing face when he had given them to her. He was so proud of himself, the great hunter! He and Leon were out in the woods even now, trying to trap more rabbits or whatever they could find. The camp needed meat. The days were shorter and hunting had to be done while there was still light. Bronwyn shivered in the cold wind that blew from the north and threw on the heavy cloak of wolfskins Leon had made for her, huddling before the fire as the rabbits cooked on the spits. Soon her men would return, hungry and cold, and a good hot meal would be waiting. Suddenly she heard a sound out there in the woods, something that didn't belong among the trees and the wild animals. It was the sound of many shod horses approaching, riding down upon the sleepy little gypsy camp.

Her heart pounding madly, Bronwyn stood up and ran over to her wagon, searching until she found her dagger. She tucked it into her sash and climbed into the larger wagon where the old woman was dozing. Lilyan was frail these days and Leon was worried his mother was ill. Bronwyn had been brewing strong teas and treating her for a fever and a lingering cough, but she knew it was age rather than any specific illness the old woman was suffering from. The sands had almost run out in her life's hourglass, and no herb or treatment on earth could arrest the sands of time.

The old woman awoke as Bronwyn entered the wagon. Bronwyn soothed her, explaining about the approaching riders. It usually meant trouble for gypsies when such a troop of riders showed up. Many times in the year and a half since she had joined them Bronwyn had seen for herself the animosity that could be quickly roused if the villagers suspected the gypsies of stealing or causing mischief.

And today there was many riders coming, she could tell and she was frightened. Most of the gypsy men, including the chief and her own husband and small son, were out in the woods. Had they, too, heard the approaching riders? Were they coming back even at this very second? She prayed they were as she clutched her dagger and waited.

She recognized him even before the dust from the horses' hooves had settled and she heard his hateful voice ringing out, calling her name. Trembling with rage and fear, she stepped from the wagon and faced him bravely. If she hid like a frightened rabbit, he would find her anyway. Maybe she could hold him off until the men returned. Surely by now they would have heard the noise and had turned back to camp to see what was going on.

She stood defiantly before the wagon and when he saw her, a wicked grin split his swarthy face and he galloped up to where she stood. Her face was as though made of stone, her eyes full of hate. He looked down at her from high in the saddle and laughed triumphantly. She cringed at the well-remembered sound and remembered the prophesy of the cards so long ago. It was Warwick, the black warrior who would bring her such grief.

"So, little witch . . . you thought you had escaped me, eh? Did you think that just because you changed your clothes and hid among these filthy barbarians, you could escape me? You were foolish then, wench!" He laughed again and prodded his huge black warhorse closer to her, reaching down to push her hood back from her grim face. She didn't move. "I must say, though, that the gypsy life does suit you. You are even lovelier than before." His black eyes bored into her icy green ones as his men kept a respectful distance.

"Have you lost your tongue, wench?" he spat, growing angry at her silence. The warriors and knights riding with him watched with increasing curiosity. They had been ordered to find the gypsies who had left Norwich the previous night. There was someone with the gypsies whom their lord sought. They were riding to Dover to set sail for France, fleeing Edward's advancing army.

The Lancasters were scattering before Edward's fury. Queen Margaret had already fled to France, taking her worthless son with her and leaving the poor insane King Henry behind. The people of England had had enough of Margaret's corrupt, quarreling court and her bribed

Parliament and had turned away from the Lancasters and the traitor Warwick, falling in willingly behind the banners that bore the white rose of York. The once great Earl of Warwick, the infamous Kingmaker, had been forced to flee like a fox before a pack of slavering hounds.

France! Warwick kept thinking as he had ridden towards the gypsy camp. That he should be reduced to seeking sanctuary abroad and throwing himself on the doubtful mercy of that damn gloating spider, King Louis, galled him. Warwick had brooded as he sought the witch and her whelp. Edward's son. He wanted them both! Especially the brat. He would take great pleasure in abducting Edward's son and his former mistress. Let Edward suffer a little, wondering what he would do with them! He would teach the man to brand him a traitor and put a price on his head! He, the Earl of Warwick and Lord of the North, a Neville, one of the greatest of all English families. He had shown mercy to Edward, and this was his reward. The hatred between Edward and Warwick had blossomed into open war that would not end until one or the other was dead.

How Warwick cursed his stupidity in releasing Edward last year! How could he have been so blinded by pity and feelings of tenderness for the boy who was no longer. *Edward was his enemy*. He would never forget it again nor would he show mercy by God!

"Well, won't you speak, witch?" he shouted, spurring his horse until it reared, attempting to scare her. Her outward calmness infuriated him. It was *as if she were waiting for something*. "So that's it—you're waiting for someone to come to your rescue. Well, it will not happen. You are coming with me to France," he said, enjoying the expression of cold fear that washed across her brown face. "You . . . and that bastard brat of yours. Edward's son. He must be quite a lad by now. About six or so, am I not right? Does he have Edward's fair coloring? His blue eyes? Will it be easy then for me to spot him among the dark weeds! *Tell me, witch! Where is the little bastard?*"

Bronwyn knew a fear greater than she had ever known before. He would kill the boy if he could, she could see it in his wolfish eyes as he leaned down from the saddle and grabbed her wolfskin cloak. With a vicious tug he pulled her to him and she started to fight, kicking, screaming and cursing him. His men watched from afar, unsure of what to do. What did their Lord want with such a gypsy wench? What were they doing here when they should be riding hard to Dover? They were already behind time and might miss the tide and the ship.

"*I have no son!*" Bronwyn cried. "*You are mistaken!* And you will not take me without a fight!" Warwick jumped from his warhorse and easily wrestled her to the ground, twisting her slender wrist until she dropped the dagger with a shriek of agony and despair.

His men looked on in astonishment as their lord scrambled in the dirt with the screaming gypsy wench. Bronwyn continued to struggle as he threw her into his saddle and jumped up behind her.

"Stop fighting or I will ruin that pretty face!" he roared, then doubled his fist and slammed it against her jaw. She collapsed then, sobbing convulsively. Warwick, cursing all the while under his breath, tied her hands to the pommel of the saddle, attempting to calm his nervous mount at the same time. His men whispered among themselves and watched, some amused, some offended. This wasn't like Warwick at all, to fight and beat a woman.

"*Now, bitch . . . where is that boy?*" he growled, grabbing her face cruelly in his hand and forcing her to look at him through her tears.

For Bronwyn it was a nightmare come true. She was barely able to keep from fainting, but she knew she must keep silent. If she said nothing, perhaps he would just take her and leave her son alone. In spite of her pain and fear, she kept praying for the men to return. Hadn't they heard her screams? Where were they? And if they came back, pray God they would leave Johnny concealed in the woods!

Warwick gave curt orders then for his men to start searching the wagons. He sent some into the woods, correctly guessing that there were others out there. Bronwyn's blood ran cold as she heard the clash of weapons even before she saw the gypsies charging from among the trees at Warwick's men, who stopped their wagon search and hastened to defend themselves. Soon the camp was filled with the sound of blade against blade, and screaming. The gypsies were no match against trained warriors with spears, maces and long swords, but with their knives and daggers they attacked the knights from behind, trying to pull them from their warhorses. Bronwyn covered her eyes with her hands and listened to the slaughter in horror, but a shout of rage in a familiar voice made her lower her hands, to see her beloved husband throwing himself savagely at Warwick, his face a mask of uncontrolled fury. Johnny was nowhere in sight.

Warwick had slid from his horse and was facing Leon, a sharp sword in his hands. Bronwyn tried to urge the stallion forward, intending to run him down, but one of Warwick's men grabbed the reins, dragging the horse back.

She looked over her shoulder and for the rest of her life she would never forget what she saw then.

Leon had no chance at all. When he lunged in for the kill, dagger upraised, Lord Warwick simply stepped aside and swung his long sword in a wide arc. Leon's head fell to the ground when the mighty blow struck. There was blood everywhere and Bronwyn screamed just once, a long, piercing wail, before the headless body crumpled to the ground and she mercifully passed out.

The next thing she knew, she was clutched in Warwick's steel arms, riding at a furous pace through the night. How long had she been unconscious? she wondered, confused. Then everything came back to her and she let out a loud moan. Leon was dead. And Johnny! What had happened to her son?

She dared not ask her captor. She must never admit to him that Johnny existed—it was the only way to save his life.

Sometime later, he asked her, "Who was that devil who attacked me? One of your gypsy lovers?"

Bronwyn remembered the wound she had once healed. *She should have let the monster die!*

She stared straight ahead into the dark, void of all feeling. There was nothing left for her now, nothing, except the knowledge that her son still lived. "That man . . . was my husband," she said tonelessly.

Warwick laughed into the wind. "You chose wrong once again," he told her. You need a man . . . a *real* man."

"*Like you, my Lord*?" she asked bitterly. "A murderer and a rapist, a brute with no heart?"

"You know me well, witch. I must admit, however, that I am disappointed that I could not find that whelp of yours and Edward's. The little bastard must have hidden well." She was frightened for her son, fatherless and now motherless as well. Many of the gypsies had died trying to save her, but she knew that those who survived would care for him. Tears poured down her cheeks as she thought of the horror of that scene, and of the destruction her presence had brought on the kind, loving gypsies. She should have died, too!

"I have no son, I keep telling you," Bronwyn said wearily. "I am alone, now that you have butchered my husband as you did my father, *you monster*!" He slapped her then and they rode on in silence punctuated only by her sobs.

France! she thought miserably. *So far away from her home and Johnny*. When and how could she escape and find her son? *If her son was still alive*. The terrible thought hit her like a physical blow. What if Warwick had not told the truth about being unable to find the boy? Sweet Christ, what would she do if Johnny were dead? What if Warwick had already killed him?

It was too much to bear and the world spun away to blackness. She welcomed oblivion gratefully. She never wanted to wake up again . . .

CHAPTER XVIII

France

IT WASN'T much of a ship—small, squat, its dark sails lowered as it pitched against its moorings, outlined against the rays of the rising sun. The sand on the beach deadened the sound of the horses' hooves as they galloped to the small rowboat that was about to leave. Warwick shouted, standing in his stirrups, and the sailors brought the small dinghy back to shore.

The next thing Bronwyn knew, filthy hands were dragging her from the saddle and she was tossed into the boat like a sack of meal, still only half-conscious. The shores of England faded away as the sailors rowed and cursed. The man who appeared to be in command spoke in a hoarse guttural voice to Warwick. "A few more minutes, milord, and we would have been gone. You're lucky."

Warwick said nothing, his square jaw set as the small boat made its way to the ship. As they drew nearer, Bronwyn could hear the creaking and groaning of the ship's timbers as it gently rocked on the water. Once on deck, for a brief moment she gazed at the brightening shore. She was leaving everything she had ever known and loved . . . dragged away to an alien land. Where was her poor little Johnny now? Tears trickled down her bruised face and she wiped them away with the edge of her cloak. How would she ever find her son again if there was a sea between them?

She turned and looked up at Warwick's dark countenance. He, too, was watching the shore recede, his expression inscrutable. "Why are you doing this to me? Why did you kill my husband?" Bronwyn asked. Her voice trembled.

He looked down at her with glittering eyes and rested his hand lightly upon his sword hilt. "I have my reasons. You can't tell me you loved that thieving mongrel gypsy! I've done you a great service, ridding you of that filthy parasite. Someday, I've no doubt, you'll thank me for it." If she had had her dagger, Bronwyn would quite readily have plunged it into his black heart. Her hatred was so apparent that he turned his dark shaggy head away. He remembered that look very well. One word more from him, and she would attack him with her claws aimed for his eyes, or throw herself over the rail into the water . . .

He caught her just in time. Their struggle was silent but fierce, and he finally seized her around the waist in his strong arms and dragged her away from the railing.

"You little fool! What did you hope to accomplish? You'd have only got a dunking and most likely pneumonia . . . and we would have caught up with you long before you reached shore," he hissed.

"Perhaps I would have drowned," she said wearily, defeated once more.

"Wench, I'm tired and hungry and in no mood for games. The next time, I *will* let you jump!" Warwick growled, then brutally shoved her toward the companion-way that led below deck. As she stumbled down the narrow steps, she cast one final yearning glance over her shoulder toward England. The ship had raised anchor and the sails were unfurled, filling with wind that would bear her far away from her home—and Johnny.

Once inside the candlelit cabin below, he threw her down on a narrow cot and left her alone with her thoughts and her fears, locking the door behind him.

She got up, trembling and rubbing her wrists that had been rubbed raw by the rope that had bound them, and ran to the porthole. Standing on tiptoe, she peered out at the distant beach and the cliffs receding rapidly into the distance, tears streaking her face. When Warwick returned, he found her still there, crying silently.

"You miss your son, do you not, my little wench?" he taunted, standing close behind her and placing his large hands upon her shoulders.

She stiffened. "*I have no son*! Whoever told you that, lied." He couldn't see her face and she was glad of it. She had never been good at lying, and she was sure he could read the truth on her face.

"No?" He sighed and caressed her tense shoulders, saying nothing for a long while. Then, "Did you know that Edward has been searching all of England for you and his son for months? And that, even though the queen has finally given him a legitimate son, he still pines for you, little witch." Warwick chuckled softly under his breath and turned her around to face him.

Her eyes were like pools of ice.

"Aye, that conniving bitch-Queen did finally give him a son last October," Warwick continued. "But he is a selfish bastard, and he still wants you and your bastard son as well. But then," he slid his hands down the front of her bodice to where her breasts heaved, "I well know the delights you can bring a man in his bed. 'Twould seem that Edward also remembers."

She shoved him away so violently that he nearly stumbled.

He glared at her with stormy eyes and then, changeable as the wind, his mood calmed and he smiled at her and gave her a mocking bow. "Sorry, milady, if I have offended you. Now if I were black gypsy, I imagine you'd be in my arms by now." Bronwyn flinched, but did not reply. "But for now, my sweet, that can wait a bit." He strolled over to a cupboard against one wall, opened it, and took some articles from inside it, bringing them to the small wooden table behind her. "Dress this cut you did inflict on me. It pains me. I recall you have great talent for healing, like all witches. You have special powers, am I not right?"

Bronwyn did not move. "Since I am not a witch, there is nothing I can do. You must tend the wound yourself." She stood there defiantly, glaring up at him.

He slapped her wickedly across her mouth and she gasped, touching her lips and feeling a slim trickle of blood. She wished she could jump at him and scratch his eyes out, but she remembered his superior strength and restrained herself. *No* she must be cleverer than he if she wanted to escape and find her way back to Johhny. So she did nothing.

He handed her a cloth and sat down in the cabin's only chair. "Tend to the wound, unless you want me to beat you."

Cringing, she did as she was told. She cleaned the deep slash and dressed it.

" 'Tis a shame you cannot just touch it and make it disappear as you did once before," he said dryly. "Difficult to believe that that was all of seven years ago," he mused, looking up into her cold face as she worked. "I suppose even witches cannot cast their spells all the time."

"*I am not a witch*!" Bronwyn said between clenched teeth. "And you have no son, either, am I right?" he threw back at her sarcastically.

426

She ignored his words. "There, it's done. But it will leave a scar," she said, contemplating her handiwork.

"And you are glad," he stated raising a hand to touch the bandage.

Bronwyn flashed him a glance of pure hatred. "You are fortunate. My husband is *dead*."

"I didn't know he was your husband. If I had, I would have brought him along with us, alive and *in chains, in the hold*."

"It was better, then, that he died. He knew you well and would have chosen death over captivity any day!" Bronwyn spat.

"Ah, I thought I recognized the dog! So it was that sniveling lute-player Edward tricked me out of all those years ago?" He slapped his thigh and laughed. "I thought I remembered that ugly face, as it tumbled from his scrawny neck!"

"He was a good man and a good husband, something a brute like you will never be!" She felt tears beginning to form again in her weary eyes. She couldn't bear to think or talk of her poor dead husband another second. She would collapse in a fit of weeping and that would give Warwick the upper hand. "Why are you going to France?" she suddenly demanded.

He cocked an eyebrow at her, surprised at her question.

"I was forced to leave England by your friend and mine, Edward. But that was *one* of the reasons. The other is that I must seek aid and refuge there. I go to France because Edward has made a treaty with Charles of Burgundy for men and support to oppose me and his greatest foe, King Louis. France has declared war on Burgundy and Louis seeks my help to keep France from completing the alliance with Charles against him. Oh, we both know how the French do love their neighbors! I am Louis's guarantee, so to speak, that Edward never has the opportunity to join forces with Burgundy. With my help as well as that of Queen Margaret's armies, Louie hopes to rid himself once and for all of the danger across the Channel.''

"And you, my lord. What do you hope to gain by this?'' Bronwyn asked caustically.

"A lot. Not only has Queen Margaret promised that her young son, who will be King of England someday if Edward were out of the way, wed my daughter, Anne, but Louis has promised me the lands of Zeeland and Holland as my reward if I defeat Edward on the battlefield. Louis will supply me with a French fleet, French soldiers and gold to finance the expedition and in return, I will rid him of Edward. Louis cannot afford to have both Burgundy and England nipping at his heels. So that is the reason I go to France.''

"Why do you hate Edward so?'' she blurted out, unable to stop the words.

He peered up at her with a strange gleam in his slate eyes, then slowly stood to his full height, towering above her as the ship swayed under their feet. The cabin was in an endless twilight, the single lantern flickering low and casting eerie shadows against the walls around them. The smell of the sea was strong in Bronwyn's nostrils. She knew she had touched a raw, bleeding nerve with him. Now he would rape her, or beat her as he had threatened. She shivered in her bright, sad gypsy gown of crimson and ribbons. Her hair had come loose back at the camp when she had lost her head scarf. It was tangled now and hung wildly about her bruised face and shoulders; she pushed the thick strands away and touched the dangling golden earrings Leon had given her for her last birthday. *Oh, my dear God, Leon is gone . . . dead! Left bleeding and alone on that cold ground . . .* She shut her eyes and the world was spinning . . .

She felt his hands on her arms and his hot lips next to her ear. "Why do I hate him so?'' he whispered, pronouncing every word as if he were branding each of them into her very flesh. "*I loved him*. I fought for him on so many battlefields. I lied for him and murdered to save his honor, so he could wear the golden circlet on his fair head. I treated him like the beloved son I never had and what has he done to repay my devotion?" His voice had risen as he spoke, his anger pulsing through him as his grip grew tighter. "I was once King's Lieutenant of the Realm, Lord Admiral and Great Chamberlain of England . . . Captain of Calais! I am as accomplished a ship's captain as I am a battle commander. This is *my* ship and these *my* men. I can sail the seas better than most sea captains! Yes, once I was all those and more. My family is far wealthier and older than the upstart Yorks! But not now. Not anymore. He has made his eighteen-year-old brother Richard, Duke of Glouchester, not only Lord Constable, but Chief Justice of both North and South Wales, and has released and pardoned that traitor Henry Percy and restored his title of Earl of Northumberland. As for me, he has not only stolen my brother John's love and loyalty, but he has also branded me a foul traitor and my lands and titles are forfeit to the crown. Even Middleham he has claimed, and branded me traitor with a price on my head!

"*I* . . . who did love him enough to give him his crown on a bloody platter! *I*, who could have killed him last year when I held him prisoner, but didn't. I gave him his freedom! Do you wonder why I have grown to hate the man so? *He will forgive all but me*!"

Warwick had never let his guard down thus before Bronwyn and it stunned her.

"But I have *you*," Warwick continued. "One thing he wants and cannot have. *I have you*! It is little enough, but it gives me some succor. I will strip your body naked and use it as I see fit, knowing that he wants you in his bed and cannot have you!"

She knew that hunger in his face well and she tried to

429

escape his arms as he crushed her to him and laid his lips possessively upon her cold, trembling ones. But it did no good to fight or kick or scream. Soon he was atop her naked, struggling body in the narrow cot. His hard-muscled body pumped at her and in the end, helpless to resist, she gave in. She no longer cared what he did to her. He had killed her husband and torn her from her small son, and she lay motionless as he had his way with her. Through her tears, she stared at the torn, red gypsy gown tossed in a heap on the floor beside the cot. She kept seeing Leon's face as the blade had struck, and wished she were dead as well.

The ship docked at Honfleur. They had followed the coastline of Burgundy from Calais to Honfleur, cautious not to alert their enemies the Burgundians of their presence. Warwick was to meet the French King there and discuss their new alliance. Louis preferred to keep their meeting secret—the French had little love for the English and he was taking a great risk in meeting the English warrior. But Louis was sly and would make a pact with the devil if it would gain him what he wanted. Louis of France, the wily spider King, would sell his immortal soul if he could, in his lifetime, see the fleur-de-lis flying over Burgundy and Charles dead.

Warwick left Bronwyn chained to the bedpost in their chambers of the inn in which they were staying when he rode out to meet King Louis. She had begged him not to bind her thus, but her pleas and promises had fallen on deaf ears. He had merely looked at her coldly and said, "This time, wench, you won't escape me. If I have to chain you to every bedpost and saddle from here to England, you will not best me!" He had turned and walked away, his bootheels clicking on the wooden planks of the inn's floor. Straining at her manacles, she glared at his back until the door slammed shut and she heard the key turn and lock her in. She screamed and cried for help all afternoon, but it did no good. No one heard her, or if they did, they didn't dare to help her.

When Warwick rode furiously back to the inn that night, he was weary, but more optimistic than he had been in a long time. He even treated Bronwyn halfway decently, letting her go to bed without so much as touching her. He had no idea that as he was sleeping, she lay awake most of the night, consumed by hatred and a burning desire for revenge, and when she did drift off to sleep, all she could dream of was escape.

She had decided, healer or no, that if she was ever to be free of him, she must find a way to kill him. She must murder him as he had murdered both her poor father and her innocent husband. She must find a way. She must!

They remained in France for three weeks. It seemed like a lifetime to Bronwyn as she mourned constantly over her dead husband and lost son. She prayed every minute that little Johnny was all right, that someone had taken him in and cared for him. She was flooded with guilt whenever she thought that if not for her, Leon and the other gypsies would not be dead now. Because of her! It was a burden almost too heavy for her frail shoulders to bear. Night after night she dreamed of her good husband; she would wake sometimes in the middle of the night, the horror of what had happened all too fresh in her heart because the dreams were so real. Over and over she relived in her dreams the way he had died. But those dreams weren't as cruel as the others in which she would dream she was back with Leon, Johnny and her gypsy family and they were all still alive and she was happy again, singing with Leon before the applauding crowds or dancing in the firelight with the gypsies. Or cooking succulent rabbits over an open fire beside the wagon Leon had furnished so comfortably for her and her son and laughing with Johnny and Leon over one of the boy's little escapades. Or making love with her husband in the still of the night, his strong arms so safely about her, protecting her from all the rest of the world. Oh, more than anything except her son, she missed the tenderness Leon had shown day after day. When she awoke from such a beautiful dream, her agony was all the greater. It was all gone . . . dead like her husband. She would never know such joy again. She would lie, shuddering with sobs, next to the man she hated with her whole soul, and would silence her tears by burying her face in the pillow or stuffing the blankets into her mouth to stifle the sound. When she found out that they were heading back to her beloved England at last, a tiny hope began to take root deep in her broken heart. Perhaps once back in England, she would find a way to escape and search for her son. It gave her something to cling to.

The crossing was a horror. She remained in the tiny, dark cabin below while the ship, sailing with the fleet of French vessels, fought the seasonal squalls and high, thrashing waves, and had to stay out of range of the English fleet. She had prayed that the English would catch up to them, but Warwick was lucky and the heavy fog let him slip past without incident. Once back on English soil, they galloped through the stormy night as the gale raged about them and the rain soaked them through to the bone, followed by grumbling French soldiers and straggling mercenaries toward Warwick Castle.

And Edward knew they were there every mile of the way. As they trudged through the mud and winter rain, Bronwyn was given hope. Edward would soon come face to face with Warwick, and she hoped with all her soul that Edward would kill her nemesis. They were headed for Warwick castle because it was the only holding Edward had not taken because it belonged to Nan, Warwick's wife, and had belonged to her father and to generations before him. Edward would not deprive a woman of her possessions, no matter that her husband was a traitor to the crown.

As they traveled stealthily onward, Bronwyn heard constant bickering between Warwick and his commanders over tactics and privileges, and grumbling dissension in the French ranks as well as the English. When you put two ancient enemies together in the same army, orders or not, it will cause trouble.

Warwick was relieved when he led his men across the castle's drawbridge over the still black moat and raised it behind them. The grounds of Warwick Castle were enormous and within its walls there was more than enough space to encamp the men they had brought from France, the horses and supplies. Soon more followers of Warwick rode in and the ranks kept swelling.

Bronwyn was left to her own devices as the days dragged on, locked in her chambers and treated like a prisoner. No one saw or spoke to her except Warwick when he had a free moment, and the servant who brought her meals. It soon became apparent that the Lancasters did not trust their old York enemy turned sudden friend, for as the summons to arms rang out, the Lancaster Lords remained silent, absent and unmoving.

Warwick ranted and raved at the noblemen he had counted on rallying to his cause and alternatively threatened and cajoled those who had come but then wanted to leave. The country was torn and divided in their loyalties once again, and Warwick was discovering that the Lancasters did not trust him and refused to take orders from him, while the Yorks hated and feared him and plotted his destruction. Warwick found himself with few on whom he could rely.

Bronwyn refused to talk to him. Her hatred had grown beyond her control. She sat in her locked chambers during the times he was gone and racked her brain trying to think of ways to escape, but there were none. She had no allies here and she knew it.

It was with mixed feelings that she looked up one day to see the door open and the Duke of Clarence, step across the threshold.

"Then it is true!" He stood by the door and studied her forlorn appearance, shaking his head in amazement. He had aged even more than Warwick. He was no longer the young rogue, though he could hardly have been any older than Bronwyn herself. He had gained weight and there were deep lines etched around his sensual mouth. His eyes kept shifting about the room as if he were afraid they were being spied upon. She noticed that he was dressed even more gaudily than when she had seen him. Failure had not changed his vain nature, nor betrayal his love of self. He was dressed in apricot satin; rings glittered on his plump fingers.

"It *is* you!" He smiled almost sadly as if to say, *Well, here we are again and look at the sorry state of affairs we've gotten ourselves into.* "When I heard that Warwick had found you and that you were with him, I could not believe it."

"And do you now?" she retorted sharply, then threw in almost as an afterthought, "my Lord Clarence." She curtsied half-heartedly. He *was* the King's brother, after all, turncoat or no.

He walked up closer to her, first checking to make sure the door was securely shut. "I've been looking for you since I heard you were here. Not as avidly as Edward has been searching for you all these months, or Warwick, but looking for you all the same. You do know that my poor brother Edward does still cherish you? That he has been worried sick ever since you disappeared last year?" George's pale blue eyes flicked across her thin face.

For the first time since she had lost her gypsy husband, she felt a faint stirring of emotion for Edward. Aye, she

434

had loved the King once and she still did. Every time she thought of her missing Johnny, she also thought of Edward, Johnny's true father. And this man, his own brother, had betrayed him!

Bronwyn glared at him and said, "Whether the King misses me or not, it would seem to me, my lord, to be none of your business. *Judas*! You have betrayed him! Why should you care how he feels? From what I understand, it was you and Lord Warwick who held him prisoner last year and then sent him into exile." She was angry, but something flashed across George's sallow face and she saw sorrow in his eyes and in his stance, and she realized that he was suffering, too. It came as a great revelation to her and suddenly her anger dissipated.

The King's brother shrugged and let his plump body sink down on a nearby chair. He rubbed his forehead with a trembling hand and looked at her with sad eyes. "Aye, and it is something I shall regret for the rest of my life, maid. I betrayed my own flesh and blood, a man who did love and trust me, and I have lived to rue that deed. I'm not asking you to forgive my great error, but try to understand. I loved Warwick's daughter Isabel, and Edward forbade me to wed her because we were cousins. But that was not the real reason. He knew that as long as he had no sons . . ." he caught the glint in her eyes and amended, "*legitimate* sons, I was next in line for the throne if something should happen to him, and that if I were to wed the Neville maid, my hold on the succession would be made much stronger. But I loved her, and married her I did. I was out of Edward's good graces and when Warwick tempted me with visions of a crown and a way of hurting my brother in return, I switched my allegiance."

He sighed again, propping his chin in his hands. She had not moved since he had walked in but still stood stiffly beside the bed, listening to his words.

"*I was a fool*! I made an enemy of my own brother and

now Warwick no longer has any use for me since he has married off his other daughter, Anne, to Queen Margaret's son. Their little scheme to brand Edward a bastard failed dismally; no one took it seriously. He shall control England through his daughter's husband now. He doesn't need me." He laughed bitterly. "Ironic, isn't it? I betrayed my brother, only to have another betray me!"

Bronwyn had been wondering all along why he had come, and now she spoke. "What do you want of me, then? We were never friends, you and I, my lord. Why are you here? To gloat?"

He looked directly into her stern face. "No, not that. When I learned that you were Warwick's prisoner, I thought I would check on you to make sure you were not being mistreated, to see if you needed anything."

It astounded her when she realized that he was actually trying to be kind. Her eyes narrowed. But why? Perhaps he was trying to worm his way back into her good graces—or Edward's? That must be it! He assumed that by seeking her out he could mend his fences with his brother.

Bronwyn laughed bitterly, turning her back on him to keep him from seeing her anger and the tears in her eyes. "To make sure I was not being mistreated, or if I needed anything?" she spat, clutching the wood of the bedpost until her hands ached. She heard him stand up behind her.

"You are too late, then, my lord! If I did have need of aid it was long before this! I am beyond help now, though I suppose I must thank you for thinking of me at all. I am nothing to a great man such as yourself," she said sarcastically.

"You mean a lot to Edward . . . still. You bore his son and I know he misses the boy terribly. By the way, madame, where *is* your son? When I heard you were here, nothing was said of the boy being with you."

She didn't trust the man but what did she have to lose?

She had already lost everything. "My son? As far as I know he could be dead now, as the good man I was married to is dead. Dead at Lord Warwick's cruel hands!" She was speaking in a matter-of-fact voice but her heart was breaking. She was afraid to show the Duke of Clarence her true feelings. How could he possibly understand? Warwick was his father-in-law and Leon had only been a "filthy gypsy." He, no doubt, would feel as Warwick had about killing such a dog. *Someday you will thank me for it*, he had said. Viper!

"You were married? And Warwick killed him?" He seemed truly shocked as he spun her around to face him. His expression was full of pity and that hurt her more than anything else. She didn't want his pity!

"Aye, my Lord, I was married. He was a gypsy, and he gave me great happiness. He showed my Johnny tenderness and love." There were tears in her eyes as she spoke of Leon, tears at the realization that she had loved him far more than she had known while he was alive.

"Now he is dead and my son . . . he is lost. I know not where he is. Warwick had only time to cut down my husband and drag me away to France. I wish to God I knew if Johnny is well, or even alive. I left him among the gypsies, my husband's people. I do not know where they are today. *There is no hope!*" She moaned and sank down on the edge of the bed, her eyes lowered as the tears ran down her cheeks.

"Nay, there is always hope, maid! I shall see if I can find the boy for you. I shall send out men as soon as possible. We shall find the poor lad, I promise!" the Duke of Clarence swore.

"You would do this for me?" she breathed, bewildered. "Why?"

"Because I do owe my brother something. And I would make amends in any way I can. I can see how distressed you are, and he is Edward's son and, thus, my nephew. It seems you have suffered enough." His voice was sincere and it touched her. As little as she liked this preening popinjay, she was in no position to turn down his offer of help.

"Thank you, my lord." She smiled at him then. "Anything you can do will be much appreciated. I am a prisoner," her voice grew cold again, "and cannot help myself, as you see, or I would be looking for my son right now. I am so worried about him, and I miss him so!" Her eyes misted again and she put her hand over them, turning away. "I pray he is safe and still alive. If he is not, I have nothing to live for."

"We shall find the boy," the Duke of Clarence restated firmly and laid a hand upon her shoulder for a brief second. "And never fear—Warwick shall not learn of the search. You can depend on it."

She composed herself then and wiped the tears from her white face, smoothed her skirts and pushed back her straying hair. Warwick insisted that she dress like a painted doll in rich and satin gowns and jewels glittering in her thick hair, but to Bronwyn it was just another of his cruel jests. How could she look beautiful when her heart was broken and the gowns hung shapelessly upon her scarecrow figure? She shuddered when she looked into the mirror and saw what she had become—thin-faced, pale and lifeless looking.

"I cannot stay long. Warwick would be angry if he knew I have spoken with you. He is not himself these days," George remarked.

Bronwyn remembered something then. "My lord, I know Lord Warwick is married. Where is his wife these days?" She had been curious about the woman all along, but had never had the courage to ask Warwick himself. Having a mistress was common enough these days; most wealthy men did, but Warwick never mentioned his wife.

"Nan? I imagine she is still in France, with Margaret

and Anne. He sent her away when the King branded him traitor. 'Tis far too unsafe for her here. And she had always hated this huge, drafty fortress. She would never come here willingly after her father died. She said the place was haunted for her, something like that. Why do you ask?'' But George thought he knew why. He had heard rumors, that Warwick had taken a mistress, which was rare for Warwick, but he hadn't known until recently that that woman was Bronwyn. It had come as a complete shock. Warwick had a strange marriage; it had been arranged when they were both children and all England knew there was little love between them. It was her wealth and titles that had always lured Richard Neville, never love or need. Warwick was a man of ice and many thought it peculiar that he kept this wench here now, of all times, with Edward breathing down his neck. But he knew that the reason Warwick craved possessing this particular wench was because the King wanted her too. It was spite that fueled his passion.

"No reason." She sighed. "I merely wondered."

"It is best that she not be here, not now."

"Because I am here?"

"Not only that." He seemed uneasy as he stood up to go.

"I am surprised you have not heard. Edward and his army are not barely a half-mile away. He has the castle surrounded and has placed us under siege since this morning. That is why Warwick is in such a foul mood. The reinforcements promised from Queen Margaret and his other allies have not materalized and they are long overdue. Lord Warwick is frightened, but would never admit it. We are trapped. There is no way we can escape, but there is also no way Edward can get to us. This is the strongest fortress in England. We could be besieged from now to doomsday unless Edward or Warwick desires a final confrontation and breaks this stalemate."

It dawned on Bronwyn then why the Duke of Clarence was being so courteous. He was afraid. His plans and schemes had come to naught and he was facing the prospect of a confrontation with Edward, unsure who the ultimate victor would be. He had burned his bridges behind him and there could be no going back—or could there?

She stared at him, a light beginning to glow in her eyes for the first time in weeks. The man she had loved, perhaps would always love, was just outside these grey stone walls.

Aye, the King's brother did have reason to be afraid, and so too did Warwick.

CHAPTER XIX

England—April 1471

FOR WEEKS, Edward's men waited patiently outside the walls of Warwick Castle. There were many messages sent between the two stubborn cousins, in which Edward demanded Warwick to surrender and he promised he would be lenient with him, and Warwick sent back word that he would see him in hell first.

It was a matter of pride and honor now for Warwick. He would win or he would die on the battlefield.

So the seige went on as the weather turned warmer with the first promise of Spring. Outside in the courtyard the birds began to sing and the sun warmed the cold earth. Bronwyn stared out her prison window hour after hour and prayed that Edward would some morning break through the massive gates and set her free from the man and the place she hated, set her free so she could find their son since the Duke of Clarence was unable to do so. But time dragged on and nothing happened. Edward's men could not breach Warwick's fortifications. They would only become targets for his expert archers who were stationed at every narrow wall-slit.

As the days passed, Bronwyn paced back and forth hour after hour. It couldn't go on much longer, she thought.

How long could Warwick hold out if Queen Margaret never landed in England with the reinforcements that Warwick so desperately needed? What would he do when he realized that *he* had been betrayed this time?

She hadn't seen Warwick in several days and she spun around, surprised, when he threw open the door one morning in April and stode into her room.

There was jubilation in his dark face and he was smiling like the cat who has just trapped a mouse. He grabbed her by the wrist and pulled her close to him. Bronwyn no longer fought him. She had resigned herself to the way things were for the present, knowing that one day her time would come.

"Pack your things!" he told her. "We're leaving here today. Immediately!"

"Leaving, my lord?" she echoed incredulously. "How? Why?" He pushed her towards the coffer at the end of her bed where she kept her clothes, obviously expecting her to start packing this very minute. She was confused. The triumphant look on his face . . . what had happened? She was too afraid to ask, but she didn't have to. He answered her unspoken questions.

"Aye, little witch, we are leaving. Edward has fled to London and my reinforcements have landed at Dover. Queen Margaret and her men are marching even now. Edward turned tail and ran . . . and now we become the hunter and not the hunted! Hurry, wench! We haven't got all day. Edward has a day's start already. He must have moved out his troops last night as soon as it was dark. Aye, Edward will run to London, his stronghold, but we'll be only a step behind him.

"This time I'll finish it once and for all. This time Edward will neither escape nor trick me! *The time has come to strike!*" His face was flushed and his eyes feverish.

Bronwyn stared at him. She had never seen the man so

excited. There was an insane glitter of hate in his black eyes and he kept muttering to himself as he strode from one end of the room to the other. He was behaving like a madman. To follow in Edward's track with the few men he had seemed sheer folly. Who knew where Margaret and her army were now? Why leave this impregnable fortress in pursuit of Edward? But she said nothing and packed as he bade her do. She had no other choice. She had been beaten too many times to cross him when he was in such a mood. Aye, like a dead leaf swept away in a flood, she must go where he led.

"It might interest you to know also, wench, that your friend, Edward's cowardly brother, has run back to the King to beg forgiveness. It seems that when our chances looked slim at best, he feared that he was not on the victor's side and remedied the situation quickly enough. He took his men and joined forces with Edward right before Edward moved out in the night. Traitor and turncoat both! I will make George regret that he did betray me!"

Bronwyn paused in her packing and said evenly, "The Duke of Clarence was never my friend and now it seems he was never yours. 'Tis no great loss, I would think."

"Oh, but I believe he was a good friend of yours," Warwick responded sharply. "After all, he did come to visit you and he also requested that I treat you with consideration and respect. He was quite concerned, in fact. Did he say anything to you about his plans? Did he discuss this latest betrayal with you?"

"Nay, my lord, he did not. That is the truth of it. And do you think I would tell you anything if he had after what you've done to me? Doubt not that in this fight between you and the King, I am *your* sworn enemy, not Edward's. I would never say or do anything to hurt the King's chances of success. I pray each night that Edward will kill you, my Lord," she said sweetly with an acid smile.

Warwick laughed, unexpectedly. "Witch, you have not changed one bit! Still the little wildcat with claws outstretched! If I did not admire your spirit and your beauty much, you would find yourself cast into the darkest hole in my dungeon. That could still be arranged if you anger me enough, so watch your sharp tongue, I warn you." His mirth had disappeared as quickly as it had come, and his face was a stormcloud.

Bronwyn finished her packing in heavy silence. Outside she could hear the blare of trumpets, the clatter of horses' hooves and the shouts of the men as the troops prepared to move out. She knew better than to push Warwick too far, and by the madness in his eyes and his mercurial temper, she also knew that right now she must not taunt him further. George had been right. Warwick was not himself.

When the time came to depart, Warwick sent for her. It was later that night and she was already exhausted by the time she was seated on her mount behind Lord Warwick. Unlike Edward, he cared little who saw her, as if he wanted her presence to be known of and spoken of so Edward would know.

Well, if George were with Edward, he already knew.

But Bronwyn soon discovered that she was not to ride all the way into London. After the first few miles, Warwick reined his warhorse back beside her bay gelding. Bronwyn had been enjoying the fresh air and exercise in spite of her fatigue after so many weeks of captivity. As much as she detested Warwick, her hopes were beginning to rise once more. They were following Edward to London, and if Edward should do battle with Warwick and win, perhaps to freedom at last.

"Witch, you are to come with me," he said in a sharp tone and, grabbing her mount's reins, he cantered ahead pulling them along behind him.

She panicked, wondering where he might be taking her.

But she had no chance to ask questions. They approached a heavy, lumbering wagon that was following behind a few others. At first, when Warwick ordered the driver to halt, she thought it was a supply wagon and that he planned to dump her, chained most likely, into the belly of it and thus get her out of the way until the battle was over.

The wagon creaked to a stop and Warwick moved his horse with Bronwyn right behind him up to its front. He grinned over his shoulder at her. "I thought that during this battle, you might want to be with your own kind, witch. I happened to run into an old friend of yours the other day who asked about you. After some discussion, she has consented to watch over you while I am otherwise engaged. And when I win, I will return for you. I'm leaving you in very capable hands, you'll see." He chuckled unpleasantly and Bronwyn suspected that whatever he had in mind for her, she would not like it. Warwick jumped down from his mount and went to talk in hushed whispers to what appeared to be a woman. It was dark and from where Bronwyn sat on her horse, nervously waiting, she couldn't hear what was being said. An old friend, he had said. Who could it possibly be? Who was this woman who was to be her jailer?

The whispers on the gentle night breeze sent chills up and down her spine. Warwick seemed to know the mystery woman well enough.

He came back to her then and yanked her roughly from her saddle. He had something shiny and metal in one hand and she could hear clinking as he shoved her up into the back of the wagon.

She cried out as something cold and hard clamped about her wrist and she realized it was a chain. He locked the other end of it around one of the wagon's inner supports and laughed down at her in the dimness of the interior. "I am sorry I had to do that, wench, but it was one of the conditions she insisted upon. I think it best as well, since your word is so easily given and broken. You would escape otherwise." He stood up and tested the strength of the chain. It was about four or five feet long; just long enough, he told her with a chortle as he stood above her, for her to leave the wagon in order to relieve herself. "You should thank me for my thoughtfulness," he told her grimly.

"So I am to remain a prisoner," Bronwyn said.

"You could hardly expect me to let you go free!"

He knelt down in front of her and peered into her shadowed face. "I am not such of a fool as to think that my victory is assured. I have accepted the fact that tomorrow when we face Edward I might lose. Did you really think I would hand you over to him so easily? Never! Whether I win or lose, he shall never see you or his precious bastard son again. If I win, I shall come back to claim you."

"And if you don't? What is to become of me?" she demanded shakily.

She heard his laughter as he jumped from the wagon, remounted, and rode away without answering her question.

Anxiously Bronwyn waited to met her new captor. The wagon was cramped and she tried to get comfortable, her mind spinning. Who was the woman? What would be her fate if Warwick should lose?

"*Well, well*! Sure enough, here is the baggage I was paid to watch, all tied up nice and pretty-like. Do you remember me, witch?" The woman had climbed in next to her from the front. Bronwyn couldn't see her face very well but she didn't need to. She was sure even before the candle was lit and held aloft, of the woman's identity.

"*Molly?*" Bronwyn gasped, drawing back. And indeed it was the woman who had delivered her to Warwick so long ago, the barmaid who had mysteriously disappeared from the Red Boar and Bronwyn's life. Bronwyn hadn't given her another thought since that terrible time. Now here she was, and Bronwyn was completely in her power. She was astounded by the change seven years had wrought in the woman. She had gotten fat, and her dark hair hung in tangled greasy strings. Her face was sagging and pasty looking in the light of the candle. Her eyes were as Bronwyn remembered, though, full of hatred and jealousy of the younger, prettier girl. Bronwyn's recent hope turned quickly to despair at the evil gloating mirrored in Molly's puffy, greedy eyes.

"Aye, 'tis old Molly, the Molly you did send into the streets with all your little schemes and haughty ways. 'Tis nice to see you again after all these years. After I was thrown out of the inn and Jack was paid off to forget all the loving devotion I had always given him, it was a hard seven years. I had to eat and at my age, few lusty soldiers and wealthy men wanted to pay for an old whore like me between their fine sheets. Not like you, pretty one." She reached out a dirty hand and touched Bronwyn's shiny, flowing hair. "And so here you be with old Molly again! So your pretty young body and your haughty ways got you no further than old Molly after all, it would seem." Molly cackled a hidous laugh. Suddenly she clamped a meaty hand about the younger woman's arm and gripped her so tightly that Bronwyn cried out in pain and surprise.

"Aye, I'm strong. All these years of being an old street whore and camp follower has made me strong, believe me. I've had to learn how to take care of myself." Her beady eyes raked Bronwyn from head to toe. "Lord High-and-Mighty there hasn't treated ye all that well, I can see. You look half starved to me, in spite of those fine clothes. He does play rough with his women, I hear tell." But, Damn, Molly thought, she is still so pretty, for all that. Time had treated Bronwyn far better than it had her. Molly was well aware that her beauty had faded long ago. Aye, time had been cruel to old Molly!

"Why are you doing this for him?" Bronwyn had finally found her tongue.

"Why money, lass. *Money*. I have to eat . . . haven't ye been listening to what I've been saying?" Her voice rose into a whine. "I'm not young and pretty like yourself. I have to beg, scratch, or spread my legs for a living. No more comfortable inns and easy days for this old nag." She chuckled, but it was a terrifying sound to a frightened Bronwyn. The woman obviously was as mad as Warwick, and hated her as well.

"*And 'tis all your doing*, my pretty. But now the shoe be on the other foot, so to speak. I've got you and I've got the only key to that lock. You'll do as I say from now on, or pay the price. Do you hear, bitch? *Do you hear?*" The words were vindictive and she squeezed Bronwyn's arm until she moaned and nodded her head. "*Good.*" Molly licked her cracked lips. "First, take off that pretty gown ye have on and give it to me!"

"*What?*" Bronwyn thought she hadn't heard correctly.

"Take off that gown. Now!" Molly's eyes burned greedily in the candlelight as she stroked the soft velvet of the wine-colored gown. "I haven't had such a lovely bit o' cloth to put upon my old bones in a long time. I want it, so give it to me. I can alter it to fit, I'll be bound."

"But what will I wear?" Bronwyn asked weakly as she unlaced the bodice and started to wriggle out of the gown.

"Oh, never ye worry, pretty bitch . . . I have just the thing back here in my chest for ye. You'll see. It'll suit you a whole lot better, methinks." She laughed and began rummaging through the chest.

When Bronwyn handed her over the velvet gown, Molly tossed at her what at first Bronwyn thought was a pile of rags, but it was in reality an old, shapeless rag of a gown. The material was patched, and so thin in places one could almost see through it. It had seen a lot of hard wear and little washing. The smell of it turned Bronwyn's stomach.

Molly held Bronwyn's gown up to herself, smiling. "Pretty. So pretty, witch. I do thank ye kindly for it. Now, put yours on."

Bronwyn obediently slipped it over her head. The garment hung on her slender frame like a shapeless tent. It was made of coarse, itchy material and Bronwyn felt unclean just wearing it.

"Molly, what is to happen to me if Lord Warwick does not return to claim me and pay you?" she asked softly. She had to be careful with this dreadful woman. She had the overpowering feeling that Molly would rejoice to see her dead.

Molly stood up and smirked down at her captive. She was much uglier than Bronwyn remembered, as though her sly, evil nature were revealed in her face. "What I will do if my lord doesn't come back to you is none of your concern. But I'll tell ye anyway—give you something to dream about tonight while ye sleep. As pretty a wench as ye be, I could get a good price for ye from one of the dockside brothels I know of, a good price. Them sailors would pay a gold piece to mount you, I dare say! Sailors do love pretty women." She laughed, a horrible, loud laugh that hurt Bronwyn's ears.

A *brothel*! Molly would sell her to a *dockside brothel*! Bronwyn's heart sank even lower than before if possible.

"Molly, why do you despise me?" Bronwyn cried. "You always have, from the very first . . . *why*? I have never done you any harm that I can recall. Why do you torment me so?" She tried to leap to her feet, but the chain pulled her back to her knees in the cramped space of the wagon. The candle had burnt down to almost nothing and she could barely make out the older woman's haggard face. If she could have reached her at that moment, Bronwyn would have strangled her, so enraged was she at the injustice of Molly's actions.

"Here, here! Calm yourself!" Molly snickered, stroking

the velvet gown with her roughened hands. She reminded Bronwyn of a great ugly cat; in a second she might start purring, she was so pleased with the dress, though Bronwyn doubted that it could ever be made to fit.

Molly's voice was spiteful now.

"You have done me more harm than you will ever know. It be so damn easy for you to get what you want from life, you whore!" She spat vindictively and Bronwyn recoiled from the spittle that sprayed her startled face. "You with your pretty, sweet face and lovely blond hair, your cat's green eyes and fair shape, your youth and your gifts! Men fight over you, love you, accept the bastards you bear them. A King and an Earl did seek you to warm their beds. And all because you are so *beautiful*!" she taunted, swiping at the girl's long flowing hair. Her hand caught a lock of it and tugged viciously as Bronwyn tried to pull away, wincing at the sharp pain.

"Not like poor old Molly here," Molly continued raving. "I got old and fat and the men no longer wanted me. I've scratched and I've stolen and I've begged just to stay alive . . . I hear you have a little boy." she said abruptly. "Well, so too did old Molly. I had me *two* fine boys. *And they be dead now*! Died of frost-bite and starvation 'cause I couldn't take care of 'em proper. That was before I came to the inn, mind you. I watched their bellies swell with hunger and their eyes beg for food and I could not help them. I buried them myself under stones in the forest and I swore that black day that I would never starve or suffer like that again. Then I found Jack. Aye, greedy Jack. I thought I had a future there at the Red Boar. Martha was a weak, spineless creature and I could handle Jack so easily. Then *you* had to come along and when all was said and done, Jack would have no more to do with me. Your fancy gentleman friend did give him a pouch of gold to send me packing as punishment for telling Lord Warwick where to find you. That was the best thing I'd ever had—old Jack and that fine inn. You took that all away from me! *Look at me now*! I dress in rags and I struggle to survive. These last years I've followed the soldiers. Men before battle, men far away from their sweet little wives and families, aren't choosy. Like a mangy, beaten dog I take what scraps they offer and am glad for them. Because of *you* am I here! *You, girlie*. And I've never forgotten what I owe you. I aim to pay you back in full one day or t'other.''

Molly sat there glaring at her, her face contorted with hate and envy.

For the first time Bronwyn began to understand. She sank back on her haunches and studied the pitiful creature before her. She was no longer angry at Molly. "Now I see why you hate me so," she whispered. She knew it was useless to argue with the poor woman, but she had to say something, defend herself somehow. "But you must believe me when I tell you that I never meant to cause you trouble. I never meant to ruin your life. I was just protecting myself. *You* led that fiend Warwick to me and I had never done you any harm. It was you who first made me your enemy.''

Molly merely grunted. She stood up as best she could in the room they had. "That is how you see it, but not the way I do, witch. You were scheming to get aholt of Jack and my place in the inn from the first time ye sashayed into the place, with your sweet, lying smile and your crafty cat's eyes and your little bag of magic tricks. Conjuring is what you were doin'! Conjuring spells so as people wouldn't know what ye were. But ye never fooled old Molly! I knew what ye were from the first, I did. *Witch*! So don't be expecting pity from me. Ye deserve none. You owe me and I'll take my price out of your pretty hide if I need to. If my Lord Warwick doesn't come to fetch ye tomorrow, then I'll sell ye. Either way makes no difference to me . . . but I'll have my revenge and some gold into

451

the bargain, maybe even enough so as I can get a small place of my own. I have to look out for myself, my pretty. Unlike you, who has men to keep her safe and warm, I have no one but myself and my wits. So don't bother to beg me to let ye go. Molly hissed and, taking the dead candle into her hands, turned and climbed back up into the driving seat. "We have a long way to go. If I were ye I'd get some sleep now while ye can." Then Bronwyn heard her clucking to the team of sorry-looking nags that pulled the rickety wagon and they lurched into sudden movement, jostling her roughly against the side of the wagon.

Bronwyn sat huddled and chained in the dark as they bounced along behind the other wagons toward London that warm April night and she thought of her small son laughing as though from far away. Then she heard his terrified sobs. *"Mama . . . Mama . . . where are you, Mama? I've looked for you and I can't find you . . . why did you leave me, Mama? I'm so lonely and so afraid. Mama!*

Bronwyn buried her head in her hands and cried harder and more hopelessly than she had in weeks. Never had things looked so bleak. She had to get free to find her son! She struggled against the chain in a sudden fury. She would have screamed if it would have done any good, but she knew it wouldn't. Molly would probably come back and beat her until she stopped. The woman had no heart.

Bronwyn drifted through dreams of herself and Leon and Johnny singing and playing before the campfire. Then she dreamed vividly of Edward and the long-ago days of their love. She kept seeing the King with his son, his eyes sparkling with pride as he raised the boy high into the air and swung him around in dizzying circles. *Oh, sweet God . . . where was her son?* Was he hungry or cold or alone? Was he frightened or hurt? *Oh, God!*

What was going to become of her now?

* * *

Dawn's pale light touched Bronwyn's drawn face and her eyes flew open. Far away in the distance she heard trumpets blaring the call to battle. She sat up, nearly bumping her head against a brace, and then heard the rattling of her chain, a cruel reminder of her bondage. She was still tired. It was barely light and she was so hungry.

"Molly? Where are you?" Bronwyn begged at the front of the wagon to get Molly's attention. They'd stopped sometime in the night and Molly had come back to get some sleep for a short while, then had climbed back up front and the wagon had begun rolling again. These were vague memories in Bronwyn's mind. She wondered where they were and what was happening up ahead.

"*Molly! What's going on?*" she called again at the top of her voice. The wagon came to a sudden lurching halt and Molly's ugly face loomed right above her.

"They've made camp up ahead on Barnet Heath. We are to go up ahead and join the other wagons along the edges of Wrotham Wood there beyond the horsecamp." Molly pointed, the reins tightly held in her strong hands. She laughed then. "Well, my little chit, it looks as if the King means to fight right here. He never intended to let us get to London to meet Queen Margaret and her army. Now the rumor is that neither Lord Percy nor Lord Stanley have arrived. Lord Warwick did summon them both in good faith but they are nowhere to be found. See out there beyond the hill to the right? See the lines of men in armor? Them to the left be English archers and behind them are knights. It seems that the King did trick Warwick into believing he had less men and cannon than he really has . . . must be thousands in his camp now and more coming every hour, it looks like to me. There be the Duke of Clarence's colors alongside his brothers' of York and Gloucester. I hate to tell ye this, girlie, but I do think that this time his Lordship will be rightly trounced. He counted on Stanley and Percy's support and men and he expected to reach London or thereabouts to join with Margaret's men. Now he'll have neither. See—the King's Banner flutters over that line of pikemen and the trumpet says it be time to fight. *Now* we're in for a time of it!'' Molly's squinty eyes glinted in the dawn, hungry for the fray to begin. It was all a game to her. She loved to see great ones at each other's throats like wild, crazed animals. It brought them down to her level.

"I'm pulling in behind that outcropping of rock there and I'll fetch us something to eat whilst we wait. From the way I see it, we won't wait very long, cause this won't be much of a battle. The King holds all the aces this time.'' She glowered at the girl's white face, then winked at her. "And after the battle's over, why, you and me will take us a little ride down to the docks!'' She laughed nastily, but Bronwyn turned a deaf ear as Molly maneuvered the wagon down through the gully into a steep ravine fronted with high, white rocks.

Molly secured the reins and looked about her. There was movement everywhere and the trumpets were calling again. Suddenly the sound of cannon boomed through the air and not too far off, she could hear the first sounds of battle—war cries and men's shouts. The battle had begun. Not much of a place for a fight, she thought with a shake of her head. Too rough terrain and far too many hills and rocks where archers might hide and rain down their deadly darts. Aye, it'll be a black day for Lancaster and Warwick, she said to herself. And a black day for the wench in the wagon behind her, too. As soon as York had won the day, Molly would sell the doxy for a pretty penny to Jamie down on the Stews Dock, and her revenge would be complete.

Warwick reined in his nervous, prancing warhorse, with a strong gauntleted hand. He was angry but proud, as well. He had taught the lad well! Aye, Edward had tricked him, true enough. He had thought to reach London on Edward's fleeing heels, hounding the arrogant pup until he caught him by the tail and whipped him well. But the pup had turned on him, instead, with sharp slashing teeth and fury in his narrowed eyes.

Ah, Edward had surprised him indeed! But Warwick was impressed by his cousin's cleverness in catching him unprepared, undermanned and weak in his defenses. *Edward, you have learned the ways of war well, he thought. You have turned into a worthy adversary!*

Then Warwick's melancholy smile faded and he lowered his visor and took his lance from the squire standing patiently below. He looked out across the sun-drenched rocky field to where Edward and his brothers Richard and George waited with their men for the first charge. Behind Warwick rode those Lancasters who had answered his call, and the French mercenaries and archers, his brother, John Neville, and his men. Lords Exeter and Oxford were to the right with their men and cannon. John Neville's heart, Warwick knew, really lay across the green fields with Edward. John had always adored his kingly, golden cousin and only Warwick's stronger blood ties and his own greater need kept him behind him and not against him.

Not enough. Not enough men, not enough artillery by far. Warwick fretted. Where was that damned Percy? Where were Stanley and all those other sniveling Lancasters who were supposed to aid him in defeating the golden lion of England?

The trumpets sang out again and Warwick steeled himself. For the first time as he gazed out across the space between him and Edward's horde, he was looking upon the White Rose banners as an enemy. How ironic that, after all these long, bloody years of strife, bloodshed and bitterness he should be fighting against that banner now, when he had always fought so bravely beneath it. He felt uneasy under the waving Red Rose. Lancaster! How he had always loathed them! How had he come to such a pass?

It's too late now, a voice in his brain tortured him. *Too late! You have made your bed and now you must lie in it. Die in it.* He shifted uncomfortably in his heavy armor and was seized by a terrible premonition as he sat there in the sun scanning the distant faces, some old familiar faces of former friends under the glorious Sun Banner. *These men he was ready to kill and maim had once been his friends and cohorts. Now they were his sworn enemies. How wrong it seemed*!

Warwick thought he could almost make out Edward's shining white Flemish armor shimmering in the morning's pale sun under a tall oak. The man in dark armor next to him must be his brother Richard. He fancied that Edward was watching him, too, across the field. He could feel Edward's brilliant blue eyes—accusing, full of pain for what they had once been to each other. *Oh, Edward, why did it have to come to this*! He laid a hand soothingly on his fretful mount's arched neck. The warhorse could smell the battle coming and was eager for the first charge. Unlike its master, was ready for the fray.

Warwick became aware then of a soundless ripple of passionate impatience rapidly moving through the men and horses behind him. He wheeled his mount in a breathtaking dancing circle and pranced down the line to inspect his men one final time. It was unnecessary and he knew it; he was just stalling for time. He'd set his command post up in the woods and made hasty battle plans as soon as it became evident that Edward had halted his forces and was ready to fight. He studied his French archers and regretted the fact that they were French. *Another old, old enemy*. All was in readiness. Serious-faced and many with fear in their nervous eyes, his troops watched and waited for the signal to attack. The knights' faces under their visors were silent and stern. All waited for his command.

God's Blood! That fence-straddler Duke of Clarence must have four thousand men with him, and Edward twice that number. Warwick looked back at his own troops. How could he trust them? They weren't his men. They were Lancaster and French.

He raised his arm as a signal to the trumpeters to sound the charge. The trumpets sounded and Warwick raised his flashing broadsword high above his head. He set spurs to his horse's heaving flanks and felt the great muscles spring into action beneath him as they thundered across the sunny field toward their fate.

But behind the metal visor, Warwick's eyes were already dead. He had no heart for this battle . . . he was haunted by memories of Edward as a boy, young golden Edward as King and all the grand plans they had once made for themselves and for England. *What had happened to change them both so? Where were their noble dreams now?*

The Kingmaker stormed into the the York lines, slicing angrily into his opponents like a man possessed. They were not men to him, these creatures who rose before him like ripe wheat, and he cut them down viciously like the Grim Reaper. More men came within reach of his flashing sword, and he thrust his blade deep into their puny flesh. A sea of fighting, bleeding men surrounded and eluded him, struck and slashed at him. Always there came more and more, like waves beating on a shore and he became confused. Yet the frenzy that gripped him did not abate. Men who later spoke of that day said that it was as if he were trying to die, as if he wanted to die. He was like a demon in their midst and there wasn't one York knight who was not trying to destroy the devil on the black stallion.

He fought on through the horde, his eyes always fixed on some vision in the distance. He sought Edward. *Edward! If he could only kill the man*, he thought in a sudden urgent burst of guilt and desperation, *he would be free of his golden spell! If he could just get to Edward* . . .

Arrows rained down upon him, some bouncing ineffectually off his armor and some lodging between the plates. Soon trickles of blood streamed down his thighs and arms. Someone drove a lance into the underbelly of his stallion and even when the horse screamed in agony and plunged wildly about, he never missed a stroke. His victims dropped beneath his wounded mount's flailing hooves or fell to the wayside, armless or headless and their cries scorched his brain. But he kept on fighting and killing and closing the gap between himself and the man in white armor just ahead of him, always just a few more feet away . . . always there, but just out of reach. For a second, he was sure he saw Edward's bright smile, beckoning and luring him deeper into the bloody fray. A sea of dying, moaning men engulfed him. A man screamed and fell next to him, his head smashed by a mace. Everywhere was the horrible carnage of war. How many, many times had he lived this same ghastly scene? How many more? He was so weary . . . but he fought on because there was no other way. There was no turning back.

A knight drove his sword in Warwick's ribs where the plates of his armor met. Warwick didn't feel it. A foot soldier lunged at him as his stallion finally stumbled to its knees and cleaved through his vambrace and the blood spurted out like a red fountain. He did not feel that, either. A halbred ripped through his bloody breastplate.

He saw Edward smiling at him in the distance as though in a golden cloud. Warwick's heart beat quickened and the world seemed to freeze around him. *There was no one on the field but Edward and he . . . Edward . . . coming closer . . . closer . . .*

An arrow whizzed past him and when he stared after it another struck him in the neck. *There was someone screaming very near to him—so near—someone . . .* he was mildly surprised *to realize the man screaming was himself.*

The noise of battle faded and he listened . . . he could hear Edward's golden laugh. Where was he? *"Edward! Where are ye?"* he cried as another sword flashed and his blade clattered to the bloody ground on which he sprawled. There was so much blood . . . pain . . .

"Edward!" he screamed as the world began to spin away from him forever. *I'm dying*, he thought. He felt no pain now, only acceptance. *Edward, I did love ye well. Edward . . .*

The young boy King, not more than eighteen, stood above him then, smiling. "I know ye did, good cousin. I know." There was forgiveness and all the old love shining in the vision's brilliant sky-blue eyes as he held out his hand, and as Warwick's gloved hand touched Edward's, he smiled. The vision dissolved in a burst of flame and Warwick closed his eyes for the last time, content.

Warwick's bloodied and broken body lay cold upon the earth in the sunlight of a warm April morning in the year 1471, all that was left of all his great dreams and ambitions.

Some time later a man in battered white armor gazed down upon him. There were tears in his tired blue eyes. This had been his protector, his enemy. *Warwick.* Edward stared down at the mutilated body. Wasn't this what he had wanted? Warwick dead. Then why did the sight tear at his heart? He turned away, overcome by the horror and nausea. His brother Richard, tired and bloody, too, supported him or he would have collapsed. The battle was over and Edward had won an astounding victory. But none of it mattered now that he had come upon the cold body of the once great Earl of Warwick.

"Come, brother. We must tend to your wound. The surgeon awaits. If we are to get to horse and stop Queen

Margaret before she crosses the Welsh border to freedom, we had best depart now, or we will lose her and her whelp for sure. Come. I will see to it that he has a decent burial. An honorable one.'' Richard's thin, serious face was full of concern and love for his older brother. He drew him away from the body and they walked slowly towards their waiting mounts and men. Edward looked back just once and tears slid down his sunburned face.

"Nay, Ned, feel no remorse or guilt. 'Tis the death he would have chosen, with a sword in his hand on the field of battle. Do not torture yourself. You could not have prevented it, brother, believe me.''

Edward nodded then and let his squire help him up upon his horse. So many good men dead. John Neville lay not fifty yards away from his dead brother, dead as well. And so many more. He looked up into the beautiful blue skies and felt the warm breeze caress his face.

As he rode away he kept thinking, it was what I wanted, wasn't it? Warwick defeated and dead at last. *It was, wasn't it?* But his heart refused to answer. He would never forget the look on Warwick's face. Whatever he had seen or thought he had seen at the end, his expression could only be described as contentment and peace. That face would haunt him forever.

CHAPTER XX

BRONWYN HEARD the clamor of battle from where she huddled, terrified inside Molly's wagon. It seemed to go on forever. She covered her ears at times to shut out the sounds, but she couldn't escape what she feared to be true. Soon she could hear the unmistakable sounds, too, of men deserting the field, throwing down their weapons and fleeing in fear. They ran past the wagon like a herd of stampeding bullocks, in flight from the advancing foe. A wounded archer paused just long enough to confirm that Warwick's forces were in full retreat.

The knowledge that Edward had won a great victory and that Warwick was most probably dead should have brought unnamed joy to her heart. But instead, she was terrified. Sweet Jesus, how she had longed for the death of that black-hearted monster and murderer! But now she feared for her future. She had no doubt that Molly would keep her word and by this time tomorrow, Bronwyn would be a whore bought and sold.

When at last the sun rode high in the heavens and an eerie silence fell over the battlefield, Bronwyn didn't have to be told what had happened. A moment later the quiet was shattered by the triumphant blare of trumpets, celebrating Edward's victory and Warwick's death.

Molly had disappeared a short while ago and when she suddenly clambered awkwardly back up into the back of the wagon, there was a wicked grin on her ugly face.

"Well, girlie, have you heard the good news?" she gloated. "Your friend Lord Warwick be naught but carrion for King Edward has won the day. His soldiers be coming now, sweeping the fields for survivors and stragglers to cart way to their filthy prisons. 'Tis not safe for the likes of us—we're leaving. Now." Her eyes glinted wickedly at the look of fear in the younger woman's eyes.

"Where are we going?" Bronwyn's mouth was so dry she could hardly speak. She still couldn't believe that it was all over, that Warwick was dead. She was in a state of shock.

"Molly . . ." Bronwyn spoke softly, her eyes pleading. "Surely you have gone far enough with this?" She rattled her chain, indicating her situation. "You have had your revenge. Please let me go and I promise that I will never tell a soul about this. But perhaps the King would reward you handsomely if I were to tell him you helped me escape Lord Warwick." Bronwyn held her breath awaiting Molly's reply. The woman was after all, greedy. The possibility of a reward might convince her, if nothing else would.

Molly burst out in derisive laughter. "Ye would like that, wouldn't ye? For old Molly to forgive and forget and set ye free?" Her eyes narrowed and she grabbed Bronwyn by the wrist. "*Over my dead body, wench*! I've waited far too long for the pleasure of getting my revenge, and I'll not be cheated of it now. Reward, indeed! I doubt the King remembers who you are! You are coming with me down to the docks and I will make sure I find ye a *good home*." With that, Molly shoved her back down on the floor of the wagon and made her way up front to start the team and the wagon going again.

"For the love of God, be merciful, Molly! I must find my son! I have to be free to find him. You were a mother once. Have you no pity?" Her cries and entreaties would have melted a heart of stone, but not Molly's. She had been through too much and seen too many sorrows; too many people had rejected and abused her. Now it was her turn to have the upper hand.

"Molly!" Bronwyn cried once more at the woman's broad back and when she didn't answer, in desperation Bronwyn lunged the length of her chain and pulled her to the wagon floor. Taken off guard, Molly for a moment lost the advantage.

"*Let me go!*" the woman yelled, struggling against Bronwyn's slender strength as she frantically searched her clothes for the key to the manacles.

"*Give me that key*! Give it to me!" she demanded as they rolled on the floor of the cluttered wagon, scratching, biting and hitting like a pair of wildcats. All Bronwyn could think of was escaping and finding her son. To obtain her objective, she would kill if necessary.

"Never, witch!" Molly hissed, clawing at Bronwyn's face and deeply scratching her left cheek. Bronwyn didn't cry out. She was determined to get that key, but Molly was far stronger than she. She was beginning to weaken and had all but given in to despair, when her hand miraculously came upon something hard and cool in a pocket of Molly's filthy gown. The key! With one last great heave, Bronwyn tossed the heavier woman off, and the key was clutched in her hand. Molly's head hit the side of the wagon, and she lay there, stunned. Bronwyn scrambled to her knees and with trembling fingers inserted the key into the lock. The manacles fell from her wrist. She was free at last!

Bronwyn tumbled head first from the wagon and leaping to her feet, she began to run blindly and wildly as if she were fleeing the devil himself. She heard the sounds of men and horses nearby and ran toward them. York or

Lancaster, it made no difference. There would be safety in numbers.

She had just come in sight of the soldiers, who stared curiously at her, when Molly tackled her from behind and threw her to the ground. Screeching and spitting, the two women rolled in the dirt, locked in a deadly, desperate struggle.

One of the soldiers, a big, burly man with a red beard, managed to separate them, laughing as if he had caught some special prize, until Molly raked her nails across his face and he bellowed in anger and rage. His humor vanished immediately as he held the two apart, shaking them like two spitting cats. He dealt Molly a stunning blow on the head and she stopped struggling. But Molly had not given up. She pointed a thick finger at Bronwyn and whined, "I only sought to stop the witch . . . she be a witch for sure! Cast a spell on me, she did. Tried to conjure a defeat for our good King Edward, as well! She cast a spell for him to *die*! Please, good sir, tell me she didn't succeed! Is the King alive? I was so afraid I be too late . . .''

The red-bearded soldier made the sign of the cross and his eyes widened in fear. He stared at Bronwyn with that look that she knew all too well—suspicion. Doubt. After a pause, he said, "Why should I believe a slut like ye?'' looking sternly at the cringing Molly who was smiling at him grotesquely, batting her eyelashes and trying very hard to be alluring.

Bronwyn shuddered in mortal terror. Her heart inside her breast turned over sickeningly.

" 'Cause I know for a fact the wench be the devil's own,'' Molly responded loudly. "She was the Duke of Warwick's whore and she did seek to help him win the victory. His *whore*, I tell ye! She is a witch! Don't look in her eyes or she'll bewitch ye, too! She can bewitch any man, she can!'' Molly babbled on and on and with growing horror, Bronwyn saw the man turn to her and study her intently as if he were starting to believe the lies.

The soldier looked from one filthy, bleeding woman to the other, narrowing his dull, bloodshot eyes. How much wine had he drunk? Bronwyn wondered, trembling with fear. It seemed the soldier and his friends, Yorkists all, had already begun their victory celebration. Some were so drunk they could hardly stand up.

"Witch, ye say? She's a witch?" he repeated slowly. "Tried to cast a spell upon our good King Edward, did she? Wanted him dead, did she?" His voice rose to a bellow then and his great hand clamped upon Bronwyn's arm even tighter. "*Warwick's whore!*" he growled drunkenly.

Molly was grinning smugly now. *I showed you. I'll teach you to cross old Molly!* her eyes seemed to say to Bronwyn.

The soldier began to drag them both towards the horses and the rest of his drunken, but suddenly silent and frightened, comrades at arms.

" 'Tis best, then, that we get the both of ye to a magistrate. Let the law decide which of ye is the witch—or if both of ye are," he chortled, tossing Bronwyn up into one of the horsemen's arms. Kicking and screaming, Bronwyn was trapped within the brawny soldier's iron grasp. Though she pleaded and wept, he wouldn't listen to her, only fondled her body, laughing at her feeble struggles.

"Got me a spitfire, I 'ave, by God!" He grinned and pinned her arms to her side. "And witch or no, she be a pretty little filly—not like yours, Will, short and fat. Ha, ha! Clean 'er up some and she could almost pass for a fine lady. Give us a kiss, wench!" Bronwyn freed one hand just long enough to slap him stingingly across his leering face. He slapped her in return and, setting spurs to his horse, rode after the others, no longer laughing.

As they galloped past the stragglers and the hobbling wounded fleeing the battlesite, Bronwyn was terrified at what would happen now. Would her nightmare of being burned at the stake become hideous reality? She feared she would never see her beloved Johnny again.

Bronwyn lay on a pile of dirty straw against the cold stones of a cell in Ludgate prison. The stone floor was damp with the moisture that seemed to seep into everything—her clothes, her hair and skin, even, it seemed, her very soul. There was no light, no warmth. She covered her nose and mouth, trying to shut out the horrible stench of the place. She had retched so many times already that she was weak and dizzy. She had no idea if it were day or night. Days and nights all merged together. *How long have I been here*?'' she asked herself and couldn't answer. Hours, days or weeks of huddling in the damp, dark cell, listening to the other women prisoners weeping and moaning around her, squabbling among themselves for a scrap of stale bread, or vomiting over and over as she had. Bronwyn's once lovely hair hung in greasy strands and her scalp itched. Her clothes were filthy, as was her whole body; she hadn't bathed since she had been locked away.

She replayed in her exhausted brain the day—or was it night?—when along with Molly and the other unfortunate women who shared her small cell she had been brought before the local magistrate. He in turn had handed them over to a priest and a group of faceless monks in black cowled robes. Bronwyn knew what their fate was to be. Mother Church was in the midst of a merciless witch hunt and great numbers of women and men were being speedily tried and sent to the stake in droves. Bronwyn remembered the poor Lollards, whom at her instigation the King had saved. She had never had to fear as long as she had had his love and protection. And when she was with Leon, she knew he and his people would protect her. But now she was nothing more than a lone woman, a woman who, like the others, stood trembling as the dreadful sentence was pronounced.

All were found guilty of witchcraft or of associating with witches and sentenced to die in flames at the stake.

In a shocked trance, she barely remembered being led away. It couldn't be happening to her . . . *not to her!* Who would look for and find her son if she were dead? The other women shrieked and wailed as they were shoved back into their cell to await the day of execution. Molly had to be forcibly dragged, screaming and kicking as she cursed the robed figures to the Hell they were bound to be going to someday for what they were doing. As much as Bronwyn loathed the woman, she had to feel pity at the injustice of it all. They beat Molly before they tossed her back into the cell, to silence her. Bronwyn helped her as best she could but Molly had given up.

"They're goin' to burn us anyways . . ." she moaned through bloody lips. "I wish they had beaten me to death! *I can't face the flames . . .*" she whimpered and hiding her eyes, began to weep. She had been weeping ever since.

But never once had Bronwyn turned accusing eyes on her and said, *It is your fault we are here in the first place.* She shared the poor woman's fears and her fate and the time for accusations and petty revenge was long past.

This had been the stuff of Bronwyn's worst nightmares—lying helpless in a cell, waiting to be taken away to feed the hungry flames. Lying in that prison, hungry, weak and sick, she had at last accepted her fate. She had always known it would come to this. She knew there was no hope. No one knew she was here. No doubt Edward thought she was already dead. No one would seek her and rescue her. Bronwyn smiled bitterly. When she had first arrived at the prison, she had tried to persuade a guard to take a message to the King, telling him her plight and begging him to help her. The guard had heard her out, and when she was done speaking, had shoved her back into the cell, laughing his head off, saying that he had heard many a grand story in his day, but hers was the best ever. Imagine a witch and whore being the King's paramour! The frustration she had felt lingered for a long time. Indeed, why should he believe her? Why should anyone?

There was no way out this time. Bronwyn prepared herself to die. The only thing that pained her now was the thought of her poor lost son. She prayed that he would be all right. She wondered if he were still with the gypsies and if he were well—if he missed her . . .

When the guards came early one morning to take her and the other women to the stake, Bronwyn was so weak, she could barely stand. A guard supported her to the wooden tumbril that would travel slowly through the town's streets towards the place of execution. Though she knew it was hopeless, she whispered "Please, sir . . . I am not a witch. Please . . . believe me! Get a message to the King . . ." But he paid no attention, thinking she was demented, and herded her along with the others, into the tumbril. Out into the bright sunlight of a glorious May day the cart rolled, beginning its long journey from Ludgate Prison to the market square where the burnings were to take place. The unaccustomed sun hurt Bronwyn's eyes and she flinched, but welcomed the clean, fresh air. She was ashamed of the filthy grey rags she wore and the way she looked, and hung her head as the cart rattled down the cobbled streets through jeering crowds.

So many years ago she remembered just such a scene . . . but then she had been only a horrified spectator. She wished to God that it were so this time, but then she lifted her face bravely to the warm sunlight. *It was her turn to die this time, her turn to suffer.* Her heart was pounding so fast she felt as if she might faint. Her old enemy Molly clung to her as the market square came into view and the crowd following them started to cheer, crazy with blood lust. They would have their sport this day! She looked out over the eager, avid faces and felt more pity than hatred. They wanted their entertainment and as long as it wasn't going to happen to *them*, why not enjoy the show? Besides, they believed the victims to be witches who deserved their fate.

"God help us!" Molly wept, falling to her knees as they pulled up before the stakes—nine of them, as there were nine condemned women. Molly stumbled when they yanked her from the tumbril and, screaming and begging piteously, she was dragged to the stake. It took two strong men to bind her securely.

Bronwyn, deathly calm, walked with dignity to her place and stood staring sightlessly into the clear blue sky as she was bound with heavy ropes to the wooden stake. Johnny, she thought, oh, my son, God be with you! May you grow up strong and brave, as your father is!

She thought of Edward then and how she had loved him, of Leon and their beautiful but brief time together. She thought of Martha and her two dear sisters. They must think she was dead already. But always her thoughts returned to her lost son and her longing for him was so great at that moment that she thought her heart must break from it.

The crowd had hushed. All the women were bound. Some were weeping. A very young girl, no more than sixteen or so, was trembling all over like a leaf in the wind, her terrified brown eyes wide, her face white.

Molly had fainted, but her bonds held her upright. Bronwyn looked over at her and felt compassion. Poor Molly. She had had a hard life, and now an ignominious death.

At least, Bronwyn reflected somberly, *she* had known happiness and love. If her son was still alive, perhaps he too would be happy one day. Bronwyn closed her eyes, shutting out the gawking mob waiting with bated breath below her . . . *waiting for her flesh to burn and her blood to sizzle in the flames.* Waiting to see her die in agony.

A man in a black hood emerged from the crowd, carrying a lit torch. A whisper of anticipation ran through the crowd and Bronwyn felt greater fear than she had ever experienced in her life. Some of the women began one last, desperate time to beg and plead pitifully.

The crowd began to chant, *"Witch! witch! Burn the witch! Sear her flesh and save her soul forever from the devil! Burn the evil from her soul!*

"Burn the witch!"

Bronwyn would never see another dawn, another summer, never love or be loved again. Never run through the cool, fragrant woods. Never see or touch Johnny again, nor Edward. Soon it would be over. She only prayed that it would not take too long and that the pain would be fleeting.

She smelled the pungent aroma of smoke as it nibbled at the fringes of the piles of wood and leaves. Soon she would see her dear father and mother again. Soon she would be with them . . .

The fire was crackling and the smoke stung her eyes as she clutched her gown with white-knuckled fingers. Her eyes were closed and she murmured a final prayer.

The hoofbeats came swiftly, their sound growing louder, stronger. Nearer. At first Bronwyn thought nothing of it. Soldiers traveling by. Nothing to do with her. She even fancied that they were a figment of her imagination born out of confusion and fear . . . the sound of approaching, thundering hooves pounding upon the cobblestones. Suddenly the roar of the crowd changed. Bronwyn's eyes flew open and she stared at the approaching riders. They were heading straight for the square! She couldn't fully comprehend what was occuring. The smoke was so thick that she could hardly see the oncoming riders. For a brief moment the smoke cleared and she saw how the crowd parted as the mounted men in long black cloaks and hoods pulled down over their faces, thundered through the opening thus cleared. They were beating at the crowd with the flat of their drawn swords and frightened people scattered noisily before them.

The four cloaked men rode directly toward Bronwyn and reined their mounts not more than five feet away from her. One man jumped from his foaming horse and, his sword flashing wickedly in the bright sunlight, ran up to her. Shoving the burning wood away, he cut her bonds and lifted her into his strong arms. Without a word he threw her upon the back of his prancing steed and swung up behind her in one swift, graceful movement. He seized the reins and set spur to his horse, galloping madly out of the crowded square as the cringing townspeople stared, dumbfounded.

"*Wait*! Molly . . .! And the others! Please, sir, don't let them burn! None of them are witches! *Don't let them burn*!" she cried, clutching the stranger's waist. "*Please*!"

His fiery horse reared as he reined in and shouted curt order to his comrades, who doubled back. Soon the other women were freed as well. In the confusion a few women ran into the crowd and disappeared and some were lifted to their rescuer's saddles as she had been.

Bronwyn caught Molly's eye for a glorious fraction of a second. Tears of relief and gratitude poured down the woman's fleshy face. She waved just once and Bronwyn waved back. Then Molly disappeared into the crowd and out of Bronwyn's sight.

Her savior urged his horse to greater speed through the twisted cobblestone streets. She could hear the other riders close behind her. No one had followed them or tried in any way to thwart the daring rescue.

A few miles out of town, her rescuer brought his mount to a rearing halt and waited until his companions caught up to them. He turned to the other men who still had their faces covered, and with a triumphant laugh raised his hand in a gesture of congratulation for a job well done. Then he looked over his shoulder at Bronwyn, who gazed at his shadowed face in stunned silence. "Well, mistress, I trust you are none the worse for your experience." He threw the hood back and smiled, dark eyes flashing.

Richard! Edward's younger brother!

Bronwyn could hardly believe her eyes. Finally she smiled tremulously back at him and stammered, "My Lord Richard . . . where did you come from? How did you know . . . ? Why . . . ?"

He laughed again. "All is well, fair maid. You are safe and you shall soon see the King. It was he who sent me. When he has accomplished his business in the North, he will come back for you."

"But how did he know where I was?" she asked, astounded.

Richard turned his horse toward London again and answered as they rode. "George told him that you were with Warwick at Barnet. It was only a matter of time before we learned that you had been taken to prison. You led us all a merry chase, I must say! I have been searching for you for weeks. I dared not return to my unhappy brother without you. He would have had me flayed alive! I bribed, spied and questioned until I found you . . . and barely in time, as it turned out! But here we are, safe at last. You have nothing to fear from now on." His voice became very soft and low. "I do know my brother Edward loves you and your son. He will be delighted when he sees you—and very grateful to me!"

Bronwyn hugged him more tightly around the waist. "As I am grateful to you for saving me, my lord! I cannot believe that I am actually *alive*!" she whispered, suddenly weak with the delayed shock of her miraculous rescue. If not for Richard's intervention, she would now be screaming in agony—or beyond screaming.

"Mistress, you are welcome indeed," he replied graciously.

Then Bronwyn's eyes grew shadowed and she added, "But I know not where our son is now, my lord. I was taken from him by Lord Warwick months ago and I have not seen him since. I don't even know if he is alive! I have been Warwick's prisoner and could not go in search of him." Much to her astonishment, she realized that he was laughing. How unlike Richard, to be so heartless! But just as she was about to tell him so, Richard spoke.

"I had best tell you now, though Edward wanted it to be a surprise." Richard turned to look at her, and his dark eyes were sparkling. "Your son is even now at the Red Boar with Martha, your sisters and their families. An old gypsy woman brought him back to them after you were abducted by Warwick. She loved the boy enough to see that he was returned to his own people. Now *that* is a story we would like to hear . . . why was the boy with a pack of gypsies?" he asked.

Bronwyn thought her heart would burst with joy. Her eyes filled with happy tears and she started to cry resting her cheek against Richard's broad back. When she could speak without sobbing, she said, "It was Lilyan, the old gypsy woman, who brought the boy back. She must have remembered what I had told her, about Martha and the Red Boar! God bless her—she is a good, kind woman," Bronwyn whispered, drying her tears and smiling.

"But you haven't answered my question," Richard persisted. "Why was he with the gypsies at all?"

Bronwyn hesitated. Should she tell the King's brother about her brief marriage and Leon's dreadful death at Lord Warwick's hands? No, she decided on the spur of the moment. One day she would tell Edward, but no one else, not now.

She sighed wistfully as she put away the memories of

Lilyan and Leon, of the gypsies she had lived with and loved. "You are right," she said softly. "It is a story worth the telling . . . and someday, my Lord Richard, I shall tell it all. Someday . . ."

Richard nodded. They reined up before the inn a short while later and the Duke watched compassionately as the small blond boy came running out to meet his mother. The two fell into each other's arms, hugging and kissing and crying with joy, the woman in her filthy grey rag of a gown and the lovely little blue-eyed boy who looked so much like his father, Edward the King.

EPILOGUE

April 1483

BRONWYN STOOD at the door and watched with sad eyes as her son mounted his grey stallion. *God, he looked so much like Edward as a young man!* she thought with a thrill of pride. *So beautiful!* Tall and straight, with a laugh that could charm the birds out of the trees and intelligent blue eyes the exact shade of his father's. Johnny at eighteen was the very image of King Edward. She smiled one last time at her son before he rode away to join his Uncle Richard to take lance and sword and follow Richard into battle against the Woodvilles. The Queen had not waited until her dead husband was cold in his grave before she started agitating for control of Parliament and the crown. Bronwyn sighed thinking of the dead King. *Oh, my sweet Edward, I miss you so. You were so loving to me and Johnny. I will always love you, Edward, until I, too, die.*

Johnny was adjusting one of his stirrups and his friend Walt, who was also going on this great adventure, was impatiently waiting for him to come along. Johnny looked up at his mother and smiled that radiant smile of his that she knew so well. He had told her the night before that she was not to worry over his welfare—that he was a man grown and had to make his place in the world. And his place, as he saw it, was fighting beside his good Uncle Richard who intended to make sure that Edward's legitimate son ascended the throne that was his by right. Edward's true son would rule the country, with Richard as Lord Protector, not that gaggle of greedy Woodvilles.

The King had died only the previous week. Bronwyn had wept for days at the sad news, and was not yet resigned to the fact that she would see him no more. Edward had died far too soon for England's good. Now her enemies were breathing down her neck again, but both Johnny and his mother knew that if Richard stood behind the young boy King all would be well. Richard was a strong, brave warrior who could lead the country through this perilous transition period until twelve-year-old Edward could take over the reins. If, however, Elizabeth got her way and her brother Anthony Woodville was appointed Lord Protector, there would be hell to pay.

As for Johnny, he knew he could never be King. But he was a generous, big-hearted lad and when he had come to her with his plans to join Richard, she hadn't tried to stop him. It was time, she knew, that he saw the other side of his world. He had lived in her world for eighteen years. When he was a small boy she had feared for him to go to court, thinking he would reject her and her peasant heritage. But now the time had come for him to take his place among the noblemen, a place to which his royal blood entitled him. She would not stand in his way.

Martha stood silently beside Bronwyn, tears in her grey eyes as she watched Johnny ride away. Jack had died years ago and now Martha and Bronwyn ran the inn together. It was a gentler place to live and work in nowadays. Bronwyn had helped to make it that way. They made a good, comfortable living. Bronwyn's sisters had both moved away to raise families of their own, but Bronwyn had remained, after finally convincing the King that it was best for both herself and Johnny if she did. He could always send for them or visit them, which he often did. Bronwyn had been happy the last thirteen years. They had been good, good years. Now they were over. She closed the door when Johnny could no longer be seen galloping towards his destiny on his grey stallion. She knew he would return someday, just as she had, just as Edward always had.

Martha said in a teary voice, "How about a nice cup of tea, dear child?"

"Aye, Martha . . . that would be nice," Bronwyn replied and put an arm around the older woman and hugged her. Yes, that would be nice.

The sound of hoofbeats faded away into the distance . . .